THE RIFT CODA

Amy S. Foster is a celebrated and award-winning songwriter, best known as Michael Bublé's writing partner, and has collaborated with Beyoncé, Diana Krall, Andrea Bocelli, Josh Groban, and a host of other artists. She is the author of the Rift Uprising trilogy and *When Autumn Leaves*. When she's not in a studio in Nashville, she lives in the Pacific Northwest with her family.

BY AMY S. FOSTER

<u>The Rift Uprising Trilogy</u>

The Rift Uprising

The Rift Frequency

The Rift Coda

When Autumn Leaves

THE
RIFT
CODA

AMY S. FOSTER

HARPER
Voyager

Harper*Voyager*
An imprint of HarperCollins*Publishers* Ltd
1 London Bridge Street
London SE1 9GF

www.harpercollins.co.uk

First published in Great Britain by HarperCollins*Publishers* 2018
This paperback original 2018

A catalogue record for this book is available from the British Library

ISBN: 978-0-00-819041-5

Printed and bound in the UK by CPI Group (UK) Ltd,
Croydon CR0 4YY

MIX
Paper from
responsible sources
FSC™ C007454
www.fsc.org

This book is produced from independently certified FSC™ paper
to ensure responsible forest management.

For more information visit: www.harpercollins.co.uk/green

For Vaughn, my warrior prince, who showed Ryn what was worth fighting for.

CHAPTER 1

"Stop scratching," my mother commands tersely. Her fingers grip the steering wheel tightly and instead of the radio that is usually playing in the car, there is only silence. Even at seven years old I can tell that she is annoyed, but mostly, she is worried. I stare down at my slender, bony wrists. Even though it is October, I am wearing only a tank top and shorts. I cannot bear the weight of actual fabric on my skin, and even this little amount is torture. I grit my teeth. I can feel my face flush and a sheen of sweat starts to form on my forehead. I want to do as my mom says, but my skin is on fire.

I need to scratch.

I stare at my legs, two skinny toothpicks. They, like the rest of my body, are covered in red, angry welts. I have had this rash for three days. Seventy-two hours. During that time, I have slept for maybe ten of them, and my parents have survived on even less. No one knows what this is. Not my pediatrician and not the doctors at Doernbecker Hospital. Nothing has helped. I've had *three* shots of different medicines—exactly three more than I like. They put some kind of lotion and then a cream on the rash. I screamed in agony and threw up because it hurt so bad. So far, everything has just made it worse. I am trying not to cry. I have cried so much these last few days that my throat hurts and my eyes sting in the corners where the tears come out. I feel like the pictures I've seen of the deserts in Africa, empty except for miles and miles of sand that go on forever. That's how I feel on the inside: like a thousand pounds of sand.

On the outside, all I want to do is scratch.

One of the doctors from the hospital has told us to go to another doctor in North Portland. A *special* doctor. This doctor only knows about skin and now my mom and I are driving there in the quiet car where I only hear my own heartbeat and my mother's occasional muttering of swear words under her breath because of the traffic.

When we get to the address, I see that it is a normal office building, white and gray. This place doesn't look all that special. In fact, it looks pretty shabby compared to the hospital and my own pediatrician's fun and fancy office that even has a fish tank. We park the car near the entry and climb out of our seats. I am slow and deliberate.

"Come on, Ryn," my mom says, a little calmer now that we've arrived. She reaches out and then pulls her hand back. If no one touches me, the rash is only itchy. If someone tries to do something else with it, even brush up against it, the rash gets angry and hurts me. Like it's mad at someone else touching me. My mom opens the door and we walk up a flight of rickety stairs and end up in a hallway. She is looking for the name of the doctor on one of the doors. When she finds it, she opens it swiftly and we move inside. There is a small waiting room and a lady sitting at a desk behind thick glass. This is the same kind of thing that I have seen at our bank. The people who give out the money sit behind a clear wall like this. Maybe this doctor really is special. My mom does not seem to notice this. She is giving the lady our name. She is talking faster than normal. I hear the lady say through the tiny holes in the wall that our visit is covered by Doernbecker Hospital. My mother doesn't understand.

"This is free?" she asks. Her accent is thicker now, the way it usually gets when she's excited. She is Swedish. I speak Swedish, too. Why is my mom arguing about paying? Who cares? Let me in there behind the thick wall where the special medicine is so I can stop feeling like this!

"Don't I have to fill out some forms or something?"

I sigh and look at a particularly large welt on my right hand.

"The hospital sent everything over. Let's just get Ryn in to see the doctor right away," the woman explains calmly. "Poor thing, she really looks bad."

"Yes," Mom snips, "of course she does. It's—it's just so unusual to not have to deal with paperwork." I know this tone. This is the tone that makes me go to my room on my own without being told to.

"Well, it seems like your daughter has a very *unusual* rash," the lady says while smiling at me. She is trying to be friendly, but I don't like her smile. It's too big. I hear a buzzing sound and a door opens. The lady ushers us inside past her desk and into an exam room. I do not want to sit. Sitting hurts. I stand in the middle of the room.

"You okay?" my mom asks. I just nod my head. I'm too tired to talk. After about five minutes, the door opens. It is not the doctor, but the lady again. She has a mug in her hand.

"I thought you could use this," she says kindly as she thrusts it toward my mom. "I know you must be very anxious about Ryn. This is a valerian and chamomile tea to calm your nerves. I don't know if they told you that while—of course—we believe in traditional Western medicine here, we also practice Eastern, homeopathic, and naturopathic medicine as well. This is a very holistic office." My mom takes the mug and says thank you, and I can see she means it. She loves all that kind of stuff with plants and yoga and juices. The lady stays and watches my mom drink the tea. No one is saying anything and it feels weird.

After a few minutes, the lady leaves again and immediately there is a light knocking on the door. She doesn't wait for us to answer. She just walks right inside. I thought the doctor would be a boy. I am happy that it is a girl because girls are better.

"Ohhh," the doctor says, looking me up and down with sympathy. "That looks sore, Ryn. Let's see what we can do about it." The doctor looks at my mom and says very sweetly, but firmly, "You should wait outside." My mom blinks. She looks at me and her eyes frown. I don't want my mom to go. I want my mom to stay. "I should wait outside," she says stiffly and she does. She actually leaves!

"I want my mom," I say to the doctor. She is a tiny woman with very dark skin and bright blue eyes.

"Well, you can have your mom or you can get rid of that rash. You choose." That doesn't seem fair at all. My mom never leaves me in the doctor's office alone. I stare for a quick minute at the doctor who is just looking at me. Her eyes are raised and her eyebrows would be, too, but she is bald there. Her skin is almost shiny.

"I guess I want you to fix the rash," I tell her.

"Excellent," she says as she walks over to a cupboard above a counter with a sink. She opens the cupboard door and takes out a package. "Now, I'm going to have to give you a shot. I am not going to lie to you. It's a big shot and it will hurt. But I promise—as soon as I give it to you, the rash will go away." My bottom lip starts to quiver. I hate shots. I've already had three! This room is cold. I want my mom. I try not to let the tears fall. Not because I care about being brave, but because the tears actually hurt my face. Doctors don't lie. If this doctor says she can fix the rash, then she can.

"Okay," I say quietly. I don't watch her as she gets the needle ready. I don't want to know how big it is. I close my eyes. I just have to get through this next part and then I will be better. The truth is, I'd probably take a hundred shots to get rid of this rash. The doctor moves quickly and without warning I feel the sting in my arm. It really hurts. It isn't the quick kind of shot the nurses usually give out. This is taking a long time. Real long. But after about five seconds, my skin stops itching. After ten seconds, I feel the doctor pulling the needle out.

I look down at my legs and the backs of my hands and I watch the bright red spots begin to fade. They disappear almost immediately. It doesn't take long at all for the entire rash to be gone. I let out a long steady breath.

"You fixed me," I tell her.

"Yes. I've made you better, but now we have to make sure the rash never comes back." The doctor is standing behind me and she places her hands, which aren't that much bigger than mine, actually, on my shoulders. "You've been very brave so far, Ryn, and now you must continue to be brave."

"I must continue to be brave," I say. At least, I think I say that. I don't remember thinking it. I don't remember agreeing with her in my mind.

"Lie down on the table. Not on your back, but your front. There is a little cradle for your face." Lying down on that table is the last thing I want to do. I want to go and see my mom, but my legs move toward the exam table anyway. I'm shocked to find that I am doing exactly what she has ordered. I feel the doctor move my hair up and away so that it is falling over the headrest. My blond locks are scraggy and unbrushed because of the rash.

"I am going to do a biopsy. That's the word I want you to remember when we talk to your mother. I have to do this in a special place, right at your hairline on the back of your neck. So first, I'm going to shave the area."

"Biopsy," I repeat. I can't really see anything from this vantage, just the middle section of her body, but it's enough to notice the razor in her hand. I feel a cool liquid on my neck and the funny tickling sensation of my hair being shaved.

"Now I'm going to give you a bunch of tiny needles to freeze the area. These won't hurt like the last one I gave you. Just lie still." I want to jump up. More shots! I don't want more shots! I want my mom and I want to get out of here but I can't move.

But I am lying still just like the doctor told me to. Why is my body listening to her when my brain doesn't want to?

I feel the teeny pinpricks go into my head. They actually don't hurt all that much, but I am getting another feeling, like, suddenly, this is all very wrong. I shouldn't be here. I shouldn't be letting this doctor do this to me. When I see her remove the large scalpel from a paper container, I lift my head up. I stare at the doctor, who seems genuinely baffled that I am looking at her.

"I told you to lie still," she says calmly. I put my face back in the cradle, but every instinct I have is screaming to get up.

The doctor gets closer and just as she is about to move into position above me I jolt up and grab her arm.

I am no longer seven.

I am no longer wearing a tank top and shorts. I am in full uniform and I am ten years older. I watch as the doctor's face morphs. Her eyes, as blue as a neon sign at night, get bigger and wider. Her body shrinks. Her hair disappears and her skin, which was already dark, becomes jet-black and reflects the fluorescent lights from above.

"You will let me do this to you," she tells me. Any warmth she may have had has been drained from her tone.

"No . . ." I say firmly, "I won't." She tries to move her hand, the one with the scalpel in it. She can't. She raises her other hand and I grab that, too, so that we are locked in a bizarre kind of dance. Her wrists are as hard as rock but I know, deep inside, that I am stronger than her. I can beat her. *I can kill her.* Yet when I kick her in the stomach, expecting her to go flying, she barely moves.

What's happening? This isn't right. My strength is waning. She is getting the upper hand. She pushes me back against the table, whips me around, and shoves my head into the tissue paper cover.

"Stop! Edo! Stop it!" I beg.

"You cannot beat me, Ryn. And why would you want to when I am about to give you such an extraordinary gift?" She sounds almost seductive in that raspy inhuman voice of hers.

"I don't want it. Please, *please.*"

But her hand remains on my neck and I am stuck. I feel the slow painful drag of the scalpel—which is also wrong. She gave me anesthetic to numb this area, but it still hurts. I scream out loud. I am squirming and kicking, but I can't get away. I begin to truly panic when I see the little black box in her tiny child-like hand. *I know* what it is. I know what it will do to me. It will change me. It will turn me into a Citadel, a soldier, a monster. She shoves it into my open wound with brutal intensity.

"No! No!" I keep yelling, begging, screaming, but it's done. I can't undo this. I can take the box out, but I can't change what it did to me all those years ago. The fight goes out of me and a single tear leaks out of my eyelid. It's hopeless.

"Ryn!" I hear another voice calling me from far away. It sounds like it's coming from another room. The waiting room? My mother? But, no, this is a male voice. "Ryn, wake up! It's just a dream! If you keep jerking your head around, you're going to open up the cut again. Ryn!

"Ryn!"

I'm asleep.

I *cannot* be asleep.

CHAPTER 2

What a shitty dream. I open my eyes and blink. It's really bright. I put a hand up to my forehead so that I can see. I can't make out anything, just two shapes, blobs really.

"She's coming out of it," I hear one voice say.

"Yeah, man, I can see that. Just back off, okay? You have zero medical training and I don't want to have to get into it with you again about all the things you aren't trained for that you insist on being a part of no matter how much danger you put people in," another voice slaps back.

I suddenly know exactly where I am.

With Levi *and* Ezra.

Are they seriously fighting right now? As far as I can remember, which all things considered, might not be the most accurate, we have Rifted onto a Pandora Earth. This is an Earth that has been randomly selected by our computer program so as not to lead hostiles—or in our case, potential hostiles—straight to our Command Center. And we were fighting. We were all fighting . . . pigs?

What the fuck?

There was me and Ezra and Levi and . . . who else? Right, the Karekins. Like Vlock. He died, though—on the other Earth. I struggle to remember where we are and so I start the running tally again: it's me, Ezra, Levi, and *not* the Karekins, but rather the Faida. We Rifted from the Spiradael Earth with the Faida Citadels who look like angels and claim to be on our side, but I have ridiculous trust issues—for very good reasons, I might add. So I can't be sure of them.

Or anything really.

I *am* pretty sure I've hit my head. My tongue feels too big and my skull, while not actively painful, seems like it belongs to someone else.

"Did we win?" I croak.

"Uh. Sure," Levi answers noncommittally.

"Did I get knocked out?"

Levi frowns, though the gesture is only apparent in his eyes. The rest of his face remains a mystery. He could be worried. He could be pissed off. Or both. Or neither. It's never easy with Levi. "You got a kind of a tusk thing stabbed into your neck." I narrow my eyes at him. I was stabbed? And I don't remember? "We Rifted out. Again. Because those pigs, or whatever they were, would not stop coming. We must have killed six hundred or seven hundred of them, but they were everywhere. It came down to numbers that we didn't have. Retreat was the best option."

I blink my eyes hard trying to get them to focus. "The pigs I remember. Unfortunately, but the rest is . . . I don't know. . . ."

Levi sighs. "I had to put you out. Sedate you. It was bad, Ryn. You lost a lot of blood."

"But you have the SenMach patches. You didn't need to drug me," I tell him angrily.

"Look." Levi's tone has just gone from sort of concerned to downright defensive. "We heal fast, but we aren't magical. The only way to accelerate the healing process is sleep. Rest. So that's what we've been letting you do for the past two hours while the boy wonder and I"—Levi gestures flippantly to Ezra—"had to hang out here with Lucifer and the Morning-stars. Hasn't been awkward at all."

"Fine. Sorry, but I'm okay now." I try to get up, but the moment I do, I start seeing little black dots bouncing around my sight line and my body suddenly feels like it weighs a ton. I sit back down abruptly.

"You're not okay, actually. You need more rest," Levi tells me. Or possibly orders me. But it doesn't matter. Rest isn't an option right now.

"I don't. I need water and some of those cubes from the SenMachs. You're the one who said I lost a lot of blood." Instead of answering, Levi just folds his arms and stares at me.

"Give her the water, Levi. And the other thing, whatever it is. Ryn knows her limits," Ezra says with authority. I'm not sure where exactly this authority is coming from, because Levi could beat him seven ways to Sunday with one finger.

"Okay," he relents as he gets the stuff out of his pack. It's only then that I realize I'm actually lying on my own bag. "But I need to examine you."

Levi holds out a canteen and the gel cubes and I snatch both away. "Like I wouldn't let you examine me," I chide. "I was stabbed. By a giant pig. You can look at my wound." I keep drinking and then I pop a few of the cubes into my mouth.

I bend my head down and Levi approaches. I suppose I should be worried about the Blood Lust activating. He's not cured and he's about to touch me, but I know that I am safe. There's too much going on. We're God-knows-where surrounded by twenty questionable Citadels. Levi's guard is up. He's nowhere close to being turned on.

And God knows I couldn't feel less sexy at the moment.

I feel his hand gently pull my hair away from the nape of my neck. His touch is tender but efficient. He seals the Sen-Mach biopatch down on my skin and into my hairline. "I could take it off to check the wound again, but I might have to hack through some of your hair. I think we should just let it be for now," he tells me as he sits back down on his haunches.

"That's your crack analysis? The Band-Aid is still on?" I ask while slowly bringing my head back up again. The water and food has helped, but I feel weak and groggy from the drugs. "The SenMach tech can do more than stitch up a cut. You know that."

Levi's lips purse. I get it. He's being protective over one of the biggest advantages we have—technology from a race of androids, the SenMachs. Still, now is not the time to be coy. I need to make sure I'm okay. I look past Levi's shoulders to the group of Faida who are, thankfully, not in any kind of defensive formation but are instead talking in low tones to one another. Although that could be equally as dangerous . . .

Worry about that later. First, get better.

"Do it, Levi."

"Fine. Computer! SenMach Computer—" Levi awkwardly spits out.

"Oh my God. Just let me." I interrupt because I already feel weird enough, and I don't need Levi's anxious fumbling to make me feel even more out of it. "Doe," I say into my cuff softly, "take bio readings from the cuff. Report on my medical status."

"I will need a drone scan to get a more accurate diagnosis," Doe's ghostlike voice says as it floats up from my wrist. Instead of saying anything, I raise an eyebrow at Levi who looks really irritated now.

"You want to risk letting the Faida see one of those?" he asks me.

"Uh, yeah, cuz I don't feel right and I don't know if it's the drugs or brain damage. So all things considered, we should take the risk."

Levi growls, but he does open up his pack again to release a small oval-shaped silver drone. He then pulls Ezra hastily over to him so that they both are blocking any view of what is happening from the Faida. I appreciate Levi's vigilance, but in this case it's unnecessary. Showing the Faida what we have might lead to an uncomfortable conversation, but they'd never be able to use our tech. It was designed for us and us alone, and it's unhackable.

The drone hovers just a few inches above my chest and then, from its middle, where the alloy has the thinnest of lines, a blue flash scans my body. When it's done, Levi grabs the thing and shoves it quickly back into his pack as if it was a kilo of heroin. He's just being plain paranoid now. I look past him to the Faida who are watching. I strain to listen, but they are speaking Faida, which I don't speak. Yet. One thing at a time, though.

"You had a deep laceration running 5.3 inches from the middle of your neck to your skull between the occipital lobes. You lost 1.3 liters of blood. I would recommend a further eight hours of rest and minimal activity. There is tissue damage that is still being healed," Doe's voice tells me with the kind of distanced candor I'd expect from an AI modeled after a robot modeled after Tim Riggins.

"Can I fight?" I ask quietly. I'm fairly sure the Faida don't speak English as we had been communicating in Roonish, but I'm not about to risk it.

"If necessary, but I would recommend against it." There's an oddly judge-y tone to Doe's voice.

"Fine. I will do my best to keep this civil," I say out loud to Doe. But it's also for the benefit of both Ezra and Levi, so they know that, at the very least, I'm going to try and talk with my mouth and not my fists. I slowly get up. Levi does not assist me because he's well aware that I've already shown enough weakness.

I stand up and straighten my spine. I plant my feet into the earth to steady myself. I'm not even sure which has me so off my game, the blood loss or the drugs. I guess it doesn't really matter. Every time I move I feel like I have to push through tar.

"You," I say to the Faida who flew me through the Rift, away from the Spiradael who were trying to kill us all. "My name is not 'human girl child.' It's Ryn Whittaker. What are you called?"

"I am Arif," the Faida says as he steps forward toward me. "And you, you are everything the Roones claimed. Still, *you are* a child."

I sigh outwardly. Arif is devastatingly gorgeous. His blond hair is curly, but not overly so, more tousled. His cheekbones are sharp enough to look like they were carved out of rock, and his eyes give the word *piercing* a whole new meaning, but I am a Citadel. I have seen wonders, and his beauty will not sway me. His words might piss me off, though.

"I am young, but I am no child. I haven't been a child for many years. The Roones saw to that. What I want to know is what you were doing on the Spiradael Earth and why you were trapped there." I fold my arms across my chest and stare.

"We were doing recon, as I imagine you were doing. A few months ago, those of us in senior command began to understand the scope of the Roones' power. Unrest was brewing within our own ranks. It was imperative that we saw firsthand what the other Citadels were capable of and if they could be persuaded to fight with us, if it came down to it."

I close my eyes for just the briefest of seconds. I don't want to appear weak. I also don't want to come across as paranoid, just in case *this isn't* some elaborate trap set up by the altered Roones. If the Faida join our cause, it could very well be the beginning of the end of the Roonish stronghold.

"Okay, look," I say to Arif, putting as much weight as possible into the soles of my boots, so I can feel the solid ground beneath me. "You seem to trust us, though I can't imagine why."

"Because we just fought a common enemy in the pig monsters, as you called them," Arif jumps in quickly. "And also, we sent a scouting party to your Earth at a Rift site in a place called Poland. We sat in on our colleagues' debrief twenty-four hours before we came here. You're just normal children. We overheard your chatter. It was hardly different from that of the adolescents on our own Earth."

I have to snigger a little at that observation. "I'd hardly say we're normal," I tell him plainly. "And I tried to tell some of my fellow human Citadels the truth, and it ended very badly. We may just be adolescents, but the altered Roones have done their job indoctrinating us."

Arif walks closer to me. I think he may want to lay a hand on my shoulder, but he draws it away slowly, reaching instead to his wings where he strokes a few speckled feathers. "Let us talk plainly," he says with far less condescension. "I have read much about your kind. I know what they did to you. I also know that we too tried to tell our fellow Citadels what was happening and then we found ourselves trapped on the Spiradael Earth. I do not think this is a coincidence."

I sigh deeply. "Just lay it out," I prod. "My head is throbbing. I am tired and I would like to believe you, but it's all a little too convenient, don't you think? That you would be there right when we needed help against all those Spiradaels?"

I hear a loud, sarcastic laugh from the unit behind him. Arif whips his head around to silence him or her. "No, wait," I ask genuinely. "I want to know what they find so humorous." A Faida woman, with hair so blond it's practically silver, steps forward regally. She's like a legit elf, but with wings.

"We've spent the past sixteen weeks on that wretched Earth with those disgusting black-eyed drones. The very idea that we would be lying in wait . . . *for you*. It's funny."

"Okay," I say, convinced she's telling the truth. I don't know why exactly. She just seems so over the whole thing, it's hard to believe that she's dissembling. Besides, her heart rate is steady. Her voice isn't fluctuating. If she's lying, then we really are fucked because the Faida would be just about the best manipulators I've ever come into contact with, and that includes the altered Roones.

"We can get into the specifics another time, when you've rested and seen to your wounds," Arif says dismissively.

"Oh, I don't think so, buddy." I keep my eyes level and my head, even though it's aching fiercely, perfectly level as well. "Time is a precious commodity around these parts, and trust is even harder to come by. I'd like to know what exactly you were doing on the Spiradael Earth and if that's a problem for you, well, we can always leave you here and come back when you feel like talking and I've gotten some rest."

"No, no," Arif says quickly, but the woman who'd spoken up earlier is now barking at him in Faida. He responds quickly in return and they have a heated but short exchange that ends with her throwing up her hands and repeating a word that sounds like *singshe* three or four times. I don't speak Faida but I'm fairly sure by the tone that this must mean *fine* or possibly *whatever*. Arif turns back around to face me.

"I understand." Arif nods tersely. "And I agree. Time is precious and our history is long and complicated. That is all I was trying to relay to you. I assumed that it was enough, for now, that we fought side by side. Clearly I was wrong." Arif sighs. He wants to go. I want to go, too, but ignorance is a trap that I won't step into willingly.

"You know, every Citadel race begins with a lie," he says thoughtfully. "Some are more elaborate than others. For us, they opened our Rifts by feeding scientific data to one of our most well-respected scientists. The Settiku Hesh came much later, but they did come."

"That's what happened on our Earth," I say quickly, wanting him to get to the Spiradael part.

"At first, it was all quite marvelous. We did not hide the Rifts from the public at large. Instead, they were celebrated," he says, "as scientific marvels. The Faida currently live in an era of peace and prosperity. We were born to take to the skies and we have done that, too. We have visited other planets, met other life-forms. You must understand, then, that when the Settiku Hesh finally did come, the Roones' offer of help was not so alien—*they* did not seem so alien . . . *to us*."

I try not to let that comment throw me. It's not so much that they've been to space, or live in space or whatever, but how does a Star Trek society find itself at the mercy of the altered Roones? What chance do we mere humans (who are basically, globally, assholes to one another) have? "So let me get this straight. You *volunteered* to become Citadels?" I ask, deliberately keeping my face neutral.

"They came through the Rift, like every other species. The aid they offered was simply too good to pass up. We were being slaughtered by the Settiku Hesh," Arif says bitterly. "It wasn't just soldiers who volunteered, but doctors, scientists, journalists. Our Citadels came from every background imaginable. It was encouraged. Perhaps if the altered Roones had made the changes conditional for only military personnel, then we might have been more suspicious. But still, even though we all had many different professions, as Citadels we became a paramilitary organization. They said it was to defend ourselves, which seemed reasonable.

"We believed so many of their lies."

"So what changed? Why was there dissension among your ranks?" I ask, all the while noting his body language, checking for any possible sign, however slight, that he is lying.

"It took years for us to catch on, such is the mastery of our enemy. The first hint that something was wrong was when we started a task force to investigate the relentlessness of the Karekins. Of course, we know now they weren't Karekins at all, but Settiku Hesh," Arif explains calmly, slowly as if I wouldn't get it. I find this tedious and I don't bother to hide it. "But it was their obsession with the Kir-Abisat that spurred us to action."

"The Kir-Abisat?" I ask, though I think I already know the answer to that one. I think whatever this Kir-Abisat thing is, I have it, too.

"The Kir-Abisat is a mutation of the genome. It allows a Citadel to open a Rift using only the sound of their own voice when matched with the frequency of a conduit, someone from the Earth they are trying to access."

I narrow my eyes. My mind begins to scramble. Can this be true? No. No way. "So it's not just, like, a sound coming from a person that's not on their own Earth?" I throw out as casually as I can.

Arif looks me up and down, as if he is seeing me in an entirely different light. "It begins that way, but it is much, *much* more."

I knew that Levi was listening from a distance. He didn't need to be beside me, not with our enhanced hearing to catch these words. Now, he moves up next to me. He folds his arms.

"But they did this, right?" he asks, fishing for more information. "They gave you this extra gene or whatever? If things were so transparent between you all, didn't you notice this particular enhancement?"

Arif huffs and shakes his head. "They said they did not. They claimed that it was a by-product of Rifting itself. We've been going through the Rifts for almost a decade. That explanation was plausible, at first."

"Okay, well," I say impatiently. "That still doesn't tell me why you all were there, on the Spiradael Earth. How did it get from a suspicion to covert ops?"

"A few of us did not like how they attempted to isolate every Kir-Abisat. So we stole information, the private encrypted files of a few of the altered Roones. And then, we learned the truth about all the other Citadel races, that they were indeed responsible for the Kir-Abisat gene and the Midnight Protocol—the switch the Roones have that can kill us all. We tried talking. We tried negotiations, but all the while, we were preparing, as any good soldier would do, for the worst-case scenario. And that's why we were on the Spiradael Earth."

"I still don't get it," I say, throwing my hands up in frustration. "Why were you fighting among yourselves? You're this progressive, open society with *spaceships*. You find out that the altered Roones have been lying to you—that they're a threat to your safety—so who is going to be on their side?"

Arif looks down at his worn leather boots. He puts both hands on his hips as if this is a puzzle that he, too, doesn't know how to put together. "They were using drugs to make us more compliant for one, and for another, many—too many Faida Citadels, unfortunately—believed that it did not matter. Whatever they did, whatever lies they told were insignificant in the face of being able to navigate the Rifts."

"How did they trap you? Why didn't your QOINS system work anymore?" Levi asks quietly. There is an edge to his voice. He is being guarded, with damn good reason.

"I believe I can answer that," the same elfin platinum-haired Faida volunteers. "They must have caught on. The altered Roones must have figured out that we were sending scouting parties out. Every QOINS system is built differently. Or rather, they improve it, upgrade it with each species. They did not know where or when we were going out, so they simply went to every Earth with a Citadel faction and sent out a signal that would blow our specific QOINS device. It's a relatively easy fix and, even better, a deterrent, I imagine, from sending out further assets."

At this, Levi begins to lead me away. He tells Arif to give us a moment and he begins to speak in Latin, hoping that the ancient dead language wouldn't be one they understand. "What do you think? Are they telling the truth?"

"I think they are. I don't think their physiology is exactly like ours, but I think it's close enough that we would have picked up on any biological cues that they were lying."

He nods his auburn head. "Okay. I agree. So what now?"

"Now we take them home—*their* home, not ours."

At this, Levi balks, but before he can say anything else, I walk confidently to Arif, and Levi is forced to jog a bit to stay with me. I know he doesn't love this plan of mine—and he hasn't even heard the whole thing. It's bold, possibly even suicidal. However, it's the fastest way to determine if the Faida can be counted as allies, and time is the one thing we can't afford to waste.

"We will escort you back to your Earth. We have technology that can mask our Rift in. We also have tech that will help us do recon. We can see if your uprising was successful. If it wasn't, then we will Rift back to the original Roones. And from there, we can start to figure out a plan."

Arif's polar blue eyes collect a gathering storm of emotions. I'm sure he wants to return, desperately, but there is also the chance that his loved ones are dead, that his colleagues have been reprogrammed and tortured and brainwashed. He's been clinging to hope for months. Hope is not such an easy thing to let go of. His body becomes oddly still, like a stone angel in a centuries-old graveyard. It is the push and pull, the want and the need. The fact that this decision is not automatic further proves that he's been telling the truth. If he had been working with the altered Roones to orchestrate this, then he would just happily take me back to his Earth where I could be easily captured and contained.

"Very well," he finally says, resigned. "Take us home, Ryn Whittaker."

CHAPTER 3

The Faida Earth had been newly programmed into our QOINS system by the original Roones and the signal boosted by Sen-Mach Tech. We were able to Rift to their Earth in one jump seamlessly. We emerge from the emerald mouth in a row, a fierce firewall of armor and feathers . . . and the sight almost makes me gasp.

It must have been beautiful here once, but it's clear that war has ravaged our surroundings. Tree trunks are splintered, hanging at unnatural angles, a forest of broken arms and legs. The dirt is pitted and scorched. There are clear impressions of bodies that had once lain there—flattened grass in gruesome shapes and then wide trails where the casualties had been dragged. The mud is marked by striations where fingers must have scrambled and scratched to get away. There is a heaviness in the air, a sorrow that is cloying. The despair might have been carried away by ravens or other woodland creatures, but those animals were frightened off and haven't returned. It is eerily quiet. I hear nothing but the increasing pulses of the Faida and their rapid breathing. I wouldn't want to come back to a home that looked like this, either.

The Rift closes and Levi crouches down and releases his drone. I do the same. We don't bother with our laptops. If we have to make a run for it, or even worse, make a stand and fight, our gear needs to be stowed.

"Doe, scan for the Faida base. How far away is it?"

"The Faida base of operations is 10.2 kilometers away," Doe says with confidence. It's strange how even though this intelligence is artificial, I am getting a sense of Doe's moods.

"Fly there in stealth mode and report back verbally as soon as you get visuals," I command.

"Okay," he responds quickly. Levi and Ezra both shoot me a look.

"Look, he kept saying 'affirmative.' It was creepy. I asked him to be more casual with his responses," I tell them both a little defensively. Levi rolls his eyes, but Ezra just keeps staring at me. I never told him the extent of what we acquired on the SenMach Earth—there was no time, with the whole deflowering me and then the going macho caveman act. I wasn't exactly in the sharing mood. And now, I don't even know what's between us. He gave me an ultimatum to stop helping Levi with his Blood Lust. The fact that he thought he could give me an ultimatum at all made me angry. He had wanted me to choose, so I chose myself. I've had enough of people trying to control me. If he wanted to talk about it, fine. But at this moment, there are more important things to focus on . . . so I just ignore him.

We stand in silence and wait. I try to focus past the Faida's anatomical machinery. I try to throw my hearing out beyond anything I can even begin to see. I filter out breath and heart-beats, growling stomachs and a low careening tone that is likely a Kir-Abisat thing, but I hear nothing else. I wonder if everyone on this Earth is dead.

"I have the base in visual range," Doe's voice says quietly. Arif looks at me and in that moment, I am anxious for him. "There are Faida on the ground and in the air."

"What?" Arif exclaims as he half flies, half jumps beside me. "What are they doing? How many are there?"

"I told you. This program won't answer your questions. It only follows my orders. Or Levi's," I say, trying to get him to back off a bit. "First things first. Doe, is there an active Rift here?"

"There is no Rift activity on my sensors."

"Well, that could be good. If the Roones had won, you would assume they would just go back to business as usual."

"Or maybe they are just exercising control. An open Rift isn't necessary anymore. The Faida know the truth. At this point, Immigrants would just be a hassle," Ezra points out astutely.

"We must go!" Arif says. He grabs my arm. I look at his hand and tense until he, very smartly, removes it. Softening his tone, he says, "Your drones are all very well and good, but unless they have the ability to see through walls, they won't be able to provide us with any real information."

"They can't see through walls, but they can pick up life signs and read heat signatures. We should at least know how many Faida we're dealing with and if there are any visible Roones," I argue.

"You want us to wait? That is unacceptable! We must know if our comrades are alive. Ryn, you can't tell me that if you were in my position you would be able to sit idly here."

I sigh and run a hand over my scalp. My hair is up, in a messy topknot. The back of my head is sticky with dried blood, and the biopatch is beginning to chafe.

No, he's right. I wouldn't wait, but I would hope that there would be someone like me there to be objective. Someone who wasn't involved emotionally and who could give me the most strategically viable option.

"It's too risky to just go barging in, though. So why don't you let Levi and me go down there. In our sensuits. We could get actual eyes on the situation."

"Go down there? There is no down. Our base is a thousand feet in the air, inside a mountain. You can't get there. And even if you could, you don't speak our language. What could you possibly learn? I know of a place where we could land undetected." Arif is almost frantic now. His wings are practically humming with energy.

"Just because you could land there before doesn't mean you can now. If your side lost, the defenses would be shored up," Levi says without hostility.

"You don't know—"

"Ryn," Doe voice says, and I raise a finger to silence Arif. "There is a squadron of fifty potential hostiles coming in from the east at 126 kilometers per hour. They will be at your location in less than a minute."

"We have incoming," I say to the group quickly as I inventory my options. If I open a Rift, we won't have any answers. If this is not Arif's faction but is instead a faction loyal to the altered Roones, we're screwed. Obviously, they have some sort of device that trumps SenMach Rift cloaking.

I reach down into my pack and grab an extra sensuit, which I throw to Ezra. "Put this on," I tell him. "Doe, have the sensuits go into stealth mode."

"What is happening," Arif says looking around wildly. "Where did you go?"

"I hope for your sake and ours that your side won, Arif. But if they didn't, don't let them take you alive." I don't feel great about throwing our newest potential allies to the wolves, but they did say they wanted to go home. If Arif and the rest lost, we are losing a squadron of Faida, which would be helpful for the sake of intel but wouldn't make much of a dent in the numbers, not really. But that's not why this is a massive risk, because if even one of them is captured and gives us up, we've lost before we've even begun. We might have forty-eight hours, tops, to warn our own people. But there is no "safe" when it comes to war. There is only risk and retreat. There is no point in retreat now. They already know we're here.

Now, there is only hope.

I listen for Ezra's heartbeat and find him. I touch him lightly on the hand and whisper, "Hush."

The incoming Faida dive and land with such intensity that the ground quivers beneath our feet. I watch Arif and his troops. They have no ammo thanks to the pigs, so they have made themselves ready by taking a stance that is mostly crouched, presumably to take off in the air with considerable force. Everything is resting on a knife's edge.

And then a Faida woman comes forward, and I watch Arif's entire body relax. His arms lower, his legs straighten, and the look on his face goes beyond relief. It is almost ecstatic.

The woman he is looking at is all cheekbones and red curls. She does not smile. Her lips tremble, though, and she stops herself by covering her mouth with a single hand. Her other hand is outstretched, as if it has just received an impossible prayer in her palm. Or maybe she waiting for Arif to take it?

Arif says something in Faida and then—as with a jolt, as

if he's just now accepting what he's seeing with his eyes—he races to her and they embrace tightly. I let go of the breath I was holding and lift my head to the sky. This all could have gone very badly. It still could. Whatever is transpiring between these two is fiercely intense. I almost feel like looking away, but there is too much at stake to allow them a private moment. Despite their intimacy, this woman could be compromised. Even worse, this could have been Arif's plan all along—to get us right here, lulling us with stories of rebellion and spycraft. I put my hands on my holster, my fingers a breath away from the trigger of my sidearm.

The two of them begin speaking in Faida. It is a language as light and airy as their wings. Words fall into and over one another. It's almost like Mandarin, but less nasal. I try to follow what they are saying, or at least the tone. For all my linguistic prowess, though, I have no idea. Finally, after a few minutes, Arif points over to where we're standing, still in stealth mode. Our cover blown, I deactivate my suit, and Levi does the same. The woman walks over to me.

"My name is Navaa," she tells me in Roonish without even the tiniest speck of emotion.

"Hello," I say matching her deadpan tone.

"Arif tells me that you rescued our squadron from the Spiradael Earth. And while I am pleased at his return, I also find the circumstances unusually convenient."

"Interesting," I tell her as I plant my feet firmly in the ground, legs locked, shoulders back. I may not look like an angel, with the hair and the perfect skin and all, but I won't be intimidated. "Because I felt exactly the same when I discovered your people were trapped on an Earth that wasn't theirs."

Navaa tilts her head to one side, eyeing me warily, as I do her. "I see," she says slowly. She doesn't trust me and I don't trust her. I'm surprised that Arif himself isn't being more cautious. How does he know that these Citadels haven't been drugged by the altered Roones, forced to forget their rebellion and made to recommit to the other side by torture, psychological simulations, or both?

"You will come with us to our base. There are many questions, on both sides. But there are no answers here, not in this wasteland. It is a place so full of death and regrets I can't concentrate."

"No, wait." Levi jumps forward. I look to him and then to Ezra, who speaks only English and Arabic. As annoyed as I am at him, I can't help but feel badly at how lost he must feel. "How did you even know that we were here?" Levi continues. "There isn't an active Rift on this Earth."

Navaa locks her eyes onto my own. "I am a Kir-Abisat. I felt the Rift open the moment you arrived." She continues to stare at me. There's no misinterpreting that look. She knows. She knows that I am Kir-Abisat, too.

CHAPTER 4

Arif carries me in his arms. I expect it to feel dangerous. I expect my own control freak issues to take over and hate that I'm at Arif's mercy, but I'm wrong. In the drag and drift of his movements, I find a sort of peace on the airy current. It's so quiet up here. There's just Arif's heartbeat and the wind, which blows like a tiny whistle.

The base is indeed set inside a mountain. It is majestic and imposing, but it is not weathered or aged. This place looks new and gleaming. From what I can see there are six stories, separated by huge panels of tinted glass and metal beams. The metal isn't silver or steel, but a sort of copper color, almost the same color as the mountain itself.

Every other floor has a massive length of decking, which must almost certainly be used as launching pads. What a sight it would be, to watch thousands of Citadels take off from this vantage. Terrifying sure, but beautiful nonetheless.

Arif angles us vertically. He hovers for a second or two, I suppose to lose his momentum, and then he softly touches down and deposits me on the concrete landing. "Navaa will want to debrief me. And then she will debrief you. I hope you will not be insulted by this security measure. I'm sure you can understand her reluctance, just as we understood yours," Arif says quietly in my ear.

"I can absolutely understand it, as long as you understand just because your girlfriend seems like she's in charge doesn't necessarily mean that she is," I warn as I watch the rest of our party land. Levi's jaw is set determinedly and Ezra . . . well, actually he looks a little joyous. And as annoyed as I am that he doesn't seem to understand the seriousness of the situation, I'm also a bit jealous that he can be like that, that he has the ability to live inside a moment without thinking of a thousand things that might be coming next.

I turn back to Arif in time for him to say, "Navaa *is not* my girlfriend. She is my wife. No one is controlling her. The drugs don't even work on her."

"Oh. Well, you must be very happy that she is safe, then," I tell him honestly. Arif just nods briefly. It seems more and more that the Faida are a reserved people, logical, tightly wound.

"I am feeling many things at once. Of course I am happy, but I am also concerned. I have no idea what happened in our absence and no clue as to how many casualties we suffered to achieve our goal."

"Understandable," I say as the massive windows slide back automatically. Navaa is at my side once again. She doesn't touch me, but we are herded nonetheless into the building. The ceilings are high enough for me to have to crane my neck to see them. There is technology here—monitors surveilling our surroundings and computer terminals. Each of the stations stands tall and isolated, almost like a kiosk at an airport for checking in. There are no desks and no seats. I guess the Faida don't sit around.

The walls are white and bare, but there are wooden beams to break up the space. While this base looks modern, it also has a strange sort of rustic feel to it as well. I suppose you get to a point in your technological evolution where you want to hold on to things from the past so that you don't get too far away from who you were. Humans haven't gotten there yet. We're still at keyboards and plasma screens.

I notice a large, wide staircase at the end of the room, but there is also a perilous-looking ledge. I peer over the edge, careful to keep my feet well away from the lip. There is a significant drop-off in the middle of the mountain, its cavernous wall lit by strips of LED lights.

"We are going up a level. It's faster if you just let me take you up, all right?" Arif asks. Right. The Faida wouldn't need elevators.

"That's fine." And once again I am swooped up in his arms. The flight is quick, maybe ten seconds or so. I'm sure I could have done the stairs in the same amount of time, but I have to admit, it's an interesting way to get from one place to another inside a building. This next level is also cavernously large, but it is broken up by a labyrinth of walls and doors. Navaa places her hand on a metal scanner, presumably a security measure to lock and unlock the doors.

"You will wait in here until we are ready to question you and your colleagues. Please don't misinterpret our wariness for rudeness. We can't afford to let our guard down," Navaa says.

"You're going to separate us?" I ask, because she was clearly addressing me and me alone.

"Protocol," she answers haughtily, while folding her slim fingers together. All things considered, I suppose I can understand that, though Levi's stance has me worried. He's deposited his weight to his feet, leaning forward just a fraction, the way he does when he's about to fight. Ezra is watching us all, taking it in, going on body language alone, but he seems to be tensing, too. I don't like the idea of us not remaining together, but as I am learning, when it comes to diplomacy, it's all about concessions, agreeing to things that leave you feeling vulnerable. "I will take your bag for inspection," Navaa orders.

Then again, diplomacy isn't always the answer. I grip the handles on my pack lightly, to prove a point.

"Well, you can try. But then I'll have to snap your wings off and open a Rift before you can call in reinforcements." There are only six Faida. I am confident that Levi and I could neutralize them. They can lock me in a room. They can observe me, as I assume they will from the two-way mirror on the far side of the room. But they are not getting anywhere *near* my equipment.

Navaa has dropped her hands. Her blue-black wings look almost flexed. Her breathing has increased. Although she is ready to fight, I can't help but get the sense that she doesn't want to. For all her bravado, there are eggplant smudges, like tilted crescent moons, beneath her eyes. She is tired.

I know the feeling.

"Navaa, let the humans keep their things. They brought us home," Arif tells her gently, placing a palm over her forearm.

Navaa answers in a lilting string of Faida. They argue gently back and forth until I see Navaa give a slight nod of her head and a weak groan of agreement. She walks briskly out the door, taking Levi and the remaining Faida with her. Ezra, though, obviously has no idea what's going on.

"Ryn!"

"It's okay, Ezra. They're just separating us for a bit. I promise—it will be fine."

His eyes are a little wild now, but he nods and follows the rest out of the room. Just before the door closes, I see Levi looking back at me, a smirk on his face at Ezra's panic.

Jerk.

The ivory-colored room has the same high ceilings as the rest of the compound. A large wooden rectangular table is shoved up against a far wall with two upholstered wooden chairs. The setup seems odd. I drop my pack to the floor to investigate. I run my hand along the smooth edges of the grain. It's thick. At least a foot, which is a strange depth for a table. I bend down and peek at the underside. A mattress is tucked into it, and a pillow and blanket are strapped there as well.

I maneuver the table by pulling it forward, then up and down. The legs bend back down the other way for stability. I have no idea how long I'm going to be stuck here. Given that I now have a bed, though, it could be a while. Clearly this isn't just an interrogation room; it's a brig. I step back and consider the walls. I notice an ever-so-slight fracture running down the length of one of them. I push it and hear a click and hiss. The wall retracts and a platform moves forward. It's a toilet and a sink. Yeah. This could be an issue. I decide that I will be cool until it's not time to be cool.

I retrieve my laptop and my wireless earbuds from the Sen-Machs. I know I am being watched, but they have no real idea what I can do, or more accurately what this computer can do, so I'm not all that worried.

"Doe," I say in a hushed tone as I sit on the bed. "*Quanti hoc possibile est in composito Faida?"* As Levi did before we Rifted to this Earth, I decide that Latin is the best option. Have at it, you angel dicks, you can even watch me pee, but you don't get to understand what I'm asking, namely, how many Faida there are in this base. Doe plays along, speaking in Latin as well, and tells me he can wirelessly connect to their computer files, but without direct access via the computer's sentient component, the data may be incomplete. I instruct him to do his best with what he's got and extrapolate if he has to.

"There are 388 Faida currently on this base. There are 622 not present but nearby." I sigh and chew my bottom lip. This is both good and bad news. I like the numbers as allies, but if Navaa decides not to trust us, I don't know how we'll get past that many.

"Can you detect any Roones here?"

"Yes. There is one Roone present, although given this Roone's location, I must conclude that he or she is being detained. The last Roone entries into the database are consistent with the rebellion Citadel Arif spoke of and I cannot detect their unique heat signatures."

Well, I guess that's good news, although prisoner or not, I'm not crazy about the idea that there's an altered Roone here.

"Can you patch me through to Levi's cuff?" I ask as I shuffle my butt around and give a little bounce. The bed is surprisingly soft. I didn't think the Faida would care much about the comfort of their prisoners, but maybe they do.

"I can. Go ahead and speak," Doe instructs me.

"Levi," I say casually. All the evidence is pointing toward Arif's account of what happened here and the current state of things being true. Navaa's suspicions about us and the timing are not unwarranted. I don't need to win her over exactly, but

I can't be acting like a spy. "Go get your earpiece and computer. Be casual about it." I wait for a few seconds until I hear his voice.

"I'm here. I'm in some kind of a cell, but unharmed. Are you okay?"

"I'm fine," I say softly in English, hoping they won't understand it. "Listen, we need to use this time productively. Start learning the Faida language and ask Doe to download all files pertinent to the altered Roones, their experiments, and the rebellion. Once you learn the language you can begin to sift through it. I do believe Arif's story, but better safe than sorry and the more intel we have, the better."

"Copy that. I assume you're going to begin to learn it as well?"

"I am, as a sign of good faith."

There is a slight lag. "If that's how you want to play it, okay. Besides, we either Rift out or let them call the shots, because we have zero advantage here."

"Roger that. Let's get to work." Without my asking, Doe pulls up the Faida lexicon on the laptop. I don't know how much time I have until someone begins to question us. I assume Arif is debriefing the rest of the Faida. I have to also assume he'll want some alone time with his wife—will that come before or after they chat with us? No way to know.

I let my thoughts drift for just a moment, wondering about Arif having a wife. What would marriage even look like when you're a Citadel? Well, it would probably look like what I've just seen with Arif and Navaa, spending the majority of your time thinking that your partner is either injured or dead. I'm not sure why anyone would sign up for that.

I spend the next four hours learning how to speak Faida.

It is a fluid language with long pronounced *O* sounds and clipped *S*'s. I memorize the many different words the Faida have for flight. *Heouine*—flight during exceptional winds. *Youshin*—flight in the dark when the moon is full. *Dawlbei*—gliding flight on a wind from the Northeast. *Kaisu*—high-velocity flight. Theirs is a language that rarely uses metaphor or simile, presumably because there are so many different words to describe what English has only one or two for. While this makes it in some ways easier to learn than a language like ours—which can be deceptively confounding—its massive vocabulary pushes even my brain to the limit.

When I am finished, I close the laptop and lean back on the wall. I look up at the cathedral ceilings. I am sure that I could leap to one of the beams, which might give me some kind of advantage in a fight, but I need to be honest with myself about the situation we are in. If it does come down to a fight, I have already lost. On some level, I trusted the Faida enough to bring them here, to their turf. It's a disturbing wake-up call to realize that I felt like this Earth was somehow safer than my own.

The large wooden door swings open and Navaa enters without asking. She doesn't say anything, but she does place her delicate hands on the thick back of a chair and lift it so that she can sit down squarely in front of me.

"So you are a human Citadel. I must admit. You aren't what I imagined."

I glare at her, my eyes narrowing as I take her in. "I don't know why. You've been to our Earth before. You've seen us already," I answer her in Faida.

Navaa gives just the briefest shake of her head. "You can do that? You can learn our language in a matter of hours?"

"I can. Is that surprising? You know what we can do.

What did you think us human Citadels were *going* to be like? Dumber? Moodier?"

Navaa folds her hands on her lap. Her fingers are so long and her nails so neatly trimmed and perfect, I'm not sure how she could possibly do much fighting with them. I look down at my own hands, which aren't exactly ugly but are dry and nicked and calloused from punching and blocking and holding weapons.

"No," Navaa answers. "I thought you would be outraged. You're adolescents whose childhood was stolen. There is little doubt that you will die young. I assumed you would be angry. Instead you seem"—she tilts her head up and looks at the wall as if it was a window—"resigned."

I lean forward on the bed, swinging my legs around. "That is true. In a way. Although I'm not necessarily resigned to dying young. I guess it's more that I've accepted what's been done to me because bitterness won't serve me. It won't help me figure out the truth, or what to do with the answers once I find them."

"And you believe that we have the answers?" Navaa asks, even though I'm not sure it was a question exactly.

"I want to know what happened here. I want to learn from your mistakes because, clearly, despite your age and experience, you made several," I tell her boldly.

Navaa raises a single, perfectly arched eyebrow. Her spine straightens. It's clear she doesn't want to relive any of it. Maybe it's pride. Maybe it's pain, but her mouth sets in a firm, straight line.

I'm being combative and I don't necessarily mean to be. I'm just feeling anxious. The Faida are so extra . . . *everything*. It worries me that they of all races find themselves in this position. I clear my throat and try a softer tone. "You don't want to have to justify anything to me. I get it. I understand how distracting my face must be to you. You think I'm young. You don't think I could possibly understand." I lean closer toward her and grab the bottom of the bed so tightly the wood creaks. Navaa looks at me for a moment, then speaks.

"I won't make the mistake of underestimating our enemies or the creatures of our enemies ever again. I don't doubt your skill or your intelligence, but you are correct. I fear your youth makes it impossible for you to grasp the scope of what is happening here."

"Well," I say, chortling back to her nervously, "that's just not true. I mean, yes, it's true that I'm finding it difficult to wrap my head around the entirety of this, but it's not because I'm young. It's because the situation is absurd and I've only come into possession of the facts—if that's even what they are—a very short time ago. That's why I'm here, to try and figure out fact from hyperbole. I took Arif at his word when he said you rebelled against the altered Roones, but I gotta say, you're not doing a lot to get the whole trust ball rolling by throwing me in a cell."

Navaa shakes her long strawberry trusses as if we're in some kind of a shampoo commercial instead of what this actually is. An interrogation. "Oh, come now," she practically purrs. "We're both soldiers. You must have known a debrief was necessary. Besides, I've never seen a human Kir-Abisat. You are untrained and therefore dangerous. I can't allow you into the general population until I have a better understanding of your relationship with Rift matter."

"Yeah," I tell her uncomfortably. "Let's table that just for a minute. The whole Kir thing—I'm just trying to get some answers to a few of the basics first. Why don't you tell me what happened here. How did you win?"

Navaa's jaw sets, making her heart-shaped face almost

square. "I would hardly say we won. We *survived*. Some of us, and just barely."

I shake my head warily. "I don't get it. You knew. You all knew what the altered Roones were capable of. How could there have been dissension among the ranks?"

"Power is intoxicating. The Faida are a proud and privileged people, and the Roones played on that pride and that sense of superiority. I couldn't have imagined that we, who had seen so much, who had persevered through eras of infighting and bloodshed, could ever be seduced into believing that some of us were better than others. That those of us who had been altered were more deserving of authority and command because of genetics, but that's what happened."

I scratch my head. "So it was ego? God complexes?" I ask in disbelief, because despite how they look, they really do seem like they'd moved beyond all that, like they were more evolved as an entire race—and not just the genetically altered ones.

Navaa huffs out a sarcastic, two-syllable laugh. "Yes, in the most basic of terms, I suppose it was. And those of us who opposed that kind of thinking were ultimately naive enough to think we could win because we had morality on our side. But we weren't *that* naive." As she says this, Navaa straightens the fabric of her uniform, as if it could wrinkle, with her palms. "Even before we told every single Citadel what we had uncovered, we began to build a weapon. A sound barrier that could block a QOINS's ability to function. It was our intention to rally the Citadels, throw out the Roones and any Karekin—excuse me, Settiku Hesh—forces they might deploy, and use the weapon, but we didn't know that so many of us would side with the altered Roones. It's not like the fighting started immediately."

I let Navaa's words bloom in my brain. I imagine all the

different outcomes and strategies and plans. The Faida are not human, and they are certainly not teenagers. They are thoughtful, cautious even. They probably would have talked, a lot, before they started killing one another. "So you told the truth and you began to get pushback. That's when you realized you might need other Citadel races and then you sent out recon parties to see if there might be any help on that front. That's why Arif was on the Spiradael Earth."

"Exactly." Navaa answers with such force that her voice bounces and echoes off the tall plaster walls of the cell. "But after Arif left, things escalated very quickly. It was only days, really. The Settiku Hesh troops started coming in alarming numbers and we had to deploy the sound blockade. After that, there was no more room for diplomacy. The war began in earnest. Between the Settiku Hesh and the loyalists we lost almost sixty percent of our Citadels, though we have re-created the formula in our own labs and we have increased our numbers back up to fifty-two percent."

"And what about the altered Roones that were here?"

"Very few were stationed on this Earth. We executed them," she says, almost casually.

"All except for one. There is *one*, right? And you're still making more Citadels. Don't you think, after everything you went through, that might not be the smartest move?" I ask her with genuine curiosity.

An ever-so-slight flicker of disgust flashes over Navaa's face. "How did you know about him?"

"Technology, from our travels in the Multiverse," I tell her honestly. The SenMachs are going to play a part in this and the Faida are going to be all over it. For now, though, I'm sticking to the topic at hand.

Perhaps surprisingly, Navaa doesn't press. Instead, she gives me a sly half smile. "We have a single Roone prisoner whose mind is so broken that he's mostly catatonic with intermittent episodes of lunacy. We keep him only to open a Rift to the original Roone Earth when the time comes for it. As for the Citadels . . . the sound blockade was a stopgap. Your naïveté, is it genuine? Or some sort of ploy?"

I throw my hands up in the air and thrust my neck forward. "A ploy for what? I want this to end. That means *fewer* Citadels in the Multiverse, not more."

Navaa grunts and folds her arms. "Do you truly not understand what a threat we are? The fact that you, a human, are sitting here on this Earth, is changing the balance of power. The altered Roones will find a way through and they will slaughter us all. It's going to take more than an army of Citadels to defeat them—it's going to take legions of armies. It *is* a risk, creating more Citadels, but believe me when I tell you that it is far more of a risk to be without them in a battle."

I close my eyes. I gently stroke the delicate paper-like skin of my lids with my fingers. I am built for war. I am built to lie. I was made to protect my Earth, but this room is getting too loud. Each one of Navaa's words feels like a lit match thrown at my face. It's just too much. There are so many worlds, hundreds of thousands of troops. I know I have to find my way through this, but I ache, and not just physically. My personal life is a disaster and I suddenly feel so crushingly alone that I'm tempted to open a Rift right in that tall, slim cell and go home to my team. I need my friends. I need people around me that I know, *really* know.

I put both hands on my head and squeeze. I can't leave, but everything is starting to buzz, or maybe it's just me. I think about it more and realize that, actually, I *am* the one who's buzzing.

"How *did* you get through the sound barricade?" Navaa's voice cuts through the noise.

I look up at her and squint. "I told you. We made friends in the Multiverse," I tell her, maybe a little too loudly, just so I can hear myself. "They gave us some toys. Don't worry, though— we're the only ones with this tech. For one thing, the Roones don't know where their Earth is and even if they did, this particular race will only share with humans. I'm not saying they're invulnerable, but they're pretty damn close."

I put my head in my hands and drag my fingernails across my scalp. I want to get out of here, but mostly I just want this woman to leave me alone. There is a steady thumping to my headache. The pain is keeping time. If I could just lie down, maybe put a pillow over my head, this screeching in my ears would go away.

I wasn't looking, so it is a surprise when I feel the weight of Navaa's body sink into the bed beside me. "Our alliance is new and fragile," she tells me softly. "And, honestly, in this moment, I am less concerned with sizing you up as a human or a soldier than I am with your Kir-Abisat gift. It is a very distinct kind of pain you are feeling right now, with a distinct presentation. Even though we are not the same species, I recognize it on your face and it tells me the Kir-Abisat is controlling you instead of the other way around."

"You can literally see it on my face?" I ask in surprise.

"Yes, but also, I can hear it. We do not sound the same, because we are from different Earths, but because we are both Kir-Abisat, there is an additional shared tonal layer. It's like the same instrument being used in two different songs. I know that does not make sense to you right now, but it will."

"All right," I concede, sighing in frustration. "But why?" I ask, trying very hard not to whine. "Why make a person do what a machine can do better? It's so . . ." I search for the Faida word. I want to say Marvel-esque, but that won't do, so I say a word that means "fairy tale" or possibly "mythic."

"Look, I cannot tell you why the Roones are so obsessed with the Kir-Abisat. What I can do is help you navigate this gift if you'll let me. By that same token, you have to trust that it can be dangerous, not just for you, but for everyone around you. You have to let me see how far this ability has progressed before I can let you around my people."

I look up into her ice blue eyes. There is distance there, but compassion, too. "I can't hurt anyone. I mean . . ." I tell her as I backpedal out of a lie, "obviously, I can hurt people, but right now the only person being hurt by the gift is me. It's like someone shoved twenty songs inside of my brain and cranked up the volume all the way."

"Yes. It's like that. But I can teach you how to turn down that noise. Help you build an internal system to turn it up or down at will. Hearing people or creatures from other Earths is not the true legacy of the Kir-Abisat, it's simply a side effect or a symptom. Always, our cells are yearning to open a Rift."

I try to take this in. Arif said as much, but it seems impossible. Literally. Like, scientifically in a world where there is no real Hogwarts, opening a door to the Multiverse defies physics.

"I can see that you are having a problem believing me. So I suppose I must show you." Navaa taps on her earpiece. "Rotesse, please drop the sound blockade for three minutes." Navaa lays a confident hand on my shoulder. I'm not loving the idea of being touched by her, especially while I don't feel at my fighting best, but I suppose I'll have to go with it.

Navaa's eyes slowly close. She takes three deep breaths. Then, the very air in the small space becomes charged, and there is a smell. It reminds me of the woods at the base when the sky goes yellow, right before a big storm breaks. Navaa opens her mouth and, well, it isn't singing as much as her own vocal cords being bowed over one another. It's more instrumental than simple humming.

I can feel the power she is pulling from me. This is my tone, from my Earth that I'm hearing, the one that's playing at the same frequency in my head. And then, I see it. At first it is a tiny dot of green. A neon speck that begins to spin out like a pinwheel firecracker. The noise in my head goes away. The proximity of the Rift is somehow dampening it. The green looms larger and larger, changing color and form from eggplant purple to jet-black. This is the Rift to my home. Navaa has actually done it.

My mouth gapes and then she takes her hand off my shoulder and the portal closes in on itself and disappears. Navaa simply looks at me with her eyebrows raised.

"How many Citadels can do this?" I ask in a rush. I don't know what just happened. I'm not even sure something *did* happen. It must have, but I can't get my mind to believe what my eyes have just seen.

"I don't have exact numbers. Eighty-seven on this Earth. I don't think the Karekin or Settiku Hesh have this ability, and I'm fairly certain they didn't give this mutation to the Akshaji because they are too unpredictable."

"That's a diplomatic way of saying they seem to like all the killing, right?"

"Yes. The Akshaji are a race we haven't had any luck with in terms of recon. Hopefully, with the humans as allies, that will change. Either way, I don't know. It could be hundreds, or thousands. I don't even know if the gift works the same way in all the different races."

"And you really don't know why? I mean it's a cool trick, but we're soldiers. They trained us to fight big scary things. How does this ability help with that?"

"I honestly do not know. My best guess is to have a force of Citadels that can ferret out and capture enemies that are hiding on an Earth they don't belong in. Rogue Rifters cannot hide from a Kir-Abisat." All I can do is sigh in frustration. The Faida may look like celestial beings, but they certainly don't have all the answers.

She must sense my anxiety. "I am offering my help. It isn't easy, but as a Citadel you already understand discipline and focus. You have the tools. I can teach you how to use them. However . . ."

"However, it requires trust, from both of us," I finish for her. She nods.

There's nothing I would love more than to trust the Faida completely, but they are wily and arrogant. Sure, I think they want to be on the same side as the humans in defeating the Roones, but I get the feeling that they want to be in charge— both during *and* after. If there's one thing I've learned in this whole crazy mess it's that I'm not giving up my power to anyone, ever again. Still, if things continue going as they are, I won't be much use to anyone in this condition. I don't think I have much of a choice.

"I can see how I would have to trust you," I begin as I fold my hands together on my lap. I want Navaa to see that I'm open, amiable. "I don't know why you would need to trust me. I can't transfer this noise into your head."

"No. But you could open a Rift and I could get drawn into it. That's why I need to get a gauge on how far this ability of yours goes. What if your trigger is emotion? What if you're angry while walking down one of our hallways and accidentally open a Rift there? I don't know what you can do, so I need you to show me, to prove you aren't a threat."

"But the sound blockade—" I begin to protest.

"You got through the sound blockade. Maybe it was your enhanced technology, but maybe not."

"Fine," I tell her because something has to give, one way or another. "What do I have to do?"

CHAPTER 5

Navaa rises gracefully from the bed and walks across the concrete floor. "Stand." Navaa has both arms reached out, palms up. I go over to her and put myself in front of her hands. "May I touch you?"

I'm not gay or bi and on this Earth pansexuality could be the norm or it could be unheard of, so it doesn't really matter, but I joke anyway, "Aren't you worried about the Blood Lust?"

"'Blood Lust?'"

"Yeah—you know . . ."

And then it hits me: she may *not* know. I think of how easily Arif took me in his arms and carried me up to the level with our rooms. He didn't even hesitate. Do they all have control over it, or . . .

"The Roones—they didn't . . . *change* you, did they? Turn your sexuality against you?"

"What? How do you mean?"

So I tell her. About the abuse we'd experienced, and how it manifested. I gloss over some of the parts—no need for her to learn about the soap opera developing between me and Ezra—but for some reason it feels good to tell someone else who would actually understand what it means to be manipulated by the Roones.

After a moment, the look around Navaa's eyes softens, but the last thing I want is pity. They don't have the Blood Lust, but then again, neither do I now.

"Do whatever you need to," I tell her quickly, wanting to be done with this conversation. Still, my instincts are hammering away at my gut like a battering ram. Not because of the Blood Lust, but just at the thought of making myself so vulnerable to such a powerful woman.

"I'm just going to place my hands on your shoulders," she tells me as she does so. "It is easy to get lost in the noise and it's important that you have an anchor in these early stages. You may experience vertigo or lose your sense of time and space. The pressure of my fingers will remind you that you are here and you are not falling."

"Great. Sounds awesome," I say in English under my breath.

Navaa chooses to ignore me, but I think she gets the tone. "Now, close your eyes and focus on the sounds inside of your mind. The pain is coming from dissonance. The strongest frequency is the one that belongs to you, but the others are fragments of tones that you have pulled along with you from the Rift. You are the boat, the water is the Rift, and the wake is all the different Earths that linger."

I do as Navaa instructs, or at least I try to. It isn't just a question of hearing all these different tones. If it was only hearing, I could probably ignore it or tune it out. But the sounds are trapped inside of me and not just in my brain. There isn't a stretch of my skin or a bone or a joint that isn't filled with noise. Navaa had been right. Giving in to this is disorienting and I am surprisingly glad of her sure and steady hands on my shoulders. "All you are hearing right now is the disparate tones, but what you can't yet discern is the rhythm. This is what regulates this ability. We are all creatures of rhythm. Our hearts beat steadily. Our pulse and blood keep the same time. There is a clock inside of every living creature that tells us when to sleep and when to awaken. This is what you must tap into. Start with your own heartbeat. Find it. Concentrate on that."

Navaa takes my hand and pushes it up to my neck, to my carotid artery, and I am grateful. I'm not sure I would have found it without being able to actually feel it first.

Thump. Thump. Thump. Thump.

Once I lock on to it, I wrap it around me like a blanket knit of heat and sinew. I find my pulse everywhere—inside my chest, in the veins running up and down my arms—and slowly, the noise, which was a constant thrum, begins to echo in the short bursts of my own beating heart.

"I have it," I tell her.

"Excellent, just keep at it. Hold on to it. Its nature will change. The Kir-Abisat is like an excited animal snarling and leaping, pulling against its leash, but eventually, your focus will make it heel. Tell me when you get to the point that aligning the noise with the rhythm is no longer a struggle."

Navaa's analogy is a good one. This ability of mine feels wild and untethered, but after a few long moments, the fight in it subsides. My head doesn't hurt. The sound is there, pulsing, but it's like hearing music in another room. "Okay, okay, it's more controlled now," I tell my guide.

"That's good. That was fast. Let's just see, shall we, if we can get you to sing one of those tones. Perhaps the loudest one, the song from home."

"Wait, what?" I ask, my eyes flying open. "I'm not ready to do that. I don't know if I *ever* want to do that. I'm only listening to you now because I don't want to walk around with an amplifier in my head all the time."

"Some people are afraid of weapons," Navaa's voice lulls just inches away from my ear. "They find it distasteful to even touch one. A soldier does not have that kind of philosophical leeway. If it's possible for you to open a Rift, then you must learn how. You cannot waste the tactical advantage."

Damn—she's right. Of course she's right. But there is something about this that terrifies me.

"I wouldn't even know where to begin," I tell Navaa honestly.

"It's a question of multitasking," she tells me. I look slightly over my shoulder at her tapered fingers and the slight curve of a wing. "It's like playing an instrument. You must always keep time; your muscles know how to keep the beat going, but then your fingers play the melody. This is no different."

I did use to play the cello. I would have never made it professionally as a musician, but I had some talent. Maybe that's why the Roones chose to insert this mutation into my genome. "Fine. All right," I relent. "You want me to sing?"

"I want you to become the tone. You start with your voice, but you must try to pull it out from every inch of your being. It should feel more like a meditation than singing a simple song."

I close my eyes again. The noise is still tethered to my heartbeat, but with considerable effort I am able to find the strongest frequency. I clamp down with my molars. This feels dumb and wrong, but I suppose I have to see how far this ability goes as much for Navaa as for myself. I begin to hum with clenched teeth, matching my own pitch to the one I hear. And then, something shifts. I feel my entire body relax as if I was slipping into a warm bath. I open my mouth and eyes and continue to sing, although that word no longer applies. Navaa is right. The frequency of home infiltrates every cell of my body. I become the tone.

Within seconds a green neon dot appears on the plaster wall in front of us. The dot begins to spread out, but only a little. It isn't the spinning pinwheel of Navaa's Kir-Abisat. This is a shimmering circle. It is a small, glimmering thing, certainly not big enough for me, or anyone else to slip through unless they were action figure size. I sing louder but the circle doesn't grow, and it doesn't change into the inky black of a Rift that's ready to take on riders.

"Stop," Navaa says loudly.

"What? I can do it. I think. Maybe?"

I turn around and face Navaa. Her heart rate has increased and there is a faint crease between her brows.

"Possibly," she says with concern. "But you shouldn't have been able to get that far. The sound blockade is up again."

I practically grunt in frustration. "Then why did you have me even try?"

"I wanted to see and now I know. Your Kir-Abisat gene has expressed itself differently. Like everything else with the humans.

"The Roones have made you stronger."

CHAPTER 6

Navaa has said nothing more about what had transpired in the cell. I don't think she's concerned that I will open a giant Rift because of a bad mood or because someone pissed me off. I'm nowhere near being able to do that, even by accident. Still, I'm quite impressed with my first attempt at opening a Rift. It wasn't anywhere near usable, but it was green. However, I am an unknown. I think she had dismissed us human Citadels as petulant and possibly easy to maneuver. Spending time with me, she is beginning to understand that while we are young, we have been forged in pain and sacrifice, just as her own people were. Our strength and my Kir-Abisat ability is not what she expected. Soldiers don't like the unexpected.

She has taken me to the floor above. Well, she flew there in the cave elevator. I took the stairs. These are the living quarters, large wooden doors running down what looks like an almost endless hallway. There are plush rugs on a wide-planked floor and gorgeous oil pictures with no frames. The Faida are confounding. They enjoy their luxuries, but don't seem to want to admit that they do.

My room is across from Levi's and beside Ezra's. I have promised Navaa that she can look at our SenMach computers, as long as all of us are present. She is concerned about the sound blockade and the technology we used to get through it. I told her that even her most gifted computer scientists would not be able to get into our system. I understand why she'd be worried, though, and there might be something that we can do to help boost the sound blockade's efficiency without it interfering with us being able to Rift out if somehow this all goes to shit (which, let's face it, is a distinct possibility given my luck).

I dump my things in my room and take a look at the accommodation. The bed is unnaturally large with a fluffy duvet that must be three inches thick. Several leather books are lined up in a built-in bookshelf, and a delicate glass lamp sits on a bedside table. There is also a tall wooden armoire. When I open the two doors, I expect to see maybe a TV, but there are only hangers and drawers. Are humans the only race to have TV? I feel like we might be. Those bear people certainly aren't sitting around watching some bear equivalent to *Downton Abbey*, that's for sure. I continue my exploration of the room and find a small electronic panel on the wall hidden behind a piece of carved wood. There are controls here, for the lights and temperature. There is also a mystery button, which I push. Suddenly, two Faida are in the room speaking about the current unrest. I crane my neck and find a holographic projection system in the corners of the ceiling. It makes sense; the two are arguing in a studio behind a large desk, so the image isn't life-size and I can tell it isn't real—more like a diorama. I press the button again. If this is what passes for entertainment on the Faida Earth, no thanks. Even if there is a way to change the channel, it seems like a pretty dumb question to ask given what's going on. Besides, my head is still pounding, and my hair and neck are sticky from the pig debacle. I have done enough today. More than enough. It's time for a shower and that insanely comfortable-looking bed.

THE NEXT MORNING EVERYONE ASSEMBLES in the mess hall for breakfast. Like everywhere else on the compound, the dining room is awash with contradictions. The tables are all rustic wood but covered in fancy, starched white tablecloths. Food is set up buffet style in large ceramic dishes over blue flame warmers on either side of the room.

The three of us humans sit together at a table in awkward silence. I'm not exactly sure what it is that I'm eating. I think it's a sort of oatmeal, it's the same color, anyway, but it tastes more of corn and cinnamon. There is enough to look at so that we don't have to look at one another. The Faida Citadels with their angel-like plumage are gape worthy. Is no one ugly on this Earth? Or even average? I don't know their long and intricate history, but if I had to guess, I would say somewhere along the way there was some kind of eugenics program. It wouldn't just explain their common coloring, but also why they would be so casual about the altered Roones "perfecting" their genome. I'm white—*super* white—but the lack of diversity among the Faida makes me intensely uncomfortable. I stare at the mushy lumps in my bowl, at the unblemished tablecloth and the wooden fork that looks like something you could buy on Etsy. I look at everything except the two young men I am seated with.

I wonder if the Faida catch this. I am hoping from their perspective the fact that we aren't gabbing makes us look more badass. I would be mortified if they knew this is teenage drama being played out in front of all of them.

When we are done, we are escorted down two levels to the science lab. This place, at least, has very little of the rustic charm that has otherwise been inescapable here. There are wood beams of course, buttressing the ceiling, but other than that there are actual stainless steel and computers. The huge room is sectioned off. On the far right, based on the refrigerators and freezers and various microscopes, I'm guessing it's for biologists or chemists or both. There is another area with equipment that I don't recognize but looks pretty high-tech—although that's pretty relative at this point considering I've been to an Earth populated by robots.

We are herded into a space with multiple terminals and what looks like a long line of data storage towers, blinking red and orange, lined up against the wall. Navaa and Arif introduce us to Hanniah, who is clearly a scientist (lab coat). Not sure if she's a Citadel, even less sure if that matters. We ask Doe to show them the code that boosted our QOINS and begin to work on their sound blockade. Ezra is intrigued entirely by this tech—even more so when one of the glowing tendrils shocks the hell out of him when he attempts to tamper with the space bar.

Ezra volunteers to stay, which is convenient because I was going to ask him to anyway. Levi and I excuse ourselves. Ezra is so enraptured that he barely notices, which leaves me feeling surprisingly relieved.

Arif catches up with us on our way out of the lab. "We have a busy day today," he says amiably. "However, one of the other Citadels can show you around the compound, even take you out of it and into the city if you wish."

I glance at Levi. We have a body language shorthand now. One slight tilt of the head. A furtive look to the right. I know we are both thinking the same thing.

"That's very kind of you, but I believe our time would be better spent debriefing in our quarters, thank you." Arif shrugs amiably, and Levi and I head to my room.

We walk there in silence and I close the massive wooden door to my quarters and lean my body against it. Levi sits on the lushly piled rug and leans against the bed.

The bed frame is so high that his entire back is bolstered by it. We don't say anything to each other, not at first. Soon enough there will be plenty of words and so we enjoy a few blissful moments of quiet.

Today we're going to do our homework. We're going to be soldiers. We're going to pore over every intel file we have on the other Citadel races. We're going to learn their languages. We're going to see how they fight. And we're going to make sure that Iathan and the Roones back on their Earth aren't hiding anything from us. I'm not about to get blindsided again.

"Okay," he says finally, snapping me out of my own head. "Where do you want to start?"

"With the Spiradaels. Those pig things ate the one hostage we had, and I want to know more about them."

"I don't think they can be turned, Ryn."

"Neither do I. I just want to figure out the best way to kill them."

"Other than getting eaten by pigs?" He holds up his hand to make it clear that's a joke and pulls out his laptop so we can begin.

We spend hours learning the Spiradaels' guttural language, which lacks any sort of flair and only a handful of words that are more than three syllables. We study the footage we have of the giant spindly Citadel race. We watch how they use their hair as a razor-like whip. We see how they block and punch. From fighting them personally, I know they don't use their legs. It's all upper body with them. I think I understand it now. It seems the joints on their arms, necks, and shoulders allow them to contort these appendages almost 360 degrees. I don't think their knees do the same, so they focus on the chest and hair to win.

Over and over again we watch their fighting style and then we practice on each other, blocking and overcoming Spiradael attacks. I never could understand why the Blood Lust never kicked in during sparring, but it never has. This is just yet another mystery of how ARC works—how specific they were when they programmed us with the Blood Lust. It never interferes with our ability to fight an enemy. It only inserts itself if we try to have a life off the battlefield. After we finish with the Spiradaels, we begin with the Orsalines.

It takes all of an hour and forty-five minutes to learn their language. They simply don't have that many words. I still can't believe the altered Roones would choose them. If their genetic fuckery is this big gift, why waste it on dumb bear people? The secret must lie in not just their strength, which I am learning is far greater than I gave them credit for, but their devotion to the altered Roones. It's religious with the Orsalines. They're zealots and that might make them the most dangerous Citadels of all.

Levi and I study their fighting style. It's actually not so much a style as out-and-out berserker mode. They don't kick, because, well, bear legs. They don't exactly punch, either, as much as they do maul. Mostly what they do is either claw opponents to death or squeeze them until their organs burst. Sometimes, they will just hurl a boulder at them. Or a tree.

Once again, Levi and I do maneuvers and I am grateful for this huge, almost empty room with its cathedral-like ceilings so that we can use the walls and beams to hang and jump from. Technically, we are stronger than the Orsalines. We have more physical strength than any other Citadel, but I would hate to be on the receiving end of one of those hugs. We each find effective ways to get out of these holds and how to keep moving to make sure their nails can't get at us. They couldn't penetrate the uniform, of course, but a lucky swipe at the neck while going for the face would lead to death pretty quickly.

After that, we hurry ourselves to the canteen, grab something that looks like a sandwich with some kind of meat and bottles of water with additional electrolytes. We've got a lot of work to do and not much time until the council we've agreed to have tomorrow.

The Daithi are the next Citadels we study. Their language is nuanced and many words are difficult to pronounce as they don't use a lot of vowels, almost like Welsh. While the pronunciation and grammar is harder to grasp, the Daithi lexicon is more straightforward than most. There are very few words that mean the same thing, and it is abnormally absent of adverbs and adjectives. It is a language of nouns and verbs, of naming and doing. This in and of itself gives us further insight into their culture. The Daithi are as small as children, but that doesn't make them any less dangerous. They are remarkably fast and their fighting style is more like a dance than combat. They move in quickly with deadly accuracy and move to another place in the blink of an eye. The Daithi rarely block. They seem to have little use for defensive fighting because in the footage we've seen where they engage, no one—not even the Settiku Hesh—gets close enough to land a punch.

Levi and I quickly realize that the only way to defeat the

Daithi is if we don't rely on sight. We need to use our other senses—smell, their heartbeats, the whirring rush of air when a fist or leg swings toward a body. This is especially difficult for me because of the stupid Kir-Abisat and the sound my own body is throwing off, but in a way, it's good practice. It forces me to learn how to dampen it even more.

Levi blindfolds me, like the Jedi I've always wanted to be, and begins to attack. The first hurdle is just getting out of the way. I focus on his heartbeat and the heat signature his body gives off. When he lunges, eventually I get the hang of spinning away, ducking and rolling in a different direction. As cool as this is, it won't actually help us defeat the Daithi. Together, Levi and I come up with strategies that will help us strike immediately after deflection. For this, we use not only combinations of punches and kicks from very strange angles, but our knives as well. Guns would be the most useful, of course. I'm never above just shooting someone, but if things go down the way they did with the Spiradaels, we're going to need to fight them off long enough to talk to them.

We don't bother leaving the room for dinner. We stuff our faces with the tasteless gel cubes provided by the SenMachs. They will give us the nutrition we need and save us valuable time. Besides, I'm not in any mood to deal with Ezra. I'm actually enjoying today. It feels good to be doing something I'm actually good at as opposed to all this fumbling around, second-guessing every word I say and how it will be interpreted.

When we move on to the Akshaji for the first time, I begin to feel truly afraid. I had been worried up till this point and anxious, of course, because of the sheer volume of puzzle pieces the altered Roones were trying to put together. The Akshaji are barely Citadels. They've been enhanced, certainly, but it's clear they see the Rifts not as a call to duty, but as a form of endless entertainment.

The language does not take us long to learn, and soon we're able to converse in Akshaj as we study their fighting. But while learning Akshaj is easy enough, learning how to defend yourself from and beat a race of Citadels with six hands at the end of six arms is another story entirely. Levi and I use the sensuits to give us the illusion of this, a visual, just so we know what to avoid and how, but other than looking terrifying, it's a fairly useless way to train as the four "pretend" arms just kind of hover. In the end, Levi and I devise a high/low strategy and just have to hope it will work.

We spar, taking turns being Akshaj. As humans, we aim for the feet and calves in an attempt to get them off balance, on the ground preferably. Alternately, we go right for the head and throat, aiming killing blows there or using the leverage of what's around us to jump up and straddle our legs around the necks. Again, guns are always a bonus, but in the case of the Akshaji, we wonder if machetes or scimitars wouldn't be preferable. It would be a lot easier to just hack off those extra appendages than try to avoid them.

It is near midnight when we finish, but our day is hardly done. We ask Doe to show us any pertinent documents about the Roones that might help us. I had Doe download their entire database when I was on their Earth—unbeknownst to them, of course. We ask Doe to look for anomalies and inconsistencies in the data when compared to the story we were given by Iathan. Doe shows us videos, official documents, health records, experiment hypotheses, the various species the Roones spliced with their own to create the "altered" Roones and the Karekin. Doe assures us that the story Iathan told us is the truth, or at least, the Roones' version of the truth. The altered Roones would have a very different take on things.

So, for all of Iathan's arrogance and posturing, he wasn't lying. We can trust him as an ally. This should make me feel better, but for some reason it doesn't. It's so obvious from the research that a civil war was inevitable. I saw it coming years before it actually arrived. Politicians at one another's throats, rhetoric and propaganda about superior species. There were demonstrations and marches and strikes. The Roones didn't like what was happening to the Immigrants. The Roones practiced civil disobedience, but it was their civility that was their downfall. There is no reasoning with crazy. There is no compromising with tyranny. None of them thought in a million years it would get to where it would, and when it did, the Roones were more offended at first than they were tactical.

When we finally finish, I feel tired in a way that I haven't for a while. It is the exhaustion of a full day of hard work, of goals accomplished and the odd clarity you can sometimes find through busywork. I stretch my legs out on the carpet, flexing the arches of my feet and rolling my neck clockwise to get the kinks out. Levi is sitting on the only chair in the room. His back is resting against it, but there is an intensity to his gaze that lets me know he's far from relaxed.

"What?" I ask him hesitantly.

"We have to talk about this, Ryn. You need to tell me what the hell is going on with you and Ezra, because it's messy and it makes us all look bad." I don't answer Levi right away. Instead, I walk over to the tall leaded-glass window. It is pitch-black outside and all I can see is my reflection. Why don't these windows open? It's not like the Faida would be worried about someone falling out. I inspect the seams, I run my fingers over the cool metal, and I hear the window shift and creak. I move my hand away and the sound stops. I wave my hand over the window again and this time it swings open fully. Motion sensors. That's the kind of thing you might want to tell a guest.

I open the remaining three windows and a cool breeze rushes in to wash away the stale air. There is the faintest smell of eucalyptus and burning wood. The night creeps in slowly like a tired ghost. It's one thing to see the hour and quite another to actually feel it.

"I had sex with him," I tell Levi boldly. There's no point in lying. Ezra and I were together—though, perhaps, the reality was our togetherness was more of a technicality. Still, I believed I loved Ezra and maybe I did or even still do, but it was an indulgent love. It was selfish and myopic, as almost all first loves are.

Yet I also cannot deny that there is—and always has been—something between Levi and me. I can't say for certain what it is, though Levi seems to have a better idea of it. I also know that he hasn't allowed himself to feel much of anything for years, which means his feelings cannot necessarily be trusted. His emotions are just unfurling. They are gilded petals, bright and shining, too fragile yet to pluck and examine.

I watch his body change with this admission. His knuckles turn white as they grip the wooden armrests. His back molars grind together, squaring off his jaw. "Okay," he says softly. "Then what happened."

I bite the corner of my lower lip. I don't want to talk about this with him. It's none of his business. But . . . it *is* his business, and he's right to ask. There's too much obvious tension among us three right now, and that puts us at a disadvantage. Whatever we feel for each other, at this moment us humans have to put up a united front here. What's at stake is just too important.

"Everything changed. I don't know," I say as I shake my head. "He said there were rules. That once we'd been together like that, we were a proper couple and that I couldn't deprogram you anymore because it wasn't right to be intimate with someone else."

I watch as Levi gives a giant exhale out, as if there had been a weight pressing down on his chest and now his lungs were finally free to let go of a breath fully. "So, basically, he gave you an ultimatum."

I undo the topknot from my head. "I don't blame him. He's not wrong," I say as I let my long hair fall. I rub my fingers into my scalp to help relieve the pain of having it pulled back all day. "He just could have handled it better. I mean, I really thought he understood me. I *thought* he would have known for sure that I don't respond well to that kind of pressure."

Levi slides off the chair and crawls toward me on the floor. "But that's because he *doesn't* know you. You guys knew each other for a couple months and there were only two weeks of that time where you were *actually* together, right? Isn't it possible that the deprogramming sort of fucked with your ability to have perspective about him? Isn't there a really good chance that the love you feel for him is mixed up with a bunch of other things?"

A laugh escapes my mouth. "And don't you think you could say the same exact thing about you and me?" I chide.

Instead of laughing with me or even cracking a smile, Levi's eyes become even more serious. "No," he says firmly enough to wipe the grin off my face. "Because *I* know you. I've known you since you were a little kid. I've watched you train. I've fought beside you. I've been amazed by your ability to keep getting back up even when I know you've been hurt really bad. You're a good friend. You're an excellent commander. You hate ice cream and except for your uniform, I've never seen you wear the color green, ever, which is probably a question that answers itself. I know you and I never would have done what Ezra did to you."

I draw my knees up and wrap my arms around my legs. I am making myself small. This conversation is rolling around inside my chest like a marble in a tin can. "Well, that's easy for you to say—*now*. But trust me, things do feel different after you sleep with someone."

Levi throws his hands up in surrender. "That's what you've got to say to me after what I just said? You think it's cool to be casually rude? Are you *trying* to pick a fight?"

I actually don't want to pick a fight at all, but his speech was somehow both totally emotional and entirely logical. He might be right. And I don't want him to be right. Still, I tell him no, but I can hear my voice becoming harried. "It's just that if you and I had sex right now, you wouldn't want me dealing with Ezra. Right? You wouldn't want me touching him or holding him." The whole time I don't let go of my legs. I'm like a little khaki blob on the floor.

"Of course I wouldn't, but the difference is, I never would have had sex with you in the first place. Don't you get that? I wouldn't do that with you until I knew a hundred percent that it was you and me and no one else. I'm a Citadel. I know how to be patient. I understand the benefits of waiting it out. We both know that your aim is pretty much useless when you're trying to lock in on a moving target."

I sigh and bring my head up. "I don't even know if I made a mistake. Was I not supposed to get involved with Ezra? Was

I not supposed to try to deprogram you in the field? Because neither one of those things felt like choices."

Levi sighs, almost sadly. "I'm not saying that," he assures me. "I know *why* you slept with him."

This ought to be good, I think to myself. "Oh yeah? Why is that?"

"Because you could. Because you had a choice. For the first time, in years, you got a say in what you wanted to do with your own body." Levi wipes his palm over his face. "I get it, because I want that power, too."

Levi isn't wrong, but he isn't completely right, either. I had sex with Ezra, yes, because I could, but also because I *wanted* to. Because I care about him. Because I found him sexy and attractive and wanted to feel him as close to me as possible . . .

I push what feels like a literal swamp of emotions aside. They are sticky, murky things. I don't need to wade through them right now. Right now, I am looking at a boy who can't do what he wants, and I hate it. It's not fair. Levi doesn't get a say. He can't own his body the way that I can own mine, and the weight of those bonds is suffocating him.

"You should take some red pills," I tell him gently. "We should get your Blood Lust under control as soon as possible, especially here." I give him a wide grin. "There're a lot of really pretty girls here."

Levi looks up, but he does not return my smile. He opens his mouth to say something and then he closes it again with a brief shake of his head. "Ryn, I . . ."

"Don't, okay?" I push the words out of my mouth in a whisper. "The timing sucks. But the timing always sucks. Let's just do this. I want to be free of it. Don't you?"

Levi looks at me as though I've slapped him.

"I don't mean free of you," I say. "I don't mean that. I mean,

I don't want you to feel like you owe me anything and I want to stop feeling like I need to fix you. I want things equal between us, normal, whatever that looks like."

Levi doesn't say anything, but he nods his head slowly. He gets up and I hear him rustling through his pack. I listen to the slow zipping of his uniform being peeled away. I keep my eyes on the floor.

We go for a full fifteen minutes without saying anything. I close all the windows but one with a sweep of my hand. Levi puts some music on by an artist I don't recognize. When he is certain the pills are taking effect, he finally walks over to me. He is wearing sweatpants and nothing else because for some reason, he seems to have an aversion to shirts. Or maybe he knows what he looks like shirtless. It's probably that.

He stands close. He stands so close it feels like he's doing my breathing for me. His eyes are green. A color I never wear, he's right about that. Green clothes feel like work. Levi's eyes are the color of a faded book cover. They are the same shade as my mother's rain boots. I notice that in his irises there are lightning bolt streaks of brown and yellow.

Ever so slowly he brings his hand to my face. He traces my eyebrow and cheekbone with his thumb. I want to tell him to stop. This is not how the deprogramming should work. Deprogramming is not about sex. Deprogramming is about feeling safe when someone you find attractive touches you. It's more about recapturing a feeling of childhood security than hormones. I want to say these things to him, but it's almost as if those green eyes of his have me in some kind a constrictor knot, one that gets tighter the more you try to get loose.

Levi's hand moves into my hair and he balls it in his fist. It shouldn't be like this. We should be watching animated films and listening to lullabies. He should be eating his favorite foods as I read a book out loud while we hold hands, but I suppose we've already done some of that stuff. Maybe there aren't any rules to this. Maybe the way I deprogrammed won't necessarily work for him. Levi is a superintense person. It's hardly surprising his process would be intense too. When he takes a step closer, I feel a twinge of guilt.

Ezra.

I just had sex with Ezra two days ago. Then I shake that thought away. I'm not Ezra's girlfriend anymore for this very reason. So what if I was with another guy a couple days ago? I could sleep with a hundred guys and it wouldn't change anything. It wouldn't make me a bad person, despite what good girls are "supposed" to do. I'm a loyal friend. I've literally taken a bullet for someone on more than one occasion. I keep this awful secret so my parents aren't destroyed. I am trying to save the world.

I *am* a good girl.

But I am not the same girl who left Battle Ground.

Levi's mouth hovers at my face and then he plunges it into my neck, breathing me in. I feel his lips brush against my ear. He had told me before that I smelled safe. Smell can be a visceral sense, so I hope that this is his way of taking additional precautions. But when he brings his head up, he doesn't waste any more time with safe. He kisses me deeply, intently. I probably shouldn't be comparing them, but I can't help it. Ezra's kisses were sweet and light and good. Levi is all fire. Levi kisses me like a drowning man clinging to a capsized boat.

I stop thinking about Ezra.

We continue to kiss, our tongues snaking in and out of each other's mouths. He picks me up in one fell swoop with a single hand and in the crook of his elbow carries me to the bed. For a moment, everything is perfect as he props me on top of the thick duvet. My hands are wrapped around his neck and his fingers are holding on to the sides of my face. And then.

And then . . .

Those green eyes change. They narrow and glare. Levi's accelerated pulse begins to get even faster. The Blood Lust. It's kicked in. I go perfectly still. I bow my head. I try. I try so hard to disappear in that moment, but there's no point. He's been triggered and I really thought that maybe we were past this. In truth, I'm more disappointed than I am scared. Still. If he kills me, I'm not sure how that would go down with the Faida. He could even be tried for murder. Citadels in Battle Ground are protected from stuff like that, but here? I have no idea. Levi yanks me up. He snarls in my face as he digs his fingers into my shoulders. He has me at least a foot off the ground. Of course, I could get away. Inside of two seconds I could have him out cold. I'm in my uniform and he's not. He wouldn't stand a chance against me.

If I hurt him, I'll ruin everything. That's the thing. That's the thing that keeps pulling me back to Ezra. He knew his life was on the line when he deprogrammed me and he did it anyway. I almost killed him. Twice. He believed in me. He somehow knew that I was stronger than my abuse and more powerful than my abusers. That's what makes this whole situation a total fucking shit show.

And now, here I am. Levi's hot, sticky breath growling up against my face. I cannot fight back. My strength is my vulnerability, and I have to hope that it's where Levi's lives, too. He keeps me in midair for a full twenty seconds. He's fighting this, I can see it. It's the inherent problem with the Blood Lust. You *can't* fight it. You have to balance on the knife edge of it. You have to surrender your body and your instincts and let that spark of innocence wriggle its way to the surface.

I want to tell him this, but talking will only make it worse at this point. Levi lifts me higher and throws me like a dart, with all his (very significant) might at the door. I manage to contort myself somewhat in the air, spinning so that my head won't hit the wooden frame. This maneuver works, sort of. I knew that my suit would absorb most of the impact, but I am not wearing my boots. So, while I've managed to angle my body sideways, to protect my skull, I have totally forgotten about my foot. When it hits the door, it hurts like hell. It makes me want to scream, but I suck the sound back into my throat because that would only excite him more.

Since I'm right here and since killing me might ruin our chance to save the world and all, I think my best option is to make a run for it. Figuratively at least. Before he can get to me, I leap up on my good foot and fling the door open. I close it behind me and hold it shut. The door is thick and solid and the handle is iron so I'm hoping I can keep Levi in there long enough for it to pass.

As soon as he realizes I've trapped him in there, he begins to scream.

"I'm gonna kill you!" Levi shouts. "You hear me, Ryn? I'm going to rip your lungs out while you watch. Open the fucking door!" Levi begins to pound and it's enough to alert our neighbors all along the hall and they come rushing out. Ezra is first. He's wearing nothing but his boxers and the look of sleepy-eyed confusion that he may just be dreaming. Levi keeps banging on the wooden planks.

"Are you afraid to fight me, Ryn? Because you should be. I'm going to wrap my hands around that pathetic neck of yours and squeeze until you turn fucking blue, you bitch, let me out of here!" There are now at least ten other Faida in the hallway. They look baffled. I don't know what to say exactly. This is the very definition of uncharted territory. The Blood Lust plays it-self out. In person. Well, that's not exactly true. The first time Ezra triggered me, I told him to run to the bathroom before it well and truly had me in its grip. I bashed my head against the floor until the pain dragged me out of it. Still, that had been just a hand on my clavicle. I think the more sexual things get, the more fierce the Blood Lust becomes.

So all this yelling and these verbal threats are unexpected. It's the kind of thing you just think. Hearing Levi say this shit out loud is both embarrassing and unsettling. My heart sinks as I see Arif and Navaa approach slowly. "This isn't him," I tell them, still holding the ever-increasingly jerking door. "This is the thing they did to us," I try to explain. The two look at each other and then me with barely veiled judgment. And then, Arif adds his own hand to the long black iron handle. Levi is just screaming now, his voice getting more and more hoarse as he continues to try and get out. Then, there is a great crunch-ing squeal, the sound you hear when a tree splinters after be-ing cut down. Levi has ripped the door off the hinges and it goes flying back into my room, crashing against the post of the bed.

Without even hesitating for one moment, Arif grabs me and pulls me down, wrapping his wings around my entire body for refuge. All the other Faida join him, creating a giant teepee of protection.

"Don't hurt him!" I yell, though the feathers muffle and dampen my scream. "If he gets hurt, he'll never get better. Just defend yourselves." I realize in that moment, I am asking quite a lot of my new potential allies. Levi is stronger than any of them, but he's not stronger than *all* of them. Also, thank-fully, the protective grid that makes their wings bulletproof seems to be a permanent modification. As Levi begins punching and kicking, I hear the distinctive buzz of an electronic force field at work.

After about a minute, the sound stops. It's pitch-black inside. I can't see what's going on, but I do feel the slight shift of air as the whirling mass of wings slowly unknits itself around me. Eventually, my vision returns. I am on my knees, curled into a ball, my hands covering my head. I look up and see the Faida have all backed away and Levi, poor Levi, is just standing there. The Blood Lust has run its course. It has hollowed him out and he looks more broken than I've ever seen him.

I know he must be humiliated. I stand up and realize, my foot. I wince and pull it up behind me. "I'm okay. Everything is fine," I tell him softly. I have my arms out in front of me, hoping he'll come to me, hoping he'll show them all that he isn't some crazy monster. He doesn't quite seem to see me, though. He is looking through me. "No one got hurt and everyone understands," I assure him. "Let's just go back to your room. We'll get you settled, you can get some sleep. You need to sleep."

My pleas seem to snap him back to reality. He swallows hard. I watch as he begins to back away. "I'm sorry. Everyone. I'm . . ." Levi's voice is barely a whisper. He hasn't been physically injured, but emotionally, I don't know how this will affect things.

As if reading my mind, Navaa walks gracefully toward him. "In truth, Levi," she says with a sweet and gentle tone that I didn't even think she was capable of, "we are all aware of what the altered Roones did to you. It is unsettling to witness, but also necessary, I think, to better understand the depravity of our common enemy. We do not judge you."

"It doesn't matter. It's cool. Let's just go back to your room," I say. I attempt to walk, but it hurts to put too much weight on my foot. I disguise my pain with a smile. I sort of shuffle toward him, dragging my painful foot behind me.

"No!" Levi says with sudden authority. "I don't want to be around you. Or anyone. I'm very sorry." And with that, Levi turns and rushes into his own room. An awkward silence weaves its way around all of us as soon as his door closes. Ezra walks swiftly over to me. I'm thinking he might be concerned. I'm thinking he may be worried that I am actually hurt. As soon as I see the furious look on his face, I know that is not the case.

He gets right up to me and whispers sternly in my ear, "I can't fucking believe you did that. Here. With them. In this place." He grips my wrist and pulls me even closer. "Your Blood Lust was nothing compared to what I just saw. Levi is going to kill you. I hope to God you know what you're doing." He jerks his hand back as if suddenly my skin is toxic and stomps away, practically slamming the door behind him. Well, I suppose I know where things stand between us now. He'll never be able to forget what he just saw and I know without a shadow of a doubt that he will never, ever, look at me the same way again. And as much as his masculine sense of entitlement disgusts me, it doesn't change the fact that his rejection rips at my guts nevertheless.

I don't know what to do. Everyone is looking at me. I go to open my mouth, but Arif speaks before I get the chance. "You don't need to explain. It seems you are injured. Can I offer medical assistance?"

As if this whole situation wasn't embarrassing enough, I'm not about to add to it by waking up one of their doctors. "No. I'm sure it's just a bruise, but thank you. Thank you all for your help with this. I'm going to go back to my room."

I hobble away before any of them can say anything else.

When I get to my room (now annoyingly without a door), I peel my uniform off and tend to my foot. I don't think it's broken, but I take all the medicine the SenMachs and altered Roones have provided in my med kit just to be sure. I don't think I'll be able to sleep at all because of what happened, but my body overrides my absolute mortification. I need to heal more than I need to brood and worry. My last thought is of Levi. The look on his face, the shame and desperation. Hatred for the altered Roones quickens my pulse. I keep my fists clenched as I drift away.

CHAPTER 7

Several hours later we are sitting at a large oval wooden table. Unlike many of the rustic pieces of furniture on the base, this one is polished with a slick lacquer that is so shiny I can see my face in its surface. I try to keep things as professional as possible given what happened the night before. The best way to do this is not to look too closely at Levi and Ezra. Denial will always work in a pinch.

I am sitting at one head of the table, the unofficial boss of the human race. I'm actually pleased to see Navaa at the other end. Maybe with two women in charge, communication will be front and center of these briefings. Navaa had very cleverly separated Ezra and Levi and seated them among the other Faida. If we are all to be on the same side, the three of us can't be seen set apart from the rest.

This is a dark, lush room with a bluish light cascading down from the unusually low ceiling. The chairs are black leather with a slim column of padding for the back. It's a highly functional piece of furniture for people with wings, but as for the rest of us . . . not so much. Still, the entire vibe of this space has a subdued elegance about it. This is a room meant for comfortable sequestration and I find this a bit surprising. Citadels aren't supposed to ever get too comfortable. Then again, on our Earth, Citadels are only soldiers. But Arif had told us that on this Earth they are other things as well—doctors, engineers, diplomats. Considering that 60 percent of the Faida Citadels were annihilated, I'm not sure theirs is the better way to go.

A large, flat glass panel emerges from the center of the table. I notice again how they like to keep their technology hidden away, beneath panels, under floors. Perhaps the Faida, with their giant, glorious wings don't like the reminder of what technology has done to them, or maybe they feel that it is somehow crass. Their posturing is disingenuous. There is only science here, all of it hard and none of it forgiving.

Navaa opens the meeting. She has an illuminated screen at her fingertips that she is using to control the images we are looking at on the panel in front of us. She brings up all seven of the Citadel races.

"Let's begin with what we can safely assume are absolute facts," she says with her usual air of authority with a dash of arrogance. "Ezra was able to bring us up to speed about his time on the original Roone Earth. Most of what he told us we already knew, but it was nice to hear that the original Roones want to stop their counterparts as badly as we do. Basically, what we are looking at is a game of numbers."

"You mean, which of the Citadel races we can get to side with our cause," Levi says. If he had any residual issues about the incident in my room, he left them outside this one. I can't help but breathe a sigh of relief. He's not about to let what happened distract any of us from what's truly important and by speaking up now, he's proving the point.

"Exactly. So, the Spiradaels." Images of the Spiradaels begin to pepper the glass in front of us. "Our team spent a considerable amount of time observing them and we have ruled that they are as brainwashed as the Settiku Hesh. It's our conclusion they cannot be turned. Humans, do you concur?"

I don't need to confer with my fellow humans to make a decision about this. Ezra, for all his knowledge of the Citadel races, never fought one or spoke to one. He never learned their language. Only Levi and I looked any of them in the eye and we had both agreed on this last night.

"We agree."

"Good. Then let's talk about the Orsalines," Navaa says as she brings several photos and video footage up on the screen in front of us. I glance over at Ezra. I see that the interface below him has been activated as well. As Navaa speaks, lines form in an iridescent white on the table, just in Ezra's eyeline. Somewhere in this room there is a mic and a translator hard at work. Not an actual person, but a program and I'm glad of it, because it means I don't have to do it myself. I have to pay attention to what's going on here and that requires all my focus.

Plus the idea of talking to Ezra right now makes my stomach roil.

"What you are looking at is over fifty-seven shrines that both our flyovers and the Roone drones have photographed. These are temples dedicated to the altered Roones. We knew they had cast themselves as deities, but we didn't realize it was to the entire planet. *Every* Orsaline believes the altered Roones are their gods, not just the Citadels."

I take a closer look at the "shrines," squinting as I inspect them on the screen. They are massive multicolored spheres, clearly representing the bald heads of the altered Roones. Some are just three or four rocks in neat pile, while others are actual structures (of a sort) with doorways. The images show Orsalines making their way in and out of them with offerings of . . . *rocks . . .*

Typical.

"We made two recon trips before the sound blockade went up," Sidra, head of the Faida's intelligence unit, offers. She speaks with a lulling cadence. This must be muscle memory for her vocal cords. No doubt she's been trained to keep people at ease, to get them to open up and offer their secrets. Torture really isn't all it's cracked up to be. Sometimes, all a person needs is to feel like they have someone who's on their side, someone who understands. Sidra, with her pearly white wings and long curly ashy-blond locks is clearly that kind of operative. "The Orsalines were living in huts when the altered Roones arrived. They were given an origin story, a bible of sorts—they aren't big readers. The Orsalines may or may not have been drugged, but they have most certainly been brainwashed. To go against an altered Roone would be akin to blasphemy."

"Levi and I were worried about this; they're zealots," I chime in. "Extremists and extremely stupid. I still find it hard to believe that given the altered Roones' MO that they would even waste their time genetically enhancing such an infantile race."

"Sometimes it's good to have foot soldiers," Donav, the munitions officer says. "Put the dumb ones in front. Let them get the worst of it. But also see what kind of damage they can do—and these guys can do some serious damage. It's a good way to make sure that your best soldiers survive." Donav's voice is a syrupy baritone. I could listen to him all day, mostly because he would be talking about guns and explosives. And also—cheekbones.

Seriously, with his red hair, he's like an insanely hot Archie Andrews with Batman's toys.

I force myself to respond to what he's saying, and not what my mind is imagining.

"Right," I say. "So my feeling is that if an entire race of people have proof—well, what they think is proof—of the divine, I don't think that's something we could shut down. Even if we got one and explained what was going on, I doubt they'd understand it."

"That's our assessment as well," Navaa said, nodding. "An Orsaline alliance is not an option. So that makes two Citadel races solidly for the altered Roones." There's a clear thread of frustration running through her voice.

"So what about the Daithi? Did you ever send a recon team there?" I ask hopefully.

"We did, but the sound blockade went up before they could return home," Sidra answers in that calm, almost seductive voice of hers. I keep the sigh I want to let go of locked inside my rib cage. That's two teams they had out and they basically cut them off before even attempting a rescue. Not cool, angel people, not cool.

"However," Navaa jumps in, "we do believe the Daithi are our best chance at an alliance. As you know from the research, which we've gained even more of since you shared Edo's computer with us, the Daithi are not a technologically advanced race, but they are a conquered people."

That's not as impressive to me as it sounds like it is to Navaa—it only proves to me that the Daithi are easily subjugated.

"They put up a fight, Ryn," Navaa says as if reading my mind. I sit up a little straighter in my chair. There are few images of the Daithi on the panel in front of me. What images do exist are tiny blurs, like a dark fingerprint getting in the way of a shot. They are fast, I'll give them that.

"The altered Roones assumed they could be easily conquered, but it took months rather than days. They made strategic strikes and had the Settiku Hesh and altered Roones scrambling . . . all *before* they were ever given any Citadel enhancements," Sidra adds.

"So you think we could get through to them?" Levi asks.

"I do believe that if we could get some of them alone and get the drug out of their system, then, yes, I think we have a very good chance," Navaa says with confidence.

"We'd have to get one first. And they are fast. They're like little bolts of lightning," I tell her with obvious skepticism.

"But you're faster," Yessenia argues. She is the chief medical officer for the Faida Citadels, so I suppose she would have the most expertise on our biological differences. "All the human Citadels are." I don't bother telling her that she's right. We are faster. The Daithi rely almost entirely on their speed. But we have a much larger toolbox, giving us both the advantage and disadvantage in that context—it's the difference between a specialist and generalist.

Navaa clears her throat. "How we proceed in further negotiations is not why we're here today. We're here to come to a consensus on which Citadel races we try to ally with. We can figure out the *how* later. So do we agree that the Daithi are our best chance?"

"The human contingent agrees," I offer, "but for the record, it's not with the same amount of confidence you have."

"Noted. Let's move on to the Akshaji."

The gruesome images of these Citadels come roaring onto the screen on the table. There is blood—not necessarily red, since not all species bleed crimson—against the shimmering purple of the Akshaj Citadels. The sinister pleasure they derive from killing is clear from these images. They don't just shoot or stab. They gut, maim, disembowel, and rip limbs, all with a sly smirk of enjoyment. Ezra turns away and I understand. He isn't built for this kind of violence. I *am* and it's not like I'm enjoying any of this.

"Before you ask," Sidra announces to the room diplomatically, but I know she's talking to me, "we did send a team, well before the sound blockade went up, and they never returned. They never checked in after the first twenty-four hours. We thought it best given the already tense situation here that we not send another unit."

"The Akshaji are unpredictable, mercurial, violent, and more mercenary than other Citadels. However, I think if we make a compelling enough argument, we could get them on our side," Navaa says with a slight tilt of her head. One of her long strawberry locks falls onto her cheekbone and she sweeps it aside efficiently.

I absentmindedly fiddle with the zipper on my uniform. She might be right—and I'm not really sure she is, based on what I've seen—but even if she is, I'm not so sure I want anything to do with these animals. They are killers. Murderers. I can't deny that I feel a certain amount of pleasure when I take out a particularly nasty hostile, but I don't wear their entrails afterward like a necklace.

Levi has even more doubts. "Why would you think that?" he interjects. "Why would the Akshaji take sides in a war they don't care about? Especially considering that, by all accounts, the altered Roones have been completely transparent with them."

Good point. I fold my arms together, waiting for an answer from Navaa.

"I highly doubt the Akshaji know about the Midnight Protocol," she says. "It would be easy to plant seeds of suspicion and doubt. They are as paranoid as they are violent." I'm not sure if Navaa is overreaching here, but it does make a certain sense.

"So basically what you're saying is we have to convince them that we are the stronger force and that eventually the altered Roones will turn on them," I ask, double-checking to make sure we're all on the same page.

"Exactly. It would be difficult, but not impossible. It is the Faida's suggestion to this joint council that we seek an alliance with the Akshaji, the caveat being we bring the Daithi in before going to them."

"Great. What's our next step, then?"

"I propose we loop in Gomda."

"Who's that?"

"He heads up the team that's in charge of deployment operations. Their sole job is to make sure that all soldiers have everything they need to survive on a mission, from provisions to ammo. Gomda and his staff are extremely thorough and I have no doubt that they will be able to help us mount an immediate and successful expedition to the Daithi Earth—"

"Wait." I interrupt her again and she clenches her jaw ever so slightly.

I don't want to run roughshod over her, so I choose my words carefully. Finally I say, "I'm impressed with the speed at which you feel comfortable deploying troops for a covert op. I also understand that time may be our biggest enemy here, but we have to go back to Battle Ground first. We need to check in with the people we left in charge, make sure Camp Bonneville is still in our control, and debrief them on everything we've learned."

Both Levi and Ezra swing their heads around in my direction at the same time. I hadn't discussed this with either one of them. But then again, I hadn't even realized how badly it needed doing until I got to this room. We don't have all the answers, not by a mile, but we have some of them. Beta Team needs to know what we know. We need the greatest tactical minds working on this problem, which most definitely includes my team and the rest of the higher-ranking human Citadel officers.

"I'm not sure that's the best idea," Navaa suggests rather haughtily. "If the altered Roones find you, this alliance will be over."

"If ARC takes back Battle Ground, then the alliance is over anyway," I say with a shrug. "Right now we control a single Rift and thousands of Citadels. If we lose that advantage, I wouldn't even know where to begin. And you have to remember, humans don't even know there are other species of Citadels, let alone that the Settiku Hesh are Roones and that *the Roones* are altered, too. They don't know *anything*. Imagine a Spiradael unit coming through and acting compliant until the intake, inside the compound. Our people have no idea how many enemies are really out there, and I'm not about to leave them so exposed."

Navaa puts her hands together, slender tapers that she squeezes tightly on the table in front of her. "If we lose you, we lose any chance of being able to Rift off this Earth safely, of forming alliances with other Citadels. At least take a strike unit of ours with you in case—"

"No way," Levi jumps in. "If a Roone sees you, then we're busted. Not to mention that we can't do things the way you did them here. We kinda tried that already and it led to a coup. We need to find another way, and maybe some of our people will have an answer," Levi argues, echoing my own internal thoughts.

Navaa frowns, as if there was no way us pitiful humans would be able to solve the problem if they couldn't.

"Enough," I say, leaning back into the seat. "We're going. Today. Navaa, please don't be offended when I tell you that I wasn't asking permission. I was simply informing you of our plans out of courtesy."

The entire Faida delegation is purse lipped, as if they had been sucking on lemons. "Thank you all," I tell them as I stand. "The briefing was illuminating. I'm really encouraged." I don't mean to sound like a smart-ass, but I probably do. And I really don't care. I can't defer to them. Not now. Not ever.

Everyone else around the table also makes a move to leave. Ezra ambles over in our general direction and we all walk out of the room together. He kept his mouth shut. I'll give him that much.

"You aren't coming, so don't even ask," I tell Ezra as we walk down the long hallway. The war room is far beneath the mountain. It had taken a good while for us to get down the stairs. At least I'll get my workout for the day climbing up them again.

"But—" Ezra begins.

I swivel quickly on my toes, turning to face him. I don't even say anything—my eyes say it all. His mouth turns into the shape of a Cheerio and then his lips flatten out. This is one battle he won't win and he knows it.

"Fine. I'll just stay here and try to get an estimate on the numbers."

"What do you mean?"

"I'll pool the recon and see if there's any way to tell how many Citadels we're looking at here and what different alliances might look like."

"Good call," I tell him honestly. Statistics are something we actually need. What we don't need is Ezra slowing us down. For a brief second I feel guilty. I know I am not being all that nice. Just a short while ago Ezra and I had been together. He put his life on the line to cure me of my Blood Lust. I had fought my way through the Multiverse to find him. I had loved him. I *had* loved him, hard and recklessly almost to the point of abandon. Now I'm finding it a struggle to even be nice. Then again, this is war. Nice can take you prisoner. Nice can get you killed.

CHAPTER 8

Levi and I open a Rift back to Battle Ground and walk out into a frigid night filled with a canopy of stars. We decided on a farm, closer to Meadow Glade than Camp Bonneville. Just a quick run and we should be back in our neighborhood. It's two thirty in the morning. Violet's parents will be sleeping, but chances are that she won't be. Violet lives only blocks from my own house. I have to be careful now. This feels as dangerous as it did when Levi and I first walked onto the Roone Earth thinking to rescue Ezra. It is imperative that no one but Beta Team sees us. Edo absolutely cannot know that we are here. She must believe that we are trekking on an adventure through the Multiverse in search of Ezra, allowing the Rift to mutate my Kir-Abisat gene even further. Otherwise . . .

No. I can't think that way. We won't get caught.

When I get to Violet's house, I spring up like a cat and then leap off a tree onto a gable, and I hang from her windowsill. I bring up my free hand and tap lightly on the glass. It only takes a second or two for Violet's face to appear. Her eyes are bright, her smile grateful. I allow myself to fall, landing in a crouch position, and Violet silently opens her window all the way and drops down wearing Nikes and oversized sweats.

She pulls me into a fierce hug. "Oh my God. You're home. You aren't dead," she whispers in my ear. Little fragments of her voice are catching. Violet is about to cry.

"We're back, but just to check in. We need to get to Henry and Boone ASAP," I tell her with urgency.

Violet lets me go and takes a step back, cocking her head at me. "Um, hi," she says sarcastically. "Remember me? Your best friend? The one who had to watch you and G.I. Joe over there. Hi, Levi."

"Hello, Violet," Levi replies with a quick flash of a smile.

"Anyway . . . I had to watch the two of you walk into a Rift never knowing if I'd see you again, so maybe just give me a minute to be happy you're safe?"

I grab Violet by the shoulders and squeeze. I don't want to scare her but . . . . "We don't have a minute," I tell her gravely.

She takes a beat. I'm sure she thought that with my return maybe this whole thing was on its way to being over, and then she sees the tension in my stance, how I'm partially pitched forward and the way my neck is jutted slightly out. Vi knows. I watch as her whole body folds into itself. Violet is a good Citadel, but she was never made for war. She can and will defend with her life. She will take lives in that pursuit, but the offensive game? Her mind just doesn't work that way.

But like I said, she's a good Citadel, and she asks no more questions. We take off into the night. We run fast. Our feet are skipping stones through backyards, over fences and guardrails, through pastures and parking lots. We get to Battle Ground Square and make a beeline for Boone's. When Violet gets him, he, too, embraces me without hesitation or worry. That's a relief—it means his Blood Lust may be cured or, at least, well under control. He also knows better than to ask questions. I will only talk when we are all assembled. There's no time to waste. Henry's house is just a few streets over. We're there in no time, and Boone goes in through the back door. They both scramble out in a matter of seconds.

Henry doesn't want to embrace me. I can see the look of relief on his face, which is then quickly replaced by something else. I have come in the dead of night. I am not at Camp Bonneville. It has taken him one second to figure out that whatever I have learned is not good. Henry is a rock star among Citadels. Levi and the boys acknowledge each other's presence with a quick nod. I can tell when my team has their guard up. Levi is nothing more than an acquaintance—a fellow Citadel, yes, but they don't *know* him. Hopefully, when they see how much trust I put in him, they'll understand that they can follow my lead.

The five of us make our way behind Henry's house, to a wooded area where there is a walking path. When we get far enough away, I don't bother with preamble. There's no need to go into Microwave Earth or Gladiator Earth. I stick with what I've learned that's of use to us. Levi joins in the conversation when necessary. Violet keeps her hands either tucked around her or at her lips, as if she's praying. Boone is pacing. Henry is stock-still, his fists flashing open and closed at various intervals.

When I am finished, no one says anything. I am on my own Earth. There is no buzzing or humming, nothing to keep caged behind my eardrums. It is not, however, silent. My fellow Citadels, all but Levi, have elevated heart rates. *Boom. Boom. Boom.*

There is something scurrying on a branch and in the thicket of trees behind us there is a rustling, not a person—no, we would have heard that. Maybe a cat or a raccoon.

"Well, that's us. Fucked. In the ass. By several partners," Boone says grimly. Then adds, "Sorry, bro," in Henry's direction. I roll my eyes. Henry is gay and he lets Boone be an idiot about it sometimes—and by "lets," I mean he doesn't kick his ass every time he makes a stupid comment. Though I will say that Boone has generally gotten better. But not tonight. Tonight, Boone is scared enough to revert back to his old juvenile patterns.

Unsurprisingly, it falls flat. No one is in the mood. Then again, I doubt Boone really is, either.

"The good news," Henry says, ignoring Boone, "is that Camp Bonneville is secure. But we have to assume that Edo is feeding everything to ARC. They know and it's just a matter of time before they sweep in."

"Not necessarily," Levi tells us all. "The altered Roones don't care about ARC, not really. They care about their work, their Citadels, and more specifically the weird buzzing gene they gave to soldiers like Ryn. They probably think the Allied Rift Coalition is just as much of a pain in the ass as we do."

"Fine, okay," Violet says, trying so hard to keep her voice calm. "But what do we *do*? I mean the magnitude of this—it's too much. Where do we even start?"

"Well, first of all, we don't make a public service announcement the way Ryn did before she left," Boone says. "We all know how that ended. The brainwashing and the drugs. We might be able to get through to a portion of the Citadels, though—twenty percent? Maybe even closer to forty." He nudges closer to Violet. A hug would be inappropriate, but I can tell they both appreciate the proximity. We've got our soldier on, but he stands right up next to her, so that their arms are touching.

"I've actually been thinking about this. A lot," Henry says, his voice a light in the darkness. *This* is why Henry stayed behind. This is why I brought Levi. We're all geniuses—I'm a leader, and Levi's brilliance lies in troop movements, tactics— but Henry thinks *beyond* the fight. "I've got a plan. I was going to start to implement it once you returned, but I think given the circumstances we should move on it. Now."

"Lay it out," I say.

"Well, we can't tell everyone, but we can tell some people. I've got transfer papers signed and ready to go. Fifty Citadels from Battle Ground that I trust. Implicitly. We send two to the remaining thirteen Rift sites and two more to each Village. We let them infiltrate. Replace the drug supply with placebos and have them cast their nets. We work Citadel by Citadel from the inside out. Two turn four, four turn eight, and so on. If our operatives think there's no way an individual can be turned without arousing suspicion, we then keep a very close eye on them. Maybe we can reboot and reprogram them in time, maybe we can't. But at least we'll know who's on our side and who isn't. I suggest we get new patches made for those that are loyal to your new fancy alliance, too. We'll be able to tell who's who if it comes down to a fight."

"And Edo and the rest of the Roones aren't going to notice when you start sending our people across the world?" I ask skeptically.

"No," Henry assures me. "I've basically been running operations here. People get transferred all the time. We just don't see it because our teams are so small. They trained us that way, not to look too hard at the numbers. The Roones won't suspect and I can cover the paper trail anyway. They won't notice. They aren't looking. The only thing Edo talks about is you, Ryn."

I close my eyes for the briefest of seconds. "Really?" I ask, though I'm not entirely surprised.

"She's always managing to slide your name into a conversation. She makes it seem casual. Trivial stuff, but she's making sure we know that she hasn't forgotten," Henry tells me.

I don't bother to respond. The altered Roones are playing both sides of a very dangerous game. Henry will know what to say to Edo to placate her just enough. The altered Roones are brilliant, but they haven't been trained like we have in evasive maneuvers. We have to assume that they don't know where we've been or this base would have been overrun already by ARC. However, the Roones tracked us in the Multiverse, so they must be using a system that the altered Roones don't have. At the very least, there's that.

I take out a flash drive and press it into Henry's palm. "This is all the intel about the other Citadel races you need to keep this place secure. Learn their languages and study their fighting styles." Henry closes his fist around the piece of tech, but before he can put it in his vest I grab his hand. "You will be unsettled by this," I warn. "You all will be. It's not going to do anyone any good by pretending this isn't scary as fuck. Denial is dangerous."

"Okay," he says thoughtfully.

"Have you taken control of the Village?" I ask the team. I would imagine that Henry's plan, to infiltrate slowly, Citadel by Citadel, would have needed a trial run and the Village here would have been the best way to test that theory. It's what I would have done, if I had thought of it first.

"Most. Not all," Violet answers. I'm a little surprised. Lovely Vi, already this is changing her.

"We need to get in there, tonight. Can you do that?"

"We do?" Levi asks in grim surprise.

I turn around and face Levi, who had been at my back. "We need numbers. Lots more numbers. We can't count on the Citadels just yet, but there are thousands of prisoners down there who want to go home. And there are some who don't. It would be nice to know who we could count on and right now it's imperative that we don't count anyone out," I tell him and everyone else calmly.

Levi grabs me by the bicep and yanks me forward just an inch. A twig breaks beneath my boot. "That is not a good idea," he says heatedly. "They aren't soldiers. What are they going to do? Whine them to death? They can't fight."

"Oh my God," I say as I shake off his hand. "Read a fucking history book. You think the resistance fighters in World War II were all soldiers? No. They were civilians. They passed along information. Observed. Moved people back and forth between enemy lines. This is a war, not a battle. We're not going to win it solely with guns."

Levi glares at me until Henry says, "I'll call it in," his low voice cutting firmly through the tension. "You guys start making your way there and by the time you arrive we'll have our people at the gate. You can just walk on through. No sneaking in required."

"Thanks. Really. Thank you all. You've done an amazing job and I'm really proud." I walk over to Violet and give her a hug. "I wish you were coming back with me, but honestly, the work you're doing here . . . you should all be leaders of your own teams."

"Just please be careful," Violet says to me as she presses her forehead up against my own. "I know I don't need to tell you, but I feel better saying it out loud."

"Roger that," I tell her as I pull away with a smile. Levi and I go to leave, but then I realize something. Something as important as everything else we've discussed tonight. "You guys," I speak out and the rest of the team turns. "This extra gene fuck they gave me—the Kir-Abisat—be on the lookout for other Citadels who have it. Like me, they'll have a weird sensitivity to the Rift, and the altered Roones will be paying extra attention to them. So far, all it does is give me a headache and make people's skin sing, but there must be a reason. We need to figure it out."

"We'll do what we can," Henry offers, "but if they're already on Edo's radar, it'll be risky. We might not make much progress on that front. You've got a few weeks before Seelye comes, but check in before that okay? As often as you can."

"Absolutely," I say confidently, because that's what leaders do. They act confident when they feel the opposite. I might never get back home, but at least I know that I'm leaving Battle Ground in the best possible hands. In the pitch-black night, Levi and I make our way north. We move at full speed, ghosts on grass and mud, outrunning the sunrise.

TRUE TO HIS WORD, Henry's Citadels—*our* Citadels—open the barbed-wire fence of the Village at our approach. They say nothing, a wordless exchange of caution that Levi and I recognize with a slight nod. I have been to the Village twice, both times in search of Ezra. I played tourist, marveling at the way ARC had imprisoned Immigrants with a picture postcard of a town meant to make them forget their own Earth and to assimilate. Humanize, regardless of species.

This time, there is no such meandering. The Village has a main street with shops and restaurants. It's too early yet for anyone to be up and about, and we take advantage of the empty road and the shop signs with old-fashioned paper Closed signs peppering the windows. We move quickly, dodging the cameras that Levi knows are there. I follow his lead. We weave in and out of areas and sidewalks.

I know exactly where I am going. If I were inclined, I might actually give myself a little pat on the back for thinking this far ahead. I had Ezra collect names before he left, to hack the system and get the identities of individuals who had been charged with infractions and sedition. At the time I thought that if ARC was closing in, I might need to smuggle Ezra back into the Village with help from some of these people. People who I knew had some understanding of the true nature of what this place was, not a quaint little town with every amenity you could think of. No. This is an internment camp and probably in the most vile depths of its underbelly, a place of torture and medical experiments.

The Village is separated into six different "neighborhoods," all with the distinctive architecture of disparate cultures from around the world—or this world anyhow. The man I am looking for—well, I suppose he's not a man, but rather a male Sissnovar—lives in the Cape Cod neighborhood. A cruel joke, really, to put a desert dweller somewhere built to reflect the ocean's landscape. But this whole thing is kind of a cruel joke, so little things like this don't bother me all that much.

Thanks to my photographic memory, I know his address: 64 Chattham Terrace. Levi knows the terrain and takes us there via backyards and low fences, well away from video feeds. We get to a small cottage covered in wooden shingles, though unlike the real Cape Cod, where this kind of siding is weathered gray from sun and salt, here it is green from moss and the dampness of the Pacific Northwest.

It is early morning—that in-between time when tomorrow balances on the knife edge of yesterday. Zaka could be awake, depending on when his shift starts in the Menagerie. He could be fast asleep. Levi and I can't risk knocking. We hop up on the porch, past a painted rocking chair, and quietly turn the knob and let ourselves in the front door. There are no locks here in the Village.

The house is tiny, but the living space is well designed. The bottom level is open even though the ceilings are low. There's a kitchen, living room, and a tiny space that could be an office or a den. In Zaka's case, he has chosen bookshelves as his main decorating theme. Every wall, from top to bottom, is lined with books. I don't see a computer or a TV. I guess Zaka, unlike some of his other fellow prisoners, hasn't been dazzled by the wonders of HBO or whatever selective media ARC allows to infiltrate their inmates' walls to lull them into complacency.

Quietly, Levi and I walk up a narrow staircase. There are three doors. I stop at the landing and listen. From the farthest one on the right I hear breathing. It is slow and deep. Sissnovars are not human. I don't know their anatomy, but it doesn't surprise me that their heart rate would be far less rapid than ours. I don't like this. I wish he had been awake. Levi and I waltzing into his bedroom is going to scare the shit out of him. He might be angry. He might feel like the intrusion means we don't deserve a few minutes of his time.

It's too late now, though. We enter his bedroom.

The room is unsurprisingly hot, the heater turned all the way up. I can feel my face flush, and the fabric of my uniform is beginning to stick a little in the creases of my limbs. I gesture to Levi to wait by the door. Ever so slowly I ease my weight down on the bed until I'm sitting beside Zaka.

"Zaka," I whisper gently. The Sissnovar stirs but doesn't awaken.

"Zaka!" I whisper a little more loudly as I touch his shoulder. Zaka's tiny eyes open, glowing yellow in the darkened room. I immediately say, "*Sest burseche-musse firche mithe dossanar mach tosse*," hoping that apologizing for coming to him in this way in his own language will set the tone. Zaka doesn't move right away. He looks at Levi in the doorway and then back at me. It's hard to read expressions on a reptilian face. He has scales where a man would have wrinkles. Slowly he brings a single finger up to his lips. I am both encouraged by this and unsettled. He's well aware that someone could be listening, but this is the first I've heard of living quarters being bugged. If ARC isn't doing it, who is? The altered Roones? Then again, it could be ARC and Henry just didn't have time to tell me.

Zaka throws off his many blankets, revealing red plaid flannel pajamas. He grabs his knitted cap from the bedpost and gestures for us to follow him. He takes us to his bathroom and turns on the tap.

"Ryn," he says in English. Levi is squashed in the corner, between a towel rack and the shower. "It is interesting to see you in my bedroom before the sun is up." A statement like that could sound pervy if someone else had said it. There is something about Zaka, though, a stillness, a statesmanlike quality that I noticed the first time I met him. It's not like I think he's above lying, I'm sure he does lie and quite well. It's more like I think that if he is lying, he's probably got a pretty noble reason for it.

"Zaka, I'm well aware that you have no reason to trust me, but I have to ask you to do something for me and it's probably very dangerous."

Zaka cocks his head to the right unnaturally, as if his tendons there don't exist. "You do not know if whatever it is you are asking me to do is dangerous or not? How can that be? You are a Citadel—you would know."

I swallow hard. I have to get through to him without giving too much away. If I reveal the extent of our situation, I could be putting him—or, if I'm completely off about him, *us*—even further at risk. "In some ways—ways I think you already understand based on that one time we met in the meadow—us Citadels are prisoners too. I know you've been written up here for something, though I don't know what. I don't care, actually. What I do care about is that I think you want to go home and we want to help you do that."

Zaka goes perfectly still. Of course he doesn't trust me; we're his jailers, and I have no idea what ARC has done to him. Or more accurately, what they made other Citadels do. His eyes are yellow, the color of daffodils and crayons. He uses them to try and get to the truth of this, to read me. I keep my hands at my sides and my legs relaxed.

"I might want to go home. I might not, but I would, of course, like the choice," he says finally.

"Look," I begin a little breathlessly, "there is something going on here. Something so big and so much more than ARC even realizes. I've been in the Multiverse, both of us have. We've traveled through it and we've learned things." At this, Zaka's head shoots up. I am not afraid. I'm fairly sure that if I was, he would be able to smell it. What I am is worried, *concerned*. I'm fairly certain that he would pick up on that, too. "I've been to a Sissnovar Earth," I say excitedly, suddenly remembering. I pull out my phone. Levi and I had taken shelter in a cave there. Primitive paintings had adorned the walls, and like any overwhelmed tourist, I took pictures. I scroll through my roll and find them. I hand over my phone and let Zaka take a look. The Sissnovar can be very still, but when he does move it's in tics and fractures. He examines the photos carefully before returning my phone.

"I have seen something like this on my Earth. Not the same exactly, but very similar," he tells me in a voice rife with melancholic nostalgia. "I don't understand, though. Why are they making you go through the Rifts?"

"They didn't make us. It's not ARC. It's the Roones—the tiny rock people you met at the intake?" I am attempting to jostle a memory from what was no doubt a traumatic time, but Zaka nods immediately. He knows.

"Are the Roones the dangerous part of this favor you want from me?" he asks warily.

"Yes. I don't want to tell you too much because the less you know, the less they'll know if they catch you. What I can say is that the Roones are the enemy and we aren't the only Citadel race in the Multiverse. They've done this before and at some point, they have to be stopped."

"Ryn," Levi growls in an almost whisper. I'm sure he thinks that's more information than Zaka needs, but I disagree. He has to be on the lookout for any of the other kinds of Citadels that might infiltrate the Village. For all we know they might be here already. I briefly describe each race to Zaka, warning him to stay away from them at all costs. At that, Zaka's body stiffens.

"I mean it," I say. "Maybe you think you and your rebel alliance pals can get one alone—force out some intel. And maybe you could, but if you did, then they would know *that you know* what they are."

Zaka places a brown-and-yellow speckled hand on the sink. He has a thumb, but only three fingers, none of which have any nails on them. He grips hard. He must be frustrated. Half a story. Lies wading around the muck and filth of truth and two jailers who come into a private space and ask a prisoner to help set them free.

"So what is it you want from me then?" Zaka asks. "*Specifically.*"

"I need you to start a resistance movement here in the Village. Figure out who you can trust, who you can't. Uncover skill sets that would be good in covert operations. Set up and hide emergency supplies. Build rooms and spaces that no one will be able to find unless you want them to. There are Citadels who know what's really going on. I'll make sure that one of them contacts you. So, in the next couple days, someone will come up to you and ask, 'I heard you're a woodworker. I'm looking for something special. It's my mom's forty-fifth birthday.' Whoever that is will be your Citadel liaison. Got it?"

"How did you know I was a woodworker?" Zaka asks me with what I think is a smile, but could be a grimace. I need to spend more time with the Sissnovars.

"The bookshelves. The rocking chair. But that's not the question you really want to ask. Go ahead, ask whatever you want. Can't promise I'll answer, but I'll tell you what I can," I say, returning the smile.

Zaka takes his hand off the sink and begins to touch his chin, the way a man might stroke a beard. "I'm not . . . *inconspicuous* here. Which is why we are currently in my toilet with the water running. I'm not sure I'm the best person for this job."

Finally, Levi steps forward. "If not you, then someone else," Levi says bluntly. "Someone who ARC would never suspect."

Zaka inhales, filling his lungs. The music of his body is a

stately song. His heart beats slowly enough for me to wonder how it even works. I have no way of reading him except in what he says . . . or doesn't say.

He carefully brings his hand out and extends his palm. I take his hand and shake it. "I hope there is honor in you, Ryn," he tells me firmly. "Not so much for myself. Whether or not I live or die is no longer of significance for me. However, the people that I recruit with this endeavor, I would not want them to come to harm."

I put my hand on my chest and bow three times the way Zaka himself taught me—a Sissnovar greeting, a nod of respect. Zaka does the same in return. He goes to turn the tap off, but I stop him with the lightest stroke of my fingers on his cool, smooth skin. "If we don't fix this, they'll kill everyone in here. I can't guarantee anyone's safety, but at least you'll have a fighting chance." Zaka nods. He turns off the faucet and we three lumber out of the small space. There is nothing more to say and so we leave, blazing a trail through the Village at such a clip I doubt any camera that managed to catch us would even know what it actually recorded. At the gates, I brief the Citadel who let us in on Zaka and the situation. She assures us she will relay everything back to Henry. We walk out of the Village in time to see the sun crawling out of the horizon like a drunk pulling himself out of an unfamiliar bed.

In a dense thicket of shrubs and trees I open a Rift to the Faida Earth. We have a plan. Now we just have to see if we have time to make it work.

CHAPTER 9

"Concentrate, Ryn," Navaa hisses in my ear.

I groan inwardly. As if I needed more of a reason to want to bash Edo's head into a million little fragments. Why did she choose me for this stupid Kir-Abisat? Is there something about me that she finds particularly special? Am I stronger? Smarter? Or is it the opposite? Maybe she only gave me this fucking gene because she felt like I'd be easy to control, to manipulate. Or maybe she just didn't like me. Full stop. I guess it doesn't matter. Feeling sorry for myself won't make the chorus of screams and cymbal crashes clambering around in my head any easier to control. In fact, it's probably the opposite.

Still, standing in this large training room with all these Faida watching me perform like a clapping seal isn't helping my morale in this department, but I understand. An untrained Kir-Abisat is a grenade with the pin halfway pulled. They need to know I am making progress. I'd probably do the same if our roles were reversed.

Doesn't make any of it easier.

"Breathe in and try again. Ezra's tone will bleed into your pores. Open yourself up to it." I fight to keep my eyes closed. Ezra's hand feels wrong on my shoulder. Heavy and awkward. I'm sure he doesn't want to be here any more than I do. But in this, he is indispensable. Which is why, presumably, he's gone along with these long hours without so much as a peep. Still, I'd much rather be with Levi going over the strategy for tomorrow's Rift to the Daithi Earth, but no, I'm here as I have been for the last three days, wrestling with the Kir-Abisat.

My eyes fly open. "I don't know how this is possible, Navaa. Maybe if you just explained how this works. The science behind it, I might be able to focus on that. It would help me."

"Do you honestly believe that we have some special insight that I've been keeping from you? Brightest Heavens! This is not amusing for any one of us. I've told you everything I know. This is the one secret the altered Roones would never write down. Anywhere. It doesn't matter. You have it. So do I. You are special, but you are not unique, so get on with it. Begin again."

"But—" I start to say even as I hear audible sighs from everyone in the room. Even Ezra seems impatient and he doesn't even speak Faida. I press on anyway. "What if it's a species? What if there's a race of people or creatures or whatever that can do this and that's where the gene splice came from originally. Shouldn't we think about finding them? They would have to be pretty powerful. Maybe they could help us."

"I doubt it," says Navaa with more than a hint of exasperation coloring her tone. "I don't think this ability is a splice, but rather an aberration, a mutation taken straight from matter in the Rift. Besides, do you believe that if there was a race capable of controlling Rifts with thought, that the altered Roones would let them live? Hardly. They alone want to claim dominion over the Multiverse. Enough stalling. Clear your mind. Start again."

Instead of answering, I do as she has ordered. Arguing only makes this process slower and more irritating. I focus on the sound coming from Ezra. It latches on to my own frequency and serpentines around it. Once they get tangled, it takes a fair bit of work to peel the layers of tones away from each other. I try and try but like a pair of ardent lovers, they seem determined to cling together.

I concentrate even harder. I clamp down mentally on our two frequencies, which simply will not separate. What I need is something that will break them apart. I pull another tone out from the vault. I don't know where I heard this one or why it insists on staying with me like a howling puppy. Still, maybe if I introduce it into the mix, it might be enough to push out Ezra's song.

I let the third tone in and sure enough, the disruption forces the two tones apart. I mentally grapple with Ezra's tone. I stuff it inside every cell that I have. I let it reverberate through my bones. This is it, I have it. I open my mouth and begin to hum, but the noise feels like it's coming out of my chest instead of my throat. I am no longer the one singing this note. The note, Ezra's Earth, is singing *me*. It's using my entire body as an instrument. I could get lost in this noise, this sea of whirling music that overwhelms me. In that moment, my blood is full of millions of spinning planets instead of cells, or perhaps the cells have become the planets. I can't tell. I am the noise and the noise is me.

My eyes fly open and I see that I have gotten to stage one of a Rift and not just a neon dot, but a huge wall of green. I want to take it further. I want to scream into the abyss of emerald. I want to punch through it with my entire being, to close it up in my fist until it strangles and turns purple and then black.

"Ryn!" Navaa's voice is one of billions. She's so annoying. Why am I even listening to her? She wanted me to be a Kir-Abisat and here it is, here I am in all my vicious glory. "Ryn, stop!" And before I know it, the breath has been knocked out of me as I go flying up and then back down, sliding along the polished wooden floor.

"What?" I ask furiously. "You wanted to know what I could do, I was doing it. You didn't have to hit me."

"I pushed you. I didn't hit you," Navaa contradicts me. I sit up, my legs are straight in front of me and I stretch my back. My whole body is stiff. I'm not used to going so long without working out, without fighting. I arch my spine and put my hands on the ground behind me and then I spring up slowly, bringing my legs along behind me so that now I am standing once again.

"I don't know how you are managing to get so far in the Rift process with the sound blockade intact. I can't be sure if it's the human Kir-Abisat or your mystery technology helping you along. Either way, Ryn, it had the upper hand. You cannot surrender to it. You must bend the Rifts to your will, not the other way around."

"Fine," I tell her as I throw up my hands in surrender, "but I can't anymore today. I'm going for a run. It's too loud in here." By way of an answer, Navaa just shrugs her shoulders and gestures to the door. Ezra narrows his eyes at me. His look reads either concern or fear. I can't tell anymore with him and that makes everything even more unsettling. I need out of this room.

Getting out of the actual Faida compound, however, is no easy thing. It takes a while to climb down over a thousand steps. Once I'm finally out of the great metal and wooden door shoved into the side of the mountain, I let loose.

For the record, I am not a runner. I mean, I can run, but I don't enjoy it, not the way some people do, *and* I am exhausted, tired to the bone. And yet, at the same time, my limbs feel like downed electrical lines. I am orange sparks and wildfire. I need to burn off this excess energy and since there are no real enemies to fight at this moment, running seems like the best option.

The forest surrounding the compound is a patchwork of black stumps and bald earth mixed with skinny branched evergreens that reach out with hundreds of needled arms. I run full out, chasing the noise in my head and the phantoms of unripened Rifts. I leap over small boulders and swing from treetops when the terrain gets too dicey.

I run for hours. Sometimes, when I find myself in an open space, I just run in circles, desperate to burn off this feeling like there isn't enough space in my own head. I run until my lungs feel half their size and my tongue goes dry. I keep going until what's left of the burning day melts like a candle, leaving behind the first blossoming tendrils of the evening. Finally, I get a sharp pain in my side, a razor cutting through my guts. When my hips feel like they are about to unhinge themselves at the joints, I let myself fall. I am not an ungraceful person, but I know I am a crumpled heap of bones and flesh and the green camo of my uniform.

I roll over on my back. Stars begin to peck into the night, tiny pinpricks through the cloudless fabric of the sky. Shit. I have no idea where I am. I don't have any provisions, either. What I do have, though, is blissful, glorious silence. Either being far enough away from the others has quieted my Kir-Abisat or I have simply worn myself to a point where nothing much is working. I could sleep here. The earth has been made soft from a recent rain. I could just close my eyes and rest and not think anymore.

I miss being alone.

But then reality hits me. Everyone would worry about me. The Faida, already doubtful and suspicious, would think me even more frivolous and troublesome. Levi and Ezra would assume the pressure is getting to me, which, all things considered, it probably is.

I'm starting to feel foolish. Like the eight-year-old who fills up her backpack with gummy bears, a pair of underwear, and a cape and tries to run away from home. There is no getting away from this. The only way this situation is going to get any better is if it gets much, much worse first. I may want to be alone, but I won't really be truly by myself for a long while. I tell Doe in my cuff to alert Arif with my position and ask for a lift home.

While I'm waiting, I drift off. I dream about the *Waterworld* Earth and its skinny stretch of land. There is someone beside me but I don't want to ruin it by looking to see who. Instead I watch the waves break and feel the sucking of the tide at my feet. There is music in the ocean, too. The surf breathes in and out. Whoever is beside me wants my attention but I don't care. The sea is endless, both empty and full. I feel a hand on my shoulder. It nudges me and then grabs. When I open my eyes, it's Arif.

"You are over eighty miles away from our base, Ryn Whittaker," he tells me, using a tone that I'm not sure is impressed or annoyed. I am surprisingly relieved to see him and happy to be out of the dream before knowing who it was that I was standing beside.

"Sorry," I tell him contritely. I rub my eyes as I stand, expecting him to scoop me up Superman style. Instead, he helps me onto a long metal cage that looks to me like some kind of gurney. I follow the lead it's attached to and see a helicopter above us. "Why can't I hear that thing?"

"It is in stealth mode. You are not the only one with fancy technology, and a hundred sixty miles is rather a long way to go just to pick up an overly athletic human girl child." I ignore the commentary and I get in the lift. Once I'm in the chopper, I make myself comfortable on one of the plush leather seats.

For a while we don't say anything. We absolutely could, because unlike other helicopters, this one really is stealth. I have super hearing and the blades and motor are practically silent. Finally, though, Arif addresses me.

"You have much to deal with, regardless of your age," he begins.

"Is that an observation or a compliment?" I ask warily, although I'm beginning to think the Faida are age obsessed. They keep bringing it up, and it's not like I can do anything about being seventeen.

Arif shrugs. "It is merely the truth. I want to say something to you, yet I am unsure as to how to say it because it involves inexperience and I do not want to offend you." I bristle a little at his wording, but he is being respectful.

"Go ahead," I tell him as I lay my hands on the slender armrests on either side of me.

"This boy Ezra, he is not a soldier," Arif begins tentatively.

"No, but it's my understanding that many of your Citadels aren't soldiers either," I reply.

"Not at first, no," Arif agrees. "But, regardless of what they were before, they were all trained in basic combat and now, well, our Citadels are soldiers first."

"Where are you going with all this?" I look briefly out the window, but there is nothing to see but my own haggard face in the black glass.

"Ezra is untrained and while he is competent enough with computers and data analysis, there are others here who can do this job. There is an unmistakable hostility between the three of you humans." I blanch immediately. I was hoping that we had done a better job covering up our personal issues. Apparently not. "Ryn, you must know, he does not belong here. Send him home. He is not ready for what will come next, and with all the pressures you are already facing, why are you adding to it? If something terrible should befall him, you would feel responsible and you would not be entirely wrong in feeling so."

I don't answer Arif, not right away. There is a truth and wisdom to his words that would be unwise of me to dismiss out of hand simply because he is the one pointing it out to me. I should have opened a Rift and pushed Ezra through it days ago. He's not safe here, but he has become a kind of touchstone for me. He reminds me how far I've come and how far I have to go. As problematic as he is, Ezra always puts people first and the cause second. One life to him is as important as a hundred or even a thousand. I can't afford to think that way, but I know, sometimes, that I actually need to.

"I'll think about it," I tell him kindly. I haven't yet mastered the art of tempering appreciation and gratitude with my position of authority. I'll add it to my list of things I have to learn in about three days while I plan a Multiverse-spanning war.

When we arrive back at the compound, Arif flies me up to the living quarters. I thank him genuinely for the ride and head straight to my room. I fill up on SenMach food cubes and shower and change. I'm not exactly looking forward to what I have to do next, but as per usual, what I want is a speck of nothing, a single dust mote among thousands, dancing in a ray of sun.

I've thought about it.

Ezra has to go.

I knock swiftly on Ezra's door. I have no idea what time it is. I didn't think to look. In a situation like this, a Citadel is never off duty, not really. When Ezra answers, bleary eyed and in his boxers looking a little confused, this point is hammered home.

"Can I come in?"

"What is it?" His words come out in a rush, and he is turning the lights on and widening the door so I can enter. "Has something happened?" He's looking around for his shirt. He has no idea where his *clothes* even are. Yeah, he has no place here. I sigh, but not too loudly, and sit down on a chair. When he sees me sit, he must realize there isn't any kind of an emergency so he calms down a little and finds his shirt and jeans on the other side of his bed. He slides his clothes on and then takes a seat on it across from me.

"What's going on, Ryn?"

I let my shoulders droop just a fraction and I look up briefly at the high ceiling, expecting my voice to echo off it. "I don't know how to say this, so I'm just going to give it to you straight. I need you to go home."

Ezra shakes his head and gives me half a smile. "Look," he says, "I know things are epically fucked between us, but it's just not important right now. What happens—or what *happened*, past tense—to us personally, we can't let it affect what's going on here."

I don't know what I was expecting him to say, but it wasn't that. His words make my face twitch a little, and so I run my

THE RIFT CODA \ 109

hands down it to erase whatever look I must be giving him. "I don't think you're getting the full scope—"

Before I can finish the sentence Ezra interrupts me. "I was so afraid of losing you to Levi that I did the one thing that would pretty much guarantee that exact thing happening. I never should have made you choose. I never should have demanded that from you and I really shouldn't have had sex with you until we had everything squared away. It was petty of me and I'm sorry."

This is the Ezra that I fell for, right here. I don't know where the hell he's been, but now he's back?

It's just making everything more confusing.

"Well, I appreciate your honesty. I just, umm . . ."

"I love you, Ryn. I will probably always love you, but it was never going to work. I mean, we're from different planets. I do want to go home—one day. But what were we going to do? Commute? We literally—and I don't mean that colloquially—don't belong together." Ezra might be the only guy in the world to give this kind of speech and use the word *colloquial* without sounding even remotely pretentious.

"Okay . . ." I begin, but once again Ezra jumps in and I involuntarily clench my fists. If he keeps talking over me, I'm not sure I'll be able to keep them in check.

"Let me ask you a question. When Levi walks into the room, what do you feel?"

I run my hands down my legs. I realize this is a mature conversation. I get that, but it's all I can do to not roll my eyes. "Nothing," I tell him bluntly.

"Come on. You know what I'm saying. When you think about Levi, what do you think?" he presses.

"I think . . . he's complicated. I think he's strong and lonely. He makes me feel safe, I guess, or safer. He's not annoying to be around anymore, and I think I understand why he was before. He's smart and he's loyal. He makes me feel tougher, but at the same time also softer. Is that the right answer?" I tell him in a long and lumbering huff. I don't like this conversation. I don't want to be discussing this with Ezra. At this point, how I feel about Levi is really none of his business. Can I just say that though? Is that rude? Or totally justified?

"Ryn," Ezra leans over and almost whispers, "that's love. It just feels different because it's a different person. It's so obvious, though—to me, at least. I knew it the moment I really saw the two of you together and how the energy changed in that room, which is why I acted like such a dick. At first I was really fucking hurt and mad, but how can I stay angry about how things went down between us, about the Blood Lust, when *all* of this is so fucking crazy? I will admit that I wanted to kill him when he hurt you the other day, but I got hurt during your deprogramming and I was okay with it because I knew it wasn't you. And that wasn't the real Levi, either. I get it now. So you don't have to send me away. You and I are going to be friends, good friends, but that's it. I'm not going to get in between you two."

"Wow, Ezra," I say, rocking back in the chair so that two front legs lift off and hover. "I appreciate the sentiment, but the mansplaining? I could do without that. Why don't you let me figure out how *I* feel? How about that?" The chair comes back down again with a hard slap on the floor. I have absolutely had it with the lectures. I admit to being a little behind the curve emotionally, but I'm not inept. I'm not a friggin' *child*. "You actually believe that I'm sending you away because . . . boy problems? Seriously?"

"Oh please," Ezra says, throwing up his hands. "There's a lot more going on here than typical romantic bullshit with you two, there's a lot more at stake. Why else would you ask me to leave?"

For a moment, I'm absolutely stunned into silence. My mouth will literally not form words. I just stare at him dumbfounded until finally, my irritation kick-starts my vocal cords. "Because there will most likely be a war *and you aren't trained*. I feel responsible for you, for your safety, and it's a worry that, quite frankly, I don't fucking need right now."

Ezra shoots off the bed and walks over to me, putting both his hands on the armrests of the chair. He holds them firmly in place and bends down so that he's inches away from my face. "No," he tells me with alarming finality. He grips both sides tighter and then lets go, spinning his body away from me.

This is new.

I'm at a loss once more, while he begins to pace. Finally he says, "First of all, let me just absolve you right here, right now, of any guilt you might feel in the future. If I die, it is not your fault. Okay? My safety is not your responsibility and you need to check yourself."

"What are you talking about?" I am genuinely ruffled here. "Of course your safety is my responsibility. Every sensitive file on that laptop, *I* gave to you. This trip through the Multiverse? That's on *me*. Levi might have thrown you in, but that's my fault, too—I should have sent you home the moment I got you instead of thinking I could just blurt out the truth at Battle Ground and everything would just be rainbows and cupcakes. *I* should have known better. I should have planned, thought ahead. It was insane to try and think that I could save you *and* everyone else at the same time. I've made a lot of really dumb calls, but that might have been the biggest . . . so far."

Ezra stops dead and looks at me disapprovingly with those big, luminous turquoise eyes of his. "You know, I'm the first to admit that I don't give you enough credit. *I was* mansplaining because I keep thinking there's a part of you emotionally that's still stuck at fourteen when this all happened to you, but you *are* so much more aware. I can see that now."

"Thank you?" I say sardonically because I know there is a very big *but* coming next.

"But"—yep and there it is—"I am still not leaving. The altered Roones kidnapped *me*. They did really fucking horrible medical things, procedures, whatever on me. And then, they threw me in a prison. So I'm not going home. I'm not going to let them get away with that. I'm in this because of them, and it has nothing to do with you. You don't get to take that away from me because *you're* worried."

"So you want revenge, basically."

"Don't you?"

The question unfurls a dozen images that begin to surface in my mind. My first battle with the Karekins. The first time I shot a man in the head. Pulling down my sweater cuffs over bruised arms around my parents. The endless training in Camp Bonneville where I had to punch my friends and all the punches I got in return. Silent dinner table conversations where I made myself small, into nothing, a grain of salt so that I wouldn't have to lie. The ticker tape of my DNA scrolling along a SenMach wall and the anguish of learning I wasn't all human. Yes. I want revenge, that's undeniable, but more than that, I want justice. I want this to stop. I am a killer, a weapon, a liar, but I've never been a hypocrite, not until tonight. Because Ezra is right. It's his life. I refuse to let anyone control me. I don't know why I thought it should be different for him.

"Fine," I relent. "You can stay—but, please, for everyone's

sake, recognize your strengths. You're most effective behind a computer. That doesn't make you any less threatening, it just makes you a different kind of soldier."

"I can agree to that, to staying out of the fray," Ezra tells me as he walks toward the door, "on the condition that you let me do some basic combat training with the Faida. I won't walk into a fight, but if the fight comes to me, I want a real chance to be able to defend myself."

"All right, that's smart." I stand up myself and walk over to him. "You know, I am sorry that . . ." My voice trails off. I'm not sorry for anything I did really. I'm just sorry we won't ever get a real chance. I'm sorry he's from another Earth. I'm sorry that there is no way for us to be together and that I just assumed our feelings would be enough to make the impossible somehow work. I am a liar. I just forget sometimes that the person I tend to lie the most to is myself. But I have to stop that now. I can't hide from the truth. The truth is here, it's arrived, inside a mountain, thousands of feet up. Reality is right here in this room.

Ezra puts a hand on my cheek and I nuzzle into it. This is hard, this knowing when something is wrong when so much of you remembers when it was just right. "Maybe things worked out exactly the way they were meant to," he whispers softly and the smell of him, still the forest and weeks-old campfires, hasn't gone away completely. "I do believe that I was supposed to meet you."

A small laugh escapes from my closed mouth. "You can't really believe in God or whatever, after everything we've seen."

Ezra moves his hand away from my face. Away from me. "I don't know about that. I just know that I'm never going to be the same. I'm different. And I'm glad."

"Me too," I tell him, and then I push the door handle outward. I need to go. Things are okay between us now, but it's fragile and I don't want to ruin it. When I get to my room, I lie down on my bed. I close my eyes, but it takes hours for me to fall asleep.

CHAPTER 10

For all his talk of staying away from the action, Ezra finds a way to make it onto the intel mission going to the Daithi Earth. To be fair, it was Navaa that really pushed for it. I have to assume Arif told her about our conversation and I believe that this is her not-so-subtle way of hammering the point home. What she doesn't know is that I have made peace with Ezra's choice. I don't feel responsible for his safety, not anymore, and if he does get hurt, it will be her fault, not mine. Well, hers and Ezra's. And maybe a little of mine. But it doesn't matter. If he wants to put himself in harm's way because he believes that the time he spent on the original Roone Earth has made him some kind of Citadel expert, then that's on him. I've advised him enough. If he doesn't want to listen to me, I have enough to deal with. On that front, Arif was absolutely right.

Ezra isn't the only civilian here. Navaa insisted that a Faida named Lujinn join us. He is apparently a professor at a university here (I ran for almost a hundred miles and never saw so much as a village, let alone a town big enough for a college, but I guess it makes sense that the compound would be isolated) who's been studying the Daithi. Even though he looks well into his fifties, he's still a strikingly handsome man with a full head of graying copper hair. There is also a Faida named Daresta who is a linguistics expert. Both Levi and I are fluent in Daithi, but she understands the nuances that we might miss given that we just basically memorized a lexicon and verbal structures over a period of hours. Neither one of these two are Citadels.

Regardless of status, everyone is wearing a uniform for protection. The Daithi are quick and deadly, but as long as we can avoid a direct hit to the head, we won't die. Probably. We make the decision to Rift in about three miles from one of the five bases on this Earth. I'm about as prepared as I'll ever be for this mission. That's the thing about this sort of work: you don't know what you don't know. We can guess and hypothesize, but we've never met this race and we certainly don't know the extent of what the altered Roones have done to them.

All in all, there are a dozen of us. Three civilians, two human Citadels, and seven Faida Citadels, including Navaa, Arif, Yessenia, Sidra, and three others whose names I make it a point to remember. They all look so similar that it's actually easier to tell them apart by their wings.

The majority of the Daithi Earth is forested. There are villages and even small cities with larger buildings and electricity. I would put their technology at about Earth's, circa the 1930s. We assume this is the Roonish influence and that without their arrival, the Daithi would still be people who stuck to a clan system. Clans are still important, but now the altered Roones are the chieftains.

We step out of the Rift and we're a flurry of activity. We sweep the immediate area and when we find that it's empty, Levi and I send up our drones. We find a village a few miles away, but where the Rift is supposed to be, there is nothing, just an empty field. According to Doe, there are no active Rifts on this planet anywhere.

Well, there aren't any active Rifts on the Faida Earth, either, so maybe that doesn't mean so much. Still, according to the SenMach tech, there are no humanoids near the Rift site. Ordinarily, I would think that the place was abandoned. But because this is the Daithi, a race known for stealth and subterfuge, I'm not convinced, and neither is anyone else on the team.

We decide to walk to the Rift's base of operations and we make our way there as silently as we can, given the civilians in our ranks. When we reach the perimeter of where the compound is supposed to be, all we see is more trees. We look at one another, not sure what exactly is going on. Doe assures us that the base is five hundred yards dead ahead. We remain hidden in a dense thicket, catching glimpses through binoculars, twin periscope views of more of the same landscape. There is no movement, no sound, not even the faint kiss of electricity. I ask Doe if there is Daithi drone activity; he assures me that there is none. Levi wonders out loud about camera feeds and Doe tells him that while they are operational, he can easily disable them. Once again I am left wondering where the hell we would be if we didn't have the SenMach tech.

I have a sour feeling in the pit of my stomach. Something here is off. We make our way carefully forward, rifles up, our feet slipping over the bracken and damp earth. When we are close enough, I can see exactly what they've done.

Clever.

The base is here all right, and so are we, or rather, our reflections. The entire compound is made of mirrors. The sheer enormity of it makes it impossible to gauge in terms of size or architecture, so once again we turn to Doe.

"I need a schematic. Specifically, where the door is. Download it to my tablet, Doe." By the time I reach around, take off my pack, and retrieve my electronic pad, the drones and the SenMach's considerable hacking skills have done their work. The entryway is ten feet from our current position. I look over the plans. I had assumed that the base was one squat mirrored structure, but it isn't. It is a many-leveled square building that fits together like a bunch of Lego bricks.

We find the door, but no handle, just a thin seam. I push it in, hoping there's some kind of spring, but no luck.

"We could always just blow the thing," Levi offers. I know he's only halfway kidding. There's no way we've traveled through the Multiverse using technology and the combined minds from nearly half a dozen Earths just to resort to explosives.

I turn to the unit. "Ideas?" I ask in Faida and English.

"Well," Ezra says boldly, "the Roones use sound to activate almost every system they have. Maybe they did that here."

"*Fosgil*," I try, which is Daithi for "open," and then, "*Doreis*," which is the word for "door." Nothing happens.

Lujinn steps forward and takes a look at the mirror, ignoring his own reflection and the inky black wings tucked behind his back. "No. It would require a password. The Daithi would never make entering their compound so easy." He begins to say a long string of words, all of which I recognize, but

I mean, if there is a password, it's hardly likely that it would be something even remotely obvious.

"*Shegail . . . Rugav Shegail*," Lujinn purrs and miraculously the door swings open.

"'Shadow born'? That is some serious high fantasy shit right there," I say to him with astonishment. "How could you possibly have guessed that?"

"I did not guess." He corrects me in the way that only a professor could, eyebrows raised, head tilted. "The term came up three times in the material Ezra Massad disseminated to us when he first arrived. They were the first Daithi turned into Citadels, the most elite of their warriors that survived the altered Roones' invasion. Interesting that the Roones would allow them to continue to use this term in the vernacular. In most cases of a conquering race, all references to opposition would have been forbidden."

"Well," Levi says as he gently pushes the door forward, "maybe they got a chance to change the password. Maybe they fought another civil war of their own and won."

"If that were true," I say, stepping inside the echoing, empty main room, "why would they be here still? There is no Rift."

"Munitions," Levi says as if it's obvious. "And because it's a hell of a good HQ considering that it's practically invisible." I don't even bother to mention the flaws in his logic, of which there are plenty. The biggest one is that if *we* ever manage to get away from ARC's stranglehold, the last place I'd ever want to be is Camp Bonneville—at least without a complete renovation to exorcise the majorly significant ghosts that would haunt me there.

We enter a large, open space that reeks of abandonment. There are rows of desks and sleeping monitors. Papers litter the floor. There are spatters of blood on different walls, as if a kid was having a go with red paint.

Something here is very, very wrong. A space can give off an impression. Plaster and concrete can cling to misery and joy. There is no joy here, only the oppressive weight of melancholy and the eerie feeling that, somehow, this pain will reach out from the carpet fibers and gut you whole.

"Doe, you've gotten access to the files in here, correct?" I say. I can tell that my speaking English annoys Navaa, but I'm not about to worry about that. I've learned her language, the least she can do is attempt to learn some of mine.

"I have. The firewalls were surprisingly easy to work through." Nothing with the altered Roones is ever easy, though. They either wanted us to see these files or didn't care if we did.

"Transfer the most recent altered Roones' logs to both my tablet and the Faida's," I say quietly. I really don't think there is anyone here, but for some reason, it feels wrong to speak too loudly in this place.

We all read the logs at the same time, and each Roonish word is a rock in my stomach.

"This says that the altered Roones believed an insurrection was imminent. That's all. Did they stop it? Who won?" Navaa asks out loud. I'm about to suggest that we fan out in groups so that we can hopefully find some answers when I hear it. It's faint, but fast. I close my fist below my lips so that they all know to keep silent. Levi has now heard what I have and he nods to me.

There is someone here, someone scared and probably about to make a run for it. The Daithi are fast, so if we lose this person, whoever it is, we might never get any answers. I keep listening, straining my ears to hear the tiny, fluttering heartbeat. It's so rapid and small it reminds me of a human baby.

When I think I know where it's coming from, I motion to the others to continue talking. Levi and I silently make our way farther down the room on the balls of our feet. I go one way and he goes another. There is a kind of dais, with a large screen behind it, presumably for making speeches and giving briefs. Levi and I whip around, coming at it from opposite sides. Our suspicions were not wrong. There is a tiny person lying flat on his stomach behind the platform. Just as Levi is about to grab his leg, the Daithi leaps and begins to scramble up a post as fast as a lizard on a tree trunk. There is a second-floor balcony and this small person, whose arms and legs are moving as fast as an eggbeater, is going to have to make a pretty giant leap to get to the railing.

Two seconds before the Daithi has to go for it, I crouch down and use the momentum of that position to send myself up, jumping ten feet in the air. It's enough to grab onto the Daithi. I wrap my hands around his tiny frame and let myself fall back down again. In a neat trick of heroics, Levi catches both of us. It's an impressive feat—even though we have done about a thousand of these exact kind of drills back in Battle Ground.

I almost want to go "Ta-da!"

The Daithi struggles and roars in my arms. He even tries to bite me, the little shit. I hold him fast and look him square in the face. I know the Daithi race is short, but this guy is barely four feet tall. He has black matted hair covered in mud and sweat. His large blue eyes are sunken in his face. This is a kid. That doesn't necessarily mean he isn't a Citadel, too, but by the way he's wildly swinging, it's obvious he has no real training.

"*Eshtad!*" I say to him calmly. *Stop.* "*Chenn aeill a'thol ohm streon thu.*" *We are not going to hurt you.* The boy slowly winds down and eyes me warily. I put my palm on his cheekbone, which is as sharp as cut flint. His black linen shirt looks two sizes too big, and his pants are being held up by a frayed rope. His scapulae and chest bones are a congregation of speed bumps on a newly paved road and his wrists are so tiny I could wrap my thumb and index finger around them with room to spare.

"Ezra, bring me some water and some protein bars," I tell him, keeping my voice steady and my eyes on the boy. The others make their way to us gingerly, knowing we must all keep our movements deliberate and open the way you should when approaching a scared animal. Ezra hands me his canteen and a bar that he has unwrapped. I keep one hand on the Daithi's shoulder and with the other I grab the food and take a small bite, proving it's not poison. I give it to the boy, who eyes it like a bar of gold that might also be an explosive. He looks at me and the bar and then at me again. He probably thinks that taking anything from us is dangerous, but he's fighting a war with his stomach and losing.

Finally, he snatches the morsel and devours it in two seconds. I give him the water, which he swigs. Navaa hands me another something, some kind of Faida cracker or cookie, and I give that to him, too. Tears leak from his eyes as he eats. I don't think he's crying because he's sad or scared, he's just . . . *relieved.*

War.

People always think that it's the soldiers who have it the worst, but I know better. I've been at this for years. Death hovers. If I die, more than likely, I'll just be shot or stabbed. I might be tortured first, but I'd probably find a way to do myself in before it got very far. In other words, my suffering would be relatively quick. For soldiers, it's black or white. But for those left behind? Mothers. Children. The elderly. Their pain is constant. Their job is to simply wait and scavenge and starve and grieve.

"What are you doing here? In this place?" I ask him gently, but with enough authority to let him know I mean business.

His eyes dart back and forth behind my shoulder. Finally, though, he says, "I was checking the kitchen again even though my mom said there wasn't any point. I thought there might be something, somewhere, I could take home to my family. Do you have any more food?" he asks brazenly.

War does that, too, strips pride away. If I made him beg for it, he would. He would do anything. The thought sickens me. "I'll give you all the food and supplies we brought if you can tell us where the Citadels went that used to live here."

"If you give me everything *you all* have, I will take you to them."

I nod my head. "Fine. You can have all our combined supplies. Lead the way."

The boy, a skeletal Peter Pan, folds his arms and locks his legs. For someone who looks about as strong as a brittle winter branch, he seems determined to call the shots. "Food first. Then I'll take you." I purse my lips, but he remains steadfast. I could play hardball with him—we could find them on our own—but what would be the point. Besides, I was always going to give him our supplies anyway.

I dip my hand into my pack and search for the small bag I keep for clean bras and undies. I empty it out in the backpack, keeping my eyes on what I'm doing. I think the rest of the team feels as awkward about looking at my underwear as I do about having them see it. Better just to pretend that it's not actually happening. Soldiering is 50 percent training, 40 percent luck and instinct, and 10 percent good old-fashioned denial.

I put my food rations in the bag and hold it out for everyone else to do the same. Navaa even produces another small plastic bag to hold more food. When this is done, I hold the bags out to the boy. He snatches them up and heaves them over his shoulder. Without saying a word, he leads us around the room to an odd door that is actually a corner. It kicks out from the bottom, opening like a mitered hatch on a spaceship. We walk through it and are outside again. The boy begins to move with alarming speed. He darts in a zigzag path, his feet nimbly leaping and pivoting over tiny rocks and gnarled roots.

The boy points a finger in the air, moving it across the velvety green tops of the trees. I take a closer look and see that there is an elaborate system of raised and angled mirrors. The Daithi have created a labyrinth using the reflections of branches and leaves to keep a wanderer confused. We pass right through what looks like the trunk of a massive oak but is really a clear path, just part of the maze. Without a guide it would have taken us hours to navigate this terrain, even with the help of drones.

After a good fifteen minutes at a brisk clip, the boy disappears through a dense hemlock thicket, or, at least it *looks* like a thicket . . .

And then, the smell.

It's so awful that bile races up my windpipe and I hold my hand up across my mouth to stop from retching and to block my nostrils. We keep moving until we emerge onto a large cleared field. I look to my right, down at the boy who points his finger forward, forcing my eyes to focus on the horrors before them.

I hear a gargled noise from Navaa that might be a scream or a word but is soon muffled by Arif's chest as he pulls her close. This must have been the Rift site. There is no Rift here any longer, just a pit half the size of a football field and filled with hundreds, if not thousands of rotting Daithi bodies. All along the perimeter of this mass grave are posts. It's the precision of it that I find just as disturbing as what they hold. Someone took the time, thought it out, planned and measured so they could get absolute symmetry. For the display.

There are wings, outstretched and nailed down. The scapulae are still attached to most of them, the bones picked clean by scavengers, but still discolored by blood and rot. Some of the feathers have been plucked and pulled by birds or trophy hunters, but it's clear enough what they are. Faida. I venture forward with Levi at my side. I walk past the posts, and when I look at Levi, I can see that the wings are proportionate to his back. They could have raised them fifty feet in the air or kept them ankle length, but no, this was deliberate. A message. The Faida that were here, the scouting party, somehow they are being held responsible. Now, the wings stand guard over this grisly horror, the ghosts of their owners absent, murdered, but still made to keep watch.

I look down at the bodies, all in uniform, mouths agape and jawbones wide. What's left of their faces is suspended in eternal surprise and pain. The smell is overpowering. It's beyond awful. The stench has clawed its way into my every opening; even the pores and my own tissues are absorbing it like putrid water. I throw up. I retch without my stomach giving me the slightest warning. It's as casual as a sneeze or a yawn. I don't even bend over all that much. I just turn my head and empty myself out.

I think I know what happened here, but I have to make sure, so I do the one thing that I want to do least in this world. I jump down into the pit. From somewhere, Levi is calling my name, but I tune it out. This is not unlike fighting, the way I have to become more machine than girl, more soldier than person. I am knee-deep in corpses. The Daithi are so small that it makes this experience all the more disturbing. I know they are not children, but with all of them here rotting and lifeless, the distinction is more difficult to make.

I turn over a body and examine it, ignoring the maggots and blackened flesh. I look at another and another. I pull burgundy patches off uniforms. The same triad symbol as mine, only with different lettering. I'll need some kind of proof later that this was actually real, that this actually happened and wasn't just a nightmare. There are no slash marks or bullet wounds. There are no bruises or scrapes on what's left of the flesh. I jump out of the pit and squat, wiping my hands in the dirt.

"At least they went quickly," I manage to say to Levi, though the sound of my own voice feels wrong, off somehow, like someone else has borrowed my mouth.

"The Midnight Protocol?" he asks, but I don't know why—he knows. We watched our own go down like this when I told everyone the truth about what ARC did to us.

"There are no active Rift sites here. No sign of Rift activity on this entire planet. They did this to them all," I say out loud. To Levi. To no one in particular.

"We should burn them," he tells me as he looks behind his shoulder at the pit. "No one should have to just rot away."

I nod and take a deep breath as I make my way back to the others. They are all pale faced and somber eyed. There might be Faida bodies at the bottom of that pile, but I am done here. If the Faida feel they must retrieve their dead from that pit of atrocity, then of course they must. I don't have it in me to help them. My shoulders are broad. I was built, born, and trained for bearing things, but not this. Never this . . . and I'm not ashamed. There is a universe of shame buried here, but none of it will ever belong to me. I assign it solely to the monsters who did this.

I clear my throat in attempt to find my voice, which I do, but it is tentative and halting. "Levi suggested that we—wait . . . where's the boy?" We all look around us, but the boy has disappeared.

"He must have booked it," Ezra says. "He held up his end of the bargain and this isn't really a place for kids."

"No, it isn't, but *he knew* where it was." I mentally switch gears in an instant as I put my hand on my gun. "And to leave the bodies like that, uncovered, exposed? And the wings . . . They knew someone would come along eventually."

"We need to find that boy," Levi says as he begins to jog through the maze. The Faida take to the sky. The three humans begin to run and, for once, Ezra doesn't ask why. He doesn't understand, but I—with an ever-increasing feeling of dread— think I do. From the air, Sidra has spotted the boy and with the help of Doe and the drones, we get closer to his position. As a Daithi, he is predisposed to disappear, but he is young and untrained. Doe's voice calmly delivers orders into my earpiece. Left. Left. Right. Left. Right. We flee over the bracken and race past uncut grasses and webs made of dead vines.

The Faida are already there as we break through to a tiny clearing. The boy has dug up a QOINS device from the earth. This one is larger than most and has a large red button on the top of it. The boy, who must have stashed the food somewhere else, has both hands in the air. The Faida have their weapons drawn.

"We arrived just as he pulled it out of the earth," Arif tells me in Faida. "He hasn't yet activated it."

I approach the Daithi slowly, holstering my weapon. "What is your name, boy?"

"Ruari," he tells me with bravado, though his hands are shaking in the air.

"Why would you call them back here?"

"They told us that more would come and if we didn't tell them right away, they would know."

"Who?"

"The bald ones, with the rocky skin—they sent giants, covered in hair. I don't know how they controlled them, but the giants obeyed them. They gathered us up, from five different villages, and showed us the bodies."

"How would they know, Ruari?" Levi asks in a tone that is gentler than I've ever heard him use.

"Like we would ever ask such a thing!" he tells us excitedly. I'm just a few feet from him now. His bright blue eyes are starting to bolt all over the place. One slip of his finger and everything we've worked for will be for nothing. In one swift movement, I take the QOINS device from him between a breath. One moment it's in his hand and the next it's empty.

"No!" Ruari screams as he starts to lunge for me. I easily hold him off with a single hand. "You don't understand. They will come back and they will burn our village to the ground and kill us all. The Citadels are gone. There is no one to protect us."

"Ruari," I tell him sternly, throwing the QOINS backward toward Levi, who catches it with ease. "They won't find out. I promise. We disabled all the cameras. We can make it look like they just broke on their own. This place has been abandoned. They only told you that to scare you. They will never find out unless you tell them."

Finally, Ruari goes still. His eyes narrow with contempt. "You don't understand. How am I going to explain the food?

The moment my mother sees it she is going to know and I can't not bring it home, we're starving." Ruari's heart begins to race. His entire body stiffens as panic sets in.

"It doesn't matter. You can tell your mother that we destroyed the QOINS." After everything these people have seen, I can't expect them to just believe that I'm telling the truth, not with these kinds of intimidation tactics at play.

Ruari shakes his head vigorously. "This isn't the only black box buried in these woods, there are dozens of them. My mother will demand that we retrieve another and report your arrival."

"Just lie, child," Lujinn steps in and says smoothly. "These monsters, they have no honor. We are trying to stop them. They need to pay for what they did to your people, and we can make that happen, but we will be unable to keep up our ruse if they know that *we know* what was done here."

Ruari considers Lujinn's words for a moment and then clearly, in his mind, comes to his senses. He is resolute. "I *could* lie, perhaps, but not to my mother. She knows me too well and we would lose whatever peace we have found. Every branch bent the wrong way, any unfamiliar birdsong would make us jump out of our skins. Each day would be filled with fear and every night would be sleepless. You say they will not find out, but you will be gone and they are very powerful. No. I must do as they have ordered."

Navaa and I steal a knowing glance at each other.

War makes monsters of us all in the end.

I bend down toward Ruari and place my hands regretfully on his cheeks. "I hope the next world treats you better than this one. I am sorry." The Faida contingent moves out of the way, circling back so that they are behind Levi and me. Ezra follows suit, though it's clear from the expression on his face he has no idea what's going on. "Rift. Pandora," I manage to whisper into my cuff.

A tiny green emerald dot spins into the inky onyx of the Multiverse, the doorway screaming into life. Ruari's eyes are so wide with fear they take over his face. The Rift is moaning, demanding an offering. Ruari looks at it and then he knows, *he knows* what's going on. "No!" He yells, "Please don't, I won't tell anyone. I promise. Please!" I pick him up from underneath his arms and pitch him into the Rift before he can plead anymore. The Rift swallows him whole and then spins away into nothingness. The forest around us becomes unnaturally quiet.

"Oh my God," Ezra says in horror. "I cannot believe you just did that."

I spin furiously to face him. "It was that or kill him. At least this way he has a chance. He could end up on an echo Earth, find a nice family, he's young—he'll adapt. He doesn't even have the tattoos on his face yet. He could blend in."

"Or he could end up on an Earth that has no air or the *Walking Dead* Earth. Or I don't know, we could have taken him with us!"

"When am I going to stop having to defend myself to you?" I hiss in his face. "That was *not* easy for me." I am so grateful that my gears shifted into drive after what we witnessed in the pit. I'm just moving on muscle memory and instinct. If I wasn't, I'd have most certainly collapsed by now, into a weeping mess. "He may be dead, but death isn't the worst thing that can happen to you. Did you see the Faida's wings out there? Did you see them all? Look at what we're fighting. We don't have the luxury of bringing home a traumatized boy who probably needs a lot of professional help that we don't have the time or energy to give him. So enough about Ruari."

"Ryn," Levi says. I whip my head in his direction praying he won't second-guess me on this, either. "We have his coordinates. When this is all over, we can go back and make sure he's okay." I sigh with relief at his suggestion.

Ezra has his arms folded. He looks forlorn. "He was just a kid," he says quietly. He's not speaking to me directly, but to the world, I guess. The world that he is, I think, just now realizing he's a part of.

"So were we once," I tell him as I check my gear and my weapons out of ingrained reflex. The shitty thing is, we can't even risk going back to burn the bodies. We can't do anything now, to suggest that we were here.

Levi comes up behind me. "It's okay," he whispers in my ear and in that moment, I do believe him. Ezra will never truly accept what I had to do today, but Levi, I know, would have done the very same.

But it doesn't mean it's okay.

CHAPTER 11

We spend the next week at the Faida base regrouping. That's what we call it, but that's not really what it is. We are recovering. Grieving. Even seasoned soldiers like the Faida who have been fighting for most of their adult lives seem only partially present. They are slow to answer questions and have taken to staring at walls. There are subtle changes in their body language, too. They will now occasionally bring a single wing around a shoulder, rubbing their jaws against the soft downy feathers.

Ezra, Levi, and I avoid one another whenever possible. We don't want to talk. There is nothing to say and every conversation feels trivial. None of us will ever be the same after what we saw on the Daithi Earth. Each body in the pit has become the slice of a razor on our skin. They are hundreds of cuts that won't clot, wounds that don't know how to heal. Eventually they will fade—they'll have to if we want to win this—but they won't disappear. They will just dissolve into our skin and turn into a constellation of agonies that we will have to carry with us forever.

I don't need any more reminders of that day, of what I saw and what I did to Ruari. Every time I look at Levi and Ezra, I see my own pain mirrored back to me in their eyes. I know they see the same so we keep our own solitary company. My thoughts are louder than they ever have been before, but I don't have it in me to talk about that day. Every time I try, the words turn to ash in my mouth before I can even speak them.

Most of my time is spent with Navaa and the business of turning me into a full-fledged Kir-Abisat, which has become her obsession. I don't blame her. It has given her something to do, so she isn't spending all day thinking about what *she's* seen. So hour upon hour she bends me this way and that, a constant stream of her urging, to separate the different frequencies I have sequestered in my brain. For these tones, I have built a memory palace. The room of this palace is my opa's study where he keeps his collection of vinyl records. He calls this place the Lab and I call it that, too. Each sound is a record stored on a shelf that I can pick out and identify by attaching it to the cover of an album.

Ezra doesn't need to stand behind me all day with his hand on my shoulder, thank God. I first need to learn to make my body buzz in just the right way to open a Rift completely. For now, the destination is not important.

It's not just the humming. My whole being has to become the noise and that's no small task. It's uncomfortable and jarring. My molecules feel like they are being poured in a blender. Each time I close a partial Rift, the sensation doesn't go away. My limbs go numb. I imagine it must be like sitting on top of an ancient washing machine set to spin (and not in the funny, sexy way that adults seem to find endlessly amusing, either). It rattles me. Literally.

However, after a week, we must all put the grief away. There is simply too much to do besides the Kir-Abisat or training or the gut-wrenching work of trying to hide from the truth of the Daithi Earth. So without much discussion, Levi and I set off for Battle Ground.

It's good to have a mission. And once we meet up with our team, they are happy to report that Henry's plan of gradual infiltration is working with impressive results. Revealing the truth one-on-one was the way to go. All the drugs were successfully swapped out with placebos, and each Citadel who's been given the facts knows at least two others they trust implicitly. More than that, they seem to know who will most likely *not* be swayed. Each day hundreds of human Citadels are recruited to our side. For now, at least, the plan is working.

When I tell Beta Team what happened with the Daithi, I do so as a cautionary tale. We have all been trained in spycraft. We are vigilant when it comes to covering our tracks, but I remind them all who taught us these tactics. The numbers may be growing exponentially in our favor, but I warn that our agents in the field cannot let their guards down. Now more than ever, we have to move forward under the assumption that while ARC might not know a thing, the altered Roones probably do. They have likely guessed we might be up to something; we just hope they don't know what.

We have to keep it that way.

From there, Levi and I also travel to visit Iathan on the original Roone Earth. Navaa and Arif really wanted to come, but I thought it best to ask the president's permission before bringing them along. I'm sure that Iathan will be more than interested in meeting with them, but it's not like I can just call ahead and ask if it's cool. These alliances are all tender, delicate things. Apart from the "Day of Pigs," as Levi has started referring to the tussle we had after we first met the Faida, we have yet to really fight alongside these people and that is where real bonds are formed. On the battlefield.

We arrive on the Roone Earth and are taken immediately to the palace where Iathan resides. Whatever it may have been in its former glory, Iathan takes no chances. He lives beneath the building, deep underground in a bunker. The city above may be rebuilding from its own civil war, but he understands there is still war in the wind and will not emerge until the threat of the altered Roones is over.

I report everything that has happened since our last encounter. I regretfully have to recount what happened with the men he sent with us to the Spiradael Earth. Losing Vlock hits him particularly hard and he takes a few moments before he is able to continue.

He is bolstered, though, when I tell him about the Faida and even more excited when I tell him that not only have we formed a burgeoning alliance, but that they have cast out the enemy on their own Earth. The fact that he didn't know this means the sound blockade works. He was aware, however, of the Daithi massacre, although he has only seen it via drone image. He presses for more information until he can tell that Levi and I aren't ready to talk about it yet and, surprisingly, he respects that.

He informs us that the most recent assets he sent to the Akshaj Earth have not returned. When I tell him that the Faida have not heard from theirs, either, he seems increasingly worried. Without the Daithi in play, we need the Akshaji. We all agree that we have to go there, although the question of an alliance is tempered by the very real possibility that we might be killed before we even get the chance to open negotiations. I offer to take a Faida contingent to this Earth, and Iathan tells me that he will happily meet with them and maybe among all four of us (Karekin included) we might be able to work out some sort of plan. In terms of our own Earth, it appears that our strategy is working. Iathan currently has a team there and they are not reporting any unusual activity in Livermore, ARC's headquarters.

Before we leave, I ask him about the altered Roone that the Faida have kept hostage. I wonder if he could be faking his condition—his apparent lunacy. Iathan responds that the altered Roones lack the ability to accomplish such a feat if the prisoner has been extensively tortured—they cannot tolerate physical pain, which is what I pretty much already know to be true. I think it's time for me to question the altered Roone myself. When we leave, I don't exactly feel hopeful, but I do feel different. I have spent the past week in the shadows, where it's so dark I don't have to see or look at anything. Being around my team and with Iathan has unfolded me, laid me flat, and smoothed out my edges. It's not exactly like I've stepped out into the sun; I don't think I could bear that kind of exposure anymore, but I am willing to let the light shine on a few bits—an ear, a cheek, a wrist—one small patch at a time.

CHAPTER 12

We return to the Faida Earth and I can tell that the trip has buoyed Levi as well. The events on the Daithi Earth had affected him differently than they did me and the others. For us, there was a profound sadness, the kind of grieving that left us breathless. Levi was just . . . angry, not that he said that in so many words, in any words actually, but I could tell. I read him up and down like a grocery list; each item was an atrocity and injustice that he kept in two perpetually clenched fists. He used the Faida training facility for ten or more hours a day, sparring with any Faida daring enough to attempt a fight. He walked around with bruises and grazed knuckles, glad I think for the pain and the proof that he could still feel it and inflict it in return. But tonight, his shoulders have fallen closer to a natural position (as opposed to being up around his ears) and he seems less far away. I think he may want to do some deprogramming. Truthfully, so do I. But we both know that we need just a little more distance. Neither one of us is quite ready yet to be so vulnerable.

The next day, I have a successful session with Navaa and I feel like it's as good a time as any to ask her about the captured Roone.

"What do you want to know?" she asks hesitantly.

"What you did to him to make him break," I answer honestly.

At that, Navaa sighs and sits on a chair. Her charcoal wings sweep the floor and she places her hands in that way on her lap that looks like she's being casual but that really means it's a conversation she would rather not be having.

"You can't possibly care what we did to him. Especially not now, not after the Daithi."

I take a seat across from her. I have been standing for three hours. I arch my shoulders back so that my spine can get a few good cracks off. "I don't care if you cut his balls off. You needed information and he needed to give it to you. I'm just wondering how extensive it was."

"Very," she tells me without remorse.

"So there's no chance he's toying with you? That it's all just a big act so that he can be on the inside when the altered Roones return?"

At that question, Navaa actually laughs. It's an unfamiliar sound coming from her, like a tinkling wind chime crashing on a warped porch. "I promise you, he is not pretending. The altered Roones are geniuses, but they are soft and arrogant. He only lasted an hour before he broke and told us everything he knew. Still, we continued and pressed for more answers, though he gave up nothing else." Navaa sweeps a stray lock casually back up into her neat braid. "Do not misunderstand me, they are calculating and ruthless, but not in that way. A Citadel could probably manage such a feat. They could not."

"I'd like to see him," I tell her as I smile slyly. "I wonder how he would react to *a human* Citadel."

Navaa shakes her head slowly. "You believe we weren't thorough? I truly marvel at your capacity for underestimating us."

"*Please* don't regale me with another story about how you colonized Mars. Seriously, I get it. The Faida are more advanced than the human race, but you personally, you are not more advanced than me." Navaa raises a single disapproving eyebrow. "This is no time for modesty. We *are* the altered Roones' greatest accomplishment. Maybe seeing a human will shake something else loose. It's worth a try."

Navaa lets a moment or two pass. She crosses and uncrosses her legs. She stares at me with unwavering intensity. I don't know what she's expecting. I've made a request and I'm not about to elaborate. I'm not sure how things work on this Earth because I have yet to see a normal (whatever that is) Faida my own age. But back home, as a teenager, I've perfected disdain with just a hint of indifference.

I can do this all day.

"Fine," she says, throwing her hands up. I'm not exactly sure why she doesn't like this idea more. I can only guess it's because the crux of it is based on the assumption that a human might be able to do something a Faida can't and they really don't like to be reminded of that. Navaa leads me out of the training room and to the stairs.

"It's eighteen stories, Ryn," she says rather haughtily. "It's a cave. The floor is built right into the mountain and used solely for detainment. It would be much faster if we flew there."

I think about the last time I walked all the way to the

bottom of the compound. "I never saw a door that far down," I comment.

"Of course you didn't. There *is* no door. It's a wall with a hidden panel built in, which reveals the entrance. You wouldn't have noticed unless you were looking. I'll need to get Sidra to clear your iris scan to gain entry or we can just fly down there together right now." Navaa is actually grinning.

She knows I dislike being flown up and down the compound like a baby. But I also couldn't possibly care less right now.

"Fine. Fly me down there. But I would like Sidra to give me clearance to that section. I recognize that you might not want me to have total access to everything on this base and I respect that. We are in your house and total transparency is not necessarily how alliances work. But, just so you know, there isn't any place in Battle Ground you wouldn't be welcome."

"Really?" Navaa says to me in a deadpan voice as she wraps her arms around me. Then, she walks to the edge, where the wood ends and the cave begins. Instead of jumping and then ascending as Arif does, she simply lets us fall backward in a dead drop. I'm sure this is the kind of thing that Boone would love. I fucking hate roller coasters because—super soldier. I get enough excitement.

But fuck her. I'm not giving Navaa any satisfaction. So instead of tensing, I purposely relax my entire body. I make her work a little harder to hold on to me. Her body shifts and I feel her wings begin to pulse. They whoosh in the air as she extends them to their fullest. I watch as the feathers move like musculature. They remind me of a song being played on just the ebony keys of a piano. We descend to the "floor" in question. It's not a proper level. There aren't even any walls. It's just a narrow tunnel built into the mountain. A single guard standing there nods at me and Navaa as we pass. Like any sentry on duty for hours at a time, his body is present, but his mind is somewhere else, daydreaming. Our arrival has snapped him back to the duty at hand and he stands a little straighter.

There are six metal doors built into the rock face. Each door has an electronic panel beside it and when Navaa gets to the middle one on the right side, she stops and lets the panel scan her eye. The lock twists and turns, metal tumbling over gears. The door hisses open a crack and Navaa pushes it all the way.

Unlike the other rooms on this base, this one is low and oppressive. It's the same basic setup as the interrogation room that I was given above. There are no mirrors here, though, no sharp objects of any kind. There is, surprisingly, a tall window, set back from the wall, any hope of direct access to it eliminated by a stretch of iron bars. The Faida gave the altered Roone a view. I don't think I would have been so kind.

"He's already crazy," Navaa says as if reading my mind. "This at least allows him to follow the rhythm of days and nights—just in case he wants to keep track of how long he has been our prisoner."

The altered Roone is sitting on the bed with his back to us, staring out the window. Unlike the gorgeous onyx of Edo's skin, his is a sickly amber color, although it may just be the dull light in here.

"Turn around, Grifix," Navaa orders. At the sound of her voice, Grifix startles and slowly, painfully, drags his body around to face us. When he's fully turned, I can see now that while a Roone's skin may be invulnerable to scrapes and scratches, it is not impenetrable. Three long cracks run down his face, permanent craters, where I suppose those of us with weaker flesh would have scars. One of these gouges stretches the length of his chin, across a sealed eyeball, and over his otherwise smooth skull. I can see the Faida causing this kind of damage, but I think it unlikely. This is not neat enough. It looks self-inflicted.

"The table is set. The table is set. The table is set, but the pages are missing. Where is that book?" Grifix says in a forced whisper. The Roones' vocal cords are also affected by the additional calcification of their genetic fuckery. They rasp and gnaw through their words, but Grifix sounds particularly rough.

"Look, Grifix. I brought you a guest," Navaa tells him as she walks closer. I can see him move away from her as she draws near. His body hunches, like closing a birthday card. He is trembling.

"Wait, wait!" he says, scrambling back. "The leaves are too green, don't you see that? They are too green! I didn't make them that way. It was God. Or maybe it was the market or maybe they are screaming." Grifix tics and pulls. He is on the edge of tears. I have to agree with Navaa. He is not faking. It's not just the nonsense he's spewing. It's his entire demeanor. This man is broken. He is terrified. He's not even completely here.

"Grifix!" Navaa admonishes with a louder voice. Grifix startles and finally looks up. At both of us. He stares at me and there is just the briefest flicker of something. Not sanity, not quite, but acknowledgment. "This is Ryn. She is a human. A human Citadel."

At this, his large remaining blue eye opens even wider. He puts a single gnarled hand up against his mouth, as if it could stop the escaping giggle. With disgust, I realize that the look that I am reading on his face is not pain or fear.

It is sheer, unabashed *joy*.

"We did it. We did it. Wediditwediditwedidit," Grifix babbles.

"Stop," I tell him grimly. I realize that my hands are balled into fists. I take a breath and stare at the pathetic wizened creature.

"We did it with red welts and pus. We did it with pictures and movies of humans rutting and fucking and sucking and then tiny broken bones. *Look at you.*" He is laughing now. Navaa takes a step closer, but even the threat of her nearness isn't enough to stop him. I think I am angry, possibly furious, but I'm not sure exactly. I definitely don't pity him. He deserves this cell and his madness. I think I feel . . . indifferent? This altered Roone is my enemy, but he is not *the* enemy, not anymore. He's a madman who will never recover and who tried to scratch his own eyes out so he wouldn't have to see the images that haunted him.

"Is she Kir-Abisat?" he asks Navaa hopefully, as if the entire world depended on her answer. She looks at me and I nod.

"She is."

At that he becomes emotional. Tears leak from the crags beside his eye sockets. "Plums and cakes. Plums and cakes, it was worth the agony, yes? Because you, child, are all the Earths everywhere. You are all the sounds at once."

The sound of his voice, like two boulders scraping against each other, raises the hair on my arms. "What do you mean?" I ask him.

"You are every sound. *You are* the sound. You're a coin dropped in a well. You don't need other shiny things. Human Kir-Abisat, you sing the music of the universe. You understand what I'm saying? Your body breaks like a dinner plate, but we managed to turn your mouth into a key." Suddenly, in his exuberance, he bounces forward and falls to the floor, grabbing my legs. "Let me see you bang the drum!" I kick him off me, but he stays on his knees swaying. "Please, Kir-Abisat, your throat is silver."

"What is he talking about? Is he making any sense to you?" Navaa asks me.

"Maybe. I think so." Honesty is not in my nature, but I realize there's no point being vague. If my instincts are right, there's no one else I can talk to about this anyway. "I think he's saying I don't need a conduit. That's what they accomplished with us. With practice I should be able to open a Rift anywhere as long as I know the address. I don't need Ezra. His frequency is already there—inside me."

Navaa looks at me in stunned silence. "Have you tried this?" she finally gets out, but her voice is smaller than usual.

"Of course not. I didn't know what this was in me until we met. And I didn't even think about it until now. But . . . I can't explain it. I just think he's right. The sounds are there, in my head."

"Plums and cake! Chimes and beetles!" Grifix screeches ecstatically.

"Let's get out of here. You don't need to be around him anymore. Unless you"—Navaa bites her bottom lip and gives me an intense, steady gaze—"want to spend some time alone with him. We don't really need him. Even if he's lying, your equipment can pretty much take us anywhere we need to go."

I look at the altered Roone. He is on his knees looking up at me, his face a decimated mountain. His people have murdered and tortured and maimed their way across the Multiverse. I briefly imagine pulling his head away from his shoulders. It would be so easy to kill him and God knows he deserves it. But nothing should be easy when it comes to this particular monster.

"No," I tell her with steely determination. "But I would like you to find a way to block that window. He shouldn't have anything to look at, not even the sky."

Navaa smiles ever so slightly, almost sadly even. "We can move him to another cell where there isn't a window."

"Yeah," I answer her while looking down at him. "That would be appropriate."

We walk out of the cell and down the dimly lit passage, which is more mining tunnel than hallway. When we get to the edge, Navaa opens her arms and I walk into her embrace. She wraps her arms around me tightly and we ascend quickly into the air.

I can do this. I can handle this newest piece of information Grifix has thrown into the mix. I will deal, somehow, with the loss of the Daithi Citadels. I can navigate my way to finding an answer to all of this.

It's just right now, in this moment, I miss my mom.

CHAPTER 13

We assemble, straight-backed and focused in the war room. The screen in front of us has been raised, casting a blue tint like moonlight on our faces in this darkened room. I have propped my elbows on the table, resting my chin slightly on my curled fists. It might look like I am asking for mercy and, given our dire circumstances, I probably would. There are just too many gods now: Jesus, Yahweh, Buddha, Kremlock the Spiradael Saint of Destruction, Morwenn the Daithi Crone of War. The Multiverse is too vast. How would any of these deities hear the pleas of one girl burrowed deep in the center of a mountain?

"Come now, one of you must have an idea about how to approach the Akshaji?" Navaa asks the room for a second time.

"Iathan has suggested we Rift to his Earth and see if we might all come up with a solution to this problem together,"

Levi reminds the room. This is not new information. We told the Faida this almost immediately when we returned.

"I would very much like to meet with the Roones," Arif says in a tone that is more threatening than hopeful. "But, on this matter, I simply can't imagine how they would help us. If they knew how to get to the Akshaji, surely they would have done so already. What they want is what all Roones want: to give the orders and let the Citadels do the grunt work."

"Arif," I warn, letting my hands drop as I slide them across the cool surface of the table. "You can't let your emotions dictate policy here. You have to separate the Roones from the altered Roones and, more importantly, the Karekin from the Settiku Hesh. They have sacrificed their entire way of life try- ing to stop the insanity of the altered Roones."

"They are not blameless, though," Navaa tells the room un- flinchingly.

"And neither are we," I tell her from across the table, the space suddenly closing in on itself as if I was right beside her and not on the other side of the room. "Every person in this room has done terrible things. We need the Roones and the Karekin loyal to them. If you don't want to discuss the Akshaj problem with them, that's fine, but they are part of this alli- ance whether you like it or not."

"I'd like to make a suggestion," Ezra says in English. The Faida read his translation and look over to him. Ordinarily, I might be a little annoyed that Ezra is trying to insert him- self here, but we've been at this for over an hour without any meaningful results. There is a chance that he is seeing some- thing we can't. Navaa blinks her eyes almost lazily in his di- rection and dips her head in a nod. "With the Daithi . . ." Ezra raises his head to the ceiling as if the heavens could provide an accurate word for what was done to them. He can't. There isn't a word. In any language. "With the Daithi no longer in play, and before we risk everything by going to the Akshaji, I think we should try with the Orsalines."

Navaa practically huffs. "We've already gone over this. We came to a consensus. The Orsalines cannot be swayed."

"Most likely that is true," Ezra admits. "But they *are* easily manipulated. I'm just suggesting the possibility of redirecting that manipulation. They've been drugged—we've got drugs. They've been brainwashed—we can do that sort of thing, too."

"Actually, Ezra," I say in Faida, turning my head to the rest of the group, "that's not a terrible idea. The problem is volume. I'm sure given enough time, we could turn them, but how many could we get to switch sides given our resources? We need thousands, not dozens."

"I'd be happy with a dozen that belong to us," Sidra says unexpectedly. "A dozen Orsalines could do a lot of damage from the inside. Sabotage, counterintelligence, discreet propaganda. We should at least see for ourselves if such a thing is possible."

Navaa exhales one long single breath that seems to go on for longer than necessary. "Because the Orsalines are particularly dim-witted and I feel confident that we can elude them on a mission, I suppose we should go."

"Agreed," I tell her enthusiastically. "We have to exhaust every option and go down every road, even if leads to a dead end."

"I can scout locations for possible entry points and create a mission brief with Sidra, Donav, Yessenia, and Ezra," Levi offers. "I'd say we'd be ready to go in less than forty-eight hours." I look at him and he is already on his tablet. His fingers nimbly crawl all over the illuminated panel. When Navaa closes the meeting, I am still staring. Even when Levi is doing nothing very interesting, he still looks so capable . . . so strong. It's the sound of the chairs being rolled back, of creaking wheels, that makes me look away. I look up and everyone is gone but Sidra, who gives me just a sliver of a smile as she eyes Levi's now empty chair. She is a master spy *and* a woman. It's not like she wouldn't know exactly what's going on.

I TAKE DINNER THAT NIGHT in my own room. I have purposely spent as many meals as I can in the common dining area because I felt like it was good for morale and for helping to cement our relations with the Faida. Tonight, though, I thought I would try to watch a holographic Faida movie on my own. Really, I just wanted an evening alone where I didn't have to make any decisions or deal with the old (literal) song and dance routine of having to open a Rift with Navaa. I start watching a film that Arif has suggested. It's about a female racer who injures her wings and can't fly again. It's good to know that some tropes are truly universal. It's not a bad movie, it's just a little boring—that is, until the love scene. I am actually shocked because I'm almost 100 percent certain that these actors are actually having sex on camera. Very loud, very enthusiastic sex . . . and since it's a holographic projection it looks as though they are right in front of me. I'm pretty sure that Arif is not a perv, which probably means this is just how they do things here in the movies. I'm not turned on as much as fascinated. I tilt my head sideways as they change positions and my mouth is kind of locked agape.

And then I hear a knock on the door.

I leap out of my seat because, although it's not like I did anything wrong here, still, *porn*. Then I decide that no, I'm not going to be puritanical about this. This is a Faida movie and if they aren't weird about it, then I shouldn't be, either. I open the door where Levi is standing, staring at me with his arms crossed. He looks behind me at the two lifelike figures going at it and even though my face is flushed, I lift my chin in greeting as if it's the most normal thing in the world to have two angels screwing in the background.

"I can hear that, you know," he informs me.

I open the door wider and gesture for him to enter. "I'm learning that the Faida are a very literal people. Not a lot of make-believe with them." Still wearing a skeptical look on his face, he warily steps inside my room.

"So this is art? Not porn?" he asks with a cheeky smile.

"I feel like it's probably both. Why don't you just come in and sit down. I'll turn this off." While it's true I had wanted to be alone tonight, I didn't quite realize what I really meant was that I wanted some space from everyone besides Levi. He's the one person here who being with doesn't feel like a chore or an obligation. I turn the movie off and he sits down on a bench in front of the tall bed. "So," he fishes. When I don't say anything, his green eyes scrutinize me. "What's up? I only wanted you to turn down the moaning, but you invited me in," Levi says, chuckling at his own joke.

"Yeah, no. I guess when I saw you I just wanted to . . ."—I pause and look up at the cathedral ceiling. There are never any cobwebs. Maybe they don't have spiders on this Earth. Interesting—"check in. We haven't really spent any time together lately. Or talked. We haven't tried any deprogramming."

Levi rubs his palms over his jeans. I notice that somewhere along the way, he cut his hair. It's not as short as usual, but it's back up above his collar.

"I don't know, Ryn. Last time we tried that I practically broke your foot and threatened to pull your guts out. I'm thinking probably we shouldn't try anything else while we're here." This is, of course, a sensible plan. Still . . .

"I get that," I assure him as I sit beside him on the bench. "But, ever since the Daithi Earth, I've felt this weird . . ." I begin to move my hands, circling them as if they were the motor that could get my train of thought going. "It's not emptiness. Well, sometimes it is, but I guess it's a kind of powerlessness? Like, I know I won't ever stop fighting, but I'm not sure anymore when I'm actually fighting. The battles aren't just physical, right? And I don't know how to wrap my brain around the idea that just being here is part of the war because I don't really feel like I'm doing anything."

Levi nods his head slowly. "You can hum a Rift open. You and Navaa are calling most of the shots when it comes to strategy, but I understand that given how we were trained, it still probably feels pretty static."

"Look," I tell him, fighting the urge to put my hands on him, not just to convince him, but because he's so solid, so completely *here*. "I totally understand, given what happened last time, why you wouldn't want to try again, but I really want to fix this for you. I want this to be one less thing we need to worry about it."

Levi looks at me, but then his eyes search the room for an answer. He must not be able to find one, because eventually they land on my face once more. And I see it. The conflict. He doesn't want to hurt me. He doesn't want the Faida to see that side of him again, but he also wants to be able to touch me. It's a powerful need, the urge to put your hands on someone you have feelings for and to let them touch you in return. It trumps common sense and reason. Levi and I, we live in the dark. We breathe in shadows and the exhaust of blood and violence. To be able to lay your head down on the chest of someone dear, to wrap your arms around them, is like a different kind of homecoming.

"I have some red pills in my Dopp kit in the bathroom," I tell him smoothly.

"Okay," he tells me with a voice that is equal parts excitement and resignation. Levi disappears for a minute or two and returns to sit beside me on the bench. I flash him a slow, secret smile and walk to the closet. I know he is watching me, and I also know there is no point in being coy. We're beyond that now. I tell my sensuit to cuff and I am naked, with my back to him. I reach into the closet and pull out my uniform. Of course it's typical with me, that instead of taking my clothes off to get things started, I need to put mine on.

I step inside one leg, bending slightly to wrestle my foot in. Then I repeat the action on the other side, bending down just a little more. I arch my back to slide my arms in and zip up the uniform as I turn around.

"I feel like that movie you were watching has given you ideas," he tells me with a sideways grin.

"Only if you've suddenly grown a pair of wings. Talk about suspension." We both laugh at that and it eases a bit of the tension, though not completely and I'm glad of it. I kind of like how it's filling the space between us, how it's heating the air and making my neck sweat a little, just under the fabric. I sit on the chair opposite him and put some music on. It's some old band that's on Levi's list of safe things. I think that it's stuff that his mom likes and listens to. His mom is featured a lot on the list and I know he feels weird about it. Still, in order to get him to feel safe, he has to get his senses to trigger nostalgia and security.

We wait in heightened silence. We stare at each other, long, languid gazes that make me bite my bottom lip and then our eyes break away to focus on something less intense. After fifteen minutes or so, he slides down the bench, getting on all fours, crawling over to me slowly. In turn, I lean back in my chair. When he gets to my legs, he rears up on his knees. It is imperative that I don't appear anxious or excited. For this to work, I must seem docile, compliant. If he in any way feels threatened, this will go very badly.

Again.

I stay perfectly still as he runs his hands up both shins to my thighs. He looks straight at me when he swiftly spreads them open like two green butterfly wings. The shock of this one, heated action makes me exhale loudly, but still, I do not move. He brings his face down and gently nuzzles his cheek on the inside of the fabric above my knee. He moves his head up and to the left, so that he is entirely between my legs. I want to run my hands through his hair and ball it into my fists, but I can't. Instead, I grit my teeth. Then, I feel his hot breath through my uniform. Who knew that just breathing in that one place could feel so incredible?

Levi puts both his hands over my own and lifts himself up slowly, dragging his face along the middle of my body. Ever so gently, he licks the front of my neck before he reaches my mouth. He kisses me hard and deep. His tongue flickers in and out of my mouth, tasting me and letting me taste him. My eyes are closed, and when he pulls away, I think he must want to put me in another position, on the floor maybe . . .

When I do open my lids, I can see that his face is an inch from my own and his eyes are blazing . . . *with anger.* I silently curse myself for making him do this. Clearly, the last time must have done more damage than I thought. In a flash, his hands are wrapped around my throat. He tips the chair back and both of us spill onto the floor. He handily slides me along the wood, away from the furniture.

This is the moment, right here. This is where I prove how far I'm willing to go, for him, for all of us. He could crush my windpipe in a second, but he is taking his time, savoring his sudden hatred. I keep my lids open, focused solely on him. I can't breathe. I feel a sudden flash of shame when I admit to myself that there is a small part of me that is relieved.

I am tired.

The road ahead seems impassable. I meant it when I said that I would never stop fighting. But if I'm dead, I won't have to fight anymore. If I die now, I won't have to bear witness to watching the people I care about die, many of whom most certainly will.

I had my few moments in the sun and now night is coming on. My vision is starting to fail, darkness is beginning to bleed into my periphery. I let my entire body go slack. I am probably going to die. I wonder briefly if I have a soul, and where it will go. We are made of energy, and energy cannot be destroyed, only transformed. Will whatever I turn into find its way back to my own Earth? As a Kir-Abisat, will I become part of a Rift?

The only thing that really keeps me present is Levi. If he does this to me, if he *kills* me, I don't think he'll ever recover. The Faida alliance might shatter. Everyone in Battle Ground is at risk. I probably should have thought of all that before. Levi keeps staring at me and all I can do is plead with my eyes. He has me. He's won. I won't hurt him.

Just as I begin to black out, his pupils change and lose their focus. He shakes his head as if waking from a dream. Immediately he takes his hands away from my neck. I take one gasping breath, filling my lungs with air. A single tear slides away from Levi's eye. It runs down his cheek like an escaped prisoner and lands on my chin.

"Don't," I croak. The pain of speaking is excruciating. I want to say *Don't worry, don't think I can't handle this, don't move, don't run.* I can't get out any of those words, though. All I can do is take lumbered, shallow breaths.

Levi slides his hand under my shoulders and lifts me up into an embrace. "I am so sorry, Ryn," he begins to repeat. It is only then, in that moment, that I realize what he hasn't.

Levi *stopped.*

There's only one way on this Earth or any other that a Citadel can stop at the height of the Blood Lust, and that is to have the link with the Blood Lust broken.

I reach up and put a finger to his mouth. "Shhhhh," I tell him, my voice trembling. "Don't you feel it? It's gone, Levi. Look. Think. It's not there anymore." Because that's how it is. The Blood Lust is always lurking, always right on the other side of an imaginary door ready to spring, but when it's gone, its lack of presence is just as visceral.

I watch this revelation transform Levi's face. First, he's recollecting, mentally sifting, and then, when he understands that I'm right, he opens his mouth and lets out a deep breath that begins and ends from the well of his entire spirit. He makes a sound like I've never heard. It's a mournful cry, ecstatic anguish.

I hold him closer to me and he picks me up off the floor and lays me on the bed. He slowly unzips my uniform and wrangles me out of it. I use my cuff to clothe me in the soft, buttery cotton the SenMachs have created. The loose sweatpants and oversized T-shirt are a cocoon of comfort and I shrug and snuggle inside them.

Levi brings up the covers and tucks me in before going

back into the bathroom. When he returns, he has a Roone ice pack that he must have gotten from my med kit. Because it's Roonish, it doesn't need to be frozen. He simply breaks the seal and the chemicals inside instantly dip below freezing. He takes off his shirt and wraps the pack inside of it before gently placing it on my neck.

Levi undresses, but he leaves his shorts on. He walks over to the other side of the bed and slides in, under the covers. I understand why he needs to be close to me like this right now. This isn't desire. This isn't about sex. I roll onto my side and he curls his body around me. His touch is light. His limbs are a layer of autumn leaves falling almost weightless around my stomach. His embrace is filled with both regret and hope. I pull him closer. I understand. Finally, he feels safe.

So do I.

CHAPTER 14

Ultimately, after much debate, we all agree that this first visit to the Orsalines will be strictly recon. Even if the opportunity presents itself to take a few of them with us, we will not. Sidra wants a working cell inside the Orsaline base. If we snatch a dozen bears, or whatever they are, they will most certainly be missed. What we are hoping for is some kind of insight into how they work as a group. Do they take time off? Do they live on or off the base? Do they get transferred? Are they ever sent through the Rift? Sidra needs a plausible way of reprogramming a cell of Orsalines away from their Earth where, somehow, they won't be missed.

It's a tall order.

Because this is strictly recon, and because we only have four sensuits, we all decide that it would be best to keep the unit small. Me and Levi, Arif and Navaa. Using the SenMach technology, we can be invisible, observing from close range, and that's what we need.

Our improved QOINS system delivers us exactly where we want to be, just one mile from the Orsaline base. Invisibility is a huge tactical advantage, but it also leads to another problem. No one can see us, which is great, but we can't see *each other*, either. We can communicate via our earpieces, but that's not exactly ideal when you're trying to be stealthy. Levi and I can get a pretty good sense of proximity if we use our enhanced hearing to listen for each other's heartbeats and breathing. The Faida will have to stick to more conventional methods. They will have to keep their heads down and watch our footprints make their way through the cracked mud and sluggish brown grass.

It's hardly surprising that the terrain is forested. We all expected that, given what we had seen in surveillance footage. What we didn't expect (though I suppose we should have) was the biting cold. It's well below zero here, and while there is no snow on the ground, it's clear from the brush and skeletal bracken that this Earth is still deep inside the winter season. Although, given what these Citadels are, maybe it's perpetually winter here. There is nothing but giant evergreens reaching up to a white sky. There are no hedges or shrubs, just trees for miles all around.

We are not kitted out for this kind of weather. The sensuits can insulate us a fair bit, but not enough. From the first moments our lungs begin to take in the frigid air, Levi and I keep to our training. We both start breathing in short, panting breaths. We begin to run in place as fast as we can. It's imperative that we keep our heart rates up and circulation going. This will burn more calories and we will have to be mindful of our nutrition, but we have no choice. I assume the Faida can bring their wings around their bodies. Must be nice, being an angel.

We make a collective run toward the base, following Doe's instructions via our earpieces. We've kept things light today, no big packs, just tiny ones holding our essentials, secured tightly under the suits.

When we see the base in a valley below us, the shock of it jolts me to a standstill. I assumed, of course, there would be some sort of structure, but I was thinking basic, like maybe a fortified shack with rough and rounded boulders. What I couldn't have imagined was a massive, sprawling temple made of stone with towers and turrets and separate courtyards between wings. It's far more Shaolin Monastery than primitive Citadel stronghold.

I grab my binoculars, as I suppose the others do as well, to get a better look at what's going on. I expect a bunch of furry soldiers decked out in uniforms and practicing maneuvers. Once again, though, what I see is very different. Yes, there are Orsaline Citadels here, but there is a bustling market outside the giant wall. Normal citizens and families are walking in and out of the ornately carved gate. Farther off in the distance, I see the unmistakable green glow of a Rift. This is not a military instillation. This is a true compound. This is the epicenter of their lives, like a medieval fortress. My guess is that the base is the village, and the thousands of Orsalines who live here are connected to the altered Roones in a way that no other race is.

I'm well aware that I don't have to point this out. My fellow comrades have eyes. "We might as well go down and take a look, see if there's anything that Sidra might be able to use," I suggest. There is just the faintest rustle as the other three collect themselves and prepare to walk down the sharply in-clined path to the stronghold.

I take the lead while Levi holds up the rear with the Faida between us. As we descend, Orsalines begin to pass us. The four of us dance delicately away, making sure to remain un-seen and holding our bodies precariously downwind so that, hopefully, they won't sniff us out, either—though who knows if their sense of smell is as acute as that of actual bears. It's not anything we read in the intel.

When we get to the compound proper, it is a bustling place. Vendors, hawking their wares from shoddy wooden stalls, range from butchers to leather smiths and even yarn brokers, selling dyed bulky skeins on fat colorful cones. We enter the gates easily. There are no checkpoints and no security. The large courtyard is surrounded by squat buildings. Children (or cubs I guess?) run in and out of open doorways ducking un-der laundry lines hung from stone posts. They all live here together. In a fortress. It would be pretty hard to kidnap any of them without drawing attention certainly.

"Stay here," I whisper. "I'm going to go inside and check out one of these houses." I nimbly creep ten feet ahead and slip inside an open door. There is a female Orsaline decked out in what may be a dress but could also just be a bunch of draped fabric under a leather apron. Bears in clothes. Jesus. It's so weird. She is chopping meat with a giant cleaver on a large table. I look around the room. There is a fire, some fairly substantial wooden chairs, and a couple pallets for sleeping. I don't even want to *think* about the bathroom situation here.

There are a few small windows with warped and bubbled glass. What there is not is any kind of technology. I don't see a TV, a radio, a phone, an oven (though I see a kind of gi-ant black monstrosity that must be a stove). The Orsalines are barely out of the Dark Ages, which is probably exactly where the altered Roones want them.

I walk out of the house and join the others. Before I can suggest that we make our way inside the actual Citadel facility, I hear a series of bells and chimes. The bells are coming from high atop several of the long, rectangular towers. The chimes are being hit by Orsalines wearing long robes, their claws lightly clanging on cymbals and gongs as they walk. Every Orsaline around me—the tiny cubs, the grizzled elderly, the round-shouldered females carrying buckets and baskets—get on their knees. As if that wasn't bizarre enough, there is a faint whirring sound, like a clock unwinding. Each stone pillar has a panel that flips over to reveal a screen. All along the high wall, panels flip as well, revealing the same.

And then, the monitors blip into life and an image of a Roone with her arms outstretched appears. She is gold—not golden or honey colored, but actually made of gold. I suppose it makes sense, gold is an ore. Her bald head shines, the light perfectly reflecting off it from different angles so it gives the appearance of a crown made of prisms and stars. She is dressed entirely in black, with a high-collared robe that's wide and curved. It's basically your average Disney villain attire. But I can see how the black would look more dramatic set against the gold as opposed to virginal white.

Still, it's basic.

She is wearing a mask of benevolence and kindness, slowly craning her neck from one side to another, her mouth agape as if she is breathing in the love of her people and exhaling virtue and mercy in return. From my vantage, she's about as believable as one of the bachelorettes playing the part of the Virgin Mary in community theater.

"All hail to the gods of Roone," the Orsalines begin to say

in unison. Their paws reach up to the heaven beseeching, their furry bodies swaying to and fro. "We freely offer up our lives to you in return for your many blessings."

Seriously?

I have seen many people at prayer, but this is different. This is primal ecstasy. These aren't just people reciting an allegiance by rote and memory. These Orsalines believe they are in the presence of the divine. "We serve you, the makers of the world, willingly with all that we have, in blood and bone. Amen." I think it's *amen*. It could be *hallelujah*. It could be something else entirely. There is no direct translation.

The bells and chimes ring once more, and the Orsalines rise and once again begin to go about their business.

"We can't leave without a full sweep, which means we need to get inside the main building," Navaa's voice faintly whispers in our ears. I look around and find a tiny alleyway that leads to a narrow strip between the buildings and the wall.

"Follow me. Let's hold hands and we can all walk together. It's a straight shot to where I'm thinking." At that, fingers grapple around my wrist until they find my own. It's Arif. Once that's done, I direct us all to this small, secluded space.

"All right, if we do this, we're going all in. That building is going to be packed with Orsalines and Roones, which means we can't risk being separated," I tell them all.

"So what do you propose?" Navaa asks haughtily. "You told us these suits would ensure our ability to do that very thing."

"They can, we just need to adjust the strategy," I tell her firmly. "Doe, program the sensuits to look like Orsaline Citadels."

Like rain on a chalked sidewalk, the sensuits dissolve and re-form around our bodies and over our faces.

"Okay," Levi says while checking out his newly padded

arms and paws. Having the sensuits cover our faces is not ideal, but it's not horrible. Not as horrible as having to *be a bear*. Of all the animals I could turn into . . . *bears*. I hate them. They serve no purpose other than to kill campers and terrify hikers.

I do begin to notice little things. We aren't all the same color for starters. Navaa is a deep chocolate brown, Levi is gray with flecks of ashy blond. Arif is sable black, and my fur is russet colored. We are all wearing a uniform (slate gray) and our triad patches are hunter green with the Orsaline letters (made of slanting lines and dashes) *KDR*. An acronym that most likely stands for Soldiers of God. Subtle.

There are no female Citadels on this Earth, so I remind Navaa to walk heavy, heel to toe.

"Not to sound racist, if that even applies here, but are we just assuming that all these bears kinda look alike and they won't notice four strangers?" Levi questions.

"Oh, I'm sure they can distinguish each other, if not by sight then scent . . . maybe. Smarter not to take any chances, which is why we should cover ourselves a little with dust and dirt," I tell him as I bend down and begin to scratch away at the hard earth beneath us so I can get a few handfuls, sorry, *pawfuls*, and pat myself all over. Thankfully, even though I now have basically two oven mitts for hands, at least the Orsalines have thumbs, or more accurately, two bonus digits so we can hold on to something—like a gun. "There are six Rift sites here and I'm sure they get transferred from time to time. I don't need to tell you all to just keep your eyes forward and walk like you belong. We'll be fine, and if we aren't, we run. At worst they'll assume we're maybe the one percent of Orsalines who don't believe in this bullshit. They won't know we're humans. Or Faida."

"That's fine, but"—Arif says as he begins to rub his back on the dirty wall behind us—"we have no idea where to look once we're inside. We cannot ask."

"No. But Doe can. Doe," I say out loud, "hack into the altered Roones' system. We'll need directions and access once we get there."

I can see Navaa's eyes roll just the tiniest bit even through the thick mass of her facial hair.

"I believe you rely entirely too much on your jewelry, Ryn Whittaker," she tells me disapprovingly. At that I just shrug, my large hairy shoulders lurching up and then back down again with about as much grace as you'd expect from an indifferent bear.

"Walk straight into the main building," Doe says through our earpieces. "There is a common room and then a hallway; go left there."

At that, our misfit team trods ahead. I concentrate on my gait, copying the others I see around me. There is a slight waddle to the way they walk, though their arms and legs are more proportionate than the bears on our Earth. Still, I move forward, trying to imagine a giant beach ball between my legs. Civilians nod at us as we pass, some even bow. I think the Citadels here have a pretty high opinion of themselves, so I don't acknowledge any of this. Instead I wonder how it is that my life could have taken such a turn that I've become Winnie-the-Pooh with two guns strapped to my thighs.

We pass other Citadel Orsalines who are standing sentry at the entry of the main building. There is a slight nod for these, my fellow soldiers, but no words. Thankfully, the Orsalines are not big on talking. Plenty more Citadels are inside, some standing guard, some training in one of two giant rings. I sneak a peek at their fighting up close. There is a lot of lunging and squeezing and roaring, as we figured. They are faster than I thought, though, and that is something to be wary of.

When we get to the hallway, Doe instructs us to pass all the other doors and head to the very last one at the end. This is apparently where all the electronic signals are coming from. There is precious little in the way of security around here, no eye scans or elevators. No one, even in this section, is using any kind of electronics to monitor anything. What there is are two burly-looking Orsaline Citadels parked right in front of the door that we apparently need to get through.

"Can you and Arif distract them?" I ask Levi. "Just long enough for us to take a look?"

"Roger that," he answers. Levi marches straight up to them and we follow, matching Levi's short, but confident stride. "You two," he half snarls in their direction. "There was a happening among the civilians. The captain asked for you specifically. Come with us, these other two will take your place."

Now, if this was any other Earth, I am sure something more detailed would have been required. "A happening" is a pretty lame way of describing much of anything, but there is not an Orsaline word for *skirmish*, *incident*, or *unrest*.

Still, because the Orsalines are stupid and cannot imagine anything of real consequence occurring with their benevolent gods protecting them, the two follow Arif and Levi down the hallway without question.

As soon as they disappear, I gently pull down on the handle of the door, fully expecting it to be locked. It's not. Maybe it's not such a surprise after all, considering that the altered Roones have this race so stymied that all they would need to do is say, "Don't open this door unless it's a total, absolute emergency," and the Orsalines would obediently comply.

I open the door just a fraction, wide enough so that both Navaa and I can get a look at what's going on. Inside this room, the altered Roones are running the show like every other command center I've seen on various Citadel Earths so far. There are monitors, computers, keyboards. The altered Roones walk purposely around talking to one another or on their comm devices. There is a large monitor showing the actual Rift and the Orsalines scattered around it, waiting for activity. While I am sure the Roones send things through once in a while for the Orsalines to get some practice in, they run an entirely different kind of show here. The Orsalines are not elite. They don't have to know strategy or stealthy tactics. They are buckshot from a sawed-off shotgun. They are useful for aiming and shooting, regardless of who or what they hit, but little else.

I know this because there is not a single Orsaline in the room. This whole place is like Oz and the altered Roones keep themselves safely tucked away behind the curtain. I hear someone coming and quickly and quietly close the door. I turn, ready to fight, puffing out my barreled chest, but it is only Arif and Levi.

"Let's go," Levi says hurriedly. "The other two went in search of their commander. They didn't seem all that bothered that we go with them."

The four of us make our way quickly down the hallway and through the melee of the large entryway. We walk in two columns out the large doorway. Before we can make it down the stone steps, though, one of the Orsaline guards actually speaks to us.

"I do not know you. Where did you come from?" the Citadel demands in a voice that is as booming as it is gravelly. *Now* they want to ask questions? Right when we're about to get out of here? Typical. I say nothing, as I am a female and there's no way I could even remotely sound like one of them.

"We just arrived. From the Sand Rift," Levi responds accordingly.

The Orsaline eyes us up and down. I'm sure he senses there is something not quite right about us, but he could never imagine what we are or that we—even as actual Orsalines—would have the balls to impersonate Citadels. He gives us a kind of head check, a thrust that must mean we are free to go about our business.

Without another word, we make our way quickly through the gate and to the path. From there, we get just far enough away to open a small Rift. We cuff back to ourselves before jumping into the onyx ocean of the Multiverse. We've learned what we needed to here.

None of it looks good for us.

CHAPTER 15

We waste no time calling a war council when we return to the Faida Earth. I can't help but touch my arms and run my palms down my thighs, thrilled with their hairlessness and the lack of padded bulk. For a few moments, we sit around the table in silence, fiddling with tablets and keeping our looks to objects as opposed to each other. No one wants to say what we all know to be true out loud. No one wants to name it and give it so much power.

Finally, the tension gets to me and I speak up. "Look," I tell the room solemnly. "It wasn't a terrible idea. We were just doing due diligence. We knew—"

"No," Navaa snaps. "We *thought*. We did not know, not entirely until today. Bright Heavens, they have them all." I know that Navaa isn't just thinking of the Orsalines, but the Spiradael and the lost Daithi, not to mention the Settiku Hesh.

"There was a chance," I counter. "If there had been some Orsalines in that control room, we could have followed through on Sidra's plan. How could we have known that they wouldn't trust a single one of them with even a version of the truth?"

"It would take weeks, if not months, to create an Orsaline cell. First we'd have to explain what a cell is. Then we'd have to help them understand basic physics. Then we'd have to prove that the altered Roones are not gods and at this point"—Navaa places a palm lightly on her forehead—"*I'm* not even totally convinced they aren't considering what they've accomplished."

"It doesn't matter," I say firmly, planting both elbows on the table. "It's settled. The Orsalines and Daithi are out. We *have* to go to the Akshaji. Immediately. We have the recon. We've done the research. I say we leave tomorrow."

"Agreed," Levi announces. "The longer we wait, the greater the risk of exposure. Right now, the one thing we have going for us is that the altered Roones don't know we're working together. We think we're screwed now, but if they find that out, it really is over."

"Can I just say something?" Ezra asks the room. "I know you all have a plan for Battle Ground and the other Rifts and it's a good one, but it's going to take time. We might not have enough of it. The altered Roones chose your planet because they knew that they could count on the world's governments to keep the Rifts a secret. Right? So what if we took that advantage away from them? What if we exposed them?"

"Like," Levi begins with disdain, "put out a press release or something?"

"Well," Ezra runs a hand through his thick, brown hair, "yeah, I suppose that would work. We have the proof. It's not like we couldn't back up our claims."

More silence. More hangnail picking and side-eyeing at the

conference table. "It's not a terrible idea," I offer congenially. I'm lying, though. It's the dumbest plan ever. "But we can't do that," I tell him without even the barest hint of condescension. Regardless of what I think of the idea, it's imperative, at all times that the humans show a united front. "It would be anarchy. Chaos. We may or may not help our cause, but it would force an international crisis and lives would be lost. Most of them civilian."

"And you don't think that every human life is already in danger on your planet? After the Daithi . . ." Ezra's voice trails off.

"They killed the Daithi Citadels and the Faida spies," I tell him resolutely. "They might be terrorizing the public at large, but they didn't murder the villagers. If we leaked this story, we would lose control of it the second it came out. God knows the kind of havoc they could unleash into a population of confused humans. Right now, we stay the course. Henry's plan is working. We don't have a lot of time, you're right about that. But chaos isn't the right response to urgency. We just have to hope time doesn't run out."

Ezra throws his hands up in mock surrender. "Okay," he tells the room. His plan is logical . . . if there was no such thing as Rifts or Citadels.

"I know where your head's at Ezra," I say in empathy. "You've handled this situation remarkably well, but think about it: you're a genius, and your genius centers around accepting that scientific anomalies are possible. Not every human is built for understanding this situation."

"You think I was *built* for accepting any of this?" Ezra asks wide eyed.

"Of course not, but you're adaptable in a way that most civilians aren't. If we told the truth, it would plunge the entire world into turmoil. Governments might even collapse, and we can't deal with a broken infrastructure on top of everything else. For now, we have to push the status quo, but don't worry. There will be a time and place to tell the truth and we'll need you for that, too."

"Okay." Ezra backs down without losing face. "I'll start working on some models for rolling out the truth."

"Great," I tell him genuinely.

"Yes, I suppose that is something you will all need to face in the future," Navaa breaks in. "But right now, today, we have some vital decisions to make. You want to leave for the Akshaj Earth tomorrow?"

"Delaying at this point would be counterproductive," Levi says efficiently.

"This is a tricky thing. But I think it makes sense," Arif chimes in. "We go in small, we have the advantage of stealth. We go in a large number and we have a show of force and the wherewithal to back it up."

"Let's split the difference, then," I suggest. "We open a Rift, and keep twenty Citadels in reserve. The four of us go to the compound in the sensuits to get an accurate picture of what it's like on the ground. If it comes down to a fight, we have a squadron to back us up and we can Rift more in if necessary."

"I don't think I need to tell you all," Sidra cuts in, "that we absolutely do not want it to come down to a fight. The goal is to isolate a few Akshaji and let them know what's happened. Show them the Daithi footage we took. They are not being drugged or brainwashed. They believe the altered Roones to be their allies. We need to prove to them that they are not."

"Agreed," I say.

"Agreed," Navaa echoes, though there is a small crease between her brows and her ice cap blue eyes look far away. This plan is far from airtight and we all know it.

We break for the day and eat in the canteen. Faida food is a mixture of beiges and creams dotted with nut browns and muted rusts. But, like everything else on this Earth, while it looks plain, it tastes rich and decadent. The Faida are vegetarians, but each dish is so hearty and delicious, I don't even miss the meat. Levi and I eat together, our faces glued to our tablets, going over Roonish documents and footage of the Akshaji. Homework. The plan might be for shit, but we'll both be as prepared as we possibly can. Ezra has disappeared to his room. I know he must be feeling isolated, but I keep reminding myself that this is his choice. He could go home right now if he wanted to and he's choosing to stay.

When the meal is over, Levi and I walk together to our rooms. Without saying so much as a single word, I open the door and Levi steps inside. The Blood Lust is gone. We are free to do whatever we want with each other. The two of us alone, in my room—the wanting of him feels stronger than ever. I have had sex only once, so I don't understand how I can feel so many things at once. There is an aching, not just between my legs, but behind my breastbone. My skin feels flushed, but it's not just heat, it's electricity. There is an urgent driving need to have him inside me, but . . . there is also an equally strong urge to send him away. I don't want to give myself up tonight. I want to belong only to me, just next to him.

And then, as if reading my mind, Levi says, "I know we can—and God knows, I want to—but tomorrow is a big day." Levi touches my face and I let the weight of my head fall into his palm. "I'm distracted. I'm not a hundred percent here and, really, I want to be totally present when we do this."

I don't need to say anything. I don't need to tell him that I get it or that I feel the same. He knows that I'm feeling exactly like he is and it's a relief. We peel our uniforms off and cuff into shorts and tees. We both climb into the giant bed from opposite sides like an old married couple. Sleeping together has become as natural as breathing to us. I roll over on my side and tuck myself into him. The bed, as big as it is, feels like a rowboat adrift on an ocean full of worries carried by eddies and currents of languages and best guesses. Levi is the steady hand that keeps the boat from spilling. Or maybe that's me, or both of us. We tangle our limbs together with the smooth white sheets. Levi's body sings the song of home and I muffle the tune by burrowing deeper into my pillow. We don't belong here, but there is nowhere else that we should be. At some point, my mind stops spinning and I fall both reluctantly but blissfully dead asleep.

CHAPTER 16

We ride once more into the screaming green mouth of the Multiverse. My body is an arrow, straight and true, and my skin leaps to catch the dark matter molecules, a swarm of bees that buzz around this emerald hive. The Faida keep their chins down and their wings tucked, barreling through like birds of prey.

When we see the Akshaj Earth, we adjust our angles in a perfectly choreographed dance and walk carefully into the horizon. Immediately, the Faida scramble into position. Some crouch behind the widespread limbs of banyan trees, others take to the branches themselves, balancing between the larger, sturdier sections, hiding in the leaves. Sidra is here, as is Yessenia. Donav has remained behind with a much larger force, ready to deploy if necessary.

Levi, Navaa, Arif, and I activate our sensuits to stealth while Levi and I send out our drones. We are two miles away from the headquarters here. Far enough to come in unseen, close enough for the reserves to get to us in minutes.

The air is thick with humidity. Already I can feel a teardrop of sweat sliding down the nape of my neck. We are truly in the wilds here—a jungle. The greens are bright enough to rival a Rift opening, and the foliage is so thick that a normal person would need a machete to navigate it. We don't have that luxury—we can't risk leaving such an obvious trail—so we'll be doing a lot of ducking and jumping. Ordinarily, this is not a big deal. Today, though, we are covered in a silky sheet and though the sun can't quite make its way down to us directly, the heat is brutal.

We will all follow Doe's directions from here. Once again, we can't see one another, but right now, at least, we don't need to. We just need to get to the base and get a good look. If we arrive separately, it's not that big of a deal, we'll still be invisible and maybe one of us will see something separately that we might have missed while trying to stick together. I take off, leaping over gnarled roots and slick patches of deep mud. I adjust my bearings by quarter turns and little skips and hops. It doesn't take us too long to arrive, but I am surprisingly put out by the effort. I sneak a drink from my canteen under the sensuit and swig a long full gulp before taking a good look at the Akshaj Compound. Like the Orsalines, this place has the feel of a stone temple. But unlike our fat, hairy Citadel cousins, the Akshaji have built something of beauty. There are gray pagoda-like spires clawing their way out of the massive, many-winged structure like an angry trussed-up wedding cake. Atop each spire is a cone of gold.

The compound itself is covered in sprawling ivy and flesh-colored roots. The structure is formidable, but even more intimidating are the Akshaj Citadels that surround it. I had seen them, of course, in grainy video feeds, but to witness them in person is something . . . else. Their purple skin is not just bright, but luminescent, as if it was made of violet-colored pearls. Their many arms moving at once is jarring. But what makes them suddenly so intimidating isn't actually their alienness. It's how they *move*.

Inside two massive rings in front of the compound, the Akshaji are sparring. It looks less like fighting than it does dancing. They are light bending, torsos swerving, backs arching all the way so that their heads touch the ground behind them as they use a pair of hands to steady themselves.

They are working with a collection of swords and knives and though I have to assume that they are practicing, they make no qualms about slicing deeply into one another. When one gets a good jab in, the others watching roar and clap. Their blood, a deep navy blue color, spatters across the stones around them. I know that as a human Citadel I am both faster and stronger, but I don't see how it can possibly be true. I feel clumsy. And small.

There must be at least five hundred of them outside. I can only imagine how many are inside the walls. If we were forced to fight them today, it would take not only our reserves at the Rift site, but probably every single one of the Faida back at the base and even then, it probably wouldn't be enough.

"Let's find each other and walk down there," Navaa whispers in my earpiece. "Perhaps there is some area of the compound where there are fewer of them, where we might be able to get some of them alone."

Doe directs us to one another. It's easy enough, we're actually not that far apart. As we maneuver closer together, my mouth begins to go dry and the sensuit is practically suffocating me. My instincts are screaming at me that this is a very bad idea. That this could actually be one of the worst ideas ever invented in the history of ideas. We are walking into a nest of the most fearsome fighters I have ever seen, soldiers that are so good they make the Karekin look like schoolyard punks. So, we go down there, covered in a friggin' invisibility blanket and just hope that we get lucky? That there's what? A little meditation garden where a couple Akshaji are just chilling out and won't cut our throats the second they see us?

I am jostled forward by Levi and Navaa. We are among them now. I am close enough to see the purple triad patches on their uniforms. Near enough to see that the acronym is HRU in Akshaj, though I have no idea what that might stand for. The uniforms are bedecked with silver and gold hoops and belts. Each one of them, male and female alike, has a piercing in the middle of their forehead and varying lengths of chains that wrap around their black hair, which is braided tightly in a topknot.

All the ostentatious decorations should look silly. Instead, it gives them a decidedly regal air, as if they are more warrior than soldier. I close my eyes and center myself. I slow my heart rate down. Here, I must be a ghost, a whisper of a thing. I just need Doe to give us a way in or some kind of location we might go to that would prove useful. I know the drones are scanning and searching, and I am well aware they can penetrate stone. We just need something, for once, to go our way.

And then, I notice heads begin to turn. First one, and then two, then half a dozen.

My heart rate begins to accelerate. They know. The fighters stop and with a terrifying intensity, every Akshaj looks in our direction.

"I can hear you," one of them spits. "Show yourselves."

Navaa practically moans. "Brightest Heavens," she hisses. "We didn't think about the one thing that we have been focused on for days. There are Kir-Abisat here."

I knew it. I knew we had overlooked a critical component. How stupid to just assume the altered Roones didn't give the Akshaji the Kir-Abisat. Why wouldn't they? Unpredictable or not, they are glorious.

When the Akshaj said he could hear us, he wasn't talking about our breathing, although they all may well be able to manage that, too. He meant that he could *hear us*, that our skin was singing a different song entirely.

We've lost the element of surprise. We've lost stealth. Our only hope, slim as it is, is that there is not an altered Roone population living here. That somehow, because they consider themselves allies, the Akshaji would not tolerate a constant Roone presence looking over their collective shoulders. Still, no one is going to die here today, not if I have anything to say about it.

"Sidra," I whisper faintly, "Rift out. Retreat. Immediately." There is nothing our reserves here can do but get us all in more trouble. "Cuff," I say boldly. The sensuit disappears back into my bracelet and I take one giant intake of breath, grateful to finally be free of its suffocating swaddle.

"What are you doing!" Navaa practically yelps. "We should run. If we move fast enough, we can Rift out before they can capture us."

The Akshaj Citadels have taken a different stance than the casual, light-footed demeanor of spectators and sparring partners. They have collectively fanned out, bracing their legs, and raising most of their arms in a defensive posture. Even with the various knives and swords, I can't help but be reminded of an elegant yoga posture.

We can't run. They'd get to us in seconds.

"If their Kir-Abisat have any kind of real gift, then they know who we are already. They'll have recognized our frequency and even if they didn't, they'll be able to if the altered Roones play it for them," I tell them in Faida, hoping the Akshaji don't speak the language, because it would be nice to have at least one advantage here. "This is our one shot to try and get through to them. If we run, if we try to hide, they will never see us as equals. *Remember where you are.*"

Levi is the first to uncuff, and then Arif and Navaa follow. I hold my head up high. I'm not afraid of dying. I mean, *I don't want to*, but that's not my real fear here. My fear is that I won't be taken seriously because I am young. Because I am a girl and human. If we lose the Akshaji, we lose everything.

"Take me to your commanding officer," I tell them in their own language. The Akshaj who had called us out comes forward. He gets close, too close, an inch away from me, sniffing and tsking as if I'm nothing more than expired meat.

"I know what you are," he says finally and with disdain. The sapphire on his forehead glints in the light, a flashing star. "You are nothing but insects and skeletons. I will take you to our Sairjidahl, but I don't think you will like it nearly as much as you might imagine." At that he lets out a giant belly laugh and the others laugh, too, a sea of snickering berry-colored Citadels who are sure we are about to die.

Before I get the chance to answer, we are surrounded. The Akshaji take hold of us with their many arms. I fight the natural instinct to shrug away, to punch or kick out. Even though their hands feel like writhing snakes on my shoulders, on my elbows, and around my stomach, I let them lead. Better that they mistake my slightness for weakness. Better that I save my energy if there is a confrontation with someone of real importance coming.

Although Levi bucks slightly, he, too, is being docile enough. Arif and Navaa stare grimly ahead, their wings tucked tightly up against their backs. The doors are already open. They are tall, at least twenty feet and made of intricately carved wood. When we are finally ushered inside, my mouth goes agape and I rush to close it.

This is no bunker or military facility. This is a true palace. The floors are a smooth black marble as slick as a sheet of ice. There are colors everywhere, bright pinks and neon oranges on wall hangings, rugs covered in tassels and mirrored pillows. The air is thick with incense and there are civilians milling around, most of them only partially clothed in sheer fabrics that showcase the fact that duplicate arms aren't the only appendages that the Akshaji have more than one of.

I'm sure it's rude to stare, but *come on*. It's going to take every bit of training I have to not let this throw me. Right in the center of the room is a huge gold leaf (or possibly solid gold—who knows when it comes to this place?) throne, and sitting upon it is a male Citadel. He is wearing a uniform, but he has more jewelry in the form of bracelets, necklaces, and layered belts than any of his fellow soldiers. Though clearly, by the way he's lazing in the chair, his arms splayed on the tiers of tufted silk armrests, he sees himself as more of a king than a soldier.

We are pitched at the leader's feet and I struggle a bit to keep my balance. I don't fall and neither do the others. One small victory in the face of what is about to be torture—possibly literally, certainly mentally. Visually, there's a mess of shit here I can't ever unsee.

"So," the man says, his voice a smooth honeyed baritone. "You are humans. Pride of the Roones." He licks his lips, his dark tongue flickering over them. "More pathetic than the Faida, and I did not think such a thing was possible." His eyes glance over Arif and Navaa, and his mouth turns upward into a cruel grin.

I'm sure that Navaa is itching to ask about her missing men and women, but I cut her off before she can open her mouth. This Akshaj has leverage on her, but he has nothing on me. I can't be baited.

"My name is Ryn Whittaker. This is Levi Branach and two of our Faida allies, Navaa and Arif. What is your name?"

The Citadel takes one hand and places it over his mouth, the way you do when you see something adorable and feel compelled to hide a smile, like it's a secret. Another hand runs over his head, and yet another two push his body up straighter in the chair.

"Allies, is it? *Really?* It's like a Gleethma and a Kizban playing with a ball of string!" And with that, he cannot hold it back any longer. He has a loud booming laugh that echoes off the walls, an infectious snark that makes everyone else in the hall start to giggle. He is acting, hamming it up by wiping fake tears from his eyes. I just stand there. It might be the one advantage I actually have as a teenage girl. *I can do disdain.* I can also do bored as fuck to perfection. I fold my arms and jut out my hip. I roll my eyes and wait.

"You know," he says while gasping dramatically for air, "there are some, I won't name names, but there are Akshaji who were actually concerned about the humans. Thank you, *girl*, for putting any lingering worries we may have had to rest.

My name is Sairjidahl Varesh and you've made me quite happy. So I won't kill you." At this, I notice the courtiers, or soldiers or guards or whatever they are, tilt their heads in our direction, pricking up their ears. Varesh places a knuckled fist under his chin and stares at me. Then, he waves a couple other hands around like he's swatting a fly. "Well, all right, I *will* kill you, but not today. Today is a happy day because you bring such good news in the form of your ridiculously feeble presence."

"Will it be you killing me? Or should I say—can it be you? That *tries* to kill me?" I ask him with real enthusiasm.

"Well," he says in a huff. "You are a rude thing. I was going to show you our infamous Akshaj hospitality, but clearly, predictably, you want to fight. I am the Sairjidahl. I would never sully my hands with your blood, but he can do it. Parth?" Varesh says and snaps his fingers.

A massive, hulking Akshaj Citadel steps forward. I keep my face neutral, but I can see out of the corner of my eye Levi's body stiffen. Parth pulls two long blades that had been scabbarded to his thighs. He then grabs two large knives that had been attached to a silver harness around his chest. He begins to whip his arms around furiously. It is a breathtaking, mesmerizing dance of steel and postures that he holds for a split second before moving into the next one. He is all beauty and deadly grace.

I consider, for a moment, my options. What I want to do is just take out my gun and shoot him in the head Indiana Jones style, but I suppose it wouldn't be very sporting of me. What I find interesting is why the Akshaji would be worried about humans to begin with? Why would we be of any concern to them? Then again, I see plenty of purple bodies around here but no Immigrants and, more importantly, no altered Roones. Navaa had said that they were paranoid to the point of mania, but I think it's more. I think they are xenophobic . . . to the extreme.

Parth moves closer. I squat down, gathering momentum in my thighs, and then I push up, jumping more than ten feet in the air. I somersault and land behind him. Before Parth can even react, I reach up and catch his neck in the crick of my elbow. I break it swiftly, like a walnut shell, using my strength and the weight of his bent-back body. I release him and he drops to the floor with a jangly thud. I turn around and face Varesh once again.

"That was not amusing," he barks and his lone voice echoes off the chamber walls. "At all."

I can't tell if he's joking or being petulant. Either way he's playing with me. I look him squarely in the eyes, narrowing my own. I give Parth's body a hard swift kick and he goes flying. The Akshaj Citadels and their minions have to duck until after a dozen or so feet Parth lands once again. This time the thud is much louder, and his body slides across the smooth floor.

"Brute force," Varesh says as he sits taller on his throne. "It's a trick, an illusion. Those bald-headed bastards gave you a gift, but you are still nothing more than a girl. You've been a Citadel for a few dozen full moons. It is impossible for you to understand the true nature of war or sacrifice."

Is there even any point explaining that the altered Roones started with me a decade ago? That in truth, I have sacrificed an entire childhood, intimacy, and family—not to mention my innocence? I fear that my protestations will only confirm his suspicions. A familiarity with suffering is not something you can prove in words, only actions.

"Despite what you think," I tell him calmly, "there is a great deal we need to discuss. I would not have come here unless our situation was dire." I make a point of sweeping my eyes around the room. Everyone has stopped what they are doing and is looking at the warrior king and me with rapt attention. Parth's body has been given a wide berth. A dark pool, looking more like oil than blood, has begun to seep from the back of his head onto the floor.

"Oh, yes, I imagine it is quite dire for *you*. We, however, will be just fine." Varesh is now perfectly still. Any thoughts he may have entertained of turning us into entertainment are past. While I might be a puny human girl, I still dispatched one of his own in under five seconds.

"Where are they? Are they here? Did you kick them out or are they prisoners?" I ask boldly.

At that, Varesh smiles, but only with his mouth. His eyes are focused. Intense.

"The Roones are treacherous cowards. They thought to control us—they killed thousands of us with the push of a button. But, *one* of their infernal miniature God machines did not respond to the command. A lone Akshaj killed every single one of them at that Rift site and warned us of their plan. And so we killed them all. Just like we executed the Faida spies they sent."

Arif and Navaa don't speak Akshaj. Which is good. We all need to stay calm. No sudden movements, no impassioned speeches. We must all act like we have stepped onto a land mine and if we take our foot off it, we die.

"The Faida that came here were not spies. I am not a spy. I promise you there is more to this story than you know. Please let me tell it to you, because whether you know it or not, we need each other."

I look over to Levi who nods his head slightly in approval. Then he goes back to scanning the room as he's done since we got here—for snipers, assassins, a sudden attack from one of the Citadel guards who are now looking at all of us with seething glares that are growing more intense by the minute.

Varesh once again places his arms on the tiered rests of the throne. "You have earned the right to tell your tale, girl, through combat. But do not imagine for one moment that there is anything that you can do for us. You are *supposedly* the greatest achievement of our enemies. And I find it very hard to believe that you are not working for them."

I gotta say, this is not how I thought this was going to go down. I had no idea that the Akshaji had broken their alliance with the altered Roones. On the surface, this is good news. But, considering the way they are treating us, it might not even matter. I begin to speak, hoping that my story is convincing enough for the Sairjidahl to even listen, let alone consider my words.

"Well," Varesh says when I have finished. "That is a compelling tale. I might even believe it. However, it does not matter. We will never align ourselves with you or anyone else, ever again. We travel through the Rifts and take what we want. You must have noticed—there are no Immigrants here."

I look around, darting my eyes quickly over the scantily clad civilians. If I was a betting sort of person, I would have said the odds were high that the Akshaji would have slaves. Their hatred of other races must run so deep that they won't even allow an Immigrant to serve them. That can't bode well for us.

"There is one absolute that I know to be true," he says to me as he leans forward, various fingers gripping at the fabric of his seat so that his body looks almost as if it's floating. "Only the Akshaji can be trusted. We are the only race worthy of being Citadels. Everyone else is weak and undisciplined."

I close my eyes in an attempt to center myself, to sift through the thoughts and offenses that are floating around this grand and ridiculous room like the billowing smoke pouring from the incense burning in the braziers. "I do believe that you are a fearsome and strong people, regardless of Roone intervention." I take two delicate steps forward. "But if you believe that you are in any way safe, that they would just let you live to conquer and pillage a Multiverse that they believe is their domain, then you are not only ignorant, but irresponsible as well, because you will get everyone here killed."

Varesh laughs once again. This time, though, it is a hollow-sounding thing, a quarter jangled in a tin cup. "We are not afraid of those skinny black-eyed dolts or the hairy snout-nosed creatures who smell as bad as they fight. The Daithi are gone—if you are to be believed—but we did not fear them, either. The Faida are almost decimated and you—you are a bunch of children. While your genetic weapons might have a slight superiority, it is easy enough to wrestle a knife away from a toddler."

"And the Settiku Hesh?" I ask bitingly. "And all the Citadels they are planning to make using races we don't even know about yet? They keep improving each crop every time. They might not come for you tomorrow, or next year even. But they *will* come. Even if it's just to train the new and improved Citadels they will likely make. They will use you for target practice. We have a chance to stop them. It would be foolish to overlook the advantage now, before they get any stronger."

At that, Varesh stands. His guards place their hands on their weapons and I can hear the faint rustle of the Faida's wings, ready to unfurl and take to the air to defend us. Varesh walks closer, a slow, predatory crawl that makes me want to back away. Instead, I hold my ground, maintaining eye contact.

When he gets just a few inches away, he does a very thorough examination of my body. He is a beautiful creature and up close, even more so. His eyes, which I thought were brown, are actually a deeper shade of a purple, like a ripened eggplant. His cheekbones are high, his nose regal and aquiline. He smells of amber and freshly plowed earth.

"You are young and so to you, it is always about the fight," he whispers almost sensually in my ear. "You leap from one conflict to the next and your blood, how it must burn and boil, taunting you, spurring you on. You ache to destroy."

"You are wrong, sir," I tell him firmly. "I ache for *freedom*. They have me under their thumb and I want sole ownership of my destiny. We *can* overthrow them. Together."

Varesh takes a step closer to me. I grit my teeth. I am learning that personal space might be a particularly human trait. "Maybe," he says, *in English*, "but maybe not." I jerk my head back as my eyes widen in surprise, and he continues. "I am not a stupid man. I know full well what is coming."

"And you're just going to let it happen? You won't fight with us because we aren't Akshaj? Like you said, you aren't stupid, you must see what we could accomplish if we align?" I know my voice has gone up a decibel. I am trying not to get excited. But Varesh has just admitted he knows what the altered Roones will do and because I don't have six arms I'm not worthy of fighting beside? That's a bunch of bullshit right there.

"You don't understand, girl. But listen to me now when I tell you that we have already lost. You seek to make me even more desperate? You want me to admit to my people that I believe that we are equals?" Once again his eyes flitter over my body, resting for just a few moments on my hands. His chin turns upward as if turning away from a noxious smell, like I got into my mother's perfume and poured the whole bottle of it on my head. "You may be able to fight, but none of you have any . . ."—Varesh stops midsentence searching—"honor. No. That is wrong. You are doing what you believe to be right, so I suppose in your own way you are honorable. What you lack is character. You have no character."

I have been accused of many things. I have been called a liar, a killer, cold and calculating. I have also been beaten, tortured, abused, molested, and experimented on and yet here I stand.

Unyielding.

I tilt my chin down but keep my eyes on him. "You want to talk about character? Honor? Well, I'm not the one who started talking in English, *Sairjidahl* Varesh," I say, emphasizing the word *Sairjidahl* because it means "supreme commander" in Akshaj and I don't think his sly use of a language that most of his people probably don't understand is particularly commanderish of him. "How much character can you have if you have to keep this conversation private from your own troops?"

His eyes narrow and his face is transformed. He is wearing a shadow. Something twisted and dark. I'm going to lose him now, if I haven't already, if I don't shut my stupid mouth and backpedal. "Look," I say through my clenched teeth. "I believe you are mistaken. There must be something I can do to prove that I have character enough to fight beside you." I practically choke on the words. The thought of having to prove anything to him makes my stomach turn.

With my contrition, Varesh's face rearranges itself. He is thinking. Pondering. Four different hands rub a thumbnail over the pads of his index fingers. "No, girl," and I once again inwardly flinch, just as I have every time he calls me "girl." "It is you that is mistaken. You want to go to war because you believe that you will win. Anyone would fight given those odds.

What you fail to understand about the Akshaj people, what *your spies* could not tell you, is that we believe combat is the only path to our truest selves. Whatever revelations are to be had in this universe are made clear only when death is riding beside us. You see, *we are* the fight. *We are* the war. To win or lose—two sides of the same coin and hardly the point."

"Well," I tell him as I straighten my spine. "Honestly? I don't think our chances are actually that good. But I don't think that trying to even the odds, to give ourselves the best possible chance to win, makes me shameful or indecent—or weak."

Varesh makes a noise, a thoughtful "hmmm," and then he turns his back on me and sits down once again on his vainglorious throne. "What if I took something from you, though?" He begins loudly, and in his own language. "What if I took something that is precious, that defines who you are? Would you still be able to find a way to fight then?"

"Like what?" I practically snort. "My life? Because if you kill me, if you kill any of us, we won't stop. None of this ends," I tell him boldly.

"Now that is stupid," Varesh exclaims with cold condescension. "If I killed you, how would you fight? But, no, I'm not speaking metaphorically. I mean, what if I actually took something that you need. Something that makes you who you are, a soldier."

"I don't know what you mean," I tell him, although my heart begins to beat a little faster now.

"Yes, I suppose I have confused things," Varesh says. "If I actually took it, it wouldn't mean much, would it? No, you would have to give it up as a sacrifice, as proof that you would keep on fighting no matter what. That losing this thing would mean you yourself would almost certainly die, but your cause may win."

"Fine," I say in a rush. "I freely offer up any sacrifice you choose if in return you agree to an alliance."

"Ryn!" Levi jumps in. "No, Sairjidahl Varesh, if there is something to be sacrificed, let me be the one to offer it. Ryn is our leader."

"I think that's the point, Levi," I tell him softly. "As the leader, this is the price."

"Exactly. She actually understands. Perhaps you are not so unworthy as I thought," Varesh says with a sickening purr. "Now, hold out your arm, Citadel Ryn Whittaker, and kneel."

Varesh is wearing a sly grin. There is absolute silence in the massive room save for the exploding sound of my heart rate soaring and the noise, the ear-shattering squeal of this Earth's tone screaming inside of my skull. Fear has kicked down my mental barricades. I don't know what he wants. Submission? Does he want me to beg? He's a thousand kinds of wrong if he believes that I won't sacrifice my pride to save everyone and everything I know and love. Besides, that isn't even pride, it's vanity.

"You can't actually be considering this, Ryn. You can't trust him!" Levi says in a panicked rush. He's switched over to Russian. As if speaking in a different language will make a difference. As if Varesh hasn't already figured out my biggest secret. I don't fear death. I fear weakness. I fear being helpless to save the people I love. "Do not take a single step in his direction or I will knock you out myself," Levi warns.

"*Nyet*," I answer stoically. "It actually makes a kind of sick sense. He needs proof that I'm not lying—that we aren't working for the altered Roones. He needs assurance that we're dedicated, that we won't switch sides if shit goes sideways and he needs to do it in the kind of bloodthirsty way that will satisfy his soldiers."

Levi looks around the room, for an answer to this or an escape, but it's pointless. We both know that there is no way out, just like we both know that, bigger picture, however he tries to humiliate me doesn't matter if it saves our lives down the line. I look over to Navaa and Arif, who may not know exactly what is going on, but who are well aware that something unpleasant is about to happen. Their faces are stone masks. But I know, if Navaa was in my place, she would do the same.

"I can't believe you're going to do this," Levi whispers.

"It's fine," I tell him grimly.

I step toward Varesh.

"Again, I will ask you to kneel. I'm not trying to subjugate you, girl, I suggest this only to save you the embarrassment of falling," he says almost kindly, as if he were the nicest guy alive and he is doing me a favor.

"I won't fall," I practically hiss back at him.

"I understand that you've been trained, girl, but you are made of flesh and bone. When your arm is severed, all the discipline in the world won't keep you on your feet."

There is a beat of absolute stillness as I let Varesh's words sink in. I honestly thought he was going to make me scrape and bow. I thought he wanted me prostrate and exposed. At the very worst I imagined he might carve into me in some ritualistic kind of proof of loyalty—a blood oath of sorts.

He wants to *cut my arm off.*

Levi explodes. He is yelling at me, at Varesh, explaining what they're asking for in Faida, and then Arif and Navaa get in on the action. Varesh just sits there, wearing a sly, wicked smile.

So this is the price for the alliance? Varesh doesn't need my arm. He doesn't even need to prove himself the stronger Citadel, for, surely, cutting off the limb of a single human girl won't do that.

I recognize in that split second that this is the only way Varesh will align with us. How else can he allow his troops to be sullied by commingling with "inferior" species without first proving that he is the master? My character means as much to him as shit scraped off a boot. Varesh is asking for my arm. If he appears weak, he may be deposed and what will the next Sairjidahl ask for? My head? I have no choice and that wily fucker knows it.

"Ryn," Levi warns, moving toward me.

"Levi, stop!" I command. "This *is* going to happen, and you will stand down!"

For a moment we just stare at each other, the fire in his green eyes intense, but I know they don't come close to what my own eyes are showing. Slowly, deliberately, he nods, and he doesn't even flinch as Arif and Navaa come on either side of him, Navaa whispering what I hope are soothing words in his ear.

Not that it should matter. Levi is a soldier, through and through, and he has his orders.

I turn back to Varesh. "You won't be able to cut through my uniform. I'll have to take the top part off," I say, trying to keep my voice from shaking. Varesh shrugs as if this is a detail he isn't interested in, though his eyes stay locked on me as I slowly unzip the fabric down to my waist. I slide it over my arms and tie the dangling pieces around my belly button. I want to throw up. I want to run away. I can't do either of these things.

The cuff is already, thankfully, on my left wrist. "Doe, move the sensuit up to the top of my bicep. Make it as tight as possible, like a tourniquet." I am aware that I am practically panting. I need to calm down. I need to slow my circulatory system as much as possible to increase my chances of survival. The cuff moves up and snakes so tightly that it almost takes my breath away.

I hold out my left arm, making a fist, because this action is a different kind of fighting, but it's a fight nonetheless.

"So you offer up your arm as a tribute to our new cause, freely and without duress?" Varesh asks in a tone more serious than I've heard from him.

No actually, you fuck. *I'm not doing this freely and this is pretty much the definition of duress. So it's going to cost you, and I hope you pay for it at the end of a Spiradael's razor hair braid.*

I need your soldiers, though. I grit out a "Yes."

Varesh lifts two of his right hands and beckons for a guard to come forward. This one is a woman. She has a look on her face that I can't quite read. Her jaw is clenched and her brows are knitted together so deeply that there is a little *v* in the center of them. I can't tell if she is sorry or annoyed. Either way, she doesn't look like she wants to do this. She gives me a slight nod, getting my permission.

I want to scream. This is possibly the dumbest and most reckless decision I've ever made, but if I back out now, they might kill us all. Shit, they may just kill us all anyway, but I don't think so. I know Varesh needs us as much as we need him, even if those under his command do not. He has played this very well. I give her the slightest of nods and she raises her sword, which is crescent shaped and sharp enough that the light bounces off the edge.

I see her arm go swiftly up and then down again. I am braced for the pain, but it doesn't come. I think at first they were playing a joke. That my first instincts had been right. It was all just an elaborate test. Then I look down and see my arm on the ground, a pale and useless thing now, a piece of meat, a sacrifice.

Then I see the red blood begin to pour out. It's making a puddle. I should be in agony. Why can't I feel this?

Levi, Arif, and Navaa rush up to bolster me, and Varesh gets off his chair and makes his way to me as well. He examines my dripping stump and the pool of scarlet blood on the marble. "Well," he says loudly in Akshaj, "perhaps you are not so weak. You have managed to stay on your feet, girl. That fact alone is proof enough that your race isn't entirely useless."

Oh my God, I could kill him. I want to kill him. I also want to pass out. I think I'm going to.

"We have a deal, correct? A bargain has been made and the alliance sealed." I push out the words. I know they are coming from my own mouth, but my mouth feels wrong, like it's on my chest or maybe in my hair.

"We have a deal. I will allow the Akshaj Citadels to engage against the Roones."

"Good," I say with more force than I thought possible given that my vision is starting to periscope. "Because I can get another arm, but I can't get another army." That comment wipes the shit-eating grin off Varesh's face. "Rift. SenMach City," I say out loud.

A dot of neon green appears just a foot in front of me. "What is this?" Varesh demands.

"This is how we're going to win," Levi barks at him. "We'll be in touch. Soon." I look down and see that my feet aren't actually on the ground. Arif is carrying me. When did that happen? The neon smudge widens and turns to purple and black in a matter of seconds. Arif wraps his wings around me. I watch, strangely fascinated, as they begin to soak up my blood.

Why can't I feel this?

There is a pull and then a drag. I am inside the Rift now, still in Arif's arms. The neon mouth is screaming at me. It's not just in my ears. It feels like the Rift has pulled back my skull and is yelling directly into my brain. I am experiencing time in two speeds. On the one hand, we are racing, whizzing through the Multiverse like a video on fast-forward. On the other hand—

Yeah. Okay. I don't actually have another hand anymore.

The thought of that, the fear and grief, pushes two teardrops into the corners of each eye. Still, time is ripped apart. There is fast-forward, yes, but also molasses slow. Each movement leaves a strange trail, an almost duplicate of the one before. My heartbeat, which kicked and hammered, is now barely pumping. I can hear it, moving in the slower time. *Thump . . . Thump . . .*

And then, the white exit. The vertical slit. There are more than one—dozens of them, the echoes, the almost identical twins of time's images. What I am seeing is not true. There is only one way out and the rest are illusions. Which makes sense. This is all an illusion. A pretense. My life, like everyone else's, only looks like a series of choices. A choice to fight. A choice to ask the Akshaj commander for help. Like it was my decision to make, my severed arm. It's all a lie. We tell ourselves that we are choosing so that our lives have some semblance of purpose and meaning. The real truth is, we are born who we are. There are no choices, only circumstances.

We are out of the Rift. I look up to the sky. It is white. Maybe it will snow. Makes sense because I am freezing. More rushing of wings and yelling, more fast and slow all at once. It was day and now it is night. I roll into the darkness. I think I may say something before it takes me. Yes, I want to say *Levi.* Maybe not. Maybe I want to ask for help. I don't know. The black swallows me whole in one gulp and I am gone.

CHAPTER 17

It is always the hearing before the seeing. That's how it goes in these situations. The beeping of machines. The hum of electricity. The quiet voices peppered with concern. Bright side, I am not in pain. Downside—I literally cannot feel anything. I can't feel my own weight. I can't even feel the clothes on my body or the sheets on the bed. It's like my brain has been shoved in a jar but somehow been kept alive.

Shit. *I am* with the SenMachs. They could probably do something like that. What if I'm actually dead and they downloaded my consciousness into an android!

Fuuuck.

I wouldn't put it past them. I open a single eye, expecting some kind of display to be right on my cornea and a readout of my vitals and status—because obviously I'm a robot now—but everything looks normal. A little blurry, but still, normal. I look down at my very own body underneath a thin blanket.

Okay, so option two—not a robot. High as hell then.

Gathered around me are Levi, Feather, and Cosmos. Feather is the closest thing the SenMachs have to a doctor. I mean, he is a doctor, just not a human one. The SenMachs are sentient machines. Feather (who I'm told was modeled after Beethoven, but looks completely and totally like a soccer dad) is the head of the biomed division. Cosmos is the "doyenne," the leader of the city. She is modeled after some British royalty person that I've never heard of. Cosmos is quite pretty, in an old Holly-wood type of way. Though *old* is absolutely the wrong word to describe any of the SenMachs. They all look like adults with baby skin. None of them have a single frown line, wrinkle, or mole (unless they were designed that way). Their skin is with-out blemish, because it's not entirely real.

I reach over hopefully, touching my right hand to my left, but it is gone. If I wasn't so completely high right now, I am sure I would be totally devastated. I had assumed they would just smack a new one on. But maybe it's not that easy. Maybe it's not even something they can do at all.

"What an exceptional story Levi has just told me," Cosmos says with near sarcasm. I say near because it's hard with the SenMachs to get real emotion across, about anything. "He tells me that you allowed a six-armed biped to cut your limb off in return for an alliance. But then I thought, no, that can-not be, for who would want an alliance with such a miserable creature?"

"Cosmos," I say, but my voice is gravelly and my throat hurts. "You watched me put a gun to my head. I threatened to kill myself if you forced us to stay here with you. You can't really be surprised that I would do something so extreme."

"Not surprised, no," Cosmos says as she looks at me with something that might be concern. There is the slightest grimace on her face, but there's an equal chance she's just annoyed. "I am disappointed—with this entire situation."

I look away. I follow the IV up and see two bags. One of blood—or something that looks like blood—and the other a clear solution. I don't want to get pissy, but I'm lying here with one arm. I kind of feel like I should have the monopoly on disappointment in the room.

"Where are Arif and Navaa?" I ask Levi, who is standing closest to me, just inches away really. I wonder if he's been like that since I was moved to this room. I wonder how long I've actually been out.

"Your Faida friends are with Neon and Doe in the physics lab. They are demonstrating the Kir-Abisat. It is quite fascinating; however, I believe the Faida to be a race that is overly pleased with themselves in general," Cosmos says indifferently. The SenMachs only care about one thing, humans.

"Really, Cosmos?" I ask while shifting my body a little on the narrow bed. "They are genetically modified flying angel people who have been to space. All things considered, they could be much bigger assholes."

At that, Cosmos raises her shoulders about two millimeters and lowers them again. This is the closest I'll probably ever see a SenMach get to a shrug.

"Your arm, Ryn. It was such a risk." Cosmos deftly changes the subject to what matters to her. The Faida are miraculous to me, but the SenMach aren't coded to give a shit about them.

"Yeah," I admit. Man, I'm high. I kind of feel like I'm going up and down on a roller coaster. "I didn't have a choice but they wanted me to think I did." I run my tongue over my dry lips. I scrunch my face because my nose itches. "But it's okay,"

I slur. "I understand now. You don't have to feel bad for me, because Varesh told me the Akshaji were the fight and I want to be the fight too. I want to be the war. *I am* the war, even with one hand, and I won't ever stop. It doesn't matter if I can't win. If we can't . . ."

I'm pretty sure the words coming out of my mouth aren't making any sense, but it makes perfect sense to me in my own head. I feel something profound with this loss. In fact, I have so many feelings right now ready to burst out of my rib cage they are like a hundred rainbows arching in the sky after rain. Something was taken, yes, but given as well. Clarity. I assume that's what this is.

Although, again, *mega* high.

"That's a very . . . philosophical, Ryn," Feather offers warmly. "But let us put this talk of war aside for now. I assume you came to us because you thought we might be able to build you a new arm?"

"Yeah," I tell him. The slow time is back again. I open and close my eyes. Left. Right. Left. Right. Morse code blinking as if looking at the room in this odd way might sober me up a little. "But if you can't, that's okay. I wouldn't be mad. It just seemed like a good idea at the time."

Feather puts a hand on my shoulder. "It was a good idea. We can do it, though it will take a little time. My team and I have been working on the problem of attaching nerve endings to our technology since you arrived."

I was ready to do this one armed, but relief washes over me. "Cool" is all I can manage. Of course, it's more than cool. My tongue isn't working. "Yessenia and Sidra," I turn my head to Levi. "They should know that we're in the place here."

"I went back right after you were stabilized and gave them our status. I tried to get Arif and Navaa to leave with me, but unsurprisingly, they aren't going anywhere." I nod my head. I don't know why Levi is worried about this. The SenMachs would happily study the Faida, but they won't help them or give them anything without our permission.

"I think we should let Ryn rest now," Feather tells the room. Levi stands stock-still, staring at me in the bed.

IT'S BEEN FORTY-EIGHT HOURS HERE in SenMach City, and Feather has finally solved the problem of attaching a SenMach arm to a living person. It's not like how I thought it would be.

It's not like *Star Wars*.

At all.

I am sitting in a chair in my room. A nurse—well, she probably isn't a nurse, but whatever the equivalent to a nurse is here—named Page has begun to shave my head. Levi has been standing in front of the window, his arms crossed, eyes narrowed. I watched the majority of my hair fall to the floor when Page used the scissors. Blond tendrils floated down like feathers, settling in little mountains around my feet. Now I am being shaved bald. There is a scraping sound, the drag and pull of the razor on my scalp.

My stump of an arm is being held up by a sling. Bits of hair are getting caught in the fabric around my neck. I look at my bare feet. I press my toes together. My legs are splayed open because keeping them closed feels like too much of an effort. Levi gives me an encouraging smile every so often, and I shift my focus every time he does. I am his leader, his commander, and right now I look like a broken doll. I want to sit up straight, I really do. I want to be fierce and stoic. But I am still sedated quite heavily. My eyes won't open all the way. I just don't have it in me and for that, I am ashamed.

I keep thinking there must be a limit to how much I can take. I was recruited at seven, activated at fourteen. Since then I have been drugged, brainwashed, abused, and lied to. I have been genetically spliced with other species. I have been turned into a weapon, a killer, a leader, a rebel, and now a leader of rebels. I have gone through the Multiverse. I have had sex, been broken up with—in the same night. I have had violent altercations with both the guys I have had romantic feelings for. I walked through a mass grave. I can open a Rift with the sound of my voice. And now here I am, with one limb that's been hacked off by our newest allies and ready to have my skull drilled into by another ally so I can get my new robot arm.

I'm afraid that at some point, I'm just going to shut down, like a phone with a drained battery. One day my capacity for dealing with all this crazy will reach its limit and I will just switch off. In this moment, as Page dries off my bald head and brushes away the tiny hairs that have settled on my neck like pins, I am afraid this moment is close. I absolutely do not want anyone inside my brain. I also don't want to go through life with one arm. Like I said, choice is an illusion. All we have are circumstances. These are mine.

Levi looks at me, his eyes as wide as two moons. He opens his mouth and then slams it shut again. Instead of saying anything, he pulls me close to him. His embrace is ferocious, and I wince a little as the IV in my one arm is jostled. He kisses my cheeks, my eyes, my ears. He keeps whispering *okay*. I don't know if he's telling me how things are going to be or if he's trying to accept that this is how things are. I pull away from him. He feels too close. We are partners, but he can't join me in this. The fact that I really want him to be right there with me, holding my hand, scares me almost as much as what's about to happen. I need him. Desperately. But this is yet another new feeling I can't afford today and so I push it down like a muffled scream.

THEY TAKE ME TO A MACHINE, a giant tub filled with a strange gel. I realize I'm going to have to go in that thing.

"I'll need some help," I tell Page. "With the gown."

"Of course," she says, rushing to undo the tabs at the back that are somehow held in place. Page gently undoes the sling around my neck and keeps hold of my stump as she maneuvers it out of the gown. In another life, getting naked in front of all these people would be embarrassing. Now, it barely registers. I might as well be a newborn, with my newly shaved head and shaking knees. There is no longer anything remotely sexual about me. I had felt powerful, strong, fully feminized, when I "offered" this piece of my body to Sairjidahl Varesh. To say I didn't think it through is an understatement. I couldn't have imagined that allowing him to do this would make me feel so violated, because I *agreed* to it. There is no female equivalent to the word *emasculate* in the English language. It hardly takes anything at all for a man to have his masculinity threatened—babysitting his own kids or letting a woman pick up the check. Is this what it takes for a woman to feel less female? Something as extreme as a body part chopped off and a bald skull?

Both Feather and Page help to guide me into the vat. The liquid is warm.

"Will it hurt?" I ask.

There is a silence. Feather is forming an appropriate response. That can't be good. "I think probably it will," he says finally. "You are getting medication intravenously, but it won't be absorbed as fast as the arm will be built. Too, we will need to cut into your brain, in order to connect the synapsis to accept this new arm as something that's a part of you—it's why your head was shaved. And there's not much we can do to numb the brain. Besides, you need to be able to feel your arm, for obvious reasons."

"Okay," I say, trying to imagine what this experience is even going to be.

"Trust me, Ryn, I know you are scared, but we have done our homework, as you would say. You must trust that we can do this successfully. A positive attitude is an important component to healing."

I want to tell him to take his positive attitude and shove it up his ass. I'm suddenly very angry, but not at Feather, not really. I'm angry at myself, at Sairjidahl Varesh. I think probably I'm also angry because I need to be, so I can fight the pain I know is coming.

I hear the door open and Feather and Page leave. I close my eyes. My chest is heaving up and down. I want Levi. I want my team. I want my mom and dad.

"Ryn?" I hear Feather's voice from somewhere. A speaker? But it sounds like it's right beside me. "I know it might seem odd, but I would like to play some music. It will help to distract you, possibly, and I always work better when a chaotic element is introduced to my coding for some reason."

"Well, you are Beethoven, right?" I say with a smile. This is not for me, but for the others watching. Like I said, it is the burden of the suffering—to make those who are helpless to do anything for themselves feel better. "Just no weird jazz or massage music."

"No, no, nothing like that. As I said. We must be positive. I have chosen Little Stevie Wonder. Here we go."

The song begins. I know it's "For Once in My Life," but only because I've heard it on a Netflix binge of *Scandal*. I hear some-thing else, screaming from somewhere far away. Then I real-ize, it is me that's screaming. The agony slams me brutally from the floaty netherworld of the drugs back into my body. It is a slicing, searing pain. I want to be brave and tough, but I simply don't have it in me. I don't know how long I keep screaming. It could be five minutes or an hour. Time becomes a slippery rope that I can't seem to keep hold of. It doesn't matter. It feels like forever and when it is finally over, I will never, ever leave that room entirely. A part of me will always be there. Screaming.

CHAPTER 18

I spend the entirety of the next day in my room doing physical therapy. I take what happened in the birthing suite and strangle it. I cover it in blankets and stupid, mundane memories like driving to work and peeing and filler episodes of average TV shows in an attempt at camouflage, so that my brain will just skip over it. It doesn't really work. The memory lies in wait for me, pouncing every time I let my focus slip.

Feather and another SenMach named Ribbon (who I am very pleased to say is Idris Elba) work to help me regain the full use of my new arm. It does look different, but that's because the skin is brand-new. Eventually it will age and freckle like the other one, just on a seventeen-year delay.

There is no scar, though, and for the most part, it works just fine. Still, I need to reacquaint my traumatized neurons with the notions of fine and gross motor skills. I throw balls, block punches, and pick up objects of various size. The arm feels like it's mine, mostly. There is still something not quite right about it. It's not that it's wrong, just different. It reminds me of when I got my ears pierced. I kept staring at them in every mirror I would pass, tugging on my lobes even though my mom yelled at me that they were going to get infected. I couldn't help it. Something had changed that I could never change back. Even if I took the earrings out, the holes would still be there.

Levi has escorted the others back to the Faida Earth. He felt it was best that they not get too comfortable here and I agreed. I do trust the Faida, but this is a very tempting place for a race like theirs. They're all peace and love among one another now, but they did their fair share of warmongering and conquering before becoming so "enlightened." Besides, whatever bullshit Ezra and I have gone through, he would want to know I am okay, and oddly enough, I think the only person he'd believe completely is Levi.

I am lying in bed that night, flexing and unflexing my hand, when Cosmos knocks and walks in.

"May I sit?" she asks politely.

"Sure," I tell her. I am a bit surprised when she actually sits on the edge of my bed and not on the chair beside it. Being that she's a robot and all, Cosmos will never have kids of her own—unless of course she decides to go through with the human breeding program and use the eggs I gave them the first time I came to this Earth. At the time, I thought it was a pretty hard-core sacrifice to forge an alliance. Ha! I showed me. So I guess she could eventually raise my own biological child. In the meantime, though, I think I'm the closest thing she might have to a daughter. She certainly acts like a mom.

"I wanted to tell you," she begins gently, remaining perfectly still on the bed, "that the troops we promised are ready, but they do need training."

"Do you want me to organize a unit to come back here? To help with that?"

There is a brief pause. Talking to the SenMachs takes some getting used to. They don't react instantaneously. Of course they could, if they wanted. Instead they choose each word carefully, after running it through several algorithms first, to gauge what the response to them might be.

"No," Cosmos says softly. Both of her hands are resting on her knees. I do that now, notice hands. "We have just finished constructing quite an elaborate simulation program. In it, we will run the troops through every single variable they might encounter. For a SenMach, a simulation would be the same as training. You *could* say that it would even be the same as experience itself, given that we do not feel fear or excitement in the way that you would. Emotions are not something we need to consider. We just need time. I understand that you do not have much left."

I sit up straighter in the bed, adjusting the pillows somewhat. "No," I have to admit. "Not so much now and even less with this whole thing," I say as I raise my left arm up.

Cosmos leans over and really looks at me. Her silver eyes glint in the darkened room. "I want to extend an offer to you," she says smoothly. "We would be willing to act as a sanctuary planet for not just the human Citadels, but your families as well. Even if this means accommodating tens of thousands of people. We have already done the math. We know what we must do to ensure a thriving human population."

I give her a broad, but melancholy smile. "That's a really kind offer. But I can't accept it. For so many reasons. I'm sure our families would do anything to ensure our safety, so they probably would come. It's not that, though. I've made promises to the Faida, even to the Akshaji, that I will fight with them to stop the altered Roones once and for all. Because they aren't going to stop. Ever. They could slaughter us all and move on to another Earth where they would just do this all over again to humans, or a different species."

"But, Ryn"—Cosmos puts her hand over my own—"like I said, we have done the math, even with these brutes—the Akshaji—the odds are not necessarily in your favor. You could very well lose, everything, to a species that is so beneath you. They are monsters, these altered Roones."

"Exactly," I say. "Trust me, if hiding out was a realistic option, I would definitely choose hiding. But if there's one fundamental truth that I've learned these past few weeks, it's that there's a big difference between being alive and having something to live for. Maybe you think you've cracked the mystery on how to get humans to coexist without killing each other for stupid reasons, and maybe really you have. But I couldn't live here farming or whatever, in this Utopia you imagine for us, knowing that I could have saved even one kid from going through what I've had to go through. I just couldn't do it. Especially if there is farming involved." I say this all with real genuine warmth. I like Cosmos and I know she is coming from a good place. It's just that she doesn't actually feel anything and I think that's all I am right now, a big ol' flesh sack of feelings.

"I understand," Cosmos says. I can't be sure, but I think there might be a twinge of sadness in that acceptance. "The troops will be ready when you need them. Feather will bring them to you."

"Feather? Why—" I begin, and then it dawns on me. Feather will come to extract the eggs and sperm from the other Citadels. More epically crazy shit I've agreed to, to win this war. "Oh," I say, not bothering to hide my surprise.

"You have ignited something in us, Ryn. We were built to coexist with humans and somehow, somewhere along the way, we've forgotten our primary function." Cosmos stands. She reaches out tentatively and touches the newly grown hair on my skull. I haven't even looked in the mirror, but it has been itchy. "It is so blond, this little bit of growth. Almost white." I run my own hands through it, there's just an inch or so. I suspect I'll get another inch by the time I leave. It does feel different, though. Softer. Like baby hair.

"I promise you, Ryn"—Cosmos's hand drifts to my shoulder—"we did figure it out. We ran hundreds of thousands of simulations, for you and your people, had you chosen to immigrate here. We know how to bring a generation of humans into this world. They will be kind, and smart and compassionate. They will understand about the value and the sacredness of human life because we will teach them about the sacrifices their parents had to make to get them here. No matter what happens in this war, part of you will always be alive."

I feel tears pooling behind my eyes. Someday, I will have a child. I will not raise her. I might not ever even get to see her. This is another gift of sorts from the SenMachs, a biological legacy. I don't know what it says about me that a robot would be a better mother than I could ever hope to be. When Cosmos realizes that I am not going to respond, she excuses herself. I look over to the window, but there is nothing to see but the dark spread of night's cover. I am alone, in a hospital bed with one inch of platinum hair, but I do have a brand-new arm.

LEVI AND I DO NOT go straight back to the Faida Earth. It is imperative that we check in at home. We arrive early morning, before shift. We choose Henry's house and he lets the others know by some elaborate code system to meet us by his house in the woods. I do not tell them what happened to my arm. Violet's only weakness is her empathy. If she knows what I have done, it might distract her from what she has to do that day, and every day, to maintain control of Battle Ground. She does wonder about my hair, though, so I lie and say it was just too annoying. I am such a good liar that Violet doesn't even question it.

Or it looks horrible and she is the one lying.

I do tell them about the alliance, breaking the news that we will need about two hundred volunteers for the SenMachs. I explain the procedure, but they hardly seem to care. What's an egg or two compared to what the SenMachs are offering in return? I will let them continue to live in this little world, this bubble of war. It serves no purpose explaining exactly what this means. Our children will literally inherit the earth. Not our Earth, but still.

Henry's plan is working perfectly. In less than a week we will control most of the Rifts and Villages. If we had more time, we could even convert the Citadels deemed unlikely to denounce ARC and the altered Roones. But we don't. As it stands, Boone thinks that by the time our fighting force arrives it will be about a seventy-five/twenty-five split in our favor. It's just a matter of days now, before Christopher Seelye returns. We need a solid plan by then. I am close to having one and I promise to send word once I do.

When we Rift back to the Faida Earth, I am met with real affection and genuine concern. Ezra hugs me for a very long time and makes a point of telling me how much he likes my hair. It is easier now between us, now that we both know that wanting someone, even loving someone, is never enough to make a relationship work. I always thought that fighting made me like an adult, but that's stupid, because kids kill people all the time. I realize that the way Ezra and I let each other go was probably the first real grown-up thing I've ever done.

The next few days are difficult. I spend hours training. First I work with my arm. I keep working until my reflexes are just as fast and my punches just as strong with both arms. Somewhere along the way I realize that my new arm is actually better, faster, and able to tolerate much more pain. There's also the added bonus of turning shit off and on by running my hand over it. I have activated the holographic Fortress of Solitude version of Doe. I started feeling silly talking to my cuff. So now, Tim Riggins is almost always beside me. At first I thought it might be annoying, having a constant presence in my room. But Doe is mostly silent and awfully pretty to look at—kind of like a painting . . . with well-defined muscles.

Doe links everything on the network with my arm. We are working out ways of controlling the lights, computers, phones, et cetera, by using certain finger and palm movements.

Finally.

I'm a magician—like Julia or Eliot.

But not Alice.

Ever.

Then I work with Navaa for my Kir-Abisat training. Sure enough, the SenMachs were able to develop a small gadget, a black disk we can attach to the hollow, curved space where our collarbones meet. It's basically like a little megaphone, boosting our own voices and frequencies as we sing open Rifts. I have managed to open quite a few with Navaa's help and we learn what the crazy altered Roone Grifix said was true. I don't need a conduit. I start singing tones from Earths other than my own, and while I can't get them to completely open, we both know that it won't be long before I can.

The rest of our time is spent in the war room. Citadels require very little sleep, but we push it, even for us. Between Ezra and Doe, we are able to make best guesses about our enemies' numbers. We run strategy and tactics. We argue back and forth like schoolyard kids about who should be in charge of what and where. We bring in Gomda and Donav to work out artillery. We think about leaving a force behind, to use guerrilla tactics if things go badly. Eventually we agree that if things go that badly, resistance cells would be pointless.

When, finally, we get a working battle plan, we bring in Sairjidahl Varesh's Akshaj faction, and Iathan comes with the original Roones and Karekins. I make a point of looking right at Varesh every time he addresses me. He is amused by my new arm and possibly impressed. Whatever terrors I face in the dead of night, in my thoughts, dripping with anxiety and helplessness, I do not let them surface. Varesh tried to break me, to split me apart. Every answer I give to him is firm and unyielding. Every question I ask exudes authority. It is imperative that he see me as an equal, as a whole human being. He's taken enough.

Our fight may be easier with these other allies, but it doesn't feel that way in the room. There are so many voices and egos trying to get their agendas across. Varesh believes we should go to the Spiradael Earth and slaughter them all. After that we should work our way to the Orsalines. I tell him that's impossible because that leaves my Earth dangerously exposed. It also leaves their Earths open to invasion with no Citadel force to protect it.

Iathan wants a parley. He believes, somehow, that once the

altered Roones see our show of force, they will back down. On this, at least, every other Citadel is on the same page.

No.

Fucking.

Way.

We will give absolutely no quarter. Every single altered Roone must die. They are war criminals, and the only talk I want to have with them is explaining to them what's about to happen during their hanging or shooting or stabbing. Whatever, I'm not picky.

After thirty hours, we finally all agree. We will fight this war in Battle Ground and while, yes, that does leave the other Earths in the alliance exposed, it is also the home of what the altered Roones believe to be their greatest achievement: the human Citadels. They'll want to secure our Earth far more than the others, so it makes sense that they would amass their troops there for the assault. The irony is not lost on me that in a bid to greedily protect what our enemies consider to be their greatest treasure, that same twisted thinking will be their undoing.

Technically there are more Karekin than human Citadels—the combined Roone/Karekin fighting force is about forty thousand troops strong. But considering that the Roones pretty much got us into this mess in the first place, I pull rank. Human Citadels make up the next largest number. I order everyone back to their own Earths. Within twenty-four hours, they must be ready to deploy.

"One last thing," I announce to the table. "We need a name. We have to fight under a different banner, but more importantly, you'll have to differentiate between the humans loyal to ARC and those that are on our side. You will be provided with new patches once you Rift to my Earth."

The table erupts with suggestions. Levi, Ezra, and I try not to laugh when the other races make suggestions like "The Rebel Alliance," "The Defenders," and "The Avengers" (revenge is on the top of Varesh's mind).

"No. None of those names are going to work and I don't have the time to explain why," I tell them all because, let's face it, there's a lot to unpack with the aforementioned monikers. "The patch will be burgundy, the same color as our fallen Daithi brothers and sisters. From now on, we are no longer Citadels. I refuse to answer to something that they've named me. We keep it simple. We're united against a common enemy. Today we agree to be a single fighting force, regardless of race. More importantly, we're free, no matter what the outcome. So, we're the United Free Army. Any objections to that?"

I admit it's not the coolest name. Again, I'm shit at naming things. But it gets the point across, and the SenMachs can make tens of thousands of patches in a very short period of time. I task Ezra with opening a tiny Rift small enough to get the message through to our robot allies, along with an outline of what's happened here.

I have deliberately kept the SenMachs away from the negotiations today. The Faida have an idea of how much technology the androids have and they are already hungry for more. How Iathan and Varesh might react . . . well, I trust them to fight with us, but that's about as far as my trust extends. The SenMachs don't need a voice here. Those troops will answer solely to me.

I am their voice.

Once again, each faction wants to weigh in on our name. *Why is it English? An army suggests infantry and the Faida are best in the air.*

"United Free Army?" Varesh snarls. "UFA? It is the sound one makes when picking up something heavy. It is stupid. Find another name."

During the long and harried hours of these talks, my capacity for patience has been climbing steadily to its limit. Varesh's rudeness takes it well beyond that.

"Enough!" I say, slamming my SenMach fist on the table. We all watch with rapt fascination as the thick wood begins to crack. A deep crevice crawls up the center of the table, branching out, with limbs and arms of its own. The assembly is stunned into silence. "Everyone gets a vote. Everyone gets a say," I tell them, barely able to mask my irritation. "But *do not* forget yourselves. The only reason we're all together right now, the only reason we have a fighting chance is because of me. I brought us this far, and so *I* am the one in charge. Each and every one of you is a seasoned veteran. I shouldn't have to tell you that there can only be one commander. Would any of you like to challenge that? If so, do it now because if you attempt to do it in theater, we will lose." I have to step up, before someone tries to push me out of the way. The table is silent. There are some formidable leaders here and I'm sure they dislike the idea of answering to anyone. They are also brilliant strategists. Most likely they are biding their time, knowing that the only person who can lead all of us, *together*, is me.

For now.

"Our name is the United Free Army. End of discussion."

Varesh leans over the table, four of his arms making delicate circles on the smooth wood. "This is not a challenge, but more of a question. I would like to know, *girl*," he asks in a sickeningly condescending tone, "why do you believe that you are more capable of leading this army than those of us with decades more experience? Just because you brought us all together does not make up for years of commanding in the field. Just because you got here first doesn't make you the best. As much as you posture, you are still a child."

The group falls silent. Varesh is the least liked of any faction leader in this alliance, which is why, I'm sure, no one has added to his dissenting voice.

But I'm also sure that they are all thinking the same thing.

"I don't need to explain myself to you," I tell him bluntly. "You can accept the terms or you can fuck off." I can feel my new hand trembling, aching to jump over the table and strangle him.

"See?" Two of Varesh's hands wave gracefully in the air. "That is the sort of vulgar answer a sullen adolescent would give. You are proving my point."

I feel a growl begin to stir in my chest, but before I can say anything further, Navaa steps in. "Ryn," she says brusquely. "I would like a private word."

I whip my head toward her sharply, prepared to give her a piece of my mind for undermining me, but the look on her face is so grave that it gives me pause. "Now?" I demand.

"I apologize, but, yes, now," Navaa says with grave determination.

"Fine," I tell her as I push my chair back and walk out the door knowing she is on my heels. We end up in the far corner of the hallway, a far enough distance where we won't be overheard. As soon as we get there I whirl on her.

"What are you *doing*?" I hiss. "Pulling me out of that room like I'm a misbehaving student who needs to see the principal! You're making this worse."

"No, Ryn," Navaa says calmly, but her eyes are wide and serious. "*You* are doing that all on your own. I can accept that you are stronger than me and perhaps even smarter than me as well. I know that your Kir-Abisat gift is far greater than mine. We all know in theory that the humans possess a superiority that we do not."

"Exactly!" I agree in frustration.

"*But*," she says in an infuriatingly calm voice, "you have not *earned* these gifts. You didn't work for them. They weren't gleaned from years of hardship or experience."

"I've experienced plenty of hardship and you know it," I assure her, though now I'm deeply offended. "It's not just what the altered Roones did to me either. That . . . that . . . *person* in the room, he cut off my arm, Navaa! And now he's questioning my ability to lead and then you call me out here. It makes it look like you *agree* with him."

"I *do* agree with him."

I take a sharp intake of breath. I feel as though I've been slapped. "How can you say that?" I say in a whisper. "How can you think that when you know how much I've had to sacrifice to make this alliance happen?"

"Because you are seventeen years old and although you are a genius, intellect is not the same as wisdom," she tells me kindly—and I hate her for it. And before I can come back with the vicious retort bubbling inside me, she holds up a hand for a moment more.

It takes all my strength not to tear her arm off and show her how that feels, but I listen.

"Now, I do believe that you are the only one who can keep us together as a cohesive unit because, as you said, it was your hard and diligent work that made it possible for us to be in that room in the first place. So I will back you as our commander . . . as long as you make a promise to me—right here, right now— that you will listen to those who have the wisdom you lack. That includes me, Iathan, and, yes, even Varesh. Do not let your ego and your need to prove that you aren't a child make you act like one. This cannot be a democracy, but it cannot be a dictatorship, either. More importantly, do not let my suffering have been for nothing. Allow me to give you the insights I learned from my many failures.

"Please, Ryn."

At first, I'm afraid that I might cry. Navaa's words have triggered my greatest insecurities. She's right. I *am* young. I am inexperienced compared to many of the others at that table. But I also truly believe that I am the only person who can keep the alliance together.

So what the hell do I do?

"If I back down now," I manage to say, "they'll walk all over me. They'll take over. All Iathan wants is revenge, and Varesh is a bloodthirsty megalomaniac. You want *them* to be in charge? If I show them any kind of weakness, they'll only see me as what they claim, a girl, and so will your people."

"You *are* a girl Ryn; you are a woman and that is good."

I shake my head, unsure of what she is saying. "How can that be good? What do you mean?"

"I have read much about human history," Navaa begins as she grabs me lightly by both my shoulders. "It is not so different from ours, centuries ago. It has always been men, going to war, thirsty for battle, enslaving those weaker than them. So this is what I mean: do not lead like a man. Lead like a *woman*. Listen. Communicate. Empathize. Be vocal. These are strengths, not weaknesses. Compromise is not a weakness, if used to further your own end. You are coming from a place of fear instead of authority. But absolutism isn't always the best answer.

"What I mean is calm down, Ryn. No one is going to take this from you, not if you act as smart as you claim to be, all right?"

I bow my head and take a deep breath. I may not be wise, but I am not stupid. Navaa is right. I've been so concerned about losing this newfound freedom I have and so terrified that someone will make me blindly follow orders again that I've forgotten that everyone here is worried about the exact same thing. That I am not alone in this. Being a leader isn't just about telling people what to do; it's about becoming the person that they need in that moment and then knowing who to be next when the moment passes.

"Okay," I relent. "Thank you. I think probably . . . no, *definitely* . . ." I take a breath. "You are right. I will always appreciate your counsel. I might not take it," I tell her with a smile, "but I promise to always listen to it."

Navaa nods her head and we both walk back into the room. I calmly take my seat and address Varesh—who I still want to punch in the skull, but I manage to push that urge away. "Sairjidahl Varesh," I begin. "I apologize for my rudeness earlier. Thank you for bringing your concerns to the table. They are valid. I am available to discuss strategy and any other concerns you may have at any time. Your experience, as is everyone's here, will be invaluable. Shall we move on?"

Varesh knits his finely shaped brows. I have not disagreed with him, so there is no reason to fight any further. He knows as well as I that to insist how capable you are for a job only makes the person pleading their own case look desperate. Since I gave him part of what he wants, he can now no longer claim that he would make a better leader.

But of course he's not going to take it lying down. "As long as you agree to listen to your betters, then, yes, we can move on," he says.

"There are no betters here, Sairjidahl," Navaa says icily. "In this room, we are all equals. Going against that fundamental rule is, as the humans would say, a deal breaker. Are you a deal breaker, Varesh?"

The entire alliance swings their heads around to look at Varesh, who has enough experience to know that this is not a battle he will win, at least not today.

"I am not," he says proudly.

"Excellent," Navaa tells us all brightly. "And for the record, I think the UFA is a fine name." And with that, finally, the others relent.

Back in control, I say, "Get your people together." The tone of that order is quiet, but undeniably firm. "We're going home tomorrow. So you have twenty-four—maybe forty-eight—hours to get squared away." I clear my throat and look at all the different colors and faces around me, at the wings and bracelets and furrowed brows.

"I guess I'm supposed to make some really inspiring speech right now. But we all know what's at stake. I don't care about the past, and I suggest that if any of you are harboring grudges, let them go. They're a distraction. The only thing any of us should care about is eliminating the altered Roones. As Varesh pointed out, *I am* young and I lack your years of experience. But maybe that's a good thing. My ideas are fresh and my strategies are forward thinking. If we work together to shape those ideas with the experience you bring to the table, then that might just be the key to besting the altered Roones at their own game. In the spirit of that collaboration, I am happy to listen to any and all strategies and suggestions if you feel you haven't been properly heard today. I hope, though, that you feel like you have. Make your peace with how we got here and get ready, because we are going to war.

"This meeting is adjourned."

Each of the delegates jumps from the table and begins to move at a brisk clip. There is a tremendous amount of work to do and very little time to do it in.

I tell Levi I will meet him back in my room after I go over some particulars with Gomda and Yessenia about setting up a triage center on our Earth. When I'm done, I make my way quickly to my quarters. Levi and I have only had a handful of hours alone. For the past few days, sex has been off the table because, well, robot arm. Tonight, though, before we head home, things could be different. My pulse starts to race a little as I get closer to my door.

When it swings open, I see Levi on the bed. He's on his back and his uniform is peeled down to his feet. That's how far he got. I walk inside the room and, unsurprisingly, he is asleep. This kind of fatigue that we are both feeling settles deep, in the marrow. I take off my uniform and manage to get the rest of his off. He barely stirs with my efforts. I climb in the bed beside him.

Timing is everything and, now, time's up.

CHAPTER 19

The first part of what is now officially called Operation Battle Ground Fury (but which I personally have dubbed Operation Fuck Those Fucks) begins with a special op, code-named Operation Sanctuary. Ezra, Levi, and I Rift back to our Earth just as dawn is breaking, blocks away from Meadow Glade. Ezra's job will be to use a drone to scan for enemy surveillance at both my house and Violet's. He will use a sensuit to go stealth to further aid his investigation. If the houses are clear, he is to knock on the door, introduce himself, and tell my parents and brother to wait there.

He will, without sounding like a deranged lunatic, have to convince my parents that something big is going on and that I will join him later to explain everything. I don't know what exactly he's going to say, but I've given him some anecdotes to help him gain their trust. He'll also use the sensuit to blow their minds. Once they see him transform into a Franciscan monk or an Ewok or something, they'll want to know what the hell is going on. They will in turn call the rest of Beta Team's parents, along with Levi's mom and sister, on a secure phone and tell them to come over. He is not, for any reason, to tell them the entire truth, no matter how hard they press him for answers. That is one thing they need to hear directly from me.

If the houses are being surveilled, he is to text me with the numbers 5–0. If that happens, then the timeline for Operation Sanctuary will need to be brought forward, though it also might mean that there is no way to accomplish the mission logistically. Luckily, twenty minutes after he arrives at my front door he sends me another text. This one is only the number 9. This tells me, with great relief, that my family has let him in and there is no one watching.

Levi and I arrive at Camp Bonneville. We don't use the train or the gate. Instead, we hop over a fence deep in the thickest part of the forested area. I don't want anyone to know that we are coming. I may not have absolute control over what's about to happen, but in this one thing, I am granted total autonomy. I get to decide the terms of my homecoming.

Levi breaks for the Rift, to gather Beta Team. I walk right into headquarters and make my way to Edo's office. All I'm going to do is tell her that I have returned, without Ezra. The next questions she asks will help us further strategize for Operation Battle Ground Fury. She is an absolutely stellar liar. Still, the manner of her queries will tell me if she is still mainly concerned with my Kir-Abisat gift or if somewhere along the way, the altered Roones found out what we are up to.

As I walk confidently along the maze of hallways that lead down to the med bay, I am greeted by many of my fellow soldiers. Some give me the knowing gaze I am sure stems from Henry's covert ops. Some are just happy to see me returned. My boots pad along the short piled carpeting. I may well never see the inside of this place again. If we lose, I'll probably die. If we win, I might insist this bunker be leveled to the ground. I don't know if we'll shut down the Rifts, but we'll definitely need a new base of operations, one that hasn't been fouled by ARC propaganda and tainted with childhood abuse.

When I get to the med bay, I swing open the door and ignore everyone else in there. I know where Edo's office is and I don't need to explain myself to a civilian. Although I doubt I would need to. Every person here has been brainwashed with the same drugs they used on us to keep us in line. When I get to Edo's door, I stop and take a breath, centering myself. I put my pack, which is just filled with the basics, on the floor. I don't want my SenMach laptop anywhere near her. I place my hand on the handle and push.

I see that Edo is standing behind her desk, her arms folded, chin tilted down. Her chair is swiveled away from me, and when I enter, I see genuine surprise on her face.

"Citadel Ryn," she says. I clench my jaw slightly at the term Citadel. Ever so slowly the chair swings around and there, wearing the smarmiest of grins, is Christopher Seelye.

Shit.

He is not supposed to be here till tomorrow. I wanted to include every soldier's family in Operation Sanctuary. It looks like it'll just be the Betas—and Levi's, of course.

"Mr. Seelye," I say indifferently. "You're here."

"Yes. I was fortunate enough to conclude my business at the Myanmar Rift early. Good timing," he tells me as he props his elbows on the desk and knits his fingers together. "I only *just* arrived."

I look over to Edo, hoping that she'll be able to give me some kind of a clue. When I left, we were all supposedly on the same side. She was going to help Henry cover for us so that I could escape. This was under the guise that she, too, was a prisoner, but now I know that was the biggest lie of all. Does she know that I know? "You just arrived? And you're here in Edo's office in the med bay? I'm surprised. I thought Colonel Applebaum would be your first stop." I level my gaze at him, narrowing my eyes as I examine him. "Are you injured?"

"Well," he says, his voice riding a sickening wave of contrived concern, "I think the more important question is, are you? You should be on duty."

I don't say anything. I look at Edo, whose bright blue neon eyes give absolutely nothing away. There are a few seconds of terse silence. "I had some pressing issues I needed to discuss with Edo," Seelye tells me lightly, as if we're old friends, in on the same joke. "Some unusual behavior at the other Rift sites. I was hoping she had discussed it with her colleagues. That's why I'm here. But again, why are *you* here?" He leans forward, the chair he's sitting on creaking beneath his weight. *"Has something happened?"*

The tiny hairs on the back of my neck stand at attention. "No," I tell him confidently. "I just had a question for Edo, but it's not important. I'll come back after my shift."

"Yeah, sure," he says as he sweeps his arms wide. I make my way to the door. "Ryn," he says with an unmistakable edge. "I like the hair." I fight the instinct to touch the arctic crop on my head. Instead I stand, perfectly still. "I always notice these things, even the tiniest details, when it comes to my favorite Citadels."

I put the biggest, fakest smile on my face. "Thanks," I tell him with as much warmth as I can muster. I open the door, snatch up my pack, and make my way out of there. I do not run even though every muscle in my body is screaming at me to haul ass. I have to stay calm. I walk up to the level of the old escape hatch. This is the one I used to get away on the very first Earth I Rifted onto. The one where the Allies lost World War II. I disable the alarm and turn the tight wheel that releases the door. Once I'm outside, I radio Levi through my cuff.

"Seelye is here early and he knows. I don't know what he knows, but he knows something is up. Both operations are now a go. Tell Beta Team that they have to get to my house. *Right now.*"

CHAPTER 20

I run so fast that I almost trip on a tiny fallen branch obscured by mud from a recent rain. Nothing is going to work here unless I calm down. I focus on my surroundings. I push my fears away and let muscle memory take over. Leap, dodge, run, jump. Okay, so Seelye knows something is going on, but I doubt he knows the full extent. I barely know the full extent and it's my operation.

We all arrive at pretty much the same time. I practically yelp with relief when I see my teammates. After a brief group hug, I notice all the cars parked haphazardly in the driveway. One SUV is partially on our lawn. I press my palm into my uniform and run a hand through my short hair. My parents are going to lose their minds. I could cuff. I could show up wearing jeans and a sweater; that might be easier for them. They need to *see* it, though.

They need to see what the truth looks like.

I study my team. They are all as nervous as I am. We've faced the unimaginable and we have hurt so many people. Everything we ever did was to protect our families from this—or at least that was the lie we believed when we were drugged into submission. It's a different kind of guilt, inflicting pain on people you love as opposed to strangers. It is sharper, like a bag of hooks, each one clinging to organs usually protected by bone.

This is the hardest thing we've ever been asked to do.

I take a deep breath and open the door and we all file inside. Our families just look at us. Mouths gaping. The silence is thick, the air almost unbreathable. I feel like I'm in trouble, like I've been caught doing drugs or shoplifting. I'm going to have to shake this feeling. I haven't done anything wrong. More importantly, I am going to have to convey that our parents haven't, either.

Finally, my mother, Vega, speaks. "Ryn, what in the hell is going on? What are you wearing? What happened to your hair? *Min Gud.*" Her words are a rushing train. I suppose I'm glad that she only said that last bit in Swedish. Usually, when she's very upset, *everything* is said in her native tongue.

"Okay," I say calmly. "I am going to tell you all what is happening. Just please don't interrupt me. I know you'll have questions, but time is critical. Just hear me out and then you can go for it."

The parents look nervous. Most of the dads are fidgeting, their thighs moving up and down like pistons. The moms are all partially covering their faces with their hands as if they know what I'm about to tell them will be something they will want to hide from. They're not that far off.

I start at the beginning: the rash, the chip, ARC, the training, the Rifts, what we fought, the Blood Lust, Ezra, Edo, my trip through the Multiverse in search of answers, and, finally, the answers that I found. I explain that war is on the horizon. I tell them plainly, honestly, that we might not all survive. I assure them that death is preferable to a life in service to the brutality of the altered Roones.

There is weeping. There are long careening wails that remind me of being inside a Rift as I am telling the story. Beta Team stands, not quite at attention, but we are stiff-backed. There can be no bending here. We understand that we must remain strong, for them. When I am finished talking, Boone's parents take a step toward him and he takes a step back. He cannot be their boy. Not now. Not yet.

"I knew it!" Flora, Levi's sister, says suddenly. "I *fucking knew* something was going on. I told you, Mom! Levi was doing a handstand on one arm. He put that fire out in the kitchen faster than the Flash. You wouldn't listen to me. You made me think that I was crazy!" Flora's hands are waving wildly. She is furious. I want to roll my eyes. Leave it to Flora to make this about her.

"I know you think this is real," my dad begins gently. He gets up off the couch and takes a step toward me. "But isn't it possible that they brainwashed you into believing all this? ARC could be the world's biggest cult. Maybe they *are* training you for some kind of war. Maybe the government is even in on it, but . . . but the rest is too insane." He takes another step toward me, as if I was a wounded animal and he has to be cautious. No sudden moves. "There's just no way that doorways all over the world to the Multiverse could be kept a secret. It's too huge." More silence. A couple of the crying parents begin to sniffle. Oh yes. Dad is being reasonable. That's a fairly rational explanation, sure. They need proof, I guess.

"Henry, I'm sorry. I'm going to have to use you to demonstrate because you're the biggest. Is that cool?"

"Depends on what you're going to do." He crosses his arms and raises a single black eyebrow at me.

"Slight emasculation. That's all."

"Well, I guarantee that there is nothing in this world that you could ever do to make me feel emasculated, so go ahead," he prods.

"Not me . . . Violet, pick him up," I tell her. She looks at her parents, who have been the most subdued throughout this whole thing. They are nice enough, but they are the kind of self-involved people that maybe should never have had kids in the first place. With her small lithe arms, Vi cradles Henry's head in one palm and runs the other down his body, settling on his rear. And then, with absolute grace and ease, she lifts him high above her head as casually as if she were holding up a banner.

The parents gasp. The crying starts all over again. "Stop!" I order them tersely. "Look, I know, it's a lot. We couldn't tell you because they used drugs to control us. By the way, you were all drugged, too. Every time you came in to meet a 'teacher' or had a 'conference,' your coffee was spiked so that you just accepted the way things were. So, enough. Take all the time you need to process this, you just can't do it here. You have to go."

"We are not leaving here," Levi's mother, Jenny, says with dogged determination. He looks a lot like her, but she has much more red in her hair. She isn't tiny like my mom or Violet's. She is built like a Pacific Northwesterner, broad and strong.

Not as strong as me, though.

"Yeah, you are. All of you. I'm sending you away. Again, this is going to sound shocking, but I'm sending you to a different Earth. One I know the Roones can't get to."

"No, Ryn, you are not sending us away. *Detta ar galen—*" my mother starts.

"We won't leave you," Henry's dad says firmly. As he is a First Nation person, I think this is hitting him doubly hard. "If you fight, we fight. That's it."

"Dad, you can't." Henry sighs.

"No one is going to fight," Violet's mother speaks up, finally. Her hands are shaking. I think it's all just beginning to sink in for her. She is a very successful attorney and barely at home. At some point Vi will tell her that this is not something to feel guilty about. That the fact that she had little parental supervision made this much easier. She didn't have to constantly lie like we did. But, again, not now. "We are going to take this to the media. I am calling CNN. The world needs to know what our government has done to you," Vi's mother announces with haughty determination.

Once again: Denial. Screams. Protestations. Everyone is yelling over one another. Each parent thinks they know what's best and in this particular case, each parent is dead wrong.

"Enough!" I yell, and everyone stares at me, most of them as if I'm just another teenage girl who doesn't know better. It takes a lot not to roll my eyes at their condescension. But I've just gone through this with Varesh and the rest of the generals, and so I'm prepared. In my most commanding voice, then, I say, "This isn't a negotiation. I'm sorry, I really am, and I've heard each and every one of you, but this is not a request." My parents look at me—*really look*. I almost feel like introducing myself. This is the first time they've ever met the real me. At home I barely speak. I certainly don't swear. I interact as little as possible because I felt like such a phony. I've been hiding for years. No more. "You are all going. Right now. To an Earth populated by robots that look like famous people. Okay? It's totally awesome and it's going to blow your minds. You don't take anything with you. You just leave."

"You can't expect us to just go, Ryn. You're our children," Henry's Korean mother says in beautifully accented English. "We will not abandon you." Well, now I know where Henry's loyalty comes from—from both his parents.

"You aren't abandoning us," Levi answers. "You're allowing us to do our jobs. We can't do this if we think you're in jeopardy. They are onto us and they know that Ryn is leading the charge. They will use you as leverage. Don't make her choose between our families and tens of thousands of Citadels around the world, not to mention the civilians that'll get caught up in this. Don't do that to her."

All I hear is breathing and the rattling drum of hearts beating. They can't bear for this to be true. They can't believe they didn't see it. And now that their eyes have been opened, I am asking them to pretty much ignore it all—*nothing to see here!*—and walk away. I realize I have put them in an impossible situation.

Well, welcome to the club.

I begin to open my mouth, but before I can say anything, Henry stops me.

"Trucks. Big trucks. They're coming," he says with his usual calm.

"I don't hear anything," Flora whines.

"Ezra, I'm going to open the Rift and give you my QOINS. Oh, and here—take my pack, too, just for now." I had dropped it at my feet and now I shove it into his arms. "Tell Cosmos what's going on. She's already offered protection. She'll know what to do," I say quickly. "Portland, 2021, casual wear," I tell my cuff and I am instantly covered in skinny jeans, a sweatshirt, and Vans.

"What is *that*?" my mother screeches.

I practically laugh. She's worried about my *clothing* after all I told them?

"That is something I got at the place you're going," I say. "It'll be cool. I promise." I hug Abel, who has said nothing this entire time. He looks shell-shocked. His face is all eyes. I quickly run my hands up and down his arms, nodding at him. We all hug our families. I wanted more time. I had so much more to say, but they have to get out of here.

"So you think I'm just going to ride this out in Robot Land?" Ezra asks me.

"I wish you would," I answer hurriedly. "But I know you won't. Just get them settled and then Rift back to the Village, as soon as you can. Levi is going to need my QOINS, and we will probably need you doing something computer-y."

"*Computer-y?*" He almost looks hurt, but I know he's just happy to be included. I throw him a tight grin, and he smiles back. No matter what's between us, it *is* a nice smile.

Even at a time like this, it's good to know he's the one looking after our families.

The team and Levi are looking at me, and now I hear the trucks, too, barreling down the driveway. "Rift. SenMach City," I tell the cuff. The Rift opens and the booming sound of it tastes like a drink of water after a day of marching through scorching heat. The great moan of the Multiverse has become part of me, as familiar as my own voice. It settles me even as it rearranges me. As a Kir-Abisat, I need it.

Our families stand before the emerald doorway in abject terror. When it goes fully black, I give a slight nod to Ezra, who assures them that he's done it dozens of times and that it's safe. Still they don't move. The rumbling motors stop, doors slam. No time. I look at my dad with pleading eyes. He has to go. He gulps, then nods, then grabs Abel and my mom and leaps. Boone's mom gasps, but others start moving, and Ezra shepherds the rest through. The Rift slams shut. I breathe out audibly and my shoulders drop just an inch. That, at least, is done.

"The rest of you need to book it. Right now. Get to the Village. As soon as Ezra gets back, you need to work in two teams collecting the UFA on this Earth," I order quickly.

"UFA? Are we getting flying saucers?" Boone asks. I don't bother to respond. There are boots on the ground and they will break down this door any moment.

"This would all be so much easier if we could just Rift from place to place on this Earth, but we can't—at least I don't think we can. The Faida Earth will act as a kind of a hub. You go to the Rift in Poland, China, Brazil, all of them—collect the UFA, and then Rift to the Faida Earth and then back here to the Village. It's going to take time, *a lot* of time, and I'm going to give you as much as I can."

"You're going to let them take you?" Levi practically whispers. He has hold of my shoulders. He doesn't want to let me go.

"It makes sense. They are going to want answers, and I can stall. Ten seconds," I warn. Levi grits his teeth. He knows full well that this is the best plan, the one that makes the most sense, but that doesn't make it any easier.

"Fine," he concedes, shaking his head. He pulls me into his arms and practically strangles me in a brief embrace. *"Don't die,"* he orders. Before I can even reassure them, they are gone. They've escaped out the back and even if there are troops out there, Violet knows all the shortcuts.

I know these soldiers will break down my door. My parents don't need to see signs of a struggle when they return, so I race to the front and fling open the door, throwing my hands in the air.

"I'm unarmed!" I scream. I look out to the rounded driveway. I don't know what or who I'm expecting. It could be Citadels. It could be Settiku Hesh or even Spiradaels for all I know. But what I see is at least fifty armed human soldiers. *Not* Citadels. Adults. They aren't wearing standard-issue fatigues, though. They are wearing all black. Almost a variation of our uniforms, with ARC patches.

They turn their guns to me. "Do. Not. Move," one of them warns me.

"If I was going to move, I'd be long gone," I spit. "I'm letting you take me in." The man who had addressed me laughs, sort of, because his mouth isn't smiling. It dawns on me in that moment that they have no idea I'm not in my uniform. Because of the sensuit, I just look like a regular kid in jeans.

A bunch of soldiers head up the steps toward me. "Wait," I say, raising my voice an octave, trying to sound even younger than I am. "There isn't anyone inside. If you need to search the place, I understand, but please," I plead innocently, "my parents will freak out if they come home and their house is destroyed." I say this to another soldier, a younger one. He looks over at the older man, who must be commanding the unit.

"We won't tear the place apart," the leader says. "Just cooperate. Be a good girl now. Don't do anything stupid."

Ordinarily, an order to "be a good girl" might result in a punch to the face. In this instance, I'm going to use my appearance (and apparently my gender) to my advantage. I know I'm on my Earth, but in this moment, I kinda feel like I Rifted to *The Handmaid's Tale* Earth. I walk slowly toward one of the dozen cars. I guess they must be Seelye's men, private guards. It makes sense that he would have them, because he's such an ungodly douche, and there's no doubt plenty of people who might want to kill him. Still, there's *a lot* of them. That can't be a good sign.

I hear the soldiers run into the house behind me. I remain calm and walk up to the man in charge. My hands are still up.

"Don't move any closer or I'll put a bullet between your eyes, Whittaker," he tells me grimly.

"Okay . . ." I say slowly. But, really, this is more of a question. He wants me to come with him, but I can't move?

"Get down on the ground. Face-first and put your hands behind your head." Wow. This is really happening. I'm, like, *being arrested*. I guess he really doesn't understand that if I wanted to kill him, I could do it in approximately 2.8 seconds by leaping over to where he is standing by the open car door. I could snap his neck, rip the door off the hinge, and use it as a shield. From there, I could handily execute his entire team.

I suppose it's actually better that he not get that.

I do as I am told. I get down slowly, putting my face in the gravel. Immediately, I am swarmed by soldiers holding me down and cuffing me. I don't know how many there are, but there are enough to make the small rocks scrape at my cheeks and leave a sour taste in my mouth. Not blood, but a sharp kick of shame. I am being touched aggressively, by many large men. I am letting them do this and I hate that.

"You can't break out of those cuffs, missy," the commander tells me. "Made by the Roones for special circumstances like this."

"I told you I was going willingly. You don't need to shackle me," I inform him, my tongue absorbing the salty earth of the gravel.

At that he does let out an actual laugh. I am yanked up, and two men on either side of me point their sidearms inches from my head. "You're a Citadel," he says, like the word is filthy enough to taint his mouth. "All you do is lie."

Strangely, that stinging piece of truth hurts more than anything that's happened so far.

CHAPTER 21

The bunker is absent of its usual busyness. There are no civilians, no intake workers or anthropologists. I don't know if Seelye has let them go or killed them—both options seem equally likely. The walls down here are thick. Even with my spectacular hearing, there is nothing. There are no screams, no jostling or yelling "Hup two three four!" There is also a suspicious lack of Citadels. I want to assume that they have now been absorbed into the UFA. Henry had ample time to brainwash and drug anyone left to oppose our new regime in my absence. Levi and the team would have planned for this, the moment I told him that Seelye knew. I just didn't get a chance to ask him what that plan was. I can only hope that they have made their way to the Village.

I am led into interrogation room C. As soon as the door is

open, four of Seelye's men take out the table and chairs. I'm not sure if this is because they don't want me having access to anything I might make a weapon out of or if their intent is the sheer indignity of the floor. Well, he's double the idiot if he thinks that a bunch of tiles are going to somehow break me down. Not after what I've been through.

I sit happily on my bum. Two men still have their guns aimed at my skull. I'm surprised when a third is brave enough to remove the handcuffs. I'm pretty sure I broke out of this exact same room on the first Earth I rifted to. They must know that the double-sided glass is easy enough for me to kick through. They take the furniture but leave a means for escape? This is a power play then. Fair enough. I can play, too.

I wait. For hours. I close my eyes and lean back on the wall. They probably know I'm not sleeping, but I also don't look worried or anxious. Inside, I am not so calm. The team has to get to every Rift site and activate each cell. I have no idea how many Citadels they were ultimately able to recruit. They also have to get to the Faida, the original Roones and Karekins, the SenMachs and the Akshaji. Hopefully, Ezra grabbed the SenMach troops when he took our families there.

On the plus side, for all the mobilizing we have to do, they also have to do the same. After a couple of hours, I sidle my thoughts away from troop movements, knowing that Gomda is a genius when it comes to logistics. He'll know where to put up camps and how to integrate the soldiers. I am determined to stay positive, maintaining that my being here is the distraction the UFA needs. ARC will know that Levi and Boone and Violet—certainly Henry—will have some answers, but Seelye knows that I am likely the only one who knows *all* the answers. This in and of itself is laughable. He's right, except

I have answers to questions he wouldn't have the first clue about even asking.

To calm myself, I begin to think of Christopher Seelye and how best to kill him. If I can keep up my feigned compliance with this kind of dedication, Seelye will want, at some point, to interrogate me himself because that's totally his jam. If he does so through the mirror, I will simply jump through it and take him. If he has the balls to actually do it in person, I will likely have to eliminate his guards as well. That's a whole lot of murder right there. Not ideal, but it's not like they're innocents if they are working for Seelye personally.

I consider my options. Because of the sensuit, they did not bother to search me. Dumb. If any one of them had given me a proper pat-down, they would have noticed that something was off. Then again, I can see why no one would volunteer for that particular job. So, while it might appear that I am a lone girl without a weapon or even a uniform, the truth is the exact opposite. I don't have my laptop—that's a bit of a bummer. Opening a Rift to the Microwave Earth and throwing Seelye inside to die a slow and painful death as the flesh melts off his bones in steaming heaps sounds about right.

I could make it quick by snapping his neck, but that seems wrong. He should suffer more. There was a time not so long ago that the idea of straight-up murder gave me pause. Those days are long gone. The Daithi gravesite ripped away pretty much any innocence I had left. I go back to my daydream.

I could use my bowie knife and cut his torso open from sternum to ball sack. Messy, certainly, but fitting. I could strangle him, watch his eyes bulge and his face go purple. His tongue would swell and fall out of his big fat mouth, but that might take more time than I have. I suppose he'll get a quick death after all, which, considering what he's done to tens of thousands of children, seems drastically unfair. I'll need something that's at least intensely painful.

A lot of those seem to involve either his eyes or below his waist.

The guards shift changes and I amuse myself with these thoughts for another hour. Sometimes I will look up at the double-sided mirror and give a little wave or a cheeky smile. They want to kill me, certainly, but they want to know what I've learned inside the Multiverse. Edo probably wants to do a bunch of tests to gauge my Kir-Abisat gift. In this, I have the upper hand. All I want from them is their death.

Eventually the door opens, and the guards once again level their Berettas at my head.

"Get up, Whittaker," one of them says, "slowly. And keep your hands up where I can see them."

I give a rather long, petulant sigh and slide up from the wall. I'm not sure why they want me to keep my hands up. I could move them faster than they'd ever be able to get a shot off. Maybe they don't actually know what a Citadel can do. Maybe that's the only way Seelye can get them to work for him.

I say nothing but walk confidently out of the door, following their instructions. Do they even realize how friggin' ridiculous they must look? Are there no alarm bells going off that these great big hulking men are pointing two guns at an unarmed teenage girl wearing jeans? Hmm . . . I guess they do know what we are capable of, after all.

Which just means they're stupid.

We take the elevator up a couple floors to the assembly level. There are two very large spaces on this level. One is a lecture hall, for, yes, lectures, but also for people like Seelye to have a place where they can spew their bullshit in front of a large, swooning audience. The other space is a training area.

This is where we do our sparring. There are six distinct combat "rings," though only two are properly roped off. The other four are simply padded platforms of various heights.

I am taken to the training area, which I wouldn't have betted on. I would have thought that Seelye would find a lecherous pleasure in hauling me in front of his men and any leftover Citadels in a bid to embarrass me, or teach a very valuable, graphic sort of lesson about Citadels who step out of line.

When I get fully into the space, I see Seelye, standing casually in one of the boxing rings. I am accustomed to his expensive tastes. Cashmere sports coats and lightly starched designer dress shirts. He never wears a tie. It's his ridiculous way of being more "relatable" to all the teens under his domain. As if somehow not actually wearing a suit negates the truth that *he is a* suit. Now, though, he's wearing jeans and a black T-shirt. His feet are bare.

As I make my way up to the ring a laugh escapes from my mouth.

"Seriously?" I ask him, not bothering to hide my amusement.

"Yes, Ryn. Seriously," he tells me with real enthusiasm. "I wanted to talk to you somewhere I knew you'd be comfortable. I know how much you love to fight. This place must have some great memories for you."

Oh yeah, I think to myself. *Like when I broke my nose, and my finger and my foot. Those three matches when I got cuffed so hard in the head I was concussed and passed out. Good times.*

"So how exactly do you see this happening?" I ask. "You want me to climb in there with you? Or . . . ?" I look to the two armed men and then back at Seelye.

"Yes, yes," he says warmly. "The rest of you are dismissed."

My mouth gapes as I let what is happening sink in. Does he hope that we'll settle this all with a friendly tussle? He is actually going to let himself be alone with me? In a boxing ring? "You probably think I'm being a little reckless here." He chuckles as he strokes his perfectly shadowed beard with his right hand. "This is a show of good faith. I trust you, Ryn, and I really want you to trust me."

I bite down on my lip to keep from exploding with laughter. I'm more likely to trust the shady dude asking kids if they want to see a litter of puppies inside his blacked-out van. This is insanely easy.

Too easy, my gut tells me.

The rest of the guards do indeed leave. I hear a whooshing sound behind me as the automated doors open and close. I am going to kill this guy, this motherfucking asshole who plucks innocent children out of their normal lives and abuses them before turning them into weapons. The prospect makes my heart beat a little faster. I'm actually excited to do this, which I suppose, makes me a kind of monster. At least I know I'm a monster though. This man. He thinks he's a hero. Still, I am curious, as to why he wants to gain my trust. What exactly does he think I'm going to tell him? Why does he think I'll tell him anything?

I spread the ropes and lithely duck inside. I rest my back against the plastic coverings, spreading my arms wide and gripping them lightly. I don't say anything. I just look at him.

"So I have a question for you," he begins. "You didn't *really* believe that we just let you take over the Battle Ground Rift? I mean, you are a genius and you understand the full scope of our influence. You don't actually think that happened?"

I tilt my head. "So you knew all along?" I ask, though I'm not surprised. "Why would you go along with it then?"

"It was an experiment in statistics really," he says as if it's the most obvious thing in the world. He begins to pace a little bit. His bare feet lightly touching the padded floor. "We wanted to know the percentage of Citadels who would remain loyal to ARC in an uprising. These things happen, unfortunately. You're all so young and passionate. This was a controlled study, giving us the ability to monitor how you dealt with the situation in a tightly contained environment. However, I am getting reports that Citadels from other Rifts are leaving their posts. So maybe it wasn't as contained as we thought."

I lift the left side of my mouth, just a little bit. I raise my brows. I don't think he knows. Actually, I'm almost fairly certain that he has no idea there are other Citadel races, and why would he? The altered Roones would then have to admit that ARC is just a front for their agenda here, and the humans are just another cog in the wheel with no real power. "That *is* strange, but I've been gone. So I really don't know what's going on." I have so much faith in the SenMach tech that I feel confident enough to play dumb. Even if their machines could pick up unauthorized Rift activity, our laptops would have masked it. Seelye is waiting for me to say more, but I simply shrug my shoulders. The best lies are always the ones that are mostly true. I haven't been here, so *how would* I know?

I look around at the cavernous empty space and widen my eyes. "But if what you're saying is true, then from what I see, there are no Citadels here. So the answer is zero. Zero Citadels remain loyal to you when the drugs are fully out of their systems and they realize they are just pawns. Drones. When they get how badly you fucked us over."

Seelye sighs as he shakes his head. "Come on now," he goads churlishly. "Are you going to stand there and tell me that you'd rather be a normal teenage girl? Glued to your phone, waiting to see who liked the picture you just posted? Hmm?" he asks with more volume when he gets no reaction. "Stop pretending." Seelye's feet cease their pacing and he looks at me levelly. "You are a legitimate superhero with access to the greatest scientific marvel mankind has ever seen. Instead of embracing that, you would rather what? Gossip about boys? Go to university for four years so that you can graduate with a mountain of debt and wonder what the hell you're supposed to do with your life?"

"Just so we're clear"—I bounce my body just a little bit back and forth on the springy ropes—"what you're saying is that I should just forget about what was done to me and all my friends—done by the way, when we were *seven* years old— because in return for the pain, the loneliness, the guilt, the shame, the violence, and the abuse, I get to be Captain America?"

"You're a smart girl, Ryn. You know your mythology—all the old standards and even the new ones too. You have an innate understanding that real heroes never ask for the privilege. It is thrust upon them, and their suffering sweetens the crusade. Yes, the rash is painful for a kid," he relents, once again beginning to stalk up and down the mat. "And, yes, being asked to remain celibate is a sacrifice, but look what you can do. Look what you are capable of. The Roones made you *better*. There's no denying that."

I can see why some people find this man attractive. He is good-looking and charming. He must be in his forties, but there is something undeniably boyish about him. What's interesting here to me is that he really believes that the altered Roones are his partners, that they consider him to be their equal in this endeavor. He really has no clue.

"Okay, let's agree to disagree on that point," I say diplomatically, white knuckling my temper. "Currently, every active

Citadel in Battle Ground doesn't share your glorious vision of the Fatherland. What are you going to do? Kill them? It might be harder than you think without the Midnight Protocol."

Seelye tilts his brown head. A shaft of sunlight streaks through one of the tall windows, putting up a barrier of light and dust motes between us. "Kill them? Of course not. I'm going to recall them. We both know they're at the Village, so let's not pretend on that front. It wasn't right, how Edo killed those kids that day. I've talked to her about it."

"Oh, yeah. I'm sure she was really choked up—felt super-guilty." I roll my eyes. "So you're just going to ask them to come back? And they're going to agree? Just like that?"

"They'll return because they'll be worried about the safety of their families." My eyes get hard. "Oh, yes—I'm not above using that as leverage to get our troops to return. Once they're back, all of you will be reprogrammed. The experiment was very useful, but it's time for it to come to an end."

My eyes narrow even tighter. Tension builds in my chest. "Murdering thousands of innocent people. That's just collateral damage then? In your actual brain, you believe that's justified?"

"Whoa whoa whoa," Seelye says, putting up his hands. "I'm not saying I'm going to hurt *anyone*—I won't need to . . . hopefully . . . with the kind of leverage I have. And that's all I need. No one is going to get killed. The Citadels will do the right thing. You may have managed to hide your family, but I can have the loved ones of every other Citadel rounded up and brought here in a matter of hours. You can't protect everyone and you wouldn't want to be responsible for spilling any more innocent blood."

"You would do that?" I blanch.

"Would you?" Seelye asks innocently.

Silently, I curse the fact that Operation Sanctuary could

only be accomplished with the Betas' families. I knew Seelye would go after our loved ones, but I didn't think it would all be happening so quickly. Seelye was supposed to have arrived tomorrow. I am powerless to help them, and I hate that feeling even more than I hate the smarmy bastard in front of me.

"Let's just stop with all the morbid doomsday scenarios, Ryn," Seelye begins warmly. "No one here is a monster. We're all reasonable people. Why else do you think I'd step into a *boxing ring* with you? I want us to be able to trust each other. I want us to work together like a real team. Mistakes have been made, I'll give you that, but we'll course correct. This work is too incredible, too important for us to get mired in the past. It's time to look to the future. Together."

I'd like to think that the altered Roones have drugged and brainwashed this guy, but I know that's not true. He's simply a true believer. He might as well be an Orsaline, kneeling every time a bell rings, praying to a golden god on a floating TV screen.

"Okay." I nod my head up and down as if I'm considering his words. What I'm considering is pulling his still-beating heart right out of his chest. "Let me just ask you, was it your idea? This whole experiment thing? Or was it Edo's? Is it possible— *at all*—that there might have been another reason she wanted me to go through the Rift?"

At this, Seelye just gives me a condescending closed-mouth smile. "Ryn, we know. We know you found Ezra. There's no way you would have come back without making sure he was safe. We know you deciphered the encoded laptop. Don't you get it? We wanted you to find it."

"And why would you want me to read those files?" I ask, genuinely interested. I mean, really, that's the one thing I never could figure out about this whole thing. I doubt Seelye knows

anything about the Kir-Abisat gene. He might think the altered
Roones are his BFFs, but I know the truth. Seelye is just a button, a dial, something they turn on and off, up or down to get
what they want. He hasn't been given the great gift of genetic
fuckery. He isn't one of the chosen. Does he really imagine the
altered Roones give two shits about a paltry human with no
special gifts? It did seem like a dangerous game Edo was playing in return for gauging my Kir-Abisat abilities—a biography
of their war crimes. Then again, I suppose they don't consider
them crimes at all.

"I told you, it was a dry run. As you know by now, the
laptop doesn't have any real information on it. It was just an
incentive. No one has ever gone through the Rifts or been to
multiple Earths. We wanted to know what would happen, if
the Citadels could handle themselves in the field and what
kind of radiation we could expect inside the Rift. You and
Levi were the first and, of course, your abilities exceeded anyone's expectations."

I physically have to chomp down on the inside of my cheek
to keep from bursting out with laughter. How moronic can
this guy actually be? Edo spun him one hell of a yarn and he
just believed her! I manage to keep myself from laughing. Instead I nod my head silently. Seelye does love to hear himself
talk and I am just going to let him. Every word he gives up
gives me something in return, although of course, he's completely ignorant of the fact.

Still . . .

What kind of game is Edo playing here? Was giving up
the laptop just a way for her to prove to me that the altered
Roones will stand with the Citadels against ARC? It seems
like an awfully big gamble for her to take, to just assume that
I would be okay with all the altered Roones had done because

of what I've been given genetically in return. It doesn't make any sense, though. *She knows me.* She knows how desperately I hate to be controlled and lied to. She can't just separate herself from ARC this late in the game. A feeling of dread washes over me.

There has to be something else going on.

Seelye smiles broadly, this time baring two full rows of glaringly white, straight teeth. "Ryn, you are a leader. People like you and they respect you. We knew that once you went through and saw all the possibilities of the Multiverse, you would understand that there is no point in biting the hand that feeds you. It's true, compromises have been made, but they are such a small price to pay for what we're getting. And by the way, what we get is everything.

"Every single thing in *every* single world."

I can't help it. I have to laugh and my giggles echo and bounce around the cavernous room, giving my outburst a darkly menacing tone. His face tightens. "What's so funny?"

"It's just—you have *no* idea. *There is no 'we.'* You are not part of the inner circle. They've been playing you, dude. Spoiler alert: there *was* something on the laptop, something that they don't want you to know and it doesn't have anything to do with traveling the Rifts." Seelye frowns. It must be dawning on him that I might know something that he doesn't and that maybe I'm not quite at the disadvantage that he thinks I'm at. "But, since this isn't a Bond movie, I'm not going to lay out my plan before I kill you. I'm just going to kill you," I tell him calmly.

Seelye's posture changes. He'd been trying to be relatable. The TED Talk guy, barefoot and amiable, superenthusiastic about his "talking points" and his "aha moments." I don't know why he thought that approach would work. Maybe he figured I'd be afraid when he mentioned my family. Maybe he really did think that I would believe that the Rifts are just too awesome an experience to walk away from. Too bad for him that he's been drinking so much Kool-Aid. Otherwise he might have stopped and considered why such a genius super soldier would allow herself to be captured in the first place.

"Well," he says, cracking his neck from one side to the next, "you can certainly try."

I wait a beat and then I leap. I bring an arm out, ready to punch him in the skull. My jump is lightning fast. Of course, he knows it's coming, but he won't be able to get out of the way in time.

Except he does.

Not only does he swivel out of my reach but in return, he gives me a kick to the ribs that sends me flying over the ropes and onto the wooden floor where I skitter a few feet. I watch from the ground as he bounds out of the ring doing a somersault in the air and landing squarely on his feet.

"I *am* disappointed, Ryn." he says with chilling calmness as he stalks over to me. I curl up on the floor, deliberately playing possum, trying to buy some time. I know what this means. I know what he is, I just don't get it. Before I can figure it out, though, he is on me like a flash flood. He picks up my left arm and bends down to whisper in my ear. "You actually thought that we would let a bunch of teenagers be in charge of the Earth's defenses? Come on. You all were nothing more than security guards really. Mall cops," he says meanly. "We're thinning the herd, making sure that whoever stays alive long enough to reach true adulthood is the best of the best."

He bends my wrist back and with one nasty jab attempts to break my arm at the elbow. There is no crack and I don't cry out. He looks at me, confused. God, I hate his face. I kick out with my feet and sweep him off his so he lands on his back with a thud.

"Funny story, got a robot arm in the Multiverse," I tell him as I rear back and punch him in the face with it. The satisfaction of that one act is enough to make me want to moan. Before I can hit him again, though, he grabs both my wrists and flings me once again. This time, I'm ready for it. I spin sideways in the air and land in a crouched position.

"Stop fighting this, Ryn," he says as we circle each other. "The Roones wanted to modify small children and we let them, for a price. It took a few years of negotiating, but finally they came around and enhanced adult troops as well. *Actual* soldiers, thousands of elite troops, all with special-ops training. Including me. Give it up. You're only going to get hurt."

I don't love the fact that there are new players on the game board. I don't doubt the altered Roones genetically modified grown men and probably some women, although there aren't exactly tons of women in special ops. I highly doubt, though, that they would ever give the adults all the same abilities they gave to us. There was a reason the altered Roones wanted kids. Seelye was too busy being Super Douche to pay attention.

"You still want to fight?" he asks me playfully.

"Yeah," I tell him, jutting my neck forward, loosening my shoulders with a little rotation in either direction.

"Too bad," Seelye says with authority. And then, with his enhanced reflexes, he pulls a gun out from behind his back. Presumably it had been tucked into his jeans, covered by his shirt. He doesn't even flinch. He just shoots me in the stomach. Not a kill shot. So we're still there. He still wants me alive. Well, he probably doesn't, but Edo sure as hell does.

I feel a sharp jolt to my abdomen, but I don't flinch. I flash him an insidious grin. Seelye does a double take. I should be bleeding. I should be doubled over. He only hesitates for a moment, though, before he starts shooting again. Again, this time, I'm ready.

I start dodging bullets. I zigzag around the room, running up the walls, flipping over equipment. There's just no way he can get me in his sights. I count the gunshots. He has to know that he won't catch me, but he still tries. Does he really think he's that much better than me? He may have been a Navy Seal or whatever in another life, but in this one, he's nothing more than an executive. While he's been flying around in the company jet, kissing Roone ass, I've been training and patrolling for eight hours a day, five days a week for three years.

When I know he's out of ammunition, I run at him.

He stands his ground, tossing his gun to the floor. He strikes first with a telegraphed jab that I easily block. I kick him hard in the sternum and now he's the one flailing across the room. He flips up like a springboard and I race at him again. This time he blocks me. He gets one good uppercut in, but when he goes to punch me again, I grab hold of his wrist and elbow him hard in the back. I follow it up with a decisive punch to his head using the back of my balled-up hand. "Cuff!" I yell and I let him watch the sensuit slide off my body and recoil back into my bracelet.

It's a distraction, and he's dumb enough to fall for it. He lets down his guard and it gives me enough time to reach out like a viper and grab hold of his neck. I keep my arm extended and lift him off the ground. "I made some friends out there," I hiss. "You're right. I'm a genius and I would never come back here unless I knew I had some decent backup." Seelye is gurgling. His face is turning purple. "What's that?" I ask innocently. "You're sorry for all the abuse and the pain and for lying to us and for being stupid enough to believe in a highly advanced species that wants to turn us into drugged-out zombie killers?" Seelye's eyes are bulging now. "Well, I don't forgive you and all of you are fucked." And with that I dig my fingers into his flesh until my nails pierce his skin. I give a mighty jerk and pull. Seelye's lifeless body slumps to the ground.

I am standing there with his esophagus in my hands.

This seems a bit extreme, even for me, but at least I won't have to hear his bullshit anymore.

I quickly drop the wet tissue and cartilage to the floor. It lands with a slick thud. I rip the T-shirt off Seelye's lifeless form and wipe my hand with it. Okay. Seelye is dead. I'm sure they'll send a replacement as soon as they can, but, at least for now, the chaos of the power vacuum can be used to our advantage.

Now, I have to book it, but I have no idea the kind of security Seelye and the altered Roones have put in place since I was first detained. I hope it's just his personal guard, even though they have probably been altered, too. Of course, this is a massive pain in my ass, but better to kill one of them than one of my fellow Citadels. Seelye had been right about one thing: I don't want any more innocent blood on my hands. If these assholes *signed up* to be altered, in secret, as part of some shadow division of ARC to put down unruly Citadels (who are just kids after all), then their blood is the opposite of innocent.

What I'd really like to do is go down to the med bay and have it out with Edo. The priority, though, is getting to the Village. I have to get an accurate fix on not only the numbers of troops we're facing, but *where* we'll face them. Seelye may have been woefully ignorant, but the altered Roones won't leave anything to chance. If I was them? I would be deploying the Orsalines, Spiradaels, and Settiku Hesh—I'd also be pretty bummed about having burned the Akshaj bridge. Right now, though, there are too many variables when it comes to finding Edo and that's presuming she's even here, so she'll have to wait. The smartest move is to get out of Camp Bonneville immediately.

There are bound to be some guards at the door. I could fight them or I could just go stealth with my sensuit. I think about the jackass who called me "little lady." He hasn't been brainwashed. He's just a smarmy asshole who got a sick kind of pleasure lording his power over me. It's a tough one, but I can't kill someone for being sexist. If I started doing that, this Earth would likely turn into Themyscira.

I tell my suit to cuff to stealth. I don't have my computer, so I assume I don't have the entire arsenal of costume changes I might normally have. I would imagine that the cuff itself probably stores a few basic sensuit settings for situations just like this and, thankfully, I see that I'm right when the silky fabric of the suit blooms over my wrist and my arm disappears.

I stand at the door and activate it. I wait, moving off to the side. No one comes in. I slide the doors open again, and this time four of Seelye's enhanced soldiers enter the room. They scramble over to Seelye, barking orders and pulling their weapons. I race to bolt through the doors before they close again. These guys might not have all the bells and whistles, but they are far from dumb. They will wonder eventually how the door opened on its own and I don't want to be around when they start asking questions.

I make it down the hall to the stairway when the alarm goes off. I now have less than a minute to make it out of the bunker. After that, the entire place goes on lockdown and I won't even be able to access the emergency hatch. I practically leap up the stairs as if gravity doesn't apply to my legs. I take them four at time at first and then as the seconds begin to tick down, I hop up entire floors.

At one point, another unit of adult Citadels comes crashing down the stairwell. I make myself flat against the wall as they pass, all the while counting down in my head. When I finally get to the ground level, I have less than twenty seconds. If I make a run for the emergency hatch, there's a good chance that I might not make it in time. If I go for the transport bay, I know I can probably get there in time, but there are bound to be a lot of troops guarding that area. I swallow my breaths. I have to be as quiet as my suit.

I decide not to risk the hatch and make a run for the transport bay. I pass by the ammunitions depot and see the massive metal doorway begin to lower down. There are troops everywhere—Seelye's guards, and a couple of regular Citadels. I'm not sure if they are from here or another Rift site because I'm moving too fast to get a decent look. It doesn't matter; they're going to be harder to maneuver around than the adults. It's my bad luck that all of them are blocking the remaining steps down to the exit.

I climb atop the railing and then use it to sail over their heads. One of my own unit of Citadels looks curiously above her head as I go past. No doubt she's heard my heart, but she has no idea what's happening, so I'm guessing that she has dismissed it as an anomaly. Invisible, flying Citadels aren't exactly a thing around here. I land and roll on my back so that I don't break my legs with the force of the landing. The door is almost closed at this point and I slide my body through it like I'm swimming through deep water.

The garage door shuts with a shutter and a bang. There are enemy troops all around me. The best I can do is start running. I take off. I hear shouting behind me. They know, of course they do, that somehow, I have managed to escape. I'd like to think that it is my superior combat and tracking skills that will allow me to escape, but not even my ego is that broad. The sensuit gives me the advantage here and I take it, gladly.

It's ten miles to the Village. There's no point in covering my tracks or doubling back. They know it's where we are holed up. I wish that I could throw a sensuit over the entire place, but it's too late for that anyhow. ARC won't know exactly what's happening inside there, but their tech will have picked up the multiple Rifts in and out. I can only pray that's all they can pick up. If somehow they are able to figure out that we are Rifting in other species and not just human Citadels, we're screwed.

I'm counting on their ignorance—that and the fact they'll use our families to blackmail us to surrender. My family is tucked away safely, but apart from Beta Team's, everyone else's is vulnerable. This means that we're going to have to figure it out before ARC gives us the ultimatum.

Damn it.

Every time I think of a solution to a problem, there are a dozen more problems imbedded in the solution. I don't have any time. There's never any time. And can I expect the human UFA to fight if they think it will cost them the lives of their parents? They're going to be pissed when they realize that I got my family out safely and rightly so. More lies then . . .

Damn it.

ARC is going to use the fact that I got the Betas' families out to their advantage. They'll snitch as soon as it suits them and then my credibility will be severely undermined and the UFA fractured.

Damn it.

One fire at a time. That one hasn't even started yet. I'll plan for it, yes, but I have to focus on the things that are exploding right now.

It's winter. It never gets arctic here in the Pacific Northwest, but it does freeze. It must have rained recently and then the temperature dropped below zero. A sheen of frost covers the underbrush, and each time I put a foot down there is a crunching sound. It's also a little slippery in the more open patches, where the mud is slick. I don't bother to mess with these dangerous spots. I vault myself into the air, grabbing hold of branches covered in sharp green needles, and swing over the spots where I might trip.

I can hear them behind me. They aren't yelling or even talking. They, like me, have become specters, whipping and racing through the forest like a whisper of a thing that was. I'm almost certain, though, that these Citadels—if that's what they even are—aren't local. More than likely they are Seelye's shadow soldiers. This gives me a double advantage. I know the fastest route. I know where to find the hidden paths.

Eventually, there is only silence behind me. I've either lost them, or they've been told to retreat. Edo wants me alive. I think she also wants me fairly cooperative. I have to assume they are going to let me think I've won this one, and since I killed Seelye, I kinda feel like I did.

When I get to the Village gate, I uncuff quickly and tell the Citadels there to let me in. They have tripled their guard, which is good to see. Also, ten Faida are there. This in and of itself fills me with relief. We have our reinforcements.

The Citadel at the gate doesn't know me, and he balks at my demand. "You aren't wearing a UFA patch," he tells me warily. I catch a glimpse of the burgundy circle on his uniform. It has two arms held up in a fist, one human, one a jeweled Akshaj, over a pair of black wings. Below it is a round lapis lazuli–shaped stone over a single silver rod to represent the SenMachs. "United Free Army" in bold lettering rings the entire thing.

"I designed that patch," I tell him as I bend over. I have to admit, I'm more than a little winded. "I'm Ryn Whittaker, let me in." The guy just looks at me and then to his friend and I realize that I don't know anyone here and for a second I freak out. What if they think I've been turned? What if the Village has already been infiltrated?

"I know this human Citadel," a Faida commands stridently. "*She is* Ryn Whittaker. Let her pass." I look at the Faida more closely. He does look familiar. Then again, the Faida are all so insanely good-looking that all their features start to blend after a while, like flipping the pages of a glossy magazine.

"Thank you. I'm sorry, I don't remember your name," I say, which is a lie. I would have remembered his name had he told me. I realize, though, as commander it's important to make those under me feel important and special, to build a bond. Really, I'm just being polite.

"I am Hayres. It is most reassuring to see that you have returned."

"To you and me both, Hayres." I nod to the others and the metal gate slides open. "Where is Navaa and the rest of the Command unit?"

"They have set up a base in a restaurant called Sugar Skull. It is on the Main Street. I can take you there if you wish," Hayres tells me in that slightly condescending way that all Faida have of talking. Like I'm a precocious ten-year-old.

"No, thank you," I tell him firmly, setting a tone of my own. "I know exactly where that place is. You can remain at your post."

I begin to walk down the road. This is a massive compound. Not only is there a village proper for the people and a menagerie for the animals that come through the Rift, but habitats—we call them "habs"—as well, specialized areas for those species who don't quite fit into either of those categories. I don't know why I had been worried about camps. There's enough housing here to billet all the troops. They certainly won't get their own houses or apartments, but they can double or triple up. Gomda will have this issue sorted, I'm sure.

It doesn't take me long to get to what they call Main Street. That's the thing about the Village, it is insidiously adorable. There are little shops and restaurants with varying architecture. One of half a dozen coffee shops is at the top end of this street in a building that is all wooden corners and sleek lines. Right next to it is a women's clothing boutique in what looks like an old gas station from the fifties.

As much as possible, the Village is self-sustainable. There are farms, gardens, and free ranges for animals that the butchers will slaughter for market or the restaurants. There are warehouses where candles, yarn, fabrics, and ceramics are made. The Village has a large and impressive bookstore, but it also has its own publishing imprint as well as a newspaper and a little TV station, but everything is censored. There is no real "art" here—only propaganda for ARC.

There are seven distinct domestic areas made to mimic neighborhoods from cultures around the world—*this world*. One of the most disturbing things about this place is that Immigrants from other Earths are forced to assimilate. They must live like humans—and if they are human, they are forced to live like humans from *here*. They must leave their own cultures behind. I suppose for some, the trade-off is fair. Their Earth might have been war-torn, ravaged by famine or disease. They might even be centuries behind us technologically.

In return for this peace and prosperity, they must remain childless—to control the population.

And they can never, ever leave.

At one time, when I thought the Rifts were unnavigable (and before I'd actually been here), I thought the Village was a good option for Immigrants. I thought that the safe haven we provided them was more generous than incarceration and certainly better than execution. And then I actually saw this place and what it demanded firsthand. This is just a really nice prison. And execution is always on the table when it comes to ARC.

Today, the street is buzzing. Species of every sort are walking with purpose, talking about what's happening. They must be hopeful that a return home is possible. Reptilian-skinned Sissnovars walk amiably beside simian-faced Maribehs. Humans are holding hands, huddled close, whispering in one another's ears.

The air is damp and cold, the sky teasing snow. I tuck my hands under my pits and press them into my chest to stay warm. Along the sidewalks and gutters there are six or seven metal garbage cans burning; great plumes of pulpy smoke waft in the air. I check one of them out to see what is being destroyed. The signs. Dual-toned posters of different species doing very mundane things. The slogans say things like HUMANITY = HAPPINESS and ENGLISH ONLY!!! I grin when I see the glowing edges of the papers buckle and double back on themselves. ARC kidnapped thousands of people and then convinced them to give up everything they believed in. In this, I must admit my own complicity. I did bring them here in the first place. I should have known better, but I didn't want to know. My anger at what had been done to me was sometimes the only thing that kept me going. The prospect of violence, of ripping something apart soothed all the parts of me that could never be put back together. My outrage could not be sustained if I felt like there were others who had it worse.

Now I know it's *all* terrible. Everyone is a victim, and at the same time, no one is. These are just average people, but they are going to fight to get out of here. They are going to risk their lives to speak their own language again and for a future generation that they may never even get to have. They, like me, have realized freedom is not the same thing as being free and that fighting is the only thing you can do with the prospect of a life in chains hanging over you—even if the chains are made of memory foam and great Wi-Fi.

I see a group of SenMachs walking together. There are two faces I don't recognize, but the other two are Will Ferrell and Carrie Fisher. Princess Leia! I grapple with the urge to run over there and take a selfie because she looks so badass in the SenMach uniform—which is similar to ours, except it's a light gray color, almost silver. The SenMachs see me and give a small salute. You might think that the robot army would be very stiff and proper, but their languid movements don't surprise me. Everything they do is calculated and nuanced because it is programmed and not learned.

I give a salute back to them and continue on my way. There are hundreds, if not thousands of people and troops on the street. My hand is still sticky with Seelye's blood, and I wipe it uselessly on my thigh. I remind myself that it is okay to be two things at once. I can be buoyed by this scene of blossoming rebellion, of so many different genders and races and colors and shapes coming together with one determined purpose; I can also be so terrified that I bite the inside of my cheek until it bleeds. The upcoming battle doesn't scare me. The fact that I lit this fire, that I am the one now in charge of feeding it and watching it burn down everything in its wake, has me practically shaking. I can't help but think there must be someone better qualified to be in charge. Then again, who has experience overthrowing a tyrannical interspecies regime hell-bent on multiversal domination? No one. So I suppose it might as well be me.

Right before I get to the large stucco walls of the Sugar Skull I realize that something is off. I turn around, resting my back lightly along the collage of plastered-in bottle caps and hand-painted skulls. I keep watching, and still I don't see what I want to.

I walk determinedly inside. I am expecting a restaurant, with tables and chairs and members of the UFA looking over plans and talking. Instead, I am assaulted with dozens and dozens of screens and holographic projections of Camp Bonne-ville and a few other Rift sites. Troops are on computers. Some are comparing notes. This is a proper Command Center. I suppose I shouldn't find the speed and efficiency with which all the races of the UFA (including our own) got this up, but somehow, seeing this here, makes it feel more real. And why did I think they would be looking over paper plans? This isn't World War II.

I clock Levi and make my way over to him. When he sees me, there is a look of absolute relief on his face. It's like his entire body lets go of a single breath. He opens his mouth but before he can say anything I blurt out, "What happened?

"*Where* are the Akshaji?"

CHAPTER 22

The entire room goes still. Everyone looks up from their monitors and tasks and focuses on me. Ezra is leaning against a table, chewing on the end of a pen. I can't in that moment understand why; it's not like he's doing any actual writing. Nerves? Navaa and Arif walk toward Levi and me. Iathan doesn't need to; he happened to be by the door.

"You okay?" Levi asks. If two hands wringing and gripping and fidgeting could speak, that's how he would sound right now. He is off. He actually sounds . . . *panicked*.

"I'm fine. They wouldn't have killed me. Edo is too curious about the Kir-Abisat." Levi turns away for just a brief second, composing himself before looking at me again.

"No, but they could have tortured you," he insists. "You have a bruise on your jaw." He picks up my left arm. "There's blood under your nails. Is it yours?" I pull my hand away.

"How did you even see that?" I look self-consciously at my uniform. I don't have a mirror, but I assume I look pretty normal. For a person who's just been taken prisoner anyway. Maybe Seelye did more damage than I realized.

Seelye.

"It's not my blood." I attempt a coy smile. "I'm not saying that I ripped out Christopher Seelye's throat," I blurt out, because technically, I could go to jail for murder, "but I'm not *not* *saying* I ripped it out either." Levi squints his eyes, processing.

"So you killed the president of this fictitious organization that has no real power. Wonderful," Iathan says, thoroughly unimpressed. "What about the *breikas*—the traitors? How many of them did you kill?"

"If you're talking about the altered Roones, I thought it best to make my way here after brutally and fatally attacking one of their leaders, fictitious or not. I could have looked for them, but, well, there's a bunker full of Citadels and only the one me so, you know, priorities. It is good to see you, all of you. But I have to ask one more time: Where is Sairjidahl Varesh?"

"Yeaaah." Levi winces so the word is dragged out slowly, like one of those scarves magicians pull out of their mouths. "We have a slight problem there." I feel my body tighten, as if every joint has suddenly been superglued together. If the Akshaji have reneged on their word—if I ended up giving my arm for Varesh's amusement, I'm not sure what I'll do. Whatever it is will involve violence and maiming. *Lots* of maiming.

"Perhaps I can explain," a voice rings out behind me. I turn and see that it is Lupita Nyong'o. Not her, obviously, but the SenMach version of her. "My name is Morning. I have been designated as the liaison between the humans and the Sen-Machs. I have been coded with additional command functions should that be necessary. However, my task here is to ensure effective communication between our troops."

"Well, that is great news. I am really glad that you all are here and I look forward to seeing Feather," I say warmly. "And our families? They made it onto your Earth without incident?"

There is a slight lag and my heart climbs up to my throat. If communication is Morning's wheelhouse, I'm going to have to explain that verbal delays like this aren't going to work. "The humans arrived on our Earth safely and they have been given the sanctuary Cosmos promised," Morning tells me without affectation. I have a feeling that these SenMachs aren't like the ones I'm used to. They were created to be soldiers. There is a hardness to Morning, a distinct inhumanness that I can't help but notice. Then again, they are, like, two weeks old. Maybe they need time to warm up a little?

"Great. So why do you need to tell me about the Akshaji then?"

"The altered Roones have created a sound blockade, much like the one the Faida have implemented on their Earth. It is possible that they even managed to use a variant of that same code and made it more efficacious. We have all been trying to find a way through the data—looking for what I believe you call a 'back door.' We have not been able to do so."

I look over to Levi and then Ezra, who just shrugs. "That seems impossible," I tell her, shaking my head. It still feels weird to have such short hair. My head feels so much lighter. "You are computers basically—no offense. It's just, I didn't think there was a system you couldn't hack into. I don't get it," I tell her, genuinely confused.

"No offense taken," she tells me matter-of-factly. "Please understand that our capabilities are limited. We are soldiers. Our primary function is to defend and to fight. We are not programmers. This could be a problem handled easily by those back on my Earth. However, since no Rift can now be opened, we have no way of allowing the data to flow freely between us."

I bow my head in frustration and dig a few fingers into my bare neck in a bid to ease the tension there. We need those troops, but it's not just that—Varesh would be overly sensitive to what he perceives as a slight. And, like with any other bully, even the tiniest of grievances would give him permission to escalate things disproportionately. He might not come to our aid, even if we find a way to get to him.

"Okay." I nod. I want a shower. I want to eat. I want some time alone with Levi, but *this is happening*—everything we've been preparing for. I am in command, which means that me, the individual, no longer exists. "We need a war council. Right now," I inform them.

As soon as I get the words *war council* out of my mouth, Gomda suddenly appears, out of nowhere.

"Ryn," he offers smoothly, "allow me to show you where we've set up the senior command post." Gomda's hand is gesturing forward and as I begin to walk, all the others follow. I am steered toward the back of the restaurant to a door that leads outside. To what I assume would be the outside patio. Instead, when the door opens, I walk into a massive tent. Tables have been pushed together to form one large one, big enough for the leaders of each delegation. There are holographic screens floating in midair around the space as well as one large one that takes up the entire back wall of the tent.

"Fantastic work, Gomda. Did you organize all this?" I ask him gratefully. "How have all the factions been settling in?"

"I delegate. However, it has been a challenge. We have emptied out certain neighborhoods so that distinct races can have their own space," he announces calmly while taking a seat of his own.

I snap my head in his direction disapprovingly. "Please explain your decision to relocate the residents. And why you would segregate the troops? We have to learn to live together if we're going to be putting our lives on the line," I tell the table occupants tersely. They have all assembled now: Navaa, Arif, Yessenia, Gomda, Sidra, Donav, Morning, Henry, Violet, Levi, Ezra, Boone, Iathan, and a Karekin general named Berj—Vlock's replacement.

"The residents were happy to vacate their homes for the troops. We thought with the Akshaji—well. We thought it best that we give them a wide berth," Henry explains. "Better to prepare for the worst but expect for the best, you know?"

"Yeah," I say. "I'm aware. Still, the Immigrants just moved out of their houses? Without incident?"

"They did, Ryn," Violet assures me, her voluminous brown hair expertly bunned at the top of her head. "*They are* scared, but they're more scared of never being able to leave here. Some Immigrants do want to stay and that's another conversation, obviously. Still, even the ones who don't have an Earth they care about going back to? Those residents have friends here, as close as family, whom they know are desperate to return. Everyone is working together."

"And we can feed all these people?" I ask no one in particular.

"We will be using stored food from the Village, but the SenMachs have sent along a literal ton of protein cubes that will keep us from starving should it come to a siege," Gomda answers evenly. Before I can ask my next question, the door opens and Zaka walks confidently through with another human woman I've never seen.

"Zaka," I tell him with real warmth. "I was just about to ask where you were." I pause for a moment, taking in his many layers of warm clothing to keep the winter chill at bay. "And who is this?"

The petite woman beside him smiles broadly but remains stock-still. "This is Glenys," Zaka says with affection. "She is not only my betrothed, but my partner in this endeavor. She and I are leading the resistance movement among the Immigrants." I deliberately keep the smile on my face. I mean, *no*, I couldn't see myself falling in love with a Sissnovar, but I suppose if I had to, I could get down with a Faida (okay, real talk, not that hard to imagine). Love adapts. Love finds a path to see through the surface, to bridge all the ways we are different and bloom on common ground. It's important that I give my immediate approval. I have a feeling we are going to be seeing this more and more. Still, Glenys is standing there awkwardly, not moving, smiling, her eyes darting at me and then to Zaka.

"Is there a problem?" I ask softly.

"I'm sorry," Glenys tells me earnestly. "I don't know what the protocol is here. Am I supposed to salute or courtesy?" A nervous giggle escapes her mouth. "I'm from a very small town in Missouri. This is all very . . . a lot."

"Just take a seat and listen," I prompt. "If there's anything pertinent you feel the need to add, you can do so. We're all getting used to this, so don't worry about feeling overwhelmed. To some degree, it's like that for all of us."

Glenys nods and they both take a seat. "So, Zaka," I begin, "Violet was just telling me that there are no problems with Immigrants rehousing. That's really the case?" It's not that I think Vi is being overly positive, but Zaka will undoubtedly feel more comfortable giving me the straight facts than a Citadel— scratch that—a member of the UFA whom he doesn't know.

"She is correct. All the Immigrants have vacated their homes willingly, gladly. They now reside in only two neighborhoods: the Cotswolds and Cape Cod. The rest of the town has been given over to your troops. Marrakech is empty, of course. In anticipation of the Akshaji."

"Look," I say, leaning across the table so I can get closer to Zaka and his fiancée. "We aren't going to ask the Immigrants to do any frontline fighting, but they may be called to defend the Village if any of the Citadels get by us after we attack. How many here, realistically, can we depend on for that?"

The entire table swivels their heads in curiosity to look at Zaka. "About a thousand. And let me tell you," he says with barely contained hostility, "if it comes to that, I pity the Citadels who would try to take this Village. We may not have altered genes, but we are more than capable in guerrilla tactics. Once again, it seems your altered Roones underestimated the very people they kidnapped to be here. More and more it seems as if they believe a person can be only one thing: a teacher, a doctor, an author. It doesn't seem that they went beyond current employment when choosing their victims. A fair number of us have many other skill sets. We have been setting booby traps and making bombs since our meeting the other night. Many of us having been secretly planning this day for years."

"I assume our people know where these traps are? We can't afford to lose anyone, especially in friendly fire," I ask him directly. "Don't get me wrong, I'm impressed. I just don't need the hassle of easily preventable accidents."

"We've got it covered. The Immigrants have it seriously dialed in—I can show you the schematics later," Boone offers. I wait a beat, wondering when the joke is coming—I'm guessing it will be of the Flintstone variety, with us all riding on the backs of dinosaurs from the Menagerie. Boone just sits back again in his chair. These last few months have changed all of us. I'm glad that Boone is taking this situation seriously, but I do miss the old him, irreverent, cocky, and even overconfident. I suppose there is no room here for humor, of any sort.

"Okay," I say, pulling at my lower lip for just a moment with my thumb and forefinger. I can't avoid this any longer. I have to know what we're up against. "Give me the numbers. And if possible, display them on the big screen so we can have a visual. Henry, let's start with the humans."

"There are approximately fifty-six thousand human Citadels. Of that number, twenty-eight thousand have been activated—meaning that the other twenty-eight thousand aren't old enough yet to have been deployed by ARC." A cold shudder runs through my body. I don't let anyone else see it though. I remain perfectly still. That's *a lot* of kids. "Twenty-one thousand eighty-seven belong to us. The rest would have either taken months to reprogram or there was something about them that the recruiters felt was untrustworthy."

I watch as those numbers appear on the screen behind me in neon green lettering. It is bright, the color of a Rift. I look at the readout and sigh. "It's unfortunate that we couldn't reach all of them," I say reluctantly. "It's disheartening to think that we might have to kill some of our own because they were loners or simply unpopular."

"Ryn," Henry jumps in, "we did the best we could given the time constraints. Maybe if we had another two or three weeks . . ." He trails off. I think he's just as disappointed as I am.

"No, I get it," I assure him. "The fact that we got as many as we did is a testament to your plan and your ability to execute it. You should all feel really proud of what you accomplished.

"As I said to Levi," I announce, switching gears because there's no point in dwelling on what could have been, "I killed

Seelye. But before I did, he told me there are adult Citadels. That the altered Roones reluctantly conceded to the US government, possibly other governments as well, and modified black-ops soldiers. I don't know how many."

"I may be able to help answer that," Morning pipes in efficiently. "Five point seven minutes after our arrival here, we sent out multiple, very sophisticated drones. They are not only capable of defending this area from an aerial attack, but they have been monitoring Camp Bonneville in stealth mode for hours. In the last thirty minutes, seventeen Rifts were opened in quick succession—presumably after you killed Christopher Seelye. Without a leader, it appears as if the altered Roones have now taken complete control. If there are 16,433 human Citadels at the base currently, we can extrapolate that there are 9,520 adult troops who have been genetically modified. That is the combined current total of humans on the base."

"Wait, just back up a minute," Vi holds her hand up. "We have to fight *double* the amount of human Citadels than we thought? You didn't want to lead with that?"

"I just found out. We're talking about it now," I say calmly. Vi can afford to freak out. I can't. "Besides, I doubt the altered Roones would give the adult Citadels as many genetic alterations as they did to us. I can't be sure, of course, but I believe that changing us before we hit puberty was part of the experiment for them. The adults were a concession. They were backed into a corner. Seelye forced their hand. We all know that the altered Roones don't like being told what to do. I fought the asshole. He was strong, but not stronger than me and that surprised him, so we can use that. Okay, let's move on; Navaa, how many Faida did you bring?"

"We brought eleven thousand troops. Nine thousand of them have combat experience, but the other two are very green. They are newly formed units. We have been training them extensively and they will follow orders." Navaa gives a slight shake of her head. "But they will need very specific orders. They don't have the experience to get creative in battle, not yet anyhow."

The numbers once again flash up on the screen, this time in a bright canary-yellow color.

"Iathan, what about your people? How many troops did you bring?"

"Well, I'm very glad you asked that," Iathan says in that off-handed way of his that sounds both indifferent and sarcastic at the same time. I don't know how he manages it. It must be a presidential thing. His blue skin looks much darker in the dim light of the tent, and his long hair has been pulled back all the way, cascading down his back in a fat bundle of braids. "We brought almost every soldier we have. If things go badly for us here, our Earth would be left dangerously exposed."

"I think we've all doubled down in that regard, Iathan. If things go badly, *none* of us are safe."

Iathan leans forward, his elbows practically digging into the table. "There is a slight difference. If we don't win here, all of us are likely to die. That would be unfortunate. However, the altered Roones will not take control of your entire planet—it would be easier for them to just move on to another humancentric Earth and start fresh, learning from the mistakes that they made here. However, they want our Earth specifically. It is their home."

"Well," Navaa growls, "it is *their* planet, too. You are *all* Roones if we are being technical. I blame your wayward brothers and sisters for many things, but I certainly cannot blame them for wanting to return there."

Once again the tension builds. Pulses quicken, spines

straighten. "Let's just stick to the data," I pivot. "Tell us how many Roones and Karekins you brought with you." This in-fighting is already raising everyone's hackles, and if I can't get it under control, soon, this war is going to be over before it starts.

"Thirty-six thousand troops—all of whom have seen battle many, many times," Iathan tells us all, but directs his words to Navaa.

The numbers go up on the board and I scrutinize them carefully.

"Do we have any idea how many we're up against? Morning?"

"There has been no Rift activity in the last seven minutes. Before that, Rifts were opening at an average of one every 1.9 minutes," Morning says with chilling accuracy. "We can therefore assume that the troops they have Rifted in to deal with this insurrection have already arrived."

"That doesn't mean much," Levi counters. "They are just as likely to stagger deployment."

There is a brief pause as Morning looks blankly in front of her. "I am not basing my conclusion solely on that informa-tion. I am basing it on the number of varying heat signatures our drones have picked up."

"Meaning what?" I rush my query, hoping Morning will catch on. She has to get better at communicating here.

"Currently posted at Camp Bonneville there are 58,733 Orsaline Citadels, 47,289 Spiradael Citadels, 27,764 Settiku-Hesh, in addition to the 16,433 human Citadels."

There is a split second of dead silence. A split second where our world fractures and unfolds—where we realize with stun-ning finality what we are up against. The numbers, in various colors, flash up on the other side of the board in quick bursts, like a razor slicing paper.

"That's 150,219 soldiers," I say out loud, to no one in particular. "How did they even know? Okay, yeah, our Citadels left their posts, but that's only twenty-odd thousand. How could they have possibly known who we brought with us? The SenMach security system should have ensured that the Rift activity and anything else happening here was locked down." I am trying to keep the panic from my voice to a minimum. I am trying to keep it level and rational, but I feel like getting up, pacing, screaming, and punching something very hard.

"Don't be so naive," Iathan says cruelly. "You believe that you turned over twenty thousand humans in a few weeks? Hardly. There are bound to be double agents here. There may even be one sitting at this table."

"Maybe it's you, *Roone*," Navaa growls.

"That's enough," I say briskly. "We can't afford to turn on each other, not now."

"The simplest explanation is that our security net was not as airtight as we believed," Morning offers. "The altered Roones did manage to create a Rift blockade that we cannot crack and one that allows *them* to Rift in and out. They may not have the exact numbers as we do, but if they've picked up on the multiple Rift openings, they would have guessed what was going on here."

"In essence, what we are looking at is that we have about sixty-nine thousand troops here, including the civilian Immigrants who have no formal training whatsoever. That number is unacceptable," Navaa says icily.

"On that at least," Iathan chimes in, "the Faida and I can agree."

"Well, not to sound all Hitler Youth here," Boone throws out, "but aren't we genetically superior to them? So what if it's almost two to one? Does it really matter? We're better than them, *and* we have robots." I smile at Boone's comment, glad that at least a part of him has remained true to his old self.

"We certainly don't need to have equal numbers, for that very reason, but we need more than we have," Navaa states. This is a fact to her, it's not even a question. "That is why I suggest that we suspend these talks so that Ryn can open a Rift using her Kir-Abisat gift. We know the gift bypasses technology. We've seen it on our Earth. If she gets the Akshaj delegation here, then we have a very good chance at succeeding."

Once again, all eyes fall to me. My mouth goes suddenly dry, and it feels like there's a hive of bees in my belly. So I'm not only supposed to be in command, but now I have to do the impossible and bring the Akshaji here?

"You know that I have never been able to open a complete Rift on my own before," I say cautiously.

"Perhaps you simply needed more motivation," Navaa hints. "I would say that our very survival would be adequate enough."

"Morning," I swivel around and look at the impeccably groomed SenMach, "you said you can't hack the blockade—does that mean ever? Or have you just not been able to *yet*?"

There is a ten-second lag as Morning's silver eyes focus on the tent wall. "There is a seventy-six percent chance that we will be able to infiltrate the sound blockade's codes in the next twelve hours. If after this time we are unable to do so, then we will need additional support from the special coding team back on our Earth."

"Those are pretty good odds," I say without trying to hide the relief from my voice. "We should wait it out."

"We absolutely should not!" Navaa argues. I hear a crunching sound, almost like footprints on hard snow. I realize it is her wings. They are no longer tucked discreetly behind her. They have risen above her shoulders. "They could attack us at any time. We are too vulnerable without the Akshaji. You must open a rift. Immediately."

To my credit, I do not balk. I don't look down or away. I keep my eyes focused on Navaa and I don't blink. Inside, I don't feel so tough. The fact that I got all these battle-hardened warriors—who are commanders in their own right—to sit down at my table and take orders from me is a miracle in and of itself. Will they be so keen to listen when my first act as leader is a failure? Possibly, but I'm in no hurry to test that theory.

"I hear you, Navaa," I tell her calmly, emphasizing the word *hear*. I promised that I would listen to her in exchange for her support, so I want to make sure she knows that I'm doing just that. "However, I've already been taken prisoner, been interrogated, fought for my life, and been chased over ten miles of difficult terrain *today*. Needless to say, I'm a little worn-out. Besides which, you know how taxing opening a Rift is." Navaa continues her cold, stern stare, but maybe this time *she's* listening to wisdom. "I have *never been able* to open a complete Rift. I certainly won't be able to do it in this condition. I promise, if the SenMachs can't break the code, I will try first thing tomorrow."

Something wordless passes between us and I pray that she uses that tactical brain of hers to see what I'm getting at. I'm basically betting the SenMachs' ability to code against my own Kir-Abisat gift—which has never quite worked. *Both* scenarios are a gamble, but I like the odds of the former much more than the latter.

"I understand your reluctance," Navaa says quickly and with less vehemence, which makes me think she is picking up on what I'm trying to say. "But, Ryn, we leave ourselves vulnerable without the Akshaji here. I know your Kir-Abisat ability is unpredictable—"

"It's not just unpredictable," I cut her off. "I haven't had enough time with it to actually make it work. It has to be a last resort. It just . . . has to be." I shake my head.

Navaa shakes her head vigorously. "We cannot win this without the Akshaji. It's that simple. What's to stop the altered Roones from attacking us right now? *Nothing.* Perhaps I'd feel more comfortable with your decision to wait if we didn't have a hundred fifty thousand enemy troops breathing down our collective necks."

"I don't think they will, though," Levi counters strongly. "Think about it, would you? Camp Bonneville is strategically advantageous. They have a fortified bunker, access to almost a thousand cameras and video feeds of the surrounding area. Seelye is gone. There's a power vacuum. But above all that, they have time. Compared to us, they have all the time in the world. They can Rift in with tens of thousands of more troops, and they think our ability to Rift is gone. They might have deployed all their Citadels, but for all we know, they could have been forging alliances on many other Earths. They could even have access to mercenaries. So why would they come here to us—to the Village—when the numbers they currently have aren't an assured victory? I'd say we have at least enough time for Ryn to rest and gather her strength if the SenMachs can't fix the QOINS."

Navaa taps a single finger on the table. I watch as a hundred expressions chase themselves around her face. Finally she sighs with resignation. "You make a compelling argument, Levi," Navaa says thoughtfully. "Very well, we will wait and use the time wisely to make sure our lieutenants are well briefed on the enemy and the terrain. They will in turn, obviously, pass this information down the ranks."

I breathe out an audible sigh of relief. "I do think that's smart," I tell Navaa gratefully. "Making sure all the lieutenants understand as much as they can not only about what they're up against, but about one another. We need them to start forming real bonds as soon as possible."

Navaa, in turn, gives me one of her famously serious no-nonsense looks as she says, "As long as I have your word, Ryn, that you will be ready to try and open a Rift tomorrow if it comes to it."

"You do," I say gravely. "Now, if there's anything else?" I look around the room. "No? Good. Then I'm going to get some rest. We reconvene at 0600 tomorrow.

"Thank you, and good luck."

CHAPTER 23

I remain standing at the head of the table and watch them all leave. I wonder for a moment if that was the right thing to do. Do leaders leave first? Instinctively, that feels wrong. I should be the last to go. The last one standing. It gets down to just me and Levi. I notice that Boone, Henry, and Vi didn't stick around. I suppose a line has been drawn. I've always been Beta Team leader, but this—this sets me too far apart.

"I have a place for us, an apartment in the New York neighborhood," he says as he gently puts an arm around me. "Let's go. Trust me, I get you're in charge, ma'am, but maybe for the next few hours, you let me take care of you?"

At first, I want to shove his arm off, to tell him that I don't need anyone to look after me. *I'm capable.* I'm capable of leading and fighting and sacrificing and more than capable of doing all of that alone.

Then I think, why should I have to?

And even more than that, the burden of leadership may leave me feeling isolated, but I couldn't have done any of this *alone*. Beta Team recruited the Citadels into the UFA. Navaa taught me about my Kir-Abisat gift and the strength of quiet, determined female leadership. The SenMachs, well, without them, we'd be thoroughly fucked, so this isn't a solo act. I might be the lead singer, but this is really a supergroup. I have to stop with the whole stoic thing.

"That sounds good," I say, resting my head on his shoulder for a brief moment. We walk out of the back flap of the tent and into the cold late afternoon. It will be dark soon. The smell of burning logs fills the air. There are people of all sorts everywhere. The Village is absolutely teeming with activity. There is a jovial mood from the restaurants and open windows we pass and an electric energy in the air that I can almost taste. I wonder about all the things that will happen, because regardless of the outcome, everything will change after tonight. The uncertainty is like the pulse of a thumping bass line, pushing everyone forward, shaking everything loose. The commander in me wants them all to get back to their bunks, to eat a sensible dinner and get an early night. The very human teenage girl inside of me knows that tonight is one of magic, of uncovered secrets, of naked bodies, booze, and singing songs so loud you think your throat might collapse. It is a night for dancing and breaking promises. It is for holding on to something, anything, and for letting go, too. War turns us into our truest selves, the parts of us we hide, the monsters we secretly think we are. We let them loose because there is no point in shame or wishing we were someone else. Our shadow selves pick away at the pretense of civility. We are about to do horrible things. We want to; otherwise, horrible things will be done to us.

We turn the corner and walk into the New York neighborhood and suddenly we are transported thousands of miles east. Brownstones and stoops and variegated rust-colored bricks. There is no distinguishing this place from the real streets of the West Village, except of course for the soldiers and the guns. There are no other species here, so I have to surmise that New York belongs to the humans. I still don't love this idea of segregation, though I understand it in respect to the Akshaji. I squeeze Levi's hand a little harder.

He takes me into a large brownstone. It's twice as wide as the one that used to be Ezra's building—or still is his building. Maybe he moved back to his old place when he got here. Ezra ducked out almost immediately after the briefing. I should have said something, but he's been keeping his distance. I don't think I can go through with tomorrow without talking to him first. I need him to know how grateful I am—that just by being the person that he was, it was enough to shake me out of ARC's dream. But maybe it doesn't matter. Maybe we've said everything we need to say.

We walk up four flights of stairs to the very top floor. "They gave us a pretty sweet apartment," Levi says as he unlocks an unusually large wooden door. "I think there is a kind of class system here in the Village. Like, I knew a person could get credits, what they use for money here, for doing extra stuff, but what in the hell would they do to afford a place like this?"

The lights turn on as soon as we enter the apartment. The ceilings are two stories high. "Wow," I say, "maybe we should have given this place to the Faida."

"No way. They went all out; they did this for you."

"Huh" is all I can manage. I don't know if I deserve the sumptuous velvet vermillion sofa or the rich leather armchairs or the bookcase, which is at least twelve feet high and stuffed with books, but I'm not about to argue. "Wait, who's they? Gomda?"

"No," Levi says as he leans against a large marble countertop. Even the kitchen is luxe. "It was Zaka. He told me today. Everything in this place was made here, in the Village by the Immigrants. They wanted you to see who they were, what they could do."

I look down at one of the amazingly intricate handwoven rugs. "They didn't have to do that." I sigh out the words.

"No one forced them. They're proud. You should say something tomorrow."

"It doesn't feel like pride," I say as I walk forward, trailing my hand along the one wall of exposed brick. "It feels like they're trying to impress me. Like, somehow, they need to prove that they're worthy or something, for us to liberate them. Which is ass-backward, because I need to be worthy of them."

Levi walks over to me and takes both my hands. "You are," he whispers. "What do you want to do? Eat? They left food. We could go over those contingency plans we have for the bunker?"

"Well, first I'd like to soak my hands in bleach to get the Seelye cooties off and then I would like to get into the bath . . . with you."

"I'm not mad at that idea," Levi tells me with a smirk. "I'll go upstairs and run the water. Check under the sink, maybe you'll find something you can use for your hands." Levi disappears up two flights of stairs that look like they're floating up the brick wall. I walk into the kitchen area and find some sort of cleaning product that I spray judiciously under my nails. I wash my hands and notice there's an electronic pad propped up on the counter. It looks like it controls the basic functions of the house, including a sound system. I don't have my computer on me, but I know it's here. "Doe, you there?" I ask my cuff.

"I am," he answers immediately.

"Cool. Connect your system to the one at my current location. When you do, play mix fifteen and make sure I'm not disturbed unless it's an emergency."

"All right," he responds. I look briefly at the wall in front of me; it's made up entirely of windows except for a sliding door that leads to a patio. The light is almost entirely gone and the sounds of the Village, music and laughter, screeching and singing drift upward. They are right there if I listen. I don't want to listen, though. Just for a little while, an hour even, I want a reprieve. I want to be on that deserted island again with Levi. I want us to be the only two people in the world.

This could be it for him and me. So far, our lives have been short but extraordinary, and tomorrow the bill might be due for such a life. If this is it, if this is all the time Levi and I have left, I want us to spend part of it loving instead of hating. I want us to create joy and life and light because tomorrow there is only darkness and blood and the stench of fear and burning things. Levi, for all his strength and power, is a broken boy. In so many ways. I don't imagine that sex will fix him. But perhaps it will allow him—this kid who's spent the majority of his life fighting, not just as a Citadel, but well before then, through a childhood that was both unhappy and unfair—to surrender. He deserves a night of letting go, of losing himself to one extraordinary and glorious moment. And I can give that to him. I can make at least one thing totally and completely right.

Besides . . .

I want him.

I don't know in what way exactly beyond tonight, but I do. I want him.

A few seconds later, my playlist starts up. It's a sultry one, the kind of music you only do one thing to—and it isn't dancing. I walk up the steps and find the bathroom is at the far end of the hall. The lights are appropriately dim and Levi is sitting on the edge of a glorious tub that is placed right in front of the window. It's kind of a weird setup. The toilet is behind a door but everything else is right out in the open. The bathroom is actually inside the bedroom. Or maybe it's the other way around.

Either way, convenient.

I duck inside and go pee quickly, knowing that the tub has to fill up. This place is crazy; the toilet has a warmer on the seat. As if this situation wasn't surreal enough, I feel like I'm in some sort of bizarre play where I'm not a soldier at all, but a supercool Manhattan socialite who's just come back from a red carpet event instead of a war room.

When I'm done, I walk toward Levi with the zipper of my uniform mostly undone. I go to zip it down again and Levi stops me. He stands and pulls me closer to him so that he can gently ease the metal teeth apart. After that, he peels the rest of my uniform off me. Now I'm just in a sports bra and underwear. I go to take those off, but Levi once again takes over. He whips the bra over my head and slides my panties down with both hands skimming my hips.

We are inches apart and I think he's going to kiss me, but instead, he just looks at me. Ten seconds ago, I could have named a thousand things that were wrong with my body, but the way he's just staring at me, I feel perfect. I reach for the zipper on his uniform, but he takes a step back and shakes his head. He undresses himself quickly. God, he's gorgeous. Every muscle is defined, he's solid, and yet there is an easiness to the way he moves, a kind of grace that comes when a person knows the exact limits of their own body.

He steps into the tub, which doesn't have bubbles, but the water is a milky blue, so he must have put something in it. Once he settles, he holds out his hand to help me climb in.

I sit down between his legs with my back to him. The water is the perfect temperature and I can feel some of the tension I've been holding start to release. I really have no idea what he's going to do. He has never had sex, so I'm half expecting him to maneuver me so that he can just slide himself in, which would be weird, but considering that we've had weeks of foreplay, not *that* crazy. Still, I am surprised with what he does next.

I feel a washcloth on my back.

I don't even know where it came from. Levi gently begins to circle my flesh. He lifts up my arms and washes each one, sliding the cloth down my ribs. There is such a tenderness in every stroke, I almost want to cry. I didn't even know that I needed this, but he did. He said he was going to take care of me and he is. He washes my thighs. He spreads them open just a little to get between them to wash there, too. He doesn't linger on any particular spot. He's really just giving me a bath. I suppose it's a little strange. This doesn't feel very sexy. It doesn't feel paternal, either, because that would be awkward. I am delicate in this water. I suppose I used to be delicate at some point, but I haven't felt that way in years. Levi is treating me like something precious, like something that if not carefully handled will break. I don't understand this at first because, really, I don't understand all that much when it comes to relationships; and then I get it. No matter how strong and fierce I am, Levi is afraid for me. Underneath my uniform and without all the tech, I am flesh and bone, easily torn apart, vulnerable. So is he, of course, but I didn't have to watch him get his arm chopped off.

I like being pampered in this way. Levi's fingers are magic when he washes my hair under the running water. It's really . . . lovely. But now that I feel nurtured and cared for, I think I'm ready to feel something else. I turn to face him, bringing my knees closer to my chest. I reach in the water for the washcloth he dropped. I lift it up and pour some soap onto it. I lean forward to start washing him, sliding it down his chest and abs, but he rips it out of my hand.

"Uh-uh," he says with a barely contained smile. "If you do that, this will be over before it even begins and I'm nowhere near ready for it to be over."

"Okay," I tell him as I lift my hands up in the air. Little droplets of scented water fall from my fingertips. Levi washes his body and I drink him in with my eyes as he does. His flesh is turning pink from the heat of the water, and his hair looks dark brown when he gets it wet and slicks it back. I bite my bottom lip and suddenly we are like two magnets. We fly together, our mouths colliding into each other. Levi braces us with one hand on the edge of the tub and effortlessly lifts me up with him as he stands. I wrap my legs around his waist and my arms around his neck. We keep kissing, devouring each other.

He gets us out of the tub and walks into the bedroom area. I feel his hardness jutting against me, so close. We are both wet and little goose bumps form on the parts of my body that he isn't touching. He eases me back onto the bed. I expect for him to stay there, between my legs, but he doesn't.

"I have wanted to do this for such a long time," he practically moans.

"Yeah, but you have to come back up here," I giggle.

"Not that. I mean, yes, *that*, later, but I'm talking about this—"

Levi drops to his knees. My ass is right on the edge of the bed and I shimmy backward another inch. A million thoughts are flying through my brain. I know exactly what he wants to do and there is this little part of me that feels like it's too much, too close, too intimate. Thankfully, there is another, louder voice inside my head that's like . . . *yes please.*

Levi grabs at both my kneecaps with open palms and separates them slowly, like he's opening a letter he shouldn't be reading. He moves in closer and throws my thighs over the tops of his shoulders. He is hesitant at first. I think he must know what to do. In theory. But here I am, open, ready, and it must be totally different from watching or imagining it. He brings his mouth slowly to the center of me. And then, whatever hesitation he has is abandoned. He uses his finger to spread me open that much wider, to get to that particular sweet spot. His tongue flickers, darts in and out of his mouth, and my back arches.

I feel like I'm melting, like I'm all body. The pressure begins to build inside of me, like a rattling steam engine in need of release. I cry out in pleasure when Levi takes his other hand and slides two fingers inside of me. He's doing something else with his thumb and tongue together, circling. I stop trying to figure it out and just let myself go with it. I feel all the muscles in my body contract and grow taut. My eyes roll back underneath my lids and I see an explosion of color there, like a Rift roaring into life. Everything is incandescent—violets and shimmering greens. I pant and grunt and call out his name. When I come, I am actually shaking.

Levi slides up my torso and picks me up and throws me back farther on the bed. I have only done this one time before and I can tell already, this is much different. Last time was soft and gentle. Now, I'm burning. Despite Levi's heart-wrenching tenderness in the bath, he's well aware of what we are both capable of, what we both can stand. I have a feeling that he, like me, likes a little pain with the pleasure.

Levi gets on top of me and kisses me again. I can taste myself on his mouth; it's like burnt sugar and salt. I drag my nails down his abs until I get to where he is rock hard. I wrap my fingers around him and squeeze just a little. He feels enormous and hot and he must be desperate to get inside of me. Levi swats my hand away forcefully. I get it. A strong gust of wind and the guy might blow, which kind of prevents me from returning the favor he just gave me. He keeps rearing up to look at me, like he wants to make sure it's really me and that I'm here and that we are indeed about to do this. Levi drops down on his elbows. I spread my legs wider to accommodate his frame.

Even though I know he doesn't want me to touch him, I have to. He understands where he is supposed to go, but given that this is his first time, I don't want him to have to worry about doing this part himself. I take all of him in my hands and guide him quickly inside of me.

The first thrust is slow. The second goes deep and hard. I yelp. It's the perfect kind of pain. Levi groans; it is guttural, like an animal, and it makes me want to pull him that much farther into me. He licks his thumb and lightly presses it to that throbbing spot between my thighs. He gently starts to move it along with his own body. I bite down on the space between his neck and shoulder. In a few short seconds, I come again—shuddering and pulsing on the bed, which makes him stop.

"Oh God," he pants. "I just have to . . . no moving . . . give me a second." I do as he asks and dutifully freeze. Levi closes his glittering green eyes, clearly trying to focus on something else. I'm not sure why. He's a virgin. As far as I'm concerned, he's already impressed me . . . twice. It's always a competition with Levi, though. He wants to hold out and I will help him. Maybe. Not helping could be just as fun.

I wiggle myself away. Levi opens his eyes. I sit up and roll over. He may think he can last. He might even have a number in mind, but he won't last long like this. I rear up on all fours and back up. I can't see him, but I hear him exhale. He places one hand on my neck and uses the other to guide my hips down to just the right angle where he can enter me. We both moan loudly when he does. This position is new to both of us and it feels insanely good.

I grip the headboard and Levi puts both hands on my ass. He starts to move faster. Our skin slaps each time it connects. Levi grabs at both hips and squeezes hard, not too hard, but hard enough to make me grit my teeth. His speed increases and we move together in perfect rhythm. I can feel it building inside of him. His heart is racing and his grunting gets even more primal. Finally, his entire body tenses and then, he comes in one long guttural moan. I sigh loudly with pleasure as he collapses on top of me, kissing my spine when his face touches my back. I roll over and bring my lips to his.

"Yes, right?" I say playfully.

"So many fucking yeses," he tells me in a tone that is part

relief and partly pure joy. "Give me ten minutes. We're going to do that again."

AT SOME POINT, we make our way down to the kitchen and eat cold chicken naked. Then we have more sex. We eat some more and we go back upstairs and have sex again. We sleep. It is the deep and dreamless sleep of the exhausted. We curl into each other like two puppies. I don't know how long we get to sleep for, but it is the best rest I have had in a while. Which is a good thing because we are awakened predawn. Our phones ring. The cuffs start beeping frantically. There is banging at the door. I sensuit my way into a long T-shirt as I race down the steps.

"What?" I ask as I yank the door back so hard that the handle almost comes off. It's Henry.

"They're coming. They're attacking," he tells me in a rush. "We have to go, right now." It takes me a second. I shake my head, trying to fling the sleep away. A part of me thinks I must be dreaming. "Ryn! Come on!" Henry shouts.

I hear Levi's feet scramble down the steps. He already has his uniform back on and is zipping it up. He throws me mine and I step into it quickly, not caring that I'm stark naked now, in front of Henry. The thought is not lost on me that I'm about to go commando. Maybe this is where the saying comes from.

"How far out are they?" Levi asks in a rush. There's no point in asking why or admonishing ourselves for getting this wrong.

No, I admit to myself. *I* got it wrong. I took a risk last night and it was a bad call. Guilt won't help the situation, but that doesn't stop me from feeling it. I have to keep my eyes on the horizon, on what's coming for us.

"They're moving fast. We might have twenty minutes." Henry tells us as we practically fly out of the apartment, racing down the streets. A siren is wailing, like an old air raid warning. We run full out to the Command Center. The generals begin to file in but the place is already full, soldiers are staring at the monitors, checking in on various patrols and teams as they fall into place. Gomda is the first person to talk to me.

"Here," he says as he hands me a version of my utility belt. "Cosmos sent a few thousand of these. They work a bit like your sensuits." I hold up the strange glowing object, a mash-up of tools and pistols attached to a fabric of starlight. When I bring it close to my waist, it locks on to my torso, winding around me. The guns end up holstered on my thighs and everything else I usually carry molds perfectly around. It's a much less cumbersome way of carrying what I need and the sensuit fabric stops glittering and turns a dark matte black.

"Do you want your rifle as well?" he asks me.

"Eventually. Let me just get my bearings," I say a little tersely.

"There's no time for that." Navaa steps forward. "Ryn, we need the Akshaji. Whatever misgivings you might have, please put them aside. The SenMachs haven't broken through the sound blockade. You're the only one who can do this."

"I know," I tell her firmly. "I apologize, to everyone, for not doing this last night. I thought we had more time, but it seems our enemy is eager to face us at our current numbers." I address the room. "Look, this isn't ideal, but to be honest, I'd much rather face them here than at Camp Bonneville. Do we have an idea of how big their force is?"

"They only left a little over one percent of their troops behind. It appears they are about to hit us with everything they have," Morning informs me rationally.

"All right. I'm going to need some space. I can't open a Rift with all this noise. Too many of you come from different Earths and it's only going to make my job that much harder.

In the meantime, we need to position our troops around the Village. They'll be coming at us from all angles. Arif," I say as I pull out both my guns and check to make sure they are loaded and the safety is off before I slide them back into the holsters as smoothly as a well-worn key into a lock. "You need to get two squadrons in the air right now. We have the drones, but we'll need eyes on the weakest areas of the perimeter to shore them up as troops fall. The SenMach troops will remain here in the Village along with the Immigrants and human soldiers. The androids aren't able to engage with humans, so it only makes sense to keep them back. Iathan?" I bark. "You and the remaining Faida are going to take positions circling the Village. Do not go as far as the forest. Bring them to you where you can see them."

"It seems like the center of the Village—where your people will be—is the safest place. Are you saying that my soldiers are more expendable than yours?" he asks, his voice dripping with aggression.

"There is no mine and yours; we are a single army, and I'm not playing favorites. I'm playing the odds," I throw out. "They don't know about the SenMachs. Fuck. I don't even know what the SenMachs can do. But they are machines, coded specifically to protect human life. You are not human. I can't risk losing them all or the advantage of them being here in the first place because they won't kill the Citadels from this planet, regardless of whose side they're on. They certainly won't attack one to save a Faida or a Roone. And I understand that it's not fair, but it is what it is. They're machines. So don't get emotional."

"Fine, I will put my people in place." He does not seem fine, though. His narrow shoulders puff outward and I can tell his face is grimacing, even through his sleek long beard.

"Great," I say, moving swiftly along. "Henry, I'm going to need you and the rest of Beta Team to stay here for now, coordinating the ops. I know you want to get out there, but I need someone calling the plays the same way I would until I get back."

"Roger that," Henry says grimly. "But where are you going to go? Look at them, they're starting to break off already." I crane my neck around to a monitor. I see a swarm of red dots, like an angry welt of hives starting to spread apart, moving to surround the Village.

"I'm going to the north end of the perimeter, where the farmland is, here," I say, tapping my index finger on a green area of the monitor. "Levi and Navaa will stay at my side, but I'll need about a thousand troops within a couple hundred yards of the area, human ones that won't give off any noise. They'll be defending the area until I get the Akshaji here, holding off the enemy if necessary." I don't bother explaining that it more than likely will be necessary because it's not like I can just whistle up a Rift. This might take a while.

"Just make sure you stick to that specific acreage. It's an area that the Immigrants didn't have time to booby-trap. Stray too far from it, though, and you'll be in trouble. Go ahead and move out," Violet tells me, "the troops will be right behind you." I nod my thanks. I want to hug her. I want to hug them all, but there is no time. There is no time for friends or history. There is only right now and my duty to this cause. I notice Ezra working at a terminal. I smile broadly at him and he smiles back, giving me a little nod. He's telling me to go, not to worry. I begin to walk, and the other two join me. I wring out my sorrows. I push away my fears. I set aside my anxiety. There is no room for fear or guilt that I didn't listen to the advice of the others. I can feel only one thing, determination, for the mission. Besides, there's still a very good chance that I won't be able to open the Rift at all. If I can't, then the call to wait for the SenMachs was the right one. But of course, it will be a hollow victory. Without the Akshaji, we are fucked. I can't believe it, but I want to be wrong.

As I take to the early morning outside, on Main Street, my troops begin to follow behind me. The sky is purple. The winter's pale light will eventually take over, like an animal rolling on its back to expose its belly. There is no goose-stepping. The human faction of the UFA is moving too quickly, as I am, through the streets and the neighborhoods, the sound growing louder as new members join us. When I am told through my earpiece that we have the number I asked for, I start to run and they follow.

I don't mean that I jog. I *sprint*. My legs pump like two pistons and my lungs begin to burn. I hear the others behind me, though it's mostly their breath, a steady drag and pull of the early morning air. Their feet are moving too fast to make much noise. Eventually Navaa simply ascends into the sky, unable to run as fast as the rest of us. I am not thinking. I am just a collection of parts, an assembly of verbs. When we reach the open field, the rows and rows of harvested crops, now naked from the season, I stop short, on my toes to keep from falling on my face.

"We're going to need some breathing room here. Take a defensive formation a hundred yards in a circular position around us," Levi shouts. The troops fan out, and Navaa lands, the ground trembling slightly at our feet as she does. "Okay. This is as secure as it's going to get. Go ahead."

Navaa puts a single hand on my shoulder. "You can do this, Ryn," she tells me firmly. "I've felt you holding back on my

Earth, afraid of the Kir-Abisat, unwilling to accept this gift our enemies have given you."

"It's not a gift," I huff. "None of this is a gift. It's ridiculous. This whole thing." Navaa remains silent because she agrees. *It is* ridiculous. Tens of thousands of people have staked their freedom and their lives on the promises made by a teenage girl with a smart mouth and a robotic arm.

"It does not matter how we got here. Here we are. Close your eyes and find the song, Ryn. That's all that matters right now."

I exhale slowly. My breath leaves my lips in a frosty cloud. In my mind, I quickly assemble my memory palace—Opa Joseph's vinyl Lab in Stockholm.

He's a hippie, not a scientist, and he's still downright revolted by the digital revolution. He's been collecting records since he was twelve. He has thousands of stacks, alphabetized in categories that he keeps on lovingly handmade shelves in the basement of my grandparents' compact home. On a single leather chair, surrounded by speakers that at the time were as big as me, my opa introduced me to the Beatles and Portishead and Edith Piaf and Jeff Buckley.

In my mind's eye I see this room, the same blond oak shelves and the thin covers of each record. I smell the damp chill of the basement mixed with the pungent aroma of my opa's weed—a vice that he will never give up.

I pull out a record. It's Nine Inch Nails, *The Downward Spiral.* The jacket's artwork looks the same, a beige-and-ochre abstract painting with a black tear. Instead of the band's logo, the writing is in Akshaj. This is their tone, living on the grooves of an unblemished disk.

All the sounds I've ever heard are stored here, associated with different artists and shelved in different sections of the

Lab. I pull the album out of the sleeve and grip the sides of it lightly. I make my entire body go still. I block out every other noise around me, all the shuffling feet and the rapidly beating hearts and the birds trilling. I take the Akshaj record out and put it gently on the record player.

The imaginary act of setting the needle down is my own self opening up. It is careful work, getting the needle in the groove, just as it is preparing my body for opening a Rift. When the first rumble of a note from the Akshaj Earth begins to play, I latch on to it. I roll it around in my head. I let it ricochet off my skull and down into the rest of my body. When I'm sure I have it, I start to hum. The noise grows inside my cells. I let it build as my voice grows louder. I keep at it, sure that it must be working, but when I open my eyes, there is only the tiniest spark of emerald for my effort.

"Shit," I say out loud. "*Shit!*"

I look over to Navaa with panic in my eyes. "I don't know that I can do this here. I think there are too many people around and it's loud outside."

"Nonsense," she says dismissively. "We don't have time for this. You *must* do it, Ryn."

"I'm trying," I tell her through clenched teeth. I close my eyes and enter the space again. This time, I can't even find the record. I know the Citadels will be here any minute, and I feel the panic rising inside of me. I grab my short hair by the roots and let out a muffled scream. It's too much. I've never been able to fully open a Rift on my own and now I'm supposed to do it here? This is not going to work.

"I can't," I tell them both, my voice sharp with disappointment. "We should just get ready, we can take them. We don't need the Akshaji."

Navaa walks directly in front of me and grabs both my

clenched fists and holds them in her own hands. I'm about to lash out, but before I can, she says, softly, "The Faida were born to fly. Most of us flew before we walked. Still, I was terrified the first time I stood on a cliff's edge without my parents. I knew logically of course that I could soar, but I was also equally sure that, somehow, my wings wouldn't work, that I wouldn't be able to catch the air. To this day, I don't remember stepping off the edge. That's because I stopped thinking. I let my fear go, I let everything go."

"I'm not afraid!" I say quickly, defensively. "I *want* to open the Rift. Why would I be afraid of it?"

"I don't think your fear comes from failure. I think you're afraid of *succeeding*. I think you're afraid of what that means. I don't blame you for rejecting this—you know it's what the altered Roones want. You don't want to give them that." Navaa moves her hands to my shoulders and practically shakes me. "But like everything else they've given you, you must use the Kir-Abisat against them. This is not for them. It's for us. All of us. Don't be afraid of falling.

"*You will fly.*"

I know what Navaa is saying is only partially true. I am afraid, but I am also stubborn. I think a part of me has always felt that if I succeeded in this, then somehow the altered Roones have won. My failure would be theirs. Now I see how epically stupid that is. It would be the same as me standing in front of a Settiku Hesh and letting them gut me because I'd rather die than use the skills that ARC gave me. I would never do that and this is no different, not really.

Once again, I close my eyes. I touch my fingertips together and lay them on my chest so that they form a triangle. I go back to the basement, to my opa's Lab. I pull out the Nine Inch Nails record once more and gently set the needle down.

This time, though, I don't just listen to the noise. I remember what Navaa told me—what she's been trying to tell me all this time.

I become the noise.

I focus the song right in the center of me, where my fingers are open. As I begin to hum, I push the sound through them, through my chest. My entire body vibrates. I lose myself. I forget my name and who I am. I am simply a sound. My lids whip open and there is the green glow of the Rift five feet in front of me. I keep singing and I watch the neon mouth open like a lazy yawn. I keep at it, focusing my hum until it's bouncing off every molecule. It feels like it's both tearing me apart, and yet somehow pulling me together. I'm both wave and particle, and I'm equally excited and scared.

The color of the Rift changes from purple to black.

There's no time for relief or pride. The three of us leap into the Rift. The sound inside is different than when we've opened one with the QOINS. It is softer, a lulling, a sweet echo of song. This is not just *a* Rift. It's *my* Rift. It's me. It's like staring in a mirror inside of a mirror. It is the sound of my own voice inside my head. I understand the Kir-Abisat now. It's not just a way to unlock the Multiverse, it's a way to *become* the Multiverse. I feel its power thrum inside of me. I understand something on such a fundamental level that there are no words to describe it. There are no words because it's a secret that's never meant to be spoken, only felt, only ridden on, like a board inside the funnel of a wave.

I used to think the altered Roones were geniuses. Now, I know they are fools. They thought they could control this, control us. But that's impossible. They can't have this. This is as much mine as my own skin. I belong to the Multiverse in a way they will never be able to. No matter what they do, they will only ever be in the audience. This is my stage, my song, my poem, my film. They could no more claim it than I could my father's portraits. I could say that I painted them, but anyone who knows my dad would know that he alone has that particular line, that way of mixing color and painting light.

I grin in smug satisfaction as I see the horizon ahead. No prison will ever be able to hold me. No chains can bind me. They will *never* be able to take me. I don't have to be afraid of them because even if they kill me, I will open a Rift with my dying breath and live forever inside the emerald waterfall of time and sound and space.

Unfortunately, my unbridled joy is short-lived because as soon as I step foot onto the Akshaj base, I see that it is empty. There is no sparring, no cajoling, no ruckus. There are only bare stretches of grass that's been worn thin and brown from trampling. Without even bothering to look at Levi and Navaa, I race up the steps of their templelike base. I throw open the doors, my heart lurching to my throat, because if the Akshaji are gone, the chances of us defeating our enemies may well be gone, too.

I never, ever thought I would be happy to see a person I so despise, but I exhale a deep, worrisome breath when I see him sitting there on his throne-like chair. He has a single leg dangled over one of the armrests and he is reading an electronic tablet. A handful of soldiers are standing sentry and just two or three servants scurrying about. To my great relief, no one is naked, but to be honest, I'd rather see a hundred scantily clad Akshaji than this near empty room.

The man in charge looks at me curiously when I clamber in with my companions. After the cacophony inside my Rift, this room is achingly quiet.

"Sairjidahl Varesh," I say, realizing that I am not only out of breath, but a little light-headed. From the corner of my eye, I see Levi look at me and then I see him reach around his back, presumably for his slim pack.

"Well," Varesh purrs. "If it isn't my favorite human."

"What happened?" I ask in a rush. Levi grabs my hand and shoves some of the SenMachs food cubes in them. "Stop," I hiss at him.

"You look like you're about to faint, Ryn. You need to eat and drink," he orders me sternly.

"I too *was* going to say that you looked especially cloud faced, but I didn't want to be rude," Varesh chimes in. I purse my lips in frustration, but then I realize that I can't afford to be off my game, not now. I shove the gel cubes in my mouth and take a long pull from the water bottle.

"Thank you," I say, maybe a little gruffly to Levi. In my defense, it's hard to act like a capable lady in charge when someone is trying to feed you. "Now, what is going on? Where is everyone?"

Varesh folds two of his arms. The other four pick off imaginary fluff from his uniform. "Why?" he asks while raising a single eyebrow. "What reason could I possibly have for not living up to my end of the bargain?"

Certain death, an arm is hardly worth thousands of lives, maybe you've been in league with the altered Roones this whole time . . .

"No reason. We had a deal. The enemy has attacked so I don't have time for whatever *this* is."

Varesh says nothing for a full ten seconds. Finally, he cocks his neck to one side and gives me a predatory smile. My fingers flex instinctively. I don't know what in the hell is going on, but I do know that the three of us can dispatch the people in this room. Now that the SenMach food has done its work, I'm ready to go.

The Sairjidahl stands slowly and walks toward me. I shift my weight to my back foot, ready to pounce. But instead of getting aggressive, he lays three hands gently up and down my back. The skin beneath my uniform bristles at his touch. "Walk with me," he says softly. This cooing, attentive version of Varesh is scarier than the manipulative, dictator one. I want to scream at him. I want to yell that there is no time for any of this, but just in case he's not a complete bastard and is following through on his word, I have to play nice.

We move toward the very end of the great hall, and by that, I mean great. It must be half the length of a football field if not more. Varesh guides me up four flights of stairs and then through layers of jewel-colored silks that serve as a sort of screen door. Once we are through, I see that we are outside, on a massive veranda. And that's not all I see.

"Your enemy is my enemy," Varesh whispers seductively in my ear. "I promised you an army, Citadel Ryn Whittaker, and there it is."

I look out and there, to my unabashed relief, are his soldiers. They are about half a kilometer away, along with the massive green tower of their Rift. It's the only area that would be big enough to stage so many men and women. I pull my binoculars off my utility belt to have a better view and what I see is an amethyst ocean peppered with gold and silver. They are drilling, sparring, and sharpening weapons. There are also rows and rows of white tents that look like sails upon this sea.

"And they're ready to go right now? You won't need shelter. We have actual lodgings for your people."

"They are ready. I began to pull them from our Rift sites as soon as we met on your Earth. I can only imagine what you think of me," he says honestly as he looks out to his people. He leans against the stone balcony with four hands. "But I am no betrayer. The things I have done, that all of us have done under the banner of the Roones, have left me with little else to offer but my sword and my word. You have both."

"Well, I'm glad to hear that," I tell him, not bothering to hide the edge to my voice. It's all very well and good for him to play nice, but my SenMach arm is a not-so-subtle reminder that while Varesh might be a man of his word, he's also cruel. This, too, I will use to our advantage. "Look at this patch," I say pointing to the new artwork we're all sporting. "Your people need to see this before we leave. They can't kill anyone wearing this symbol. If there's time, there are patches for all of you, too."

Varesh studies the wings and fists velcroed to my chest. "I see that we are included in your coat of arms."

"Of course you are." I look him straight in the face and hold out my hand for him to shake. "Welcome to the United Free Army."

CHAPTER 24

It's one thing to open a Rift for three people, it's another thing entirely to open one for over twenty thousand. Luckily, I don't have to do this alone. I am not the only one with the Kir-Abisat gift here. The other races still need a conduit—a human in this case to get them to my Earth. There's Navaa, of course, and 433 Akshaji with the same ability. No kind of tech is a match against the Kir-Abisat, regardless of conduits, though, thank God. When we begin, the sound is incredible. It is a symphony of tones. It makes my teeth rattle and my veins thrum. The Rift we open is a fucking monster—a Day-Glo kraken with emerald tentacles ready to consume us all. When the Rift turns to a shimmering onyx, it is time to go.

Being inside a Rift with thousands of other people is what I imagine a drug-fueled outdoor concert would be like. A roaring, thumping sea of arms and legs and bodies all moving together in ecstatic unison. I say I imagine because I've never been to a festival like this due to my job and also because I hate annoying people on drugs.

When I see the bright white slit of light indicating the end of the tunnel, I shift my body. I'm not sure what to expect on the other side. I put both hands on my guns and use the kick of the barometric pressure to give me a boost. I fly out of the Rift, spinning sideways in midair and landing safely in a squat—just in time for a Settiku Hesh to take a swipe at me. I leap up and back, vaulting in the sky. Before I land, I manage to shoot a Spiradael squarely between the eyes.

The Citadels are everywhere and I need to get back to the Command Center so I can see where we are at and, more importantly, where I can shore up our defenses with our new reserves.

"Doe!" I scream, because I can barely hear my own voice above the screams and weapons fire. "Patch in the Akshaj comm units to central Command. Tell the team I'm on my way down there and that we have our reserves."

I wait a beat or two for Doe to get this done and then I say, "Varesh, follow me. I don't know how your command structure works, but leave a squadron or unit or whatever behind here to pick up the slack, the rest of you can follow me into town."

"Acceptable" is all he replies. Okay then.

Levi, Navaa, Varesh, and I make a run for the populated part of the Village. There's a significant part of me, the down-and-dirty soldier, that aches to stay behind in the fray, but as the leader here, I need to get back to headquarters, at least for now. It's imperative that I get a clear picture of the attack and work out a way to get the upper hand.

I take off at full speed with Levi and Varesh's troops behind me. Navaa shoots into the sky. There are literally thousands of troops in battle. When I can, I take out an Orsaline or a Settiku Hesh. With the human Citadels, I am more cautious. When a particularly frenzied one makes a run for me, I duck his punch and step on his thigh, throwing my body over his head, taking him down with me by the neck. I put him in a chokehold until he passes out. Some of the human Citadels, most probably, can be saved if given time and deprogramming. The others are past redemption and will have to be executed.

But that's something I hope we can figure out later.

We leave an exponential number of Akshaji in our wake as we go. I watch them fight with a precision and grace that is almost distracting. They are gorgeous and spellbinding. It's no wonder to me at all why the altered Roones would have chosen them. They already look like gods, even without genetic enhancement.

When I finally get to Main Street, I am jolted by an explosion. A residential housing block has been blown. Henry tells me through my earpiece it's the local resistance movement. I knew they had booby-trapped certain areas, but if some of them want to live here afterward, they can't just go around blowing up buildings. Even though I am the leader here, this is their Village. I have to hope they know which targets are acceptable collateral damage.

Before I can get to Sugar Skull, I feel a sharp tightening around my shin. Then I'm yanked backward. It's a Spiradael. More specifically, one's razor hair braid. I land on the pavement with a thud, my teeth cutting into my bottom lip. I whip around to look at him and see he's got a gun in his hand. He gets a shot off, but I'm already on my feet.

"Doe, I need protection for my hands!" I order and immediately the sensuit unfolds up my body. I dodge another bullet by shifting sideways. This gives me enough time for the tech to do its thing. Both hands are covered in a chain-mail-like material all the way up to my neck and down to my bra line.

I grab the braid with both hands and leap. The Spiradael is still shooting but I'm moving too fast for him to lock on. When I get close enough, I turn around so that the wrapped hair is in both hands behind my right shoulder. I give a strong yank and I hear a sickening crack and what sounds like a bunch of wet towels being lifted off a sopping floor. I have actually taken his entire head from his shoulders. I catch Varesh's eye as he's plunging three swords into the heart of an Orsaline. I'm not sure how he got through the uniform. That is definitely a worrisome detail for later. He gives me a nod of approval, which I surprise myself by enjoying for a minute. He is not a guy I should be trying to impress.

I take just a few seconds to watch the SenMach troops at work. While they don't have our speed, they certainly have our strength. Unsurprisingly, they fight without effort, punching and parrying as if they were casually swatting away flies. They don't have the grace of the Akshaji, but there is a fluidity to the way they fight that is mesmerizing. No time for that, either, and I keep moving.

The block surrounding the Command Center is mercifully clear. Wisely, they've put on a lot of guards to keep the area safe. With Varesh's people, this eye in the hurricane should last a while. I walk into the restaurant and see my team conferring with other UFA members as they give commands. I am happy to see that it's not just humans doing tactical. The Faida, Roones, and Karekins are all watching monitors and giving orders.

"Everyone!" I say loudly to the room. "Some of you have already met him, but for those of you who haven't, this is

Sairjidahl Varesh of the Akshaji. He's added his own twenty thousand troops to the cause, so I'd say that puts us in a much better position." An explosive cheer erupts from the room.

Well, slap my ass and call me Diana. I feel like Wonder Woman.

Probably shouldn't be thinking that way. This is serious. I wipe the little grin off my face. "Henry, where are we at?"

"We're holding them off, but there's just so many of them."

"Where's most of the fighting happening, though?" I ask as I look at a giant screen that seems to be aggregating troop numbers and conflicts. I'm assuming this is the work of the drones and Morning's skill set.

"It's still mostly in outlying areas. About eight thousand have breached inside the town itself. We're handling it, but taking casualties," Boone says.

"I assume Yessenia is in the gym facility, overseeing triage?" I ask, still looking at the large map of the town and the pulsing red dots that shift and grow every second.

"She and Feather, along with a Roone healer, are in command there. I'm trying to make sure that we save as many enemy human Citadels as we can, but in these conditions, it's really hard," Vi tells me sadly.

I put a hand on her shoulder and give it a good squeeze. "It's fine. I know everyone is doing what they can." After getting a grasp of the holes in security, I make a decision. "Okay, let's send an additional ten thousand Akshaj troops here," I say, pointing to the far northwest of the town. "Varesh, you are welcome to stay here, or you can take point on that if you want."

"Always, I prefer to fight," he tells me with a sparkle in his eye. He is waiting for my orders, for me to tell him where to put his troops. I never thought we would get here, but here we are. Together. I can't stand the sight of him, but I am glad that he's on our side. More than glad. Relieved. War makes hypocrites of us all one way or another.

"Okay, it looks like we are most vulnerable in this section." I point again at a small area west of Main Street. "And here," I say, laying a single finger at the area of the Village where the habs are. "The Immigrants inside those habs haven't chosen a side, but they deserve our protection, so let's send fifteen thousand integrated troops out there, to defend that position and . . . wait." The enemies' dots start to move rapidly. They had been in an imperfect circle around the entire Village enclosure. Now they are on the move. It looks like sand falling around a marble.

"What are they doing?" Iathan asks, as if he's personally insulted that they've changed tactics.

"How have Zaka's efforts been going?" I ask no one in particular.

"They are surprisingly very effective," Henry says, clearly impressed. "They mined two massive acres of farmland, here and here." I look and wince a little when I realize just how close we were to those mines when we opened the Akshaj Rift. "They set up nets and falling tree trunks with spikes and shit in the forest. They are good."

"Do we have an estimate in terms of casualties on the other side?" I wonder.

"Eighteen thousand six hundred fifty-five," Morning tells me with her usual precision. "That number is far less in our faction. Our casualties have been minimal." I nod my head and drag the breath into my lungs. Our injuries and fatalities are lower only because we are being more cautious. The combined ARC and Citadel forces don't care about their losses.

They'll just throw as many armed soldiers at us as they can until they wear us down.

"Right, okay," I begin thoughtfully, "so they have no idea how many we are and every time they tried to flank us, they got blown up or spiked or whatever. They were testing us with acceptable losses. But now they moved . . . see? From the way they are positioning themselves it looks like they're about to double down with a full frontal assault. They're gonna blow through the front gate."

"If it was just bodies, I'd say we had a decent shot, but they've got Settiku Hesh tanks, ten of them. We don't have any MANPADs," Henry cuts in quickly.

"What is a MANPAD? I don't know this word," Iathan remarks grimly. Because I speak all of the languages of the Citadels now, I hadn't realized how much most everyone in the room is dependent upon the SenMach translating program. Still, there are some words that can't be translated.

"It's an acronym for man-portable air defense—a shoulder-held rocket launcher," I explain.

"The UFA members were able to get a lot of weapons out of their respective armories before they Rifted out, but there wasn't time to grab anything with that kind of firepower," Henry says almost apologetically. "Besides, we don't really use that kind of stuff. We've never needed it before now."

"Can't worry about it now. So here's what we're going to do. I want our best snipers on every window, on every rooftop on Main Street. If this is how they're attacking, they're going to have to basically roll through town," I order, still thinking as I'm talking. I'm trying to wrap my head around the sheer numbers involved. "Navaa, your people are our best chance at taking out those tanks. Assign a squadron to every vehicle.

You're going to have to overwhelm each one with numbers. It's dangerous, but we can't have all those tanks in play."

"I'll get that going," Arif says as he walks away, immediately on his earpiece directing his troops.

"We'll evacuate the buildings and snipers based on how many armored vehicles get through. Boone," I say, and he immediately takes a step forward. "I'm going to need you and Vi to stay on that in here, maneuvering troops from Command in real time, based on their firepower. Varesh, Iathan, Morning—your soldiers, along with ours, are the infantry. It's basically going to be a brawl in the streets."

"I like this plan," Varesh says smoothly. "We should be fighting hand to hand. That way I will know our enemies are truly dead." There is a moment of terse silence. I think we all like a good fight as much as the next guy, but we're talking almost two hundred thousand troops in a very small area. We not only need to win, but we need to keep the Immigrants safe, too. Speaking of Immigrants—

"Where is Zaka?" I ask, looking around.

"He's gathering up all the resistance fighters from the Village. He's tasked me with being his envoy in here," Glenys says without hesitation. Now that she's had a taste of what war really looks like, her trepidation is gone. Although the puffiness under eyes suggests a decided lack of sleep, she seems much more confident. She even *looks* taller.

"Good, tell him to position his people behind us on the front line. Look," I say as I drag a hand through my short hair, still unused to its cropped length. "I know a lot of you still want me to stay behind here at Command. And maybe if they were coming at us from all angles, I might have reconsidered my position. But there is no real tactical play here. We just have to let them run through us and take them down as they do. The troops need to see me out there."

"I agree with you, Ryn," Navaa says thoughtfully as she glares at the monitors. "Your presence in theater will galvanize the troops and make the other humans wonder about your determination. The remaining Citadels under ARC's command will only have to look at you to understand that there must be some sort of basic truth that they are missing."

I can't help but snort a little at that prediction. "That would be nice," I say hopefully. "But we can't count on that, so let's move, people, and stay on the comms," I tell everyone. The different parties scramble and I finally get a glimpse of Ezra in the fray. He is working with a SenMach, presumably on the sound blockade problem. Our eyes clap on to each other. I had wanted to say something to him, but now I have no idea what that something might be. I will always love this boy, this brave soul who taught me that training and super soldiering has very little to do with where real strength comes from. Real strength comes from the exact opposite, from knowing the odds are stacked against you, but you raise your hand anyway and step forward. Ezra smiles and gives me a slow nod. We don't need to say anything to each other. We know.

When I walk outside, the sheer volume of people is overwhelming. We are thirty deep and a quarter of a mile long, zagging around buildings and statues and even some apartment buildings. I take my place in the middle of the street, front of the pack. When they come, I will be the first thing they see.

Before it even gets that far, there is a barrage of pulses and screams. The Faida are doing their job from the sky, taking out the tanks. The tanks don't use bullets, they use lasers. So, from

this distance, it sounds like I'm listening to *Star Wars* from another room.

"We have secured three vehicles," an unknown voice says in
my ear.

"Affirmative," I respond. "Commandeer them. Start firing
on the enemy and the other tanks," I order. There are more
whooshing screeches as the lasers slice through the air in stac-
cato bursts. There's an explosion and smoke drifts from the
south. So. It's not only lasers then, but missiles as well. I have
to assume that the only reason they haven't relied on a blitz is
that missiles are messy and concussive for both sides. Lasers
are far more precise. Besides, I'm thinking a Faida might just
be fast enough to catch one and throw it back at them. I bet
they don't want to test that theory.

"We've overtaken two more," a voice says through the earpiece. "That's five. We have half."

"Keep at it. Keep taking them out and use these things
against them." I try not to wince every time I hear the booming flash of an explosion. The entrance to the Village is still
too far from me to see, and even if it wasn't almost a mile
away, it's on a decline, curving down from our position.

I put my hands on the guns strapped to my legs. The
screaming is louder now, and then there are shots, silencing
the moans.

"We took possession of a sixth vehicle, but the remaining
four are headed your way. They'll be in visual range momen-
tarily."

"Good job, we'll take over from here," I say as I look to the
horizon. "Take your wounded to Triage and meet us back here
on the line."

The thunder and rumble of the tanks invade the air a minute or so before we actually see them. I crack my neck and roll

my wrists, limbering up my body for what's coming next. We have about five seconds before they start firing. "Vi," I say in my earpiece. "Send out two teams of Gammas, Ros, Kappas, and Omegas to deal with those tanks. They cannot be allowed to get any closer. We're too packed together. They'll just pick us off. I imagine, since I'm still hearing weapons fire, that the Faida in the tanks are doing a fair bit of damage to the Citadels?"

"We managed to take out thousands of the enemy in this capacity," Morning breaks in. "Many of them human." This is the first time I've heard any kind of emotion in her voice.

"I don't like this any more than you do, Morning, but we can't expect our allies to risk their own lives being gentle with the human Citadels. We'll do what we can on our end," I tell her briskly.

Finally, the tanks come into view, and in a flash, each team Vi assigned to take out the vehicles sets upon them furiously. I want to keep watching, hoping they'll do their job, but I just have to trust them, because the enemy that outran the fire from the commandeered tanks are yards away. They charge at us all and I run to meet them. My legs pump with increasing speed and I leap in the air with one arm held out. I manage to get a young Citadel down by cutting her off at the neck. Before she can get up, I give her a massive wallop on the skull. She's not dead, but she's incapacitated.

Before I can turn around I feel a great pressure around my entire body. One of the Orsalines has me in his grip. I inch toward my gun, hoping he won't break my ribs before I get there. I pull out a pistol and place it solidly behind me, beneath his chin, moving my head away as I pull the trigger. I fall out of its embrace . . . and I just stop for a second.

I have never in my life seen anything like this. The sound

is deafening. I knew of course that war was loud, but not like this. It's not just the metal clang of bullets firing out of chambers or lasers whizzing in the air, but the grunting and breathing and screaming from both sides. The ripping of limbs, of skin slicing open and blood dripping. I cannot believe we are killing one another. I can't believe that they made us do this.

But I don't have time to ponder the insanity of this because another Orsaline comes at me, his claws digging into my uniform as his open jaw and pointed teeth lunge for my carotid. Then I see his head chopped cleanly off. I turn and look. It's Varesh, who gives me a slight bow and continues on his campaign. I suppose this makes us even. Sort of.

No. Not ever.

I use the dead carcass of the Orsaline for cover. I place it in front of me to act as a shield and begin to fire my gun. I shoot one more Orsaline in the head, and then another. In rapid succession I take out three Spiradaels and four Settiku Hesh. I drop the body so I can reload. I barely have time to get a clip in when another human Citadel jumps down and gets me in the jaw with his elbow. I wish I had time to explain that we aren't the enemy. That he needs to stop and that nothing is what it seems. But he's lost to the fight. I doubt he'd listen, anyway, regardless of the brainwashing and the drugs. The best I can do is empty my entire clip into his chest. This won't kill him because of the uniform, but it does slow him down long enough for me to put him in a sleeper hold.

I reach into my belt for another clip, but before I can reload, I hear something that makes more than a few of us stop in our tracks. It's hoofbeats on the pavement. I narrow my eyes and look behind me. Zaka and twenty of his resistance fighters.

Riding.

Unicorns.

This is everything my fantasy-loving, Chronicles of Narnia–reading girlhood self could ever ask for and it's absolutely bananas and glorious. As if the sight of that wasn't surreal enough, at least fifty large catlike animals, something between a jaguar and lynx, dart through the line past me and immediately start to maul the enemy. "Zaka?" I ask in confusion. "This is beyond amazing but *what* is going on?!"

"A surprise. You know I work in the Menagerie, yes? Well, I've been training these beasts since they were kittens. They are much smarter than the large cats you have on your Earth. I've trained them to avoid the humans—well, retrained. I must admit that wasn't always the case. We didn't know you would eventually be on our side."

Zaka rides on past me with guns in both hands, shooting Citadels and the ARC soldiers cleanly in the head. And if all that didn't completely blow my mind, the next thing I see makes me actually squeal. There is a screeching bellow from the skies. The Faida are swarming, acting as snipers, but now, there is something else flying with them. Massive birds, with wings outstretched at least six feet. They sort of look like pterodactyls, but they are orange, with red necks and yellow spots. "And the birds?" I shout with wonder.

"Bycheters," he manages to yell back to me, though it's obvious he's distracted. What was once a war between genetically enhanced super soldiers has turned into a circus spectacle. I'd love to be able to watch this *Animal Kingdom* vs. *Aliens* thing, but a smart smack to the face with the back end of a Spiradael braid brings my focus once again to the task at hand. A Settiku Hesh has me in his sights. I squat and leap up, a single foot landing on his face. I keep stomping and stomping, grinding my heel into what's left of his nose until I'm sure he's dead.

The onslaught is unrelenting. No matter how many I take

down, it seems like there are ten more to take his or her place. I can feel my body weaken. I don't know how much longer any of us can take this. It's not the physicality of the killing that is beginning to exact its toll, but the sheer volume. The body count is relentless. It is the gentle tapping of a nail on a thin plaster wall. Soon, it will pass all the way through and the wall will crack in spider veins and I will never be smooth again.

And then, as if in slow motion, something else happens. I hadn't been paying attention to the tanks. I had assumed we gained control of them, but I see one has moved past us, up the street, and is aiming directly at Sugar Skull.

"Vi," I scream. "You have incoming. Get out of there!" I yell, but my words sound like they have been swallowed up by a crashing wave. I was sure I yelled a warning, but time seems to have been ripped apart as if everything that's happening has already happened and now I'm living inside a memory, unable to affect the outcome.

The tank fires two missiles in rapid succession. The boom from the weapon echoes in the chaos, bouncing off the walls of the buildings and the mass of soldiers themselves. I watch the smoke billow from the launcher on the hatch. I see the sleek gray balloon of the projectile fire into the restaurant. In my periphery, a human Citadel tries to take aim, but I dodge and shoot her squarely between the eyes. So much for saving our own.

I watch as members of the UFA start to overwhelm the tank, ripping the metal conveyor-belt-like wheels apart and shooting the gunner.

I practically fly back toward the Command Center, stepping on dead bodies, even leaping on an Akshaj's shoulders so that I can get a higher position to make a cleaner jump, but it's too late. The missile enters a window and in two or three agonizing seconds before I can get there, the entire place explodes. I wasn't thinking. I'm too close.

"Shield, Doe!" I yell, though I'm not sure what exactly that will do. The thin metal gloves and breastplate that I had practically forgotten I had been wearing slide forward in a nanosecond and form a rigid plank of silver big enough to protect me from the brunt of the blast. Glass flies all around me and the energy from the explosion itself pushes me entirely backward at least a foot. My ears ring from the proximity of the blast, and everything sounds like my head's been shoved underwater.

The whole thing must have lasted five seconds, maybe six, but because time skipped out of place and fell apart the moment the tank fired, it felt like both forever and also instantaneous.

"Vi!" I scream, though I can't really hear my own voice. "Boone!" A Faida runs past me, his wings ablaze. I step into the smoky shell of what was once our Command Center. A few charred beams are still standing, but everything else is a mass of bricks and melted plastic. There are burned bodies flung everywhere, presumably those who were right at the heart of the blast. I walk over the uneven debris, tripping once or twice on a body part or a piece of broken wood from a table. My eye catches what is left of a SenMach. One entire side of her has melted so that she is only half a silver skeleton. The other half has melted into a stew of wires and rods. Then I notice that she is on top of something, a hand. I wade through the rubble and pick up the body and throw it behind me. And there, with just a few burns, is Ezra.

Shit.

I had thought he would have evacuated farther away once

the fighting started, but I should have known better. "Ezra!" I say loudly. There is blood pouring from a gash on his forehead and there are burns where his body was exposed after the SenMach's bio flesh burned off. I bend down and gently touch his face before reaching around to check his pulse. I moan with relief when I find one.

"Ezra, get up," I say, slapping his face lightly, just enough to wake him. His eyes blink open, but he's unable to focus.

"Ryn?" he asks hoarsely.

"Yeah, but you have to move. Right now, to the gym . . . the triage center. I can't take you there. I have to look for Boone and Violet," I say in a rush as I quickly check his head and neck for serious trauma. "You can move, right? Wiggle your toes and fingers."

He manages to open and close his hand a few times. "I think Ruth Bader Ginsburg just saved my life," he tells me groggily as I help him sit up.

"What?"

"I mean, not her. Obviously. But the robot her. She just jumped on top of me when you radioed in that the missile was coming. She didn't even think. She didn't even give me time to thank her or say anything."

Ezra sounds out of it. Or at least I think he does. My eardrums haven't quite recovered from the blast.

"The SenMachs—their job here is to protect humans. She was literally made to do that very thing. I'll make sure that Cosmos knows one of her own saved you." Ezra finally stands, though he is unsteady on his feet. He puts his hands out, palms down as if the air itself can steady him. "I need you to run, Ezra. You have—"

Ezra cuts me off before I can continue. "No," he says adamantly. "I'm staying here. I can help you look for Violet and Boone. I know you don't think I can do anything . . ."

I put a thumb over his lips and pat his face, wiping a drop of blood that is about to fall into his eye. "Shhhh," I say softly. I take both my hands and pull his forehead to mine for just a moment. "You're hurt and I have so much more to do. You have to be away from here. You have to be safe." I laugh a little to myself at the idea. "Or at least . . . safer. Please, I am not ordering you. I'm asking you. Just go. Please be one less thing that breaks my heart today." I think he must see it in my eyes, the desperation, how I'm white knuckling this whole thing. When he met me, I was just an ordinary super soldier girl. He's seen our misfit escape plan turn into a full-scale war that I'm commanding. But it wasn't that long ago that I was almost broken, that I wept at his feet and traced his boots because I couldn't touch him when I found out what they did to me.

"Okay," he says, taking my hands away. He pulls me close to him and then winces when he realizes that he actually is hurt and that his arm is burned. "Just watch your six." He smiles. "That's army talk. I learned how to talk army." I nod and push him gently away. I watch as he leaves through the open wall, and then I turn around to walk deeper into the restaurant to find my friends.

The smoke intensifies the farther in I get. I hear yelling, someone asking for help, and I know it's wrong, but since the voice is speaking Roonish, I keep walking. I just need to make sure my friends are okay. I keep yelling their names. I start coughing because the air deeper inside is so thick with smoke that it's making my eyes water.

"Ryn!"

It's Boone. I look up to the sky briefly in relief, though I don't know why. If God is real, he doesn't live here. Not in this place of acrid smoke and bodies wrenched apart.

"Where are you? Keep talking so I can get to you!" I tell him.

"Here! Over here!" he says frantically. I follow his voice, picking up pieces of foundation and wood, throwing them behind me as I go. Finally, I get to him. I see that he is on his knees in front of an odd-shaped sack. I bend down, my eyes watering. I wipe the tears away and I see that it is not a sack but a person.

Violet.

At first, I don't understand why she is lying there. Doesn't she know there's an actual war going on and we don't have time to let an injury keep us from doing our job? I squint my eyes to try and see better, what could be keeping her down? Then I realize that there is only half of her. From the waist down, Vi is gone.

This is okay. This is fine. The SenMachs gave me a new arm, they can give her new legs, a pelvis, it can be done . . .

"Get her up, Boone! Why are you just sitting there? The SenMachs can fix her. Carry her to Triage," I bellow.

"Ryn," he says, his voice breaking on my name. "She's gone. She died the second the missile hit. I was across the room. I . . ."

"Don't be fucking stupid, Boone. She can't be dead. It's Violet . . ." I wipe her long brown hair away from her face. The smoke must be clearing, escaping out of the hole where the roof used to be, because it's becoming easier to see. Her eyes are looking up and her mouth is open, almost in surprise. This is my best friend's face, but this is not my best friend. Everything that makes Violet Vi has disappeared, it has been wiped away. There is no compassion or tenderness in her eyes. There's no sweetness to her lips. And her hair, it's so messy. Violet's hair is pristine, either falling with the precision of a straight ruler down her back or up in a perfect ballerina bun atop her head.

Her skin looks a waxen, ashy gray. This is not my Violet. This is just a body.

I harden my stomach muscles to stop myself from collapsing. I clench my molars because I absolutely cannot break down. "Where's the rest of her?" I demand.

Boone just shakes his head. I want to shake *him*. I want to smash his head in. I love Boone, I really do. But Violet—Violet is worth a hundred Boones. Why does he get to be alive? I slow my breathing. I realize I'm panting. That is absolutely the wrong thing to think, and if Vi knew, she would punch me in the nose. Boone and Violet have loved each other for years. I can't imagine that anyone would love her more than I do . . .

Than I *did* . . .

But I suppose it's possible that Boone does.

Did.

"Okay," I say to him as I make my way around her. I realize in that moment, finding the parts of Violet that are missing don't really matter. She's gone. "Boone, babe," I say to him gently, "we need to get out of here. The rest of this building is going to come down any moment."

Boone doesn't respond. He doesn't move. I think he may have even forgotten to breathe. I kneel down beside him, the rubble digging into my uniform uncomfortably. My face is crying. It is the only part of me that seems to accept what has happened. I bend down and kiss Violet's head. She tastes of metal and ash. My lips imprint whatever is left of my humanity. War is a feral beast. It is death and fire and blood. There will always and forever be before Violet died and after.

And the after, at least for right now, the *me* after is no one. I am not a person anymore. I am the steel tip of a blade, the hollowed-out place inside a bullet, the crashing atoms colliding inside a laser. I am all punches and kicks and the pull of a trigger.

"Boone!" I yell as I shake him.

He turns his head slowly to look at me. "I don't know what . . ." Now he looks bewildered, almost drunk. "What am I supposed to do?"

I yank him up by the shoulders. I pull him up so hard his feet dangle in the air for a split second before they touch the earth again.

"Fight," I tell him coldly. "We fight and we kill them all."

At first, Boone's head shakes like he doesn't understand. And then he looks at me. His face changes. His features harden. His eyes narrow. I give him a smile, not of happiness but in understanding. He returns the sinister grin. Boone is back, or at least a part of him—the deadliest part. We bolt outside the Command Center. I don't bother to look for him, or Levi or any of the others. What I am about to do next belongs solely to me.

I once again return the sensuit so that I can deal with the Spiradael's unique hair situation, and after that, I switch off. I empty both guns into the heads of my enemies. When my ammo is gone, I just use my hands. I leap from each one to the next. I tear heads off shoulders. I pitch bodies to throw targets off balance and stab Citadels in the throat and skull and eyes. Since I know their uniform will slow my efforts, I devise a way to rip it off them from the neck down. Once that's done, it's easy enough to plunge a fist into a rib cage and pull out a still-beating heart.

And this arm, this beautiful flesh-and-metal hybrid of an arm that was once a compromise, a way to bargain to this very moment, is so much more. It is stronger, faster, deadlier. It is just so . . . *extra*, as am I. I am more than a mere soldier now.

I am a cause. I am a precise instrument of death, and I will not stop unless someone or something can stop me, and that doesn't look like that is going to happen any time soon.

I don't know how long this lasts. I am covered in blood of all colors and I have taken my fair share of licks along the way, but I don't feel the pain. I don't feel anything. I do notice that my opponents are fewer and fewer. I also notice that if I can get a Settiku Hesh by the feet, I can pick him up and bash his head back and forth on the ground on either side of me—the way the Hulk likes to do.

Eventually, I realize that I am all alone. I look down around me at a pile of bodies. Dozens and dozens of dead Citadels and ARC's so-called expert black-ops soldiers. I have no idea where I am. Three of Zaka's cats race by me, drawn by a whistle. A riderless unicorn passes a few seconds later. She gives me a slow, melancholy look with her massive black eyes as she saunters by.

"Morning—status? I've taken out every combatant in this area, where are the rest?" I ask.

"Hold," she tells me immediately.

I wait in the middle of the fleshy wreckage. It doesn't occur to me to move just yet. The only thing that occurs to me is to do more fighting. I wipe the edge of my knife blade on my uniform and put it back in my belt.

"We have killed all Orsaline, Spiradael, and Settiku Hesh Citadels. We have captured forty-three percent of the human Citadels. They are currently being taken to a holding facility. Boone Castor has overseen the execution of Seelye's Shadow Citadels-9—three hundred twenty have been killed."

"And how many casualties on our side?" I ask forcefully. I care. Of course, I care, but now, after Violet, the number feels almost unimportant. It seems like incredibly, miraculously, we've won. It doesn't feel like we've won, though, not without Vi.

"Comparatively few. Dead, 14,339. Injured, 22,655." I repeat the number in my head. It does seem small compared to their losses. "Levi is okay? And Henry?" I ask.

"We're fine," Levi's voice cuts in. "We're in the triage center. Helping with the injured. Only the critically wounded are here; the rest have been taken into the neighborhoods by other team and unit members. We're all medics. Seems like that part of the training was universal."

"Why don't you meet us here, we can debrief," Henry adds.

"No," I say with authority. I step on the bodies that surround me, not bothering to expend the energy it would take to jump over them. "I want an elite integrated team to meet me by the front entrance. At least five hundred troops."

"Ryn," Levi says smoothly, "I don't think you understand. We won. The altered Roones are holed up in the base, we can get to them later."

"Did any of you think that was a request? Because around here, we call that an order," I say calmly, though my tone is clipped, bordering on hostile. Right now I don't have to be nice or accommodating. I have to finish this. "Nine thousand three hundred twenty adult Citadels. There *were two hundred more* at the base. We haven't won shit until we get the altered Roones. So let's go get them."

"I am in agreement with Ryn Whittaker," Varesh says boldly in my ear. "These Citadels are merely foot soldiers. This war is not over until every altered Roone is dead."

I begin to make my way to the entrance of the Village. I eat some gel cubes and drink some water, knowing that I have depleted far more of my energy than my adrenaline will let me realize.

"Fine, we'll meet you there," Henry chimes in, albeit grimly.

I stand and wait in the open field. The quiet is unnerving. Birds have fled and the thousands of bodies around me are still. I don't look down. I have had enough of death. I keep my eye on the horizon and my focus primed on the work we have yet to do.

Eventually, the troops I've asked for fall in behind me, and from above, the Faida are circling. This new unit has over two hundred human UFA members, while the Akshaji, Karekins, Roones, SenMachs, and Faida make up the difference in equal numbers. Levi is here. He awkwardly moves forward, perhaps in an attempt to hug me, but I jolt backward. I cannot fathom the thought of tenderness right now. Levi reads my body language instantly and hands me my pack instead.

Varesh, Berj, and Morning have also joined. A good portion of Morning's face has been melted off, presumably in the explosion that killed Vi. I notice that Iathan also has joined us, and I fight the urge to groan out loud. He was in the Command Center, too, but apart from a slight limp, he managed to escape unscathed. He lived and Vi didn't. It doesn't seem fair at all.

Navaa is in the air. Henry has opted to stay behind to identify and separate the dead. Fallen members of the United Free Army and the human Citadels will be buried here or taken to their own Earths. Nonhuman Citadels will be thrown into a Rift going to the Microwave Earth where their skin will melt off and all that will remain of them will be a pile of yellow bones.

The Faida have offered to carry the original Roones. They are efficient enough soldiers but are unable to run as fast as we can. I am grateful for this because I don't want to waste any time waiting for them to catch up. Once we've collected ourselves, we head straight for Camp Bonneville. The drones will accompany us, too, but given our speed, I doubt they will get there before us. The forest is a blur. I remember setting off, but by the time we arrive, I don't recall the actual journey. I wonder briefly if it will always be like this or if it's just a kind of hangover, from the war, from grief. I lead us around back to the ancient escape hatch. I expect it to be closed and locked, but it is wide open. I take out my gun—now reloaded with ammo that Levi provided. I move a single foot to step inside and then set my foot back down again.

"What are you waiting for?" Varesh demands. "They are here! Move!"

I whip my head around and give him a look that silences him. After today, I really don't know what my face is capable of.

"Morning," I say softly.

"Yes, Ryn?"

"Are the drones picking up any life-forms here at all?" Morning looks blankly at the open hatch. "Morning, you have to be faster with these answers, okay? We aren't on your Earth. Ten seconds could be life or death."

"Understood," she tells me plainly, "I was just double-checking the data."

"And . . ." I fish.

"There is no one here. The base is empty."

All around me there is murmuring. The Akshaji are furious. The Faida are bewildered, but Iathan and I catch each other's eyes.

"We weren't monitoring the sound blockade during the battle, were we?" I ask out loud to everyone, to no one.

"We were," Morning insists. "It did fluctuate, but we assumed it was our doing. That we had weakened the defenses with our coding."

I holster my gun and begin to pace. "Obviously that's not what happened," I tell them all with a sigh. "That's probably what they wanted us to think, but they used this. It was a win-win."

"Elaborate," Varesh demands.

"All this . . . All this terror and death was about the experiment. The only thing the altered Roones cared about was gauging the human Kir-Abisat gift. Could it override a sound blockade? That's all they really wanted to know and I proved it to them when I got the Akshaji. We have to assume they were monitoring it, either from here or the Akshaj Earth."

"How is that a 'win-win' as you say?" Navaa asks, shaking her head. "They lost over a hundred thousand of their own troops. How could that be perceived as any kind of victory?"

I laugh and I'm sure I sound half-mad, but I don't care. "Navaa," I say, not bothering to hide my disappointment in the way that I address her. "Don't be naive. *They are indifferent.* One dead Citadel is the same as a thousand or ten thousand. All of you are inferior now, can't you see that? Now that the altered Roones know our potential, they can start again, with humans on another Earth, and this time, *all* of them will get the Kir-Abisat gene. You think they care about creating really good soldiers? Ha!" I spit. "I can open a door to the Multiverse, on my own, without a machine or a conduit, using only my throat. That achievement is all that matters to them now. The rest of you? You're obsolete. You might as well die."

I can see the look of shock and horror spread among the group. They know I'm right and they also know, as I do, that we have been played. We slaughtered thousands. We did their dirty work for them by eliminating their inferior subjects. We thought this was about liberation. For the altered Roones it was only about data and a clean slate.

Mostly.

The win-win part is why we're looking at an empty bunker.

"They want to go home," Iathan spits. He knows exactly what I'm talking about because, after all, he's a Roone, too. "This wasn't *just* about tying up loose ends. It was a distraction. We left precious few behind," he whispers frantically. "I warned you that this could happen!" His words are sharp, threatening even. I don't look away. Instead, I narrow my eyes with a threat of my own. He knew the risks. We all did. I'm not about to give him an apology, and I pray he's not dumb enough to ask for one.

"So they are on the Roone Earth? *All* of them? The one where this all started?" Varesh asks.

"Yes . . . and that's where we're going. Right now," I say to them all.

"Uhhh," Levi begins. "Yeah, maybe we call for reinforcements?"

"We don't need them," I say confidently. "In fact, the Sen-Mach contingent won't be coming. We can't risk the altered Roones getting access to their tech."

"That would leave you with only four hundred twenty troops," Morning chimes in quicker than I've ever heard a Sen-Mach speak. "I advise against this. There could be thousands there. You may be vastly outnumbered."

I shake my head vehemently. "No. Our first mistake, our biggest mistake, was thinking like soldiers. They don't think like soldiers, they think like scientists. They observed, they recorded, and then they took advantage of a chaotic situation."

"You honestly believe they won't have thousands of Citadels with them?" Navaa asks doubtfully.

"Well, maybe a thousand, but we can deal with that. We go

in fast and dirty—surprise them. I doubt they'll be expecting us this soon."

"Yes, we should go, right now," Iathan says rather frantically.

"Look," I warn. "You have to be calm now. Precise. *Clever.* I'm sure the altered Roones have plans within plans within a propaganda brainwash plan. They've been waiting for this day for a long time. They must have sympathizers that remained behind and as president, you're bound to have opposition. We cannot let them address the public. Hopefully, they're taking some time to put their strategies in place, but if they have started to implement them . . . well . . . it's vital that you act presidential. That you act like their claims are not only illegitimate, but laughable. Now, I don't think they will have a significant presence there. Not yet. If they do, we take *our very* significant presence back tomorrow when the troops have rested. Your Earth will not fall into their hands as long as you project total and absolute confidence, which, given how you generally come across, shouldn't be much of a stretch."

I thought the comment might win one of Iathan's playfully condescending laughs, but I get nothing. His face is grim. "These are my people, Ryn. An entire planet at the mercy of those monsters . . ." Iathan trails off.

I take a deep breath in and look at our bedraggled crew. Navaa has an angry cut running down the right side of her entire face. Varesh's skin is more red than purple, tinted scarlet from his enemies' blood. Levi has eggplant-colored bruises around his throat. Iathan himself has half of his beard missing, along with a sizable chunk of his hair sliced or lasered off. I don't even want to think about what I must look like.

"Iathan," I tell him as gently as I can. "We're all monsters. But let's go save the world anyway."

CHAPTER 25

We use the Kir-Abisat to Rift onto the Roone Earth. My voice
commingles with a dozen others and the Rift tears into the air
in front of us as easily as a loose seam being ripped apart. The
upside is that we will get past any sort of blockade the altered
Roones may have put up. The downside is that the Kir-Abisat
is not as precise as the QOINS system so we end up Rifting
onto the Roone Earth about a mile out of town. There is no
way to mask this opening from Roone scanners. They know
we have arrived the moment we step onto the sandy ground.
But I have thought of this contingency, too. We release our
drones and Doe works quickly to hack into their mainframe,
uploading our own Faida-programmed sound blockade, bolstered by the SenMachs' firewalls. They might be able to hack
this eventually, but for now, we have them trapped.

I have only been here once, under heavy escort. I got to see almost nothing but the city itself and, even then, I was surrounded by Karekin guards who blocked any view I might have gotten. I am surprised that the Roone capital is basically in the middle of what looks to be a desert—not Saharan or anything, as there is some vegetation, but a place that reminds me a lot of the Joshua Tree National Park that my parents drove us through one painfully hot summer on our way to Disneyland. Dad was ecstatic and I . . . was thirteen.

We're a long way from all that.

From here, Iathan takes point. He knows exactly where we are and the fastest way to get to where he figures the altered Roones are at—his bunker inside the capital. I send out the SenMach drones. Obviously, I would have preferred to not take any of their tech with us, but Morning assured me that it would self-destruct (most spectacularly, she added) if it fell into enemy hands. The drones go up and we start to run.

The Roone soldiers are pushing it as fast as they can. For the rest of us, it is a mild jog. When we approach the city proper, Iathan directs us to a power station. The building is white, a little on the art deco side, and surprisingly intact. Since much of the city was ruined during their civil war, I have to assume this would be one of the priorities to rebuild. A soldier kicks down the metal door and Iathan wonders out loud if the Sen-Mach tech can infiltrate the entire grid and power it down if necessary. I have my laptop again and so I'm thinking that yeah? Probably? It would be a great advantage tactically if we could shut the altered Roones out of their systems.

I ask Doe and he wants me to put the laptop down on the ground, in front of one of the station monitoring systems. I don't bother to ask why I haven't seen a single employee here.

It seems weird, but then again, these are the Roones. They probably think that such a job would be beneath them—much better to have an automated computerized system.

Big mistake there.

Once the laptop is down, white glowing tendrils crawl out of the keyboard like that terrifying long-haired girl from all the *Ring* movies. We all wait anxiously to see if Doe can accomplish the task.

"I have entered the system undetected, though your presence has been noted. Additional troops have been sent to the perimeter of the capitol building. They also know about the sound blockade and are working to override it." Doe's voice rings out clearly in the nearly empty room save for a few pipes and levers.

"How many are they? Do you know?"

"I do not. It was a verbal command, but noted in their logs," Doe answers without affectation.

"And our drones, in stealth," I wonder out loud, "will they be detected by the altered Roones?"

"There is a ninety-seven point six percent chance they will not be," Doe answers quickly. The SenMachs are all getting used to the idea now that they can't wait seconds to answer vital questions, even the ones that don't have an actual body.

"Let's get an accurate count from the drones," Levi cuts in. "We wait here, see how many we're dealing with and go from there. If there are too many, Ryn, if we're outnumbered to the point of recklessness, then we have to come back with more troops of our own."

"Agreed," I say as I give the command. We walk outside again, to where the rest of our troops are positioned and wait. It doesn't take long.

"There are 417 sentries outside the capitol building. Our

scans have picked up an additional 1,128 heat signatures inside," Doe reports.

"That's good news," I say to the group. "I don't know how many altered Roones there are. I'm guessing not very many. Iathan, any intel on the actual numbers of your rogue faction?"

"There were only six hundred twenty created here on this Earth. I cannot say if they made more in the years following their banishment," he tells us thoughtfully. I wonder in that moment what his thoughts are. Six hundred twenty responsible for the deaths of hundreds of thousands. It's almost inconceivable.

Almost, but not quite.

There weren't very many Betas, either, and look how much we did.

Vi.

I clear my throat. I cannot think about that. About her. Not yet.

"I doubt very much they created more," Navaa chimes in and thankfully breaks my train of thought. "They presume that they are chosen. They consider themselves to be gods. And while they think nothing of enhancing a species's strength or mental acuity to gauge the results, ultimately, they believe they are far superior. Too superior to ever re-create their own genesis."

We all nod our heads in agreement with that assessment. "Is there any kind of back door to the bunker?" I ask Iathan.

"There is only one way in, through the front entrance," he tells me while stroking what's left of his beard. I think he must get in that moment that it is only half there as his eyes widen in surprise. He takes a knife from his utility belt and begins to hack away at what's left of it. "We considered an emergency escape route, but concluded that it would leave us too exposed. *Spies*. When we were fighting our war, they were everywhere. We couldn't risk that kind of weakness in our last line of defense."

I bristle a little because that seems like an epically stupid tactical assumption. There should always be more than one way to get in and out of your foxhole, but I don't bother to say it out loud. It doesn't matter now.

"Let's use that to our advantage then," I tell the other leaders. "We take out the 417 outside. We use Doe to jam the comms and cut the power. They won't be able to go anywhere."

"I feel it prudent to remind you that if they have with them a human who possesses the Kir-Abisat gift, the blockade will be useless," Doe warns. "They could escape."

"I don't think they do," I say thoughtfully. "They didn't give it to the adult soldiers Seelye made them alter and I was kind of their test subject, right? But, either way, we just get in there as fast as we can. Varesh and Navaa, your troops will take care of the guards outside the building. The rest of us will rush the place. If possible, those of us taking the bunker will avoid combat entirely to preserve our energy until we're inside the facility. Agreed?"

Everyone backs the plan and we go. It's about twenty blocks to the Capitol and although there is no secret entrance to the building, there is a way to get there underground, through the tunnels that run the fiber optics. We take left and right turns seemingly at random. I'm sure that we are going to get lost in this maze, but Iathan and his soldiers know exactly where we are going.

We end up in another government building directly across from the Capitol. I assign a team of twenty to act as snipers. The Faida can do this from the air as well. The Roones that are working at their desks and inside their offices scatter and duck.

Iathan reassures them to remain calm. I pay no attention to them or their frantic, nervous energy. I stick to the mission. I race out of the door as fast as my legs can carry me. Bullets whiz by me, but I am vaulting and leaping up the steps in a fashion that is too unpredictable for any of the guards to get a lock on me. I don't focus on where the shots are coming from or even who is doing the shooting. I have one mission—to get inside as quickly as possible—and I must have faith in the troops I have ordered to give us cover to handle the job.

I ignore the carnage of the Citadels going down around me. The Akshaji are making quick and vicious work of their targets, shielding themselves from bullets and lasers with a flurry of arms while the others punch and stab and slice the enemy. Every instinct I have tells me that it is wrong to run, that I should be standing my ground here, and supporting my allies. I also know that we might only have a few minutes before the altered Roones find some wily way to evade us once again.

The power is out in the Capitol, a large white columned building with lapis lazuli tile, the same color as Iathan's skin. I remember all this from before, but I don't really care about the architecture. I care about getting down to the bunker, where I know our true enemies are. There are two elevators and we cram as many bodies inside as we can. When the elevators are jam-packed, I leap up and punch my way through the hatch at the top so that I can ride it down with an additional ten members of the UFA on top. Doe allows power to these two elevators alone. The rest of the bunker will be dark. And silent.

I crouch down, holding on to a piece of metal as the elevator descends deep underground. The speed creates a sort of vacuum. I can't hear much and my ears pop as we go down.

It sort of feels like an amusement park ride actually—if there was such a ride that started out in a free fall but ended up in certain violence. I can't imagine there would be too many people lining up for that one.

When the elevator finally stops, the strange innocuous ding tells us we've arrived. The doors open and the Citadel guards—mostly human, but some Spiradael that are posted here—immediately open fire. They must have heard the elevator make its way up or down and were lying in wait. Not that it matters. The UFA begin to do their thing and the Citadels don't stand much of a chance.

The eleven of us who rode down atop the elevator burst through ten seconds later, surprising those few troops left in the narrow hallway. I take advantage of its dimensions by springing from one concrete wall to the other. I am relieved that it's not completely dark down here—there is a red strip of emergency lights that give an otherworldly feel to what is already a majorly alien situation.

My boots leap to the right and I use both palms to get me to the next wall where I can jump again, above the fray. I finally land on one of the special-ops fake-ass Citadels. I have enough momentum now that I kick him so hard in the face I hear his neck snap.

I take a bullet to the shoulder. It misses my head only because I keep moving. I pull my guns out and just start picking them off. Sorry, Christopher Slimy Pants Seelye. Your wannabe Citadels aren't nearly as fast as me. They might have years more experience, but that hardly matters at the end of a gun. You got played by Edo. Ha. I mean, I hate Edo, but I kind of love that she and the altered Roones pulled this one off.

Part of me expected that this would be more of a challenge and I guess I'm a little disappointed that it isn't. Fish in a barrel. Oh, they give it their best shot; one even rushes me and manages to get me on my ass. He draws up his nine-mil to shoot me in the face. I snatch it away so fast his eyes bulge. I raise an eyebrow and hit him with such violent, deadly force in the temple, his brain bleeds. When the hallway is clear, I see that Levi has caught up to me.

"Whoa," he whistles. "You are on a fucking tear. I'm really glad you are on my side."

"Me too." I flash him a smile. "Iathan!" I bellow. "You lead."

We follow the Roone, taking care of Citadels as they approach, but now we have the drones in stealth mode down here with us, too. There isn't anything we aren't prepared for. We get to the situation room. The doors are barred. I do know this place well, since we launched our first operation against the Spiradael Earth from here. The space is massive, more chamber hall than war room. Half is a proper command center and the other half is a huge oblong receiving room where Iathan is all presidential-y. It always seemed a bit more like he was president of a banana republic, though, since he has a chair-like throne on a dais.

He and Sairjidahl Varesh should spend some time getting to know each other.

I move toward the door, but Iathan places a hand upon my own. His skin is cool and hard.

"Please, Ryn Whittaker, if you will allow, the Roones would like to be the first to confront our countrymen," Iathan says with genuine humility.

"And then what are you going to do? Call each other names?" I ask. I'm really not trying to be combative, but this is no time for a debate.

"No," he says, standing up a little straighter. "Of course not. We are going to arrest them. They will be put on trial publicly for the entire world to see. For the entire Multiverse. They will spend the rest of their lives in prison."

"Hmmm," I say as I look to the door. That would be the most civilized way of dealing with the altered Roones certainly. I have often worried about my role as Citadel, playing judge and jury, getting to decide who lives and who dies. I was never comfortable with it. Perhaps a life imprisoned, away from their experiments and their Citadels' adulation, would be punishment enough. Maybe death is too easy.

Then again . . . I don't really trust *any* of these assholes.

"Nope. Sorry." I kick down the door and there is more shooting, lasers this time. The Settiku Hesh will guard the altered Roones with their dying breath. There are only about fifty of the suicide soldiers here, though. They put up a valiant effort, but the Akshaji brutally dance through them, cutting them down as if they were nothing more than streamers at a house party. I purposely hang back and wait, focusing my attention on the hundreds of altered Roones, all that's left of their kind. Even now, even when they know that they have been beaten, they are watching this all as if it has nothing to do with them, as if at the end of this, our allegiance will naturally turn once again in their favor.

When the Settiku Hesh have all fallen, our entire unit faces them in the large space. I don't quite know what they are waiting for and then I realize they are waiting for me, for my orders.

"Varesh?" I ask smoothly. "May I borrow one of your swords?" The altered Roones are physically no match for any Citadel, but they do have a natural defense, skin as hard and impenetrable as polished stone. Varesh hands over one of his bejeweled blades, hilt first with a tiny bow.

I walk over to the altered Roone closest to me.

"Please," he pleads, "we gave you such a gift. We—"

I don't bother to let him finish. I cut his head off with one brief slice and then . . .

It is a slaughter.

In the chaos, I see Edo, backed all the way into the corner; she is onyx, the color of night, the color of a Rift's final scream. I leap over to her. I will have my revenge, not for me—not really, I've accepted who I am—but for Violet, who never in a million years should have been chosen to be a Citadel in the first place. When I get to Edo, I just stand there, blocking her escape. Her huge blue eyes are defiant and calculating. She is trying to find a way out of this, configuring variables, weighing her options. In short order she will know, though: there is no way out.

She *will* die.

When the room grows silent, I know my people have completed their mission. There is only one altered Roone left. I drag her heavy body to the middle of the room.

"Iathan!" Edo barks. "You have turned into a barbarian. How could you let these outsiders execute us like this? I demand a trial. Bring me an advocate, immediately."

"Are you actually asking for a lawyer?" I say, my mouth agape.

"Ryn, enough," she tells me, as if I am a dog, as if I can be brought to heel with a command. "There is no more victory here today. How many of your brothers and sisters have you slaughtered in the past few hours? Can you even count them? Dozens? Hundreds? I taught you better than this. We were unarmed. Defenseless. And now, you're going to kill me? For what? Why?"

"Good point," I say, playing along. "Maybe we should ask the Daithi contingent their thoughts. Oh wait. We can't do that, *can we*, Edo?"

Edo's expression changes in an instant. She knows that tack won't work, appealing to my better angels, so she switches to another. "Do not pretend that you don't enjoy the power I gave you." Edo is tiny, but she lifts up on her tiptoes to whisper in my ear. "You love it." I close my eyes for a brief second. The hatred I have for this woman is visceral. It is clawing at my insides. It's making my fingers tremble. "Every single species we chose, all of you, were nothing but amoeba. Barely evolved, baby steps from the primordial ooze. You might not have asked for it, not implicitly, but the state we found all of you in, it would have been irresponsible to walk away without changing your sad state of existence. We made your world better and we can make it better still—and not just your world, but every world there ever was and ever will be. Despite what you've seen or heard, I never wanted to be a god. I wanted to be a mother, a mother to thousands of children who could open up a doorway to the Multiverse with a song.

"I wanted *you* to be the gods."

I may be young, but I know my history. These are the words of dictators and tyrants. They step into power and blame the victims for handing it over. No one ever thinks that they will end up the martyr. Bright-eyed brides sold by their fathers and shackled to boiling pots and mewling babies, Jews herded onto cattle cars, men of color strung up on fat oak branches for daring to question their place, Muslim women stoned for adultery, indigenous people the world over forced to bend to the will of conquerors because honor and knives, voices of dissent, artists and poets and journalists who dare to tell the truth are no match for cannons and guns.

And my sweet Violet with her long legs and agile arms turned into a soldier because they thought her grace would be deadly on the battlefield. No child wakes up and imagines themselves to be anything other than the hero of their own story.

I reach out and grab Edo's fat neck with my fingers and squeeze. "You have lost the privilege of speaking," I growl. "You are a liar and a murderer and an abuser of children. You are filth. You may think all of us species were begging for it. But it is your species that is almost extinct. So—survival of the fittest. Ultimately, wherever you place yourself on the evolutionary scale, you will die knowing that you were wrong." There is a gurgling sound as words—or maybe air—try to come out of her mouth.

"Ryn," Iathan says firmly as he walks slowly, deliberately to my side. "You have had your way in this. You have executed them all save for Kredolain. Let us have her, please. Let us show our people what happens to those who think they are above the law."

"Who is Kredolain?" I ask, maintaining my grip and not bothering to look back at Iathan.

"Edo. Kredolain DoMiskavix. She was one of the three leaders of the rebellion," he says with a weary sigh.

"Really? Well, you aren't making the compelling case you think you are with that new bit of information."

"Actually"—suddenly I feel the dull nuzzle of a firearm push into the back of my skull. Iathan, the Roone bastard, has aimed a gun at my head—"I'm not particularly interested in making *any* sort of a case to you. You have done your job, Ryn. Now let me, as the president of this country, do mine."

"If you pull that trigger, you will die," I tell him without emotion. I've been carrying the weight of expectant death on my shoulder like an old handbag all day. When I try to reach for a feeling, there is only surprise. I find that I am rather shocked at my own heart's relentless beating.

I'm alive.

For now. Nothing is certain in this game, and so I don't attach any kind of real emotion to this fact because it may only be temporary. Because of this, Iathan's threat is disappointing more than it is scary. As if my command here was something he indulged, but never truly respected.

"I am willing to die to do what is just and right," he says, though his voice falters. *He's* the one who's scared.

"There is no way to put the genie back in this bottle. Where was your sense of justice and morality when all this began? You can't be the better person now, it doesn't work that way." I tell him calmly squeezing a little harder. Edo's eyes bulge.

"Ryn!" Iathan screams. "Ryn, stop please. I don't want to do this!"

"No one wants this," I say sadly. Edo begins to slump, her impossibly heavy head giving way to gravity. I know on an intellectual level that I am wrong and Iathan is right. He is the leader here. Edo is a Roone and his people deserve some kind of closure for all that they have endured. I just can't seem to let her go, even as I feel her life slipping away and the barrel of Iathan's pistol dig into my head. I have moved beyond reason. I think I may have lost my mind.

"Ryn," I hear Levi's voice from somewhere close, but I can't see him. I can't stop looking at Edo, the woman who violated me in every conceivable way. "Let her go. Listen to Iathan . . ." There is a distinctive thread of panic weaving through his words. Levi never panics, and this jolts me enough to slacken my grip just a fraction.

"Please!" Edo gurgles.

I tighten my grip at her pathetic word.

"Ryn!" Iathan warns. I want to take my hand away, but I can't. It's like my brain is frozen.

And then, a shot. The singular whistle of a laser. I drop Edo to the floor and spin around. Iathan is at my feet with a scorch mark on his carotid and a pool of blood forming rapidly around us. I look up and see, to my surprise, Berj, with his arm still outstretched and his gun in the air.

"Our people do not need any more reminders of the past," he says sadly, "and Kredolain certainly does not need a platform to spew any more of her lies. She will manipulate every Roone she comes into contact with. She is too dangerous to let live."

Edo, who is also on the floor, is taking deep, gulping breaths. "You have the nerve to call me the traitor," she wheezes. "You just assassinated your president." Her hand is clutching at her throat and she is trying to move backward, away from me. "Karekin, you will pay for this." Edo looks wildly around. "Why are none of you arresting him?" she asks the Roones and Karekins in the room.

"Because," I tell her in Roonish. "I am the commander of the United Free Army and these troops belong to me. Berj was protecting his superior officer. He is the opposite of a traitor."

At that, Edo laughs. It is the sound of boots walking over bits of sea glass. "The United Free Army? Really, oh my," she manages to get out condescendingly.

"I don't see what's so funny. Iathan, for all his flaws, was a good man. Misguided and arrogant, but not rotten to the core. Not like you."

"Oh, enough, Ryn," Edo waves her hand dismissively. "If you are going to kill me, then do so," she announces while getting on her knees. "I die happily, knowing that you are the legacy I leave behind. You have already reshaped the world, many worlds in fact. You have torn them apart, but you will find that putting them back together again is not so easy. And in those moments, when hundreds of thousands are looking to you for guidance, you will think of me. You will realize that you and I are far more alike than we are different. After a time, your hatred will lessen and you will regret what you have done this day, but I will already be gone, as will my ability to absolve you." She bends over, exposing her jet-black neck. "Go ahead," she barks, "chop my head off."

I get down on my knees and grab her by the shoulders. "You still think you have bestowed some great gift, don't you? That we are all somehow better because of you? No, Edo, I am not better. I just . . . *am*. And I will not spend the rest of my life hating you less. I will spend whatever years I have left trying not to hate myself. And knowing that I never chose this, that you did all the choosing, is what will save me, one day."

I take both my hands and place them gently on her cheekbones. She doesn't like this. She doesn't like me to be so close, so intimate, and so she balks, her bright blue eyes shifting. I have learned this about the altered Roones—they want to observe. They are serial voyeurs, always keeping a safe and acceptable distance. They believe they are parents, that they are *our parents*. But this is false. They are zookeepers. They are Oppenheimer and Groves, watching the first atom bomb tear apart a fragile New Mexican desert from behind a concrete shell.

I am desperate in that moment for Edo, or Kredolain, to experience the full weight of these "gifts" she has given me. I want her to know what it means to be the mother of a god, truly. If she had read any mythology at all, she would have known it never ends well for her kind. That in fact, a god cannot become a god without murdering her creators. I move my mouth an inch away from hers. I think she supposes I might kiss her. And I will. In a way.

I begin to hum. I let the song build. I let the Multiverse collect itself from every atom and neutron and photon inside my cells. I let them dance in my blood. I can feel Edo start to pull away from me. But she made me so strong, and she can't get free. I can feel the panic in her. A beheading is one thing, but to die in this way, that is something else. Yet I keep singing. I sing into her mouth and I hear a scream as the Rift starts to open in the center of her tongue.

My song builds. I keep just the right tone and the precise volume for this to happen. Edo's entire face disappears inside the swirling neon green helix of the newborn Rift. It does indeed take her head. Pieces of her onyx skull fracture into such tiny fragments they become mostly dust. And then the rest of her body lifts up and follows suit, swirling and folding and dissolving.

Edo is nothing more than a pile of sand in front of a purple Rift no bigger than a chair. I close my mouth. The Rift bleeds back to green and then pops away like a soap bubble. The altered Roones are dead. The United Free Army has won the privilege of its name.

I take a handful of what remains of Edo and shove it into a leather pocket on my uniform. She was right about one thing—I have torn worlds apart. I will need reminding every day how not to turn into her when I help rebuild what I have destroyed.

CHAPTER 26

I return to Camp Bonneville and sleep for twelve hours. My slumber is a light switch. One minute I am on, moving through the bunker, talking, advising, ordering, and the next I am in a makeshift bed, completely off. There is no in between. There are no circling thoughts, or plans, or wondering what to do next. My body retreats. I do not dream.

When I finally awaken I see that Levi is on his tablet in the cot next to me. I sit up and rub my face and scratch at my short hair. I haven't slept so long since, well, I can't remember. Probably it was before the chip was implanted.

"Hey, Sleeping Beauty," he says as he lowers the tablet. I notice he's not in his uniform anymore, and I also notice that I actually slept in mine. Gross. "Feel any better?"

"Oh, yeah," I say without enthusiasm. "I feel great." Levi rolls his eyes. Neither one of us will feel anywhere close to great for a long while. "I'm going to hop in the shower, and after that, let's take a walk, okay?"

"Sure," he says with a salute. "I'll be here." I peel myself off the bed and walk to the locker rooms where I take a long hot shower and leave my uniform among a pile of a hundred others in the laundry bay. I know that I'll have to put it on again for what's coming next. We all will. I make a mental note to ask Henry who can be assigned this monumental task. The laundry is the least important thing on a list a mile long I have running in my head. I'll get to it, but for now, I just need to be outside, away, even though it's cold and sprinkling with rain. I turn my sensuit into a pair of comfortable jeans and a cozy sweater. Instead of walking back to the bunk room, I ask Levi to meet me outside.

Together, Levi and I walk the distance to the Rift. We don't say anything. He just keeps his arm around me, occasionally putting his lips to my hair. We must look like an ordinary couple out for a little hike. God, I wish that were true.

We arrive at the massive emerald green tower of the Rift. The place is absolutely deserted. We don't need guards here anymore. Of course, we never really did. It was always just a way to test us, the extent of our abilities and how far we would be willing to go to protect Battle Ground. The door has been closed, but not locked. I sigh one long breathy exhale and lean my head on Levi's shoulders.

"So many kids are dead," he says quietly. "We could never keep this a secret, but now that we're on the other side of it, I can see why they wanted to. It's going to change everything. Where do we even start?"

"We start with the truth. And I'll do that," I tell him while I squeeze his hand. "I won't be like Edo and her people. I'm going to step forward and put myself right in the middle of it."

Although even thinking about that—press conferences and interviews and all the questions—makes my stomach lurch.

"But, Ryn," Levi says grimly, "it's not just about the truth. Every single government on Earth was complicit in recruiting child soldiers. The whole system has to be dismantled. You get that, right? That we're the ones that are going to have to enforce this change and most people are not going to be down with that idea. At all."

I lift my head and stare into the Rift. "Oh, I know. That's why I already had Doe hack into every secure government mainframe so they can't just nuke us all. They can't even do anything actually. They're locked out. They'd have to use carrier pigeons to move their own troops."

Levi looks long and hard at me. "So what you're saying is that we actually run the world right now? Like, for real?"

"Yeah, but you're still thinking about this from the outside in. The change has to start right here. *From* this place."

"What do you mean?"

I let go of Levi completely and take two steps forward. "We take people through. *We show them.* Not just the scientists and historians and anthropologists and journalists, but the poets and priests and the imams and rabbis and the skeptics. We prove how incomprehensibly huge the Multiverse is and how our teeny part takes up just a fraction of it. That's how we get things to change. By offering something more, something incredible."

I don't need to look at Levi to know he's folding his arms. I can tell by the tone his voice takes. "You're putting a lot of faith in mankind."

"But it won't just be mankind, will it? Who's going to argue with an angel?" I say cheekily. "We don't have to do this alone." I turn to him. "We can't. We shouldn't. We need our allies. We have Navaa and Cosmos and Henry and Zaka—Varesh can fuck off, but we ask for help and we make things better."

Levi looks thoughtful. There is still daylight, but the sun is so weak that the neon green of the Rift illuminates his face. "Yeah, but better for us isn't better for everyone. Human immigrants, from other countries on *this* Earth have a hard time. Maybe all this enlightenment is too much to ask."

I walk into his arms and hold him. Or, rather, I let him hold me. "Probably," I say as I look up at him. "But just imagine, an Earth where no one suffers, no one gets sick or goes hungry or kills each other over land. We can give that to the world. I mean, we have to try."

"And if people don't like it? If people like the world the way it is now?" I realize he's playing devil's advocate, but now he's just being annoying.

"Then we send them to another one," I say with a smile (although, really, I'm not joking).

I can feel Levi nod his head. "Okay. It's not perfect, but let's try it. Together."

I look up at him, deep into his eyes, and kiss him on the lips. "Always," I whisper. "You're stuck with me and, full disclosure, I might not be completely sane."

"It's too late," he tells me, his face breaking into a wide-open grin. "I already love you."

At that, my heart seems to settle a little deeper into my chest. "I love you, too," I whisper back.

It feels so good to say those words out loud, without a caveat or a "one day"—without worrying that I don't deserve it, that I'm not good enough or the things that I've done have made me despicable. Love isn't something that you have to earn, although perhaps it is something that you have to be worthy of. I know now . . .

I *am* worthy.

I look to the shimmering ripple of the Rift. I wanted my freedom and I got it, or at least a version of it. Because it's never going to be complete. I am tethered to this towering, luminous doorway. Forever. And I suppose that some might not see that as liberation at all, but I do. The Rift is a choice now and a privilege. I turn to Levi. "Let's start right now. This doesn't need to be here anymore. *We* get to decide where and when to open up the door," I tell him gently. I keep hold of his hand, though, and walk him closer to the Rift. I stare into its swirling emerald waves. I can hear its song, spilling out from every direction and seeping into my skin. It doesn't tug at me. It knows it can't have me that way anymore. The Rift that almost killed me, almost killed us all, is now our greatest hope of surviving. "Doe!" I shout with pure glee. "Shut this thing down."

There is a slight lag and then it is simply gone, without a trace, and the battleground is empty.

ACKNOWLEDGMENTS

It isn't easy saying good-bye to Ryn. I've lived with her in my head and in my heart for years now. I've watched her grow, mature, evolve, and step up to become a fearsome defender and thoughtful leader. Just as it is with my own children, I had no idea what she would become but I always knew what she was capable of.

I have to thank, first and foremost, my incredible agent, Yfat Reiss Gendell, who had to wait five whole years until I managed to deliver a manuscript that she could sell—and sell it she did, like a total rock star. The entire team at Foundry Media is amazing, but I have to give a special shout-out to Jessica Felleman for her patience and many, many discussions about Ryn and her world.

David Pomerico at Harper Voyager is just about the best

editor a girl could ask for. David believed in the Rift way before it was even called the Rift. He has stood behind me and beside me to help me build this incredible world. There are so many others at Harper who have been instrumental in this journey. Notably, Priyanka Krishnan, another incredible editor (and SDCC partner in crime), Caroline Perny, Kayleigh Webb, and Pamela Jaffee.

A lot of people have helped me sell this trilogy, so I'd like to thank the teams at Wunderkind, BookSparks, Section 101, and Sneak Attack Media.

Personally, I'd like to acknowledge my Ride or Dies: Lisa Rockower (who has read every iteration of every single one of these books; whew, that is real friendship), Sam Brickman, and Claire Coffee, who is just about the most amazing book narrator in the world and a dear friend. I would also like to thank Kiki Teal Littlestar, life coach, friend, and badass entrepreneur. She made me a Perlena once I joined her co-working space, and that has been such a gift. To know that as a woman I have a safe place where I can always go to write, vent, learn, and be part of a community is such a blessing for me as a writer. In fact, I'd like to thank all the ladies of the Perlene for sharing so much of their fantastic energy with me and for giving me such unwavering support.

I'm also part of a greater writing community at large. So, I would like to give a shout-out to some fellow writers who along the way have shown up for me. Sam Maggs, Danielle Page, James Dashner, Margaret Stohl, Melissa de la Cruz (and the Yallwest folks in general), Tamora Pierce, April Henry, and my sometimes con husband, Richard Kadrey.

A final thanks to my parents and the rest of my very large and wonderful family. Finally, I want to say thank you so very much to my husband, Matt, who is not only an excellent beta reader but who gives me the space emotionally, physically, and practically to write every day. And to our kids, Mike, Eva, and Vaughn, who inspire me every day. I love you all.